We hope you enjoy this book. Please return or renew it by the due date.

You can renew it at www.norfolk.gov.uk/libraries or by using our free library app.

Otherwise you can phone 0344 800 8020 - please have your library card and PIN ready.

You can sign up for email reminders too.

11.3.23

# THE SURVIVOR

*Also by Simon Conway*

Damaged
Rage
A Loyal Spy
Rock Creek Park
The Stranger
The Saboteur

# THE SURVIVOR

## SIMON CONWAY

HODDER &
STOUGHTON

First published in Great Britain in 2022 by Hodder & Stoughton
An Hachette UK company

1

Copyright © Simon Conway 2022

The right of Simon Conway to be identified as the Author of the Work has been
asserted by him in accordance with the Copyright, Designs and Patents Act 1988.

Grateful acknowledgement is made for the permission to reprint
excerpts from the following copyrighted material:

'Death & Co' from the collection *Ariel* by Sylvia Plath © 1965
All rights reserved. Used by permission of Faber and Faber Ltd

A CIP catalogue record for this title is available from the British Library

Hardback ISBN 978 1 529 33434 0
Trade Paperback ISBN 978 1 529 33435 7
eBook ISBN 978 1 529 33437 1

Typeset in Plantin Light by Hewer Text UK Ltd, Edinburgh
Printed and bound by in Great Britain by Clays Ltd, Elcograf S.p.A.
Hodder & Stoughton policy is to use papers that are natural, renewable
and recyclable products and made from wood grown in sustainable
forests. The logging and manufacturing processes are expected to
conform to the environmental regulations of the country of origin.

Hodder & Stoughton Ltd
Carmelite House
50 Victoria Embankment
London EC4Y 0DZ

www.hodder.co.uk

For Nick Sayers

'The dead bell,
The dead bell,

Somebody's done for.'

Sylvia Plath, 'Death & Co'

# I

## In search of Angry Bear

There is something obscene about the manner of their arrival.

Jude Lyon, an officer with the UK's Secret Intelligence Service (MI6), flies into Central Africa on a Boeing A380 double-decker with air stewardesses who swish down the aisles in tight-fitting Christian Lacroix-designed uniforms of an 'aeronautical' style. Even in Economy the seats are comfortable, the wine is full-bodied, and the cheese is on the cusp of runny.

The wingspan of the plane is so wide that the tips extend over the chaotic encampment that presses up to edge of the runway and threatens to spill onto it in a floodtide of human misery. Landing, the reverse thrust scours the makeshift roofs, stripping away plastic sheeting and sending it billowing in its wake. More than fifty thousand people displaced by fighting are huddled inside the airport perimeter.

As he sits staring out the window at the camp, Jude struggles to contain his anger. He's angry with himself for failing to protect the people of his country against a barrage of attacks that have devastated large parts of London. The anger is born of danger and fear: tensing the muscles in his arms and legs, clenching his fists and teeth, and sending a pulse through his head that thumps like a drum. Its intensity disturbs him. He has always regarded himself as sane. He's never felt the urge to murder anyone in a shopping aisle or mow down a crowd from behind the wheel of a car. By and large, he has slept undisturbed by conscience. But lately he has been having doubts about himself.

It feels like he might burst into flames.

Jude's fellow traveller, Yulia Ermolaeva, flew in on an expensive seat at the front of the aircraft's top deck and he can see her ahead of him in the queue for Arrivals, surrounded by the families of the local ruling class who are returning from a Parisian shopping expedition.

She is wearing a khaki safari suit that looks like it was designed for the Masai Mara, and limping slightly. There are itchy stitches on the back of her thigh from where a fragment of grenade shrapnel clipped her in a London tower block. Jude is also wounded, his midriff bandaged from where the psychopath Guy Fowle knifed him. They have both been indelibly marked by the London attacks, minds and bodies scarred, friends and loved ones lost. But the necessity for speed in their response means that there has been little time for grieving.

'Shall we continue?' asks a man standing behind him.

Jude sees that a significant gap has opened between him and the person in front of him.

'Pardon me,' he says and moves to make up the distance.

They are waiting in line for a tent that has been erected between the plane and the terminal building, where Jude can see medical auxiliaries in blue scrubs hold temperature gauges to passengers' foreheads before letting them pass.

'Are you here to save us?' the man asks politely in impeccable English. He is tall and slightly stooped, bald on top with tight grey curls above his ears.

'No, I'm not.'

'You are here for our minerals?'

'No.'

The man seems unconvinced. 'This is not a tourist destination.'

'I'm looking for someone,' Jude tells him.

This is more to the man's liking. 'Does this person want to be found?'

It's an interesting question. 'Not by me.'

He's come to this troubled country at the headwaters of a tributary to the Congo River in search of a Russian hacker named Angry Bear.

'Should I want you to succeed?'

'Yes,' says Jude, who is desperately trying to prevent a world war. 'Lives may be saved.'

'Do you mean the lives of foreigners and those of my countrymen who flew in at the front of this plane? Or do you mean the lives of the hungry people here at the airport?'

'Ordinary people in my own country,' Jude tells him. 'But elsewhere too. Even here.'

'I wish you luck then,' the man says in a serious tone.

Along with his passport and vaccination certificate, Jude hands over a barely legible landing card that he scrawled before landing. He has seen the room where they store the landing cards in a neighbouring country: floor-to-ceiling stacks gradually being assimilated into a termite mound.

Waiting outside the terminal building there is a black, armoured SUV without insignia. It is owned by PMC Valkyrie, the private military company that until recently was a proxy army for the Kremlin but has now been declared an illegal military formation by the Russian president. With the black SUV is a police escort in a pick-up truck with a machine-gun mounted on the flatbed behind the cab.

Jude gets in the backseat beside Yulia.

The journey from the airport is, by reputation, one of the most volatile on the continent. It passes through a market, which spills onto the road, funnelling the traffic into a single lane. Sullen crowds press up against the ballistic windows as they edge forward, and the policemen shout at them to get away with little apparent effect. Legionnaires keep watch from the top of an armoured personnel carrier that's parked in the midst of the throng. It's hard to imagine what they'd do in the event of a riot, other than lock themselves inside their hardened steel box and wait it out.

Eventually, the convoy eases out of the market and accelerates into town, passing mud-brick buildings and garishly painted shipping containers turned into shops, mango trees coated in red dust, and crumbling colonial facades.

The Valkyrie compound is down a side street near the old armoury where a couple of years before four tonnes of sweating, woefully ignored fifty-year-old dynamite finally blew up. Someone has done a passable job of rebuilding the perimeter walls and plastering the cracks. Which is more than can be said for the carcass of the Parliament building, which is only a couple of blocks away. The team commander is an overweight Belarusian in a stained khaki T-shirt with the orc-skull Valkyrie insignia on it. He shambles across the parade ground towards them and introduces himself as Stas. With him are two non-commissioned officers and thirty or so soldiers from the poorer parts of Russia and its client states. Two deafening diesel generators deliver twenty-four-hour electricity and there is a ten-metre-wide satellite dish streaked with red dust mounted on the roof of a two-storey building.

Stas clearly believes that Yulia has arrived straight from Moscow and stares at her as if she is by turns exotic and terrifying.

'Show us where Angry Bear worked,' she demands, imperiously.

Stas leads them into the building. He shows them to the windowless room from which the hacking operation that targeted London was run. It's been ransacked. Nothing is salvageable. Angry Bear took an axe to the servers, hard drives and banks of monitors before she fled. That was just after a Tailored Access team from the US National Security Agency traced her from a laptop in Downing Street to here via a series of staging servers that were spread across the planet.

She didn't make it far into the jungle.

Two weeks after her departure a ransom note was delivered to the compound gate demanding a million US dollars in used twenty-dollar bills in exchange for Angry Bear's safe return. Stas shows them the location of the cash drop-off, pointing with a length of dried reed at a wall-mounted map. He tells them it's about a hundred and twenty kilometres north of the city but there's no tarmac, so it's a six-hour journey on crushed laterite that has been churned up by trucks and hollowed out by rains.

'We think it's a small group of bandits hiding in the forest.'

It's a broad green expanse divided by rivers like the veins on a leaf, with only the occasional settlement to hint at human habitation. From the tone of his voice, it's clear that Stas has little enthusiasm for venturing into the interior. 'She must have told them that she was valuable.'

She is undoubtedly valuable. Angry Bear is one of the coders behind Grom, a nation-breaking weapons platform designed to cripple the critical infrastructure of a nation that was built by a murky alliance of Russian military intelligence, PMC Valkyrie and an anarchist hacker collective known as the Protean Bears. As a means of delivering mass destruction, malware may be prosaic – Grom lacks the apocalyptic flair of nuclear winter or the Greenland ice-cap melting – but it does show how quickly the veneer of civilisation can be stripped away and an entire society plunged into a pre-industrial era of tooth and claw. Guy Fowle used it to launch a wave of attacks in London that caused a widespread collapse of law and order and very nearly resulted in the entire city being covered in a radioactive cloud.

The UK is now on the highest threat level in expectation of further attacks. Fowle is on the run and Angry Bear may be one of the few people with an idea of how to stop him.

'You have the ransom money?'

'The currency dealer delivered it this morning,' Stas confirms. He shuffles down a corridor and shows them into an adjacent room, where a trestle table is stacked with packets of plastic-wrapped bills with a total weight of fifty kilos. 'None of my men have been paid. They're getting restless. The sooner you get this out of here the happier I'll be.'

'What are the terms?' Jude says.

'Two people in one vehicle carrying the cash,' he replies. 'You hand over the money at one location and an hour later the prisoner is released two kilometres away and told to follow a path that leads to you.'

'How do we know that she will be released if we hand over the money?'

Stas shrugs. 'Kidnapping is a business here. You can call it thieves' honour.'

'Thieves' honour?' Yulia says, incredulously.

'It's the way they do things.' He looks at Jude. 'I can lend you a driver.'

'Oh, no,' Yulia says. 'It's Russian money and I want to see it delivered.'

'In that case, Yulia and I will go alone,' Jude says.

'I can give you a map and a GPS,' Stas says with a shrug. 'After a certain point, there is only one road.'

'Do you have an armoury?'

Stas unclips the ring of keys from his belt and unlocks a steel gun cabinet. 'Help yourself.'

Jude browses the shelves and adds a blunt-nosed Russian Gyurza pistol, two cardboard boxes of 9mm ammunition, a smoke grenade, an anti-personnel grenade, a plastic-wrapped slab of C-4 explosive and a box of detonators to his messenger pouch.

Yulia lifts an eyebrow. 'Are you planning to start a war?'

'I like to prepare for the worst.'

'The worst has a habit of following you around.'

## 2

# Rock Ape rises

Lee Chapeaux, Member of Parliament for a visceral northern constituency that has turned its back on the vapid politics of aspiration, stands six-foot-and-three-inches tall in the nation's capital with his fingers curled and his bandy legs about shoulder width apart, feeling the power rising to his groin from the native soil beneath him. He is flanked on one side by the Noble Boys, a squad of the finest working-class chaps from the fighting parts of England, and on the other by the hard-pressed nurses and paramedics who have found in him their greatest champion. Behind him is the red-brick Victorian façade of one of the capital's recently hard-pressed and full-to-bursting hospitals.

'I have asked you to come here today to announce my bid to be the next Prime Minister,' Lee announces to the jostling pack of hacks and paparazzi with his widest smile, side-stepping the thorny issue of territory and sovereignty. Prime Minister of what exactly? A united or fractured Kingdom, a greater or lesser Britain, with or without Scotland or that bit of Ireland that defies all understanding – matters best left for another time. 'I have chosen this place to make my announcement as a symbol of my success in protecting this country from our enemies. While the mob ran riot in our streets and Russian saboteurs ran amok and Londoners fell sick and the ruling elites hid behind their Whitehall barricade, ordinary people from the rest of the country mobilised in response to my call and created a human chain around our hospitals. It's time for the right-thinking people of this country to follow their example, to stand up for what's ours.'

It surprises Lee that there are still people out there, fellow parliamentarians amongst them, who believe that voters are swayed by arguments. What they don't seem to grasp – as he does – is that politics is war. Voters are friendly forces, and your sole objective is to crush the opposition. You find enemies wherever you can. If necessary, you make them up. When the rioting broke out across London, Lee saw his opportunity. He hired a bus to transport his men to the capital to defend the hospitals, just one bus from his constituency to begin with and then a convoy from across the nation. Patriotic folk determined to do their duty. And when the news broke that the Prime Minister had lost his battle to the shitting disease, Lee again saw an opportunity. The Prime Minister is dead. The top job is vacant.

'We are in a floodtide in the affairs of men,' Lee says with a chestful of air, because a dash of Shakespeare never goes amiss, 'and now is the time to ride the wave of fortune.'

'What about the Foreign Secretary's accusation that these are unsightly and illegal squatter camps?' a journalist calls out.

The Foreign Secretary is a measly cunt who couldn't fill a sandbag or drag a wounded soldier to safety. His name is Nigel Featherstone, and he is what is left of the *cabinet of dunces* that the dead PM surrounded himself with because he preferred sunny optimism to hard truths. Nigel is due to announce his rival candidacy and parade his reassuring, choir-singing wife before the day is out.

'How would gravy train Nigel know?' Lee replies, in mock-outrage. 'He spent the crisis hiding in Brussels with his cowardly euro-mates. Where was he when we needed him? Absent from post! You're welcome to tour the camp. I think you'll find it's very hygienic. My friend Ezra paid for the drinking water, the soap and the Portaloos!'

The senior members of the Cabinet may live in fancy grace-and-favour homes, but they don't own them. As his friend, the freewheeling business tycoon Ezra Gullet, likes to say, 'We bought it for them, Lee. We own Downing Street, and we own them.' And as he repeated over the phone last night – 'Lee, it's time to move in and hang our own wallpaper.'

'Do you regret saying that the Russian president is the world leader you most admire?' another journalist shouts.

'No,' Lee brazens it out. Always tell the truth when you must and lie sparingly. 'I admired his strength of purpose. But he went bad, didn't he? He lost his way. Look at what has happened to London. It's a disgrace. It makes me incredibly mad. We had no money and no fuel, no internet or power, and people were dying of sickness. Law and order collapsed. That's why I'm so proud of the patriots who rushed to defend our hospitals.'

'Do you mean the so-called Noble Boys?'

'I mean anyone who acted the good Samaritan.'

'Do you condemn those who set fire to mosques and synagogues?'

'Of course, I condemn any act of vandalism. You won't print that though, will you?'

'And the vigilante attacks? Do you condemn them?'

'I support anyone who comes to this country and is prepared to integrate and demonstrate their loyalty. At the same time, we can't be having foreigners who we know nothing about holding a knife to our jugular. We need to take back control.' He waves his hand. 'That's it, boys and girls. Thank you for coming.'

He's having a cheeky cigarette around the back by a loading bay when the reporter who asked the first question finds him. Denzel, his ever-present campaign manager, moves to block her approach but Lee waves him away.

'Mister Chapeaux,' she says.

'Call me Lee.'

'I'm Indirabala Bhatt. And you can call me Bala.'

'I know who you are.' She writes for the *Yorkshire Post* from their London bureau. He's aware that she's been studying him for several months. At first, he assumed she was coming from a place of contempt. Then he wondered if she might have been encouraged by the Security Service to spy on him. But she seems surprised by something in him. He quotes her copy back at her: '*Since his heroic strut onto the political scene, former special forces soldier and inner city ne'er-do-well Lee Chapeaux has cast himself in Shakespearean terms: from Afghanistan, where he fought with valour, in the manner of*

*Prince Hal finding within himself Henry V, to London, where he stood up to the rioters, as proud as a latter-day Coriolanus.'*

'You liked that, didn't you?' she teases him.

He knows from her bio that she's originally South African, a descendant of Punjabi labourers imported to Natal by the British in the nineteenth century. She has only recently become a UK citizen. A modelling contract paid her tuition fees on the prestigious journalism course at Johannesburg University. She is tall and willowy with a mane of hair that tumbles to her shoulders and slim-cut jeans, enough to stir the loins of any full-blooded imperial adventurer.

'I don't believe that it ended well for Caius Marcius Coriolanus.'

'He let his pride destroy him,' she says with a smile.

'That won't happen to me.'

'Have you spoken to the Foreign Secretary?'

'Yes, we've spoken.' He pats the granite step beside him. 'Come on.'

Bala sits. 'And you've agreed to dismantle the camps?'

She has the kind of face that invites confidences. 'Certainly not,' he replies, 'but it so happens that our work is done here.'

'What did you talk about then?'

'The attacks, obviously, I told him that we can't be relying on foreigners to run our key industries. We need to protect our land, our weald, our common space. We're only just beginning to learn how close this country came to total catastrophe at Sizewell.' There is still a cordon around the nuclear power station at Sizewell on the Suffolk coast and thousands of people have been evacuated amid rumours of a partial meltdown in the reactor caused by one of the cyber-attacks. 'And we're told we're going to have to wait a year for the Koreans to deliver us new transformers!' Only three of the six super-transformers that supply London with electricity are back up and running, meaning daily load-shedding is the norm, with rolling blackouts across the city.

'What did Mr Featherstone have to say for himself?'

Lee snorts derisively. 'Nigel told me that a systemic cyber-attack was on the government's risk register, but what of it? It was on a spreadsheet! What difference did that make? Where was the contingency planning? Horrendous! And we still don't know if it's over. Guy Fowle is still loose. And there could be tens or hundreds of Russian sleepers in our key industries. We face an existential risk. We could be attacked again, at any minute.'

'You're getting a lot of coverage with that claim,' Bala says. 'Some say that you are inciting violence.'

It is only three days since an operations room supervisor at the Fawley oil refinery, the largest in Britain, was badly beaten by an incensed mob outside his home in a usually quiet cul-de-sac in Southampton. The supervisor, who is of Corsican extraction, is still in intensive care and it's touch-and-go whether he will be permanently disabled. There have been scores of incidents ranging from vandalism of homes to physical attacks targeting 'foreign-looking' workers in the last two weeks.

'The threat we face is real,' Lee replies. 'It's not hypothetical. It's clear and present danger; we must do something about it. That means ensuring the people in the control rooms of this country who are pushing the buttons that give us electricity and fuel and drinking water are people we can trust.'

'What do you make of the government's offer of amnesty to any Russian illegals who hand themselves in?'

'Has anyone handed themselves in?'

'Not to my knowledge,' she says. 'And No. 10 is refusing to comment.'

'All the more reason to get me into No. 10 so the truth can come out.'

'Do you think it's likely you will be the next Prime Minister?'

'I think it's possible.'

'And are you prepared to meet face to face with the Russian president?'

'No true Englishman has ever been frightened of any foreigner. Of course I'll meet him. He needs to explain himself. If these attacks really were the acts of criminal elements of his own security services, then he needs to provide the evidence and commit to some house cleaning. If he continues to shelter them and not hand them over, he's complicit and we're on a very dangerous path.'

She frowns. 'Are you threatening military action against Russia?'

He ditches the grin and gives her his most sombre look. 'If there are any further attacks, there will be grave consequences and I'm not ruling anything out.'

Her expression turns playful. 'Is it true that at Hereford your nickname was Rock Ape?'

'How did you find that out?' He laughs, wistfully. 'Yeah, it was.'

'Can you explain?'

'Before I did SAS Selection, I served with the Royal Air Force Regiment.'

As a young soldier, he'd been a member of a casualty extraction team in Afghanistan, securing helicopter landing sites under fire. He'd seen more than enough blood and carnage to give him an acute sense of the absurdity of life.

'Go on.'

'It's a case of mistaken identity from Aden in the 1950s. After a night drinking in the mess, two officers of the RAF Regiment decided to go out on a night-time shooting spree and bag themselves some Hamadryas baboons, known locally as rock apes. In the darkness, one of them shot the other. When he was asked why, he said that he mistook him for a rock ape.'

Her phone beeps an alert.

'Excuse me.'

'Please go ahead.'

She glances down at the screen and Lee allows his eyes to roam the contours of her body, the lowland uplands and the upland summits, and imagine the plains and deltas that lie beneath her clothes. When she looks up, Lee sees an amused expression on her face. 'The bookies have lowered the odds on you.'

'I bet you're thinking you should have put some money on me?'

She smiles archly. 'What makes you think I haven't?'

'It's going to be fun.' Lee delivers his most raffish grin. She is beautiful and bright. He has been single for far too long. 'I'm sure we can find a seat for you on the battle bus. Want to come along for the ride?'

# 3

# Ransom

Jude and Yulia drive through an abandoned rubber plantation, past mottled ranks of trees with white milky liquid spilling over the cups like candlewax. Beyond the plantation, jungle presses up to the edge of the road, large heart-shaped leaves hanging over the furrowed red clay.

The further they get, the worse the condition of the road. The potholes get deeper and closer together, so it feels like hitting oncoming waves in a boat, each crest followed by a sudden trough. The bottoms of the craters are full of muddy red water that is the consistency of Campbell's soup.

Jude can see that Yulia is preoccupied. In the last two weeks she has lost her husband and her life has been turned over. Her current status is unclear. It is possible though unvoiced that she has defected to the West.

They stop to let a troop of monkeys pass, the alpha stopping to watch them from the middle of the road while the others cross. Jude glances left and right and in the mirrors. The jungle feels ripe for ambush. For Jude, this is no time for reflection; there is just the uncertain now.

Eventually the road ends. Jude parks in a clearing beside a wooden shelter with three open sides and a thatched roof. They get out. He looks at the map and his GPS.

'Now what?' Yulia asks.

'We wait.'

She sits on a log beneath the shelter and starts applying mosquito repellent to her wrists and the back of her neck. Jude considers the foot trails that disappear into the ancient and ageless jungle like muddy tunnels.

'Under other circumstances I might have suggested that we take the money and run,' she tells him.

'Under other circumstances, I might have agreed.'

'Please, darling, you're such a bad liar.'

The air is so thick it's like being smothered in a steaming towel.

There is none of the usual Checkpoint Charlie drama of a prisoner exchange. There is theatre, nonetheless. The kidnapper sent to collect the cash arrives on a scooter, slipping and sliding along one of the trails towards them. He looks painfully thin and barely out of his teens.

The boy parks the scooter beside the Land Cruiser and puts it up on its stand. Together they consider the task of transferring the money from the car to the scooter. Eventually, Jude walks over to the shelter and pries one of the rough planks loose. He lays it across the back of the scooter and secures it with bungee cords. He then spends twenty minutes transferring the bricks of cash to the plank and strapping them together with canvas straps. When he is done, the stack of money is as wide as the scooter is long. The boy climbs on the scooter and switches on the engine. He gets about fifty metres down one of the trails, a different one to the one he arrived on, before the inevitable happens; the weight of the money strapped to the back tips the scooter over on its side in the mud.

'Heaven help us,' Yulia says.

Jude goes after him.

The boy is trapped. He stares up at Jude with scared, bloodshot eyes. Jude reaches out and takes his hand, dragging him out from beneath the scooter. They stand beside each other, contemplating the toppled stack of money. Jude offers a cigarette from a packet he brought with him in his messenger bag. Jude very rarely smokes, but in other not dissimilar circumstances he has learned their use in kidnap situations. The boy accepts one.

There's no way he's going to drive the money out on the scooter. The boy finishes the cigarette and flicks it into the mud. Then he gestures for Jude to help him. Together, they get it back up on its wheels. They push it back and forth in the mud to turn it around and wheel it back to the clearing beside the car.

'What now?' Yulia asks from the shelter.

When he looks back, he sees that the boy is holding a pistol in his right hand.

He steps up to Jude, who stares down the shaking barrel and then into the boy's eyes. He carefully raises his hands in surrender. He's trying to figure out where the boy got the gun from, under the seat of the scooter perhaps?

'I think he wants the car.'

Yulia sighs. 'We're being mugged by a child.'

Jude's hands sweep in from either side like a clap. His left fist strikes the boy's right wrist at the same time as his right hand grabs the top of the barrel and twists. The force of the blow breaks the boy's grip and flips the gun.

The gun is now in Jude's hands and pointing at the boy.

They stare at each other.

'That was very brave, darling,' Yulia says. 'But it is not clear what you have achieved.'

'I'm not partial to having guns pointed at me.'

'Yes, but what now?'

She has a point. Jude sighs and ejects the round. He tucks the gun in the back of his trousers and walks over to the scooter. He loosens the straps and carries the muddy bricks of plastic-wrapped cash back to the Land Cruiser while the boy watches, holding his bruised hand against his chest.

When Jude is finished, he goes over to sit beside Yulia on the log.

The boy is staring at them as if they are beyond understanding.

'How old do you think he is?' she asks.

Jude takes the car keys out of his pocket and throws them to the ground at the boy's feet.

'Skedaddle,' he says.

The boy gets the message. He jumps in the car and starts the engine. They watch, fully expecting it to get stuck, as the car squeezes down one of the narrow trails, sliding and revving in the mud, breaking branches across the bonnet and leaving them in its wake. Eventually it drives out of sight and, not long after, the jungle swallows the sound.

'That feels like a million dollars well spent, darling.'

It starts to rain.

Jude stares at the scooter. 'Do you want to ride pillion?'

Yulia rolls her eyes. 'It will soon be dark.'

'I could request an extraction.'

There is an Increment team on standby at an airfield in Cameroon ready to rescue them if necessary.

'Let's wait and see what happens,' Yulia replies. 'Perhaps there is such a thing as thieves' honour. Besides, I'm bored of other people.'

Jude sympathises. For the first time since Guy Fowle tried to kill him, close protection officers are not shadowing him. It feels like a form of liberation.

# 4

# Mashenka

Jude collects fallen wood for a fire, twigs to begin with and then branches, many of them wet. He plants the larger branches like stakes in a semi-circle in front of the shelter. Then he rips away the rest of the planks from the sides of the shelter and breaks them across his knee.

'How are you going to light it?' Yulia asks.

He breaks off a piece of C-4 from the slab in his pouch and rolls it into a ball in his palms. He puts it down on the ground an arm's length from the shelter and builds a pile of twigs and smaller branches over it. It burns fiercely when he lights it, hissing and letting off an acrid smell. He starts feeding pieces of plank to the fire.

Once it has got going, he puts his jacket around Yulia's shoulders and they sit together on the log beneath the dripping thatch, staring into the crackling flames. Eventually she leans into his shoulder and says, 'You take me to the nicest places.'

'Never the same place twice.'

'With you, life is never dull,' she concedes.

Around them the dripping jungle turns from green to grey as the light fades. The sound of insects rises gradually to a roar. Yulia produces a silver flask from one of her many pockets. She takes a sip and passes it to him.

He sniffs it. 'What is it?'

'Black strap rum.'

It smells of burnt wood and caramel, and tastes rich and smoky.

'I am being courted by the Venezuelan ambassador,' she explains. 'He flies it into London from Caracas in the diplomatic pouch.'

'Do you miss him?'

'The ambassador?'

'Valery.'

She looks surprised. 'My husband? Absolutely not! I mean, he had a certain piratical flair but age and disappointment coarsened him.' She holds out her hand for the flask. 'And I don't miss my FSB minders.'

When he had commenced surveillance of her, the British intelligence services had been under the impression that Yulia was the bored wife of a military intelligence officer. Jude was told the FSB minders were there for her husband, who was under diplomatic cover at the Russian Embassy in London. But it turned out the minders were hers, ostensibly to protect her but to watch her also. She was a senior officer in the Russian Foreign Intelligence Service, the Sluzhba Vneshney Razvedki.

'By the end there were three agencies involved in our marriage: the SVR, the GRU and the FSB,' she explains. 'It didn't make for a tranquil home life. I suppose I should be over the moon that he is gone.'

'But you're not?'

'Darling, there is a psychopath out there somewhere with the means of breaking entire nations, our two countries are on the brink of war, our romantic assignation has run its course and there's only so much rum.'

Jude hears movement in the darkness and stands up. He imagines some enormous beast barrelling towards them. A woman crashes through the branches of the improvised stockade and throws herself down in front of the fire. She's covered in mud and her clothes are torn.

'You're Yulia Ermolaeva,' she says, when she looks up. She has dark eyes with luminous whites in a filthy face. There are twigs and leaves in her hair.

'I am,' Yulia replies. 'And your name is unknown to me, which is not a satisfactory state of affairs.'

'Your husband was dick!'

'He was.'

'I'm fucked,' the young woman says. It's surprising how expressive her face is. She looks around. 'What now?'

'We wait for morning,' Jude says. 'And then we walk back to town.'

She looks incredulous. 'Are you serious?'

'Yes.'

'I don't believe it. What kind of stupid operation is this?'

'The usual kind.' Yulia passes her the flask. 'Have a drink.' The young woman stares suspiciously at it. 'For the sake of God!' Yulia snatches it back and swigs it before returning it to her. 'Russia paid good money for you. Why would we poison you now?'

The young woman wipes her face with the back of her hand and takes a sip and then another.

'I am not going to call you Angry Bear,' Yulia tells her.

'You can call me Mashenka.'

'Goldilocks? Really?'

'It's what my father named me. He was dick, too.'

'Well then, Mashenka, perhaps you can tell us why you decided to team up with Guy Fowle and almost start a war?'

'You think I had choice?'

'We all have a choice,' Yulia tells her. 'It's what makes us human.'

'That is very fucking profound,' Mashenka says.

'You're beginning to annoy me,' Yulia tells her.

'You're already annoying me,' Mashenka snaps. 'I can see why you married dick.'

Knowing better than to say anything, Jude gets up to turn the branches so that a fresh side faces the fire.

At least it has stopped raining.

# 5

# Black site

Jude wakes to the thump of helicopter blades and a searchlight skimming the tops of the trees towards them. He climbs to his feet and steps out from under the shelter with Yulia and Mashenka rising behind him. They are lit up. An American Black Hawk looms out of the sky and lands, bouncing on its wheels. A SEAL team fans out to take protective positions while a second Black Hawk circles overhead like a sleek black wasp. The team leader runs up to them and shines a red-lensed torch in Jude's face. He is wearing a helmet camera and a Chief Petty Officer's rank slide.

'Confirm that you are Mr Jude Lyon?'

'Yes, I'm Lyon.'

'You're other government agency.'

It's a statement not a question. The Chief switches the torch beam to Yulia's face, 'Ms Yulia Ermolaeva?'

'Also, other government agency,' she replies.

A SEAL assaulter puts a black cloth hood over Mashenka's head and another ties her wrists with cable ties. They lift her and carry her back to the helicopter.

'I have orders to transport you along with the prisoner,' the Chief says.

'I'm not going anywhere,' Yulia says.

'You have a better suggestion?' Jude asks.

She rolls her eyes. 'I want a shower.'

'They have showers where you're going, ma'am,' says the Chief. 'And hot food.'

She looks at Jude and shrugs. 'Shall we?'

'Please.'

She crouch-sprints for the helicopter with Jude behind her. They climb aboard onto the second row of seats behind the machine-gunners. The turbines roar and the helicopter's deck shudders beneath them as they lift off.

The next time Jude wakes, the deck is tilting, the pitch of the blades changing, the roar of the engine increasing: they have left the jungle behind and through the window he sees desert and long shadows rushing up towards them. The chopper hits the ground with a bone-jarring thud, throwing everyone back on the seats.

'Move!' one of the crew yells. They unbuckle and scramble out, running across the sand at full tilt. Behind them the second helicopter lands.

They shelter from a hot, dry wind by a mud-brick wall and watch while one of the pilots climbs up onto the roof of the helicopter to inspect the rotors and a fuel truck trundles past a neglected artillery gun towards it.

It's not long after dawn.

The Chief points to a solitary hill with peaks of barren rock about a mile away and tells them that there are enemy combatants massing on the other side of it.

'Where are we?' Yulia asks.

'That's classified.'

'This is ridiculous,' says Mashenka from inside her hood.

Judging by the terrain, Jude guesses that they have reached the edge of the Sahel, the belt of tropical steppe that stretches across Africa, and which the Arabs call the coastline of the Sahara.

'How much further?' he asks.

'Another couple of hours that way,' the Chief says, pointing north-west.

Which means they are probably heading for Niger or Mali.

'Why aren't they using the bloody artillery?' Yulia asks.

The Chief shrugs. 'They don't have the right ammunition. Generals cut deals with different suppliers and so they have hundreds of different weapon systems and everyone has the wrong ammunition.'

When the truck is finished it drives off and parks in the shadow of a tree on the edge of the landing zone.

'Back on board,' the Chief says.

The chopper vibrates with increased power and rises, swinging out over a refugee camp and beyond it a ditch that surrounds the settlement like a medieval moat. They rise higher, the terrain receding into illusory smoothness.

The US base is the only facility for miles. At first, it's a black mark on an undisturbed horizon, a tiny oasis in the emptiness, but gradually it becomes clearer. A sandcastle of concentric anti-vehicle berms, coiled concertina wire and watchtowers beside an airfield with nothing else but sun-scoured desert for as far as the eye can see.

They circle the runway before landing to allow a Reaper with a twenty-metre wingspan to take off. As the drone rises slowly into the bright blue sky, the chopper touches down and taxis towards the twelve-foot-high mud walls. Military Police lope towards the chopper and surround the hooded prisoner. Their shouts are drowned out as the helicopter's turbines roar and it taxis towards the other end of the runway.

Jude and Yulia jump out and follow the MPs as they hustle the prisoner towards the wall and through a small metal door into a narrow channel between concertinas of razor wire. In a khaki tent, Mashenka is pinned to the ground and MPs in surgical gloves cut away her filthy clothes and shake powder all over her. Naked, covered in white powder, she is lifted up and carried to a doctor, who shines a torch in her mouth and pokes around with a lolly-stick.

Mashenka bites it in two and gnashes her teeth at them.

'We've got a biter,' one of the MPs says convivially.

'You are now in a military facility,' another MP tells them, after relieving Yulia of her satellite phone. 'You will be escorted at all times. This way.'

He leads them past Mashenka and two waiting lab technicians. Outside, the air has a whiff of diesel and burnt plastic. They go through another metal door in a mud wall into an enclosure filled with six large tents. The MP marches up to the nearest tent and holds the flap open for them.

Inside, soldiers in desert fatigues are sitting in camp chairs or lying on cot beds. One of them, wearing a sergeant's stripes and name badge with *Coolidge* on it, looks up from her laptop and says, 'We've got two beds for you down the back of the tent. I suggest you get some sleep. We'll wake you when we're ready for you to see the high-value prisoner.'

'I was promised a shower,' Yulia says.

'The water's pretty cold this time of the morning,' Coolidge says. She has a shaved head and cold, colourless eyes. 'It'll heat up again by lunchtime.'

Yulia sighs. 'Lunchtime, then.'

Jude takes her by the hand and leads her down the central aisle between cot beds. The last two on one side are unoccupied. Jude pulls them together and they lie down, fully dressed under rough blankets, with their noses inches apart.

'This just gets better and better,' Yulia whispers. She closes her eyes and soon she is asleep. Jude remains awake for a time, conscious of people in the tent around him.

Jude wakes to find Yulia sitting wearing a towel on the edge of her cot and using another as a turban.

'This is Keisha,' Yulia says.

Jude looks over his shoulder at the next cot where Coolidge and another woman are sitting. He recognises her as one of the hackers from the US Army Tailored Access team that set up shop at Downing Street while Guy Fowle ran amok at Sizewell.

'I'm Jude,' he says, feeling in need of a toothbrush.

'Nice to meet you properly,' Keisha says. She has two cornrow braids and is wearing jeans and a green T-shirt with *USAF* on it in large black lettering.

'Keisha is what passes for authority in this place,' Yulia says.

'I am,' Keisha replies. 'What can you tell me about the prisoner?'

'She recognised me,' Yulia replies, 'and she knew my husband.'

'And did you recognise her?'

Yulia shakes her head. 'I've never seen her before.'

'We have sent her fingerprints and DNA to Moscow. They are going to want to talk to you when they have the results.'

'Of course,' Yulia says. 'Do you have a hairdryer?'

'You just need to go stand out in the wind, you'll get the best blow-dry of your life,' Coolidge says, cheerily.

Yulia looks unimpressed.

'When can we speak to the prisoner?' Jude asks.

'Now.'

'I will get dressed,' Yulia says. 'Look the other way. You too, Jude.'

When Yulia is clothed, Coolidge leads them from the tent enclosure towards a gate at the entrance to another compound with twelve-foot-high mud walls topped with razor wire. Armed MPs open the gate and allow them in.

Inside, they go down a narrow passage between outer and inner walls. The inner walls are decorated with murals remembering 9/11, Fallujah and Benghazi.

'The facility holds up to twenty high-value prisoners,' Coolidge explains. 'We have eleven currently. Yours takes us up to a dozen.'

She opens a beaten-metal door onto a courtyard with two single-storey concrete buildings separated by a gravel path. There are two MPs sitting in the shade of camouflage netting.

'We'd like to speak to number eight, please.'

'We'll bring her down,' one of the MPs replies.

'You better watch out,' the other says. 'She's a biter.'

They walk down the path between the two rectangular buildings. Each is divided into ten cells with a number painted in black above the door. They continue to a door in the wall at the end of the path. On the other side is another smaller compound with two side-by-side geodesic domes coated with dust.

The second dome has a steel floor, a desk that is bolted to it and four camp chairs. Above the desk there is a canopy of diffuse orange light criss-crossed by black aluminium struts. Coolidge arranges three chairs in a row on one side of the table and another chair for Mashenka on the other.

'There you go,' she says. 'I'll leave you to it.'

They sit and wait for the dust to settle.

Mashenka is escorted in by two MPs, who press her down in the chair and take two steps back. She is wearing an orange jumpsuit and shackles, and her head has been shaved, revealing a smooth, childlike brow. She stares sullenly across the desk at them.

'This will go a lot easier if you cooperate,' Keisha says, briskly.

Mashenka snorts, 'Easier for who?'

'How long have you been in Africa?'

'Too fucking long.'

'What is your role in the hacking group known as the Protean Bears?'

Mashenka rolls her eyes. 'I am official porridge taster.'

'Who do you report to?'

'Daddy Bear.'

'Who is Daddy Bear?'

'Really?'

'Yes.'

She laughs. 'Father of Baby Bear.'

Keisha sighs and signals to the MPs. 'Take her back to her cell. Let her stew.'

# 6

## Desert voices

They hear from Moscow the following afternoon. Another twenty-four hours where Jude frets about the possibility of a new Grom attack on UK soil and the search for Guy Fowle continues. Keisha gives Yulia her satellite phone back and walks her outside the accommodation tent into the sunlight. She points at the vast blue sky.

'We'll be listening.'

'I'm sure you will,' Yulia replies and strides towards the shade of the perimeter wall.

'Do you trust her?' Keisha asks Jude, who has joined her at the entrance to the tent.

'Yes,' he replies.

Keisha looks sceptical. 'You are too close to her.'

*Is that what the problem is?* Jude wonders.

They haven't shared a bed since Istanbul, back when Yulia's thug of a husband was alive and Guy Fowle was behind bars. And she's recently told him that their romantic assignation has run its course. But he was close to her, once. Physically, at least. In the preliminary stage of their courtship, which was conducted via the message portal of a bespoke dating site for married women, she had sent him a series of images, anatomical close-ups in high definition, that were provocatively intimate and anonymously clinical. They had yet to meet face to face but there were several distinct parts of her – she referred to them as *'hills, caves and ridges'* – with which he became intimately familiar. Of course, from the outset he was alive to the possibility that the images were not of her body but someone else's. He had been tasked by his employers with seducing her and there was always going to be a risk that she would spot him for what he was, an agent of a foreign power engaged in a honey trap operation. When she let him explore her for real and he discovered that the images were genuine, he felt blessed.

Keisha agrees to let Yulia lead in the second round of questioning. The same venue and the same tableau: Keisha, Jude and Yulia on one side of the folding table and Mashenka on the other, the two MPs standing guard at her shoulders.

'These are the facts,' Yulia says in English. She is wearing a pair of reading glasses and in front of her there is a sheaf of faxes that arrived from Moscow shortly after the satellite call and are already curling in the heat. 'You are Maria Alfyorova.' Mashenka is staring intently at the ceiling of the dome and acting like she would rather be anywhere else in the world. 'You are twenty-five years old, and you were born in Krasnoyarskiy Kray near Lake Tiberkul, not so far from the Mongolian border. In many ways, your early life is a sad tale.'

Mashenka's nose twitches, as if she has smelled something unpleasant. She is clearly no stranger to being questioned by authority figures.

'You grew up in the Strict Community, a doomsday cult with a taste for polygamy and exotic punishment. Apparently, they are still waiting for the great plague.' Yulia sifts through the faxes until she finds the one that she is looking for. 'You were taken into the care of the state at age thirteen. According to the report from the Ministry of Labour and Social Protection, the elders of the community believed that you were exhibiting signs of demonic possession and were planning to drown you in a formal ceremony.'

Mashenka shrugs.

'Perhaps you were too much for them to handle,' Yulia muses. 'After all, such communities are not so well equipped to handle angry young women. Neither it seems was the state. Sadly, our orphanages remain places of neglect and threats. You were quickly designated as *neobuchaemy* – uneducable – which is usually reserved for the mentally disabled. You showed a talent for escape from successive institutions. You soon came to the attention of the police: there are reports of violence and theft with no apparent remorse. Your name is then linked with a gangster with a violent streak from a Siberian crime syndicate. Of course, the next step is prison. How was it for you in prison, not so easy I think?'

Mashenka scowls.

'And yet, I can say that for the purposes of the state it worked. You did not go back to prison. The next reference that links you to an institution is altogether more benevolent. You enrolled as a student of computer programming at the St Petersburg State University. Apparently, you excelled. Bravo! It is so good to see a previously unprepossessing individual with a hardscrabble upbringing turn their life around. But . . .' Yulia's hand snatches at the air. 'But! Something is off. According to their records you were not state sponsored or special quota, instead you were a paid admission student, which raises the question, who paid? A bene-factor you met in prison perhaps?'

Mashenka harrumphs and rolls her eyes.

'After St Petersburg, equipped with an excellent degree and specialist skills that are much in demand, you returned to Siberia, perhaps at the suggestion of your mysterious benefactor? I under-stand that there is a name for hackers that work on the frontier in the east, Promysloviki Bears. And the connections between hack-ing and organised crime are well established. It is therefore no surprise that, according to state records, you are listed as the co-owner of a once successful but now defunct chain of sushi restaurants on the oil frontier, and your fellow co-owner is Juri Malenkovich, an *avtoritet* – authority – in the Tambov Gang of St Petersburg.'

Mashenka is indignant and finally breaks her silence. 'I never went inside one of these restaurants. I hate fish.'

'Now we're getting somewhere,' Yulia says. 'My colleagues in the FSB tell me that the restaurants were a front for a money-laundering operation, and they believe that you and your fellow conspirators were responsible for a succession of hacking operations that raided Moscow-based cryptocurrency exchanges. You hacked the exchanges and rinsed the money through the restaurants. You did very well, and you made a lot of money. But . . .' Again, Yulia snatches at the air. 'Something happened! It all came crashing down around you. What happened, Mashenka?'

She glares defiantly at Yulia. 'What do you think happened?'

'I think that you got greedy, and you didn't do your research properly, that's what happened. You hacked an exchange called Vr. The distinctive feature of the exchange was that it did not ask customers for their ID. This did not cause alarm bells to ring? Like I said, greedy but also stupid. Because the start-up capital for Vr was provided by the oligarch Oleg Solokov, banker to senior officers in the military and the intelligence services. He cried foul. And so, you came to the attention of the GRU and in due course my husband. He made you an offer you could not refuse. You didn't want to go back to prison. Therefore, you agreed to work on Grom.'

'I told you your husband was dick. Do you have gum?'

Keisha passes her some. Mashenka chews thoughtfully for a minute or so and then says, 'I'm not going back to Russia.'

'That's not for you to decide,' Yulia says.

Ignoring her, Mashenka looks at Keisha. 'What's the shape of deal?'

'The United States government is prepared to offer you immunity from prosecution in return for complete and truthful testimony,' Keisha replies, to Yulia's obvious irritation. 'The conditions of the immunity will depend on the value of the evidence and its impact on the United States.'

'I have very valuable evidence,' she says. 'I know name of trusted custodian of Grom network for eastern seaboard of United States.'

'That's the kind of detail that we want to hear,' Keisha tells her.

'I want to live in Las Vegas. Long way from the sea. I hate fish!'

'Like I said, the more you give us the better it will be for you.'

'Your lawyers must speak to my lawyers,' Mashenka says, 'then I give you the prize.'

# 7

# Anywhere but here

'Maria Alfyorova is wanted for terrorism offences in the United Kingdom,' Jude reminds Keisha as they head back to the accommodation area.

Keisha doesn't break stride. 'My government wants Mashenka for different reasons.'

Jude protests, 'London was nearly destroyed. Fowle is still out there and may be about to strike again.'

'He doesn't have access to the app any more. The phone was destroyed.'

'We have a witness statement from Candida Taunton, the mother of one of Fowle's children, that says during the period he had the phone in his possession, he transcribed details from the Grom app into a notebook, including the means of activation of illegals.'

'You mean the not-so-reliable statement from a grief-stricken junkie?'

Jude struggles to contain his frustration. 'We have no idea how many other attacks he has written down and are ready to go, or have already been activated but are yet to happen. I need more time with her.'

'You'll get your chance,' Keisha replies.

'Before you fly her out of here?'

'Of course, and if we come to a deal with her, you'll get information as she shares it. And who knows, maybe one day she'll answer for her crimes.'

It comes as no surprise that Mashenka's law firm Grub, Mesiles and Torres is registered in Panama, a jurisdiction renowned for secretive offshore transactions. The partner handling her extradition and immunity is a jovial Texan named Bobby Torres who has been exiled in the Colón Free Trade Zone for twenty years. He wears a cowboy hat on the conference call convened the following day.

'I'm done reviewing the documentation sent to me by the US attorney general's office,' Bobby says from a window on Keisha's laptop. 'But I'll tell you, I've still got some outstanding questions. When I get satisfaction on that, I'll be sure to let you know.'

'What exactly are your questions, Mr Torres?' Keisha asks.

'My client is very specific about Las Vegas and the lifestyle she envisages. I just need to sort a few details of the financial remuneration and the blanket nature of the immunity. Nothing y'all need to worry about.'

'Of course,' Keisha says.

'But more importantly, my client would like reassurance that she will be treated fairly if she fully cooperates but – I'm emphasising the *but* here – the Protean Bears remain at large. She will do all she can, but she has made it clear that the bears are very impressive individuals who may evade capture. They are protean both by name and nature.'

'We can offer fairness,' Keisha says. 'As long as she is truthful and tells us everything she knows.'

'I'm sick of this place,' Mashenka says, leaning in between Jude and Keisha to speak to the screen. 'I want to go to Las Vegas.'

'You just hold tight, young lady,' Bobby says, in a fatherly tone. 'And stay safe. I'll get you moving just as soon as I can.'

That night they are startled awake by the banshee sound of a siren. Jude sits bolt upright, reaching for his pistol as he swings his feet off the cot. All around him soldiers are tumbling out of theirs, grabbing at body armour and helmets. He grips Yulia's hand.

'Put your boots on,' he tells her.

Sergeant Coolidge appears out of the darkness and says, 'Follow me.'

She leads them across the compound and through several gates to a staging area beside the runway that is guarded by the SEAL team. They kneel in the sand. Two Black Hawks have their rotors turning and the air is full of dust.

'What's happening?' Jude shouts above the roar of the engines.

'There's a convoy of enemy combatants heading this way,' Coolidge shouts back. 'We've been told to prepare to evacuate.'

The gate behind them rattles open and a line of twelve shackled prisoners, including Mashenka, with hoods over their heads are marched over to the helicopters and made to climb aboard. The Black Hawks lift off and rise into the night sky.

In the silence that follows, they listen to rumours swirling in the darkness around them. The convoy has fifty technicals with more than two hundred fighters aboard. They are Islamists or people traffickers. They have sworn to behead the foreigners. They are less than twenty kilometres away.

'It seems that we are less valuable than the prisoners,' Yulia says.

'Don't you worry,' Coolidge reassures her. 'The cavalry are here.'

Moments later, the sky erupts – shafts of white light on the horizon.

A fraction of a second later the sound of the explosions hurtles across the desert like a freight train, and they can feel the percussion wave in their chests.

'Arc light,' someone yells.

Somewhere out over the desert a B-52 Stratofortress is bombing the convoy. Jude pulls Yulia close, and she buries her head in his shoulder while the bombs continue to fall. The pummelling goes on for several minutes and then stops as suddenly as it started.

Yulia lifts her head. 'Is it over?'

'It's over,' Coolidge says, standing up.

As they are walking back to their tent, the returning helicopters with their cargo of prisoners fly low over the compound and land on the runway behind them.

# 8

# The first ballot

Lee is heading back to London on the battle bus from a rally of
the faithful in a Brexit lorry park as big and bright as Wembley
Stadium when the results of the first round of MPs voting are
announced.

The Noble Boys start howling like wolves.

Six candidates have fallen at the first hurdle having failed to
secure the support of at least 5% of their fellow MPs. Only three
now remain. In order of greatest vote share: Nigel Featherstone,
Fabian Pees and Lee Chapeaux – the elder statesman, the posh
whippet, and the youthful insurgent.

Who cares if he's third? He's through to the next round! Lee is
whooping with his arms in his air. Without thinking, he grabs the
nearest person and hugs her tight. The dizzyingly familiar smell of
orange blossom and cedar wood: with a start, he realises that it's
Bala. He releases her immediately.

'I'm so sorry,' he says, fighting to suppress a grin that threatens
to reach from ear to ear.

'That's okay,' she replies, also grinning.

His insides do a somersault. *Ping!* The message is sent and
received: inbox to inbox. They both want to do that again.
Preferably without an audience or the hindrance of clothing.

'I have to . . .'

'Go on.'

He leaves Bala with Denzel, his campaign manager, and walks
the length of the bus, swaying from seat to seat with a cheerful
smile, acknowledging the uproar with a wave and the occasional
squeeze of an intern shoulder. They look like plump puppies –
boys and girls – asking to be squeezed. They'll all be drunk and up

to mischief tonight. He feels a frisson of excitement at the prospect of spending the evening with Bala.

At the back of the bus, surrounded by an exclusion zone of empty seats, is Amanda Chappell, the backroom adviser to his largest financial backer, Ezra Gullet. She looks up from her tablet as he approaches. He has always found there to be something intimidating about her immaculate demeanour, and his efforts at teasing Ezra about it have always met a stony wall of silence.

He sits beside her, careful not to touch her.

'I really hope that you're not as stupid as the clown show of people you got round yourself,' she tells him with customary blunt-ness in an old-school Boston accent that has ditched the letter 'R' unless it's in front of a vowel. 'Nigel has half the votes cast and just successfully coalesced the anyone-but-Chapeaux caucus around him with his "heal the nation" spiel. If they stick with him, he is assured a place on the final ballot. Fabian is nipping at his heels and has the edge on you because MPs have always preferred their radi-calism delivered by an aristocrat not an upstart usurper.'

*Usupah.*

Lee shakes his head. 'When will they stop taking "went to Eton" as a qualification to run the country?'

'Are you sure you want to be Prime Minister?'

'Of course I do.'

She looks unconvinced. 'You don't have enough allies. Fabian would offer you a seat at the Cabinet table if you agreed to drop out of the race. Maybe you should be content with that.'

It was Ezra who'd told him it was PM or nothing. Ezra said the balance of power had shifted so far in No. 10's favour, no other government department was worth lobbying any more.

'The public love me,' he says, waving at the passing country-side. 'You were the one who told me that. And not just working people but entrepreneurs, the self-employed, and even sectors of management.'

'And as I also told you, the public are not the Party. The polit-ical Party are mercurial and according to my polling undecided. Besides, it counts for nothing unless you get through to the final round when the Party membership gets the opportunity to vote. Right now, you are in the hands of your fellow MPs and your cheeky-chappie act isn't going to cut the mustard.'

'You do know how to piss on a guy's shoes,' he says, wondering where she picked up *cut the mustahd*? Perhaps it's an Ezra expression.

'I'm not paid to flatter your ego.'

'That much is clear. How are we going to deal with Nigel and Fabian? You must have some dirt on them?'

'Actually, no. Nigel is as boring in private as he is in public. And Fabian's mental ferocity finds physical expression in his marital bed only. Besides, it's a dangerous road to go down. What if they retaliated?'

'What of it? I've got nothing to hide. Although my sins may be numerous and varied, they have been thoroughly raked over and laid out for all to see.'

'Are you sure about that?'

She clearly knows something. 'Come on, what is it?'

'What do you know about your new journalist friend?'

'Bala? I like her. You've seen what she's just written about me. *Chapeaux's campaign is like throwing open the shutters and tearing down the curtains in Miss Havisham's decaying mansion. It's the shot in the arm that every British person needs.* You can't ask for more than the nation waking up to that, can you?'

'How much do you know about her?'

'She's straight talking, bold and sassy. She knows her mind.' She also has a body to die for but he refrains from saying that. 'I like her a lot. Why?'

Amanda sighs. 'The rainbow nation has very progressive sex status laws.'

'What's that supposed to mean?'

'She's not what she seems.'

'Tell me!'

'Despite what it now says in the birth registry and on her passport, she was born a man.'

Which is not what he was expecting. 'I see.'

'I have Bangkok hospital records that detail the work she has had done,' she says, matter-of-factly. 'Breasts obviously, a tracheal shave, jawline, and brow-bone sculpting. As far as I can tell, that's it.'

She returns her attention to her tablet, swiping through graphs that might be stocks or polling numbers or morbidity rates or God knows what. Lee sits for a while and then gets up, feeling like he's been dismissed. He heads back towards the front of the bus.

# 9

# A walk on the wild side

Ezra Gullet throws a party that night at Wolfhanger, his 1930s mansion on the Wentworth Estate, a sprawling flat-roofed modernist castle with sweeping elevations and a curved staircase in a steel-framed glass turret.

The Breaky Bottom flows.

Sparkly-eyed Ezra is not a tall man, though he is fleet of foot. He skips up the final steps at the foot of the grand staircase so that he can reach Lee's shoulder. He proceeds to try to squeeze the life out of it with one hand while he raises a glass of award-winning Sussex fizz with the other and proudly tells the assembled guests that Lee has broken the mould of British politics. Lee feels bashful and unexpectedly short of anything to say. He waves it off. Cue cheering and clapping and backslapping. He glimpses Bala at the back of the room but before he can do anything about it, Ezra is steering him through the crowd in the opposite direction. Denzel falls into step beside them.

They pass through several reception rooms. On one of the largest televisions that Lee has ever seen, Nigel Featherstone is holding an 'impromptu' press conference on the runway at RAF Brize Norton before boarding a plane to Moscow. He is calling for a new international treaty on cyber-warfare: 'Without being sure of the source of the attack or having a legal framework that defines what constitutes an act of war, proportionate response like sanctions or counter-attacks are almost impossible to implement.'

'Dull!' Ezra exclaims.

Lee smirks. 'Fingers crossed he comes back waving a bit of paper!'

'It's clear blue water between him and us,' Denzel says.

'Come on,' Ezra tells them. 'Last bit of work for the day.'

He leads them towards his study.

'Do you want a password?' Ezra calls out as they approach Tito, the long-serving head of his protection detail. He's about the same size as Lee but bulkier in the chest.

'That's okay, Mr Gullet,' Tito replies. 'Only your mother could love it but I've grown accustomed to your face.'

'You're a charming fellow, Tito, like Lee and Denzel here. Three big, charming fellows. Will you vote for Lee?'

'Of course, Mr Gullet. I joined the Party like you said.'

'All the more reason for us to get Lee through to the final round! Now we want to be undisturbed while we're talking to our foreign friend in there.'

'No problem, Mr Gullet,' Tito says, opening the door.

For a study, it's thin on learning. Ezra has entirely dispensed with books. Instead, the walls are lined with calfskin leather on three sides. The fourth is floor-to-ceiling glass. A woman in a midnight-blue headscarf is staring out at a stand of floodlit lace-bark pines at the far edge of the manicured lawn that mark the boundary between the garden and the golf course beyond. She turns when they enter.

'This is Alysha Volkova,' Amanda Chappell says from behind Ezra's desk. 'She's from Damascus but married to a Russian and carrying one of your shiny new blue passports.'

Lee is less than pleased. 'Why am I here?'

'Don't worry, Alysha is our kind of Russian,' Ezra explains in a placatory tone. 'She hates that bastard in the Kremlin. Don't you, Alysha?'

'He is a thief and a mass murderer,' she agrees.

'And what do you want me to do about that?' Lee asks.

'For too long, the Russian people have tolerated an autocratic leader because of the security that he offered. Nobody in Russia wants to go back to the chaos of the 1990s. But where is the security now? The criminals are running amok. The intelligence agencies are at each other's throats. The streets are full of anarchists. The president's position is very precarious. It wouldn't take much for him to fall. In which case, someone must take his place.'

'What has that got to do with you?' Lee asks.

'I am an intermediary, nothing more. I support a candidate. A nationalist and a former soldier like you, a man of pragmatism. He has seen first-hand the damage that expeditionary wars do. My candidate would prefer Russia to have a new relationship with the West.'

'I want that too,' Lee says.

'He would like to meet with you to negotiate a new security agreement based on mutual benefit. He would like you to be his friend.'

'I've said it before, Ms Volkova. I'm not frightened of being seen with anyone. I'll go an extra mile for peace and even mutual benefit.'

'That will be music to his ears.'

'But if I'm wronged, I'll fight and woe betide my adversary.'

'He respects that,' Alysha says. 'Which is why he is content to wait until you are in Downing Street for a meeting.'

'I'm a long way from Downing Street.'

'He would like to help you with that.'

'I don't need help,' Lee says with his chin out.

Alysha bows her head. 'Forgive me.'

'Provided that your candidate is a legitimate person and there are no security reasons why I shouldn't meet him, I am content to do so.'

'Thank you,' she says, 'and thank you for your time.'

Ezra guides Lee out of the study. Back in the main body of the house, the partying has turned raucous. They can hear the whooping and yelling of the Noble Boys and the campaign kids rising from the basement swimming pool.

'I have a good feeling,' Ezra tells him before he can say anything. 'Excuse me while I go and say farewell to our guest.' He squeezes Lee's forearm and heads back the way they came.

'What was that about?' Lee demands.

Denzel shakes his head. 'No idea.'

'Have you seen Bala?'

'She was heading for the terrace.'

'Can you kill the lights out there in three minutes? I'm going off duty.'

'Of course.'

'And keep an eye on the campaign kids, I don't want anyone drowning in the pool tonight.'

'I'm on it,' Denzel says. 'Don't you worry. I'll see you bright and early tomorrow.'

'Thanks.'

He finds Bala alone with a half-empty glass of fizz on the table in front of her. She looks sad. He sits opposite her and holds out his hands. She takes them in hers and turns them this way and that, studying his walnut knuckles that tell the tale of his youth, bouncing from one fistfight to another.

'People feel safer with you on their side,' she tells him, solemnly.

'To be honest, they mostly act nervous.'

She nods her head. 'They don't want you on the other side.'

Abruptly the garden lights go out.

She gasps. Above them, the sky is full of stars.

'Shall we go for a walk?'

'I'd like that.'

She undoes the straps on her heels and removes them and he follows suit, taking off his shoes and socks. He places them neatly beside hers on the flagstones. They walk barefoot across the lawn, feeling the bounce of the grass between their toes, heading towards the dark outline of the pines.

'You know, don't you?'

'Yes,' he replies.

'I should have told you sooner.'

'Why?'

She looks surprised. 'It doesn't bother you?'

'Why should it?'

With a free hand, he'd burn all social rules. He reaches out and holds her hand. They walk amongst the pines towards the fairway. His irritation with Ezra for the unexpected and unwanted encounter with the Russian/Arab woman is banished. He feels a wave of contentment. With his free hand he reaches out and touches the smooth and distinctively mottled bark of the nearest pine. Abruptly, he pulls Bala to him against the tree. He feels the trunk against his shoulders and the firmness of her body pressing against his. They kiss and he is almost overwhelmed by the softness of her lips and the urgency of her desire against the upward curve of his thigh.

They kiss for a very long time. Later they make love on the fairway beneath the stars.

# 10

# Grom OS

'Grom is stealth weapon,' Mashenka explains in the morning with the ink dry on her deal. She's out of the shackles but still in Guantanamo orange. Even so, she has made the costume her own: rolling up the cuffs on her sleeves and ankles; and cinching her waist with a black keffiyeh scarf. 'Specification for prototype requires that operating system and application software is optimised for use with small mobile device, phone, or tablet, to allow covert deployment. Criteria include drop-down target country list and menu of options. Each option is bundle of targets including energy, water, waste, health, material goods, maritime and land-based supply chains, communications, and capital. Design is intended to exploit vulnerability of tightly coupled infrastructure, in which behaviour of one element is closely connected to other elements and is not resilient in the face of non-linear events. By selecting option, you trigger sequence of attacks to carefully calculated timeline with cascading impact.'

'That worked,' Yulia says, grimly. In contrast to the prisoner, she looks frayed and sleepless after last night's events.

'In London, yes,' Mashenka replies, enthusiastically. 'Test worked very good! I saw significant gain of function with multiplier effects.' When she sees the expression on Jude's face, she looks at Keisha. 'I don't like having him here.'

'Tough,' Keisha says. 'You shouldn't have trashed his home-town and killed his friends.'

'I want to go to Las Vegas.'

'You'll get to Las Vegas,' Keisha says, 'but not until I'm good and ready to send you there.'

Mashenka gives them an angry look.

'Keep talking,' Keisha says.

She rolls her eyes but resumes. 'In addition to pre-loaded Grom bundles there is build-your-own option like pizza toppings. That is what Guy Fowle did and to his own timeline. That is why it was difficult to predict what outcomes would be. To be honest, he made cascade effect work even better than bundles. True implication of biological agent chosen, for instance, only becomes clear when taken in context of nuclear reactor meltdown, as incapacitated population is unable to flee.'

Yulia grips Jude's arm tightly while he struggles to contain his anger.

'Tell us about the nature of the attacks,' Keisha asks.

'First type of attack is malware. As well as Grom operating system, Protean Bears design malware. Programme called DarkMatter hijacks logic controllers of industrial systems to make everything look fine when in fact is totally fucked, like oil terminal or nuclear reactor, and other programme is DataSlay which lobotomises servers and erases data across any connected systems including Cloud-based back-up. This you use on banks and financial institutions, and government too. The malware is customised for individual target and loaded onto ready-to-use USB sticks and carried by courier on continuous patrol in state of heightened readiness. Is operate like home delivery. You click on option and after short time courier delivers. Simple. Very difficult to counter with pre-emptive action.'

'And the second type?'

'This is kinetic, guns and bombs to destroy stuff. Again, pre-placed and ready-to-go, all it needs is password and kapow! Attack is initiated.'

'And who does the initiating?' Yulia asks.

'Both types of attack require human beings, obviously. For malware they often must be physically inserted by trusted employee in closed systems that cannot be externally hacked via internet and for kinetic is to make physical attack. We get human beings from GRU via Valkyrie. They build network of human assets in key infrastructure, and we must integrate

43

into operating system. Is very complicated: hardware, logistics, finance, administration, communications, you name it. This includes weapons caches, safe houses, and identities . . .'

'Tell us more about the human assets,' Keisha says.

'Grom uses three types of assets in each country to initiate the attacks,' she replies. 'First type is illegals, Russian sleeper agents who have been embedded as employees in key infrastructure. This includes GRU Spetsnaz operators, so-called stay-behind teams with special military skills. Second type of asset is coerced, by means of blackmail and extortion with threat of physical injury or exposure of secrets. These are identified and targeted by GRU officers in entrapment operations . . . you know . . . drugs, rent boys, cash for favours. Kind of people are politicians, bureaucrats, police, army, and people working in key utility companies. Mostly men, of course. Men are so stupid.' She gives Jude a pitying look. 'No offence.'

'And the third type?' Keisha demands.

'Service providers. People who work in organised crime, like Albanian mafia for instance. This allows for degree of flexibility and alternative means of achieving aim, if for instance weapons caches or safe houses are compromised by enemy action.'

'You must be very proud,' Keisha says, dryly.

Mashenka smiles and tips her right hand, emoji-like, in a guiding gesture. She delivers the sales pitch: 'Hybrid character of attacks, range of available supplies and secure capability, simple password system and autonomous means of initiation make Grom very effective as both first- and second-strike weapon.'

Yulia is furious. 'You built a weapon of mass destruction without any safeguards governing its use! There's nothing to stop it being used again and again. It's utter stupidity.'

They stare at her long enough for her to drop her hand and look intently into the corner of the dome with an aggrieved expression on her face.

# 11

# Two bears don't live in one lair

'Tell us about Scary Bear,' Keisha says, opening a folder and passing three A4-sized laminated prints across the table.

The first photo is of the hacker known as Scary Bear lying dead on a mortician's slab in London with dark lesions visible on his neck. In the second, Scary Bear is lying on the tiles in the almost-empty swimming pool of a Chelsea mansion where Guy Fowle throttled and drowned him. In the third photo, which has widely been shared on the web in the aftermath of Fowle's escape, Scary Bear is at a winter barbecue, standing in a forest clearing with the Russian president.

'That crazy fucker in the Kremlin,' Mashenka says, 'this is all his fault.'

'Let's concentrate on Scary Bear,' Keisha says. 'Who is he?'

'He called himself Fyodor.'

'That's it?'

'Just Fyodor: I don't think is really his name.'

'Why did he have the Grom app on his phone?'

'He had app because of testing user experience of *doverenniye litsa*,' Mashenka explains, 'that is trusted custodian of network.'

'Custodian? You used that word before.'

'Is basically Triggerman.'

'Triggerman?'

'Firing Key Operator, whatever you want to call it. Somebody must press the trigger. That is to activate the Grom bundles and distribute the USB sticks and cash. Each country or region has one custodian.'

'And Scary Bear, aka Fyodor, was the UK custodian?'

'Temporarily, for purposes of acceptance testing phase only,' Mashenka explains. 'Is soft launch in live environment. Plan is to activate some of Grom assets in UK and measure response times.'

'Why the UK?' Jude asks.

'Because you are isolated with bad economy, lousy infrastructure and shitty government that covers stuff up,' she replies as if the answer is self-evident. 'If during the testing phase we knock out a few systems, is like background noise, maybe nobody take much notice and we have proof that the app works. I didn't know that your idiot of a husband, Yulia Ermolaeva, and that troll Dmitri Troshev would make stupid plan on the side to break Guy Fowle out of prison or that Fowle would kill Fyodor and steal his phone.'

'What was your role?' Yulia asks.

'I am just there to analyse test data results.'

'What does that mean?'

'Is glitchy. Grom system is at prototype stage and requires manual review.'

'And you didn't think the death of Scary Bear and the theft of a phone containing the app constituted a glitch?'

Mashenka pulls a face.

'Why didn't you stop the test?' Jude demands.

'How could I?'

'You were able to affect the outcome of the test,' Keisha says. It's a statement not a question.

Mashenka denies it, emphatically. 'Absolutely not.'

'You hacked into the Treasury's server, and you spoke with the British Chancellor Gabriel Morley on several occasions,' Jude says, grimly.

'You made Morley give up my location and sent an illegal to kill me,' Yulia adds.

Mashenka shrugs. 'You are not dead.'

'I escaped. The only reason I am here is because of the brave actions of a young woman and two police officers who sacrificed their lives to protect me.'

'My friend Gretchen is dead because of you,' Jude says.

'I did what I was told to do.'

Yulia is incensed. 'You have no sense of responsibility, do you?'

Mashenka protests. 'There was nothing else I could do! Don't you understand? You say it was glitch but how could I know that? In scheme of things, Scary Bear is expendable like me. How do I know Fowle is not also GRU asset? I don't have full administrator permissions. I can't see whole system. There is no big red SCRAM button with STOP written on it!'

'Utter stupidity!'

'Second-strike facility is designed for retaliation when command chain is destroyed. Once initiated it cannot be stopped. You're SVR, you should know this. Like I said, no stop button!'

'So you just sat back and watched it all unfold?'

'By the time I'm sure the whole thing is one big cluster fuck, is too late to do anything about it!' Mashenka shouts. 'Then I just want to get the hell away from it all!'

Keisha intervenes, 'Stop!'

Yulia and Mashenka stare at each other across the table.

'How did you meet the man calling himself Fyodor?' Yulia asks.

'After I get arrested by GRU and your dick husband threatens to send me to the gulag, he tells me I have to work for Protean Bears,' Mashenka says, sullenly. 'I'm like, who the fuck is that? He tells me go home and someone will contact me. But when I get home Fyodor already there and my boyfriend has fled never to be seen again because Fyodor is fucking scary.'

'But you went to work for him?'

'What choice did I have?'

'And what did you do for him?'

'Access: breaking and entering. All systems have holes, ins and outs, so for me it's just question of finding them. It was like with currency exchanges, I find back door, usually left by programmers during design and development process, and I open it. I get him in. When he's in, Fyodor trashes everything. That's his skill.'

'What of the other Protean Bears? How big was the team?'

Mashenka shrugs. 'Protean Bears' philosophy is – never have two bears in one lair. So maybe there are twenty bears or fifty bears, or maybe not? I don't know. Is compartmentalised with tight cell structure. Each bear speaks with no more than two other bears.'

'When we hacked your computer and before you managed to erase the hard drive, we inserted a web-shell and sent out a network ping,' Keisha says. 'We had one response from a computer near to Donetsk Airport in the Donbass region of eastern Ukraine. It also happens to be the last known location of the Prizrak – Ghost – Unit of PMC Valkyrie. Who is in Donetsk?'

'That is Khmer Bear. She is Test Coordinator and third member of cell. I heard she helped GRU design NotPetya. But I never meet her face to face.' NotPetya was the name of a notorious piece of malware that was used in Ukraine in June 2017 to take down government ministries, the Post Office, energy companies, airports, railways, and banks. The malware quickly spread beyond Ukraine's borders, disrupting global supply chains and ultimately costing the world economy $10 billion. The Russian GRU Unit 74455, also known as Sandworm, was widely believed to have been responsible for the attack. Mashenka gestures at Yulia. 'Khmer Bear is one who tells me to give your location to undercover asset.'

'Who does Khmer Bear report to?' Keisha asks.

Mashenka looks at Yulia. 'Chilly Bear, who is general secretary of Protean Bear collective.'

'Also Siberian?'

'Exactly. Protean and Promysloviki.'

'And where do we find Chilly Bear?'

'He is wherever the hardware is. Protean Bears operate online but still depend on physical command and control server in real world.'

'Where is that?'

'Somewhere secret with lots of power and data-processing capacity. Also, beyond reach of subpoena or legal summons.'

'But most probably Siberia?'

'I've heard that,' Mashenka admits.

'And who does Chilly Bear report to?' Yulia asks.

'In Moscow? The president!'

Yulia is incredulous. 'Directly to the president?'

'No, of course not, via Thirteenth Directorate.'

Judging by the expression on her face, Yulia isn't aware that there is a so-called Thirteenth Directorate.

'Tell me about the Thirteenth?' Jude says.

'Is new, specialising in hybrid warfare. That's all I know.'

'This is bullshit!' Yulia snaps.

Mashenka shrugs. 'If you say so, you are queen spy. But I'll tell you, if you want to know what was on Fyodor's app – whether he had full access to global illegals network, for instance – you need to go to Moscow.'

'There's a certain amount of scepticism about your claim not to have known what your husband was up to,' Keisha tells Yulia, when the MPs have returned Mashenka to her cell.

Yulia bristles. 'I hate to break it to you, darling, but people in marriages often keep secrets from each other.'

'I need to speak to Langley,' Keisha says. She gestures for them to leave.

They go out and stand by the mud wall behind the domes.

'Have you got one of those cigarettes?' Yulia says, angrily.

'Sure.'

Jude lights one for her and one for himself.

'What are you going to do?' He asks.

'Mashenka is right. I need to go to Moscow. I need to find out if there really is a Thirteenth Directorate and track down so-called Khmer Bear.'

'Is that safe for you?'

'No.'

'Then don't go.'

'It's where the answers are.'

He knows there's no point trying to convince her otherwise.

Keisha emerges from the dome and walks over to them. 'Mashenka is being transferred to mainland USA for further questioning.'

'She is a Russian national,' Yulia protests. 'You can't just kidnap her.'

'She's getting what she wants. She's leaving for Las Vegas in the morning.'

'I paid money for her!'

'I've arranged a flight for you both to Darmstadt in Germany. That's what you want, isn't it?'

Yulia flings the cigarette away in disgust.

# 12

## *Kompromat*

The buzzer goes at three a.m. and Lee rolls out of bed thinking it's stand-to back in Helmand and then, moments later, that there's a significant and more embarrassing risk it might be a former lover turned needy or sentimental at his door. He doesn't want anything to interfere with the joyous vibe that has enveloped him since the night at Wolfhanger. Besides, he's due to get up in a few hours and drive to the constituency and he could do with more sleep. Irritated, he pads naked across the living area of his Barbican apartment and scowls at the screen of the videophone.

Amanda Chappell.

So, it's not a WYD – what ya doin' – booty call.

He has no choice – her boss Ezra pays the rent and knows full well that he'd do almost anything to keep the 'Cromwell' of Cromwell Tower in his official address – he presses the button. He considers answering the door naked but pulls a pair of white briefs on instead. The elevator rises. When he opens the front door, she breezes past him in a cloud of expensive perfume without so much as a furtive ogle of his washboard and the dark curls that reach his navel. She does, however, take a glance in the direction of the bedroom, where Bala is spread-eagled on her tummy with her long brown limbs akimbo on the white sheets. Amanda offers him a raised eyebrow and heads for the far side of the living room. If she is impressed by the view from the thirty-fifth floor, she isn't letting on. She turns on her heels and faces him.

'Ezra believes in you.'

He scratches his head. Surely this could have waited until morning.

'What do you want, Amanda?' he asks. 'Frankly, I'm kind of busy.'

'I see that.' She has a way of looking at you that makes your testicles shrivel. 'How long do you think you are going to keep this a secret?'

'I thought we might go public,' Lee says, cuffing it, 'hold hands on the breakfast shows and maybe a spread for a magazine.'

Surprisingly, she doesn't seem opposed. Lee can practically see her doing the calculations. Weighing the odds. She's entirely unflappable. 'When?'

He gives her a lazy grin. 'I thought maybe wait until after the leader is chosen . . .'

'Ezra thinks you have a chance of winning this.'

'Of course he does.'

'If you make it through to the next round.'

'And there lies my problem.'

'Provided that you agree, Ezra has authorised me to take action.'

She has his full attention. 'What kind of action?'

'Material has come into our possession that shows Fabian profiting financially from the recent carnage in London, selling shares in nuclear energy when the government lost contact with the control room at Sizewell.'

Interesting. 'It's less than forty-eight hours since you told me that it was a dangerous path to tread.'

'I didn't have the level of information then that I have now.'

'And where did this new level of information come from?'

'It's probably better if you don't know anything more than what I've told you.'

'I see.'

'So, what's your decision?'

She says it with sufficient seriousness that he realises she intends him to consider it a devil-at-the-crossroads moment. He laughs at the melodrama. What's there to consider? 'Hell, yes.'

She nods, crossroads moment done, guitar restrung, etc. 'I'll prepare a measured statement for you to give, and share it with Denzel. When the time comes, try not to sound triumphalist.'

'Message received.'

'In the meantime, you should be ready to go public about your new friend at a moment's notice. I'm not worried about Fabian but as the acting Prime Minister, Nigel Featherstone has the resources of government to bring to bear against you. We can't afford to let him, or the security services, take an unanticipated sideswipe at you.'

'Bring it on,' he says with his chin raised.

'I'll speak to *Hello*. They owe Ezra.'

'Thank you.'

'You can thank me when you're in Downing Street.'

After she's gone, he returns to the bedroom, where Bala is awake, sitting with the sheet tucked under her armpits and covering her breasts.

'You really might be the Prime Minister,' she says.

That's when it really hits him. They grin simultaneously, as surprised as each other. 'Yes.'

'Did you mean that about going public?'

'Yes.'

'I'm not a trophy.'

'Oh yes, you are.'

'Oh no, I'm not. And I'm not a fetish either.'

'I can feel a stirring,' he leers.

'Be serious!'

'Come to Downing Street with me.'

'How can I be a journalist from Downing Street?'

'Join my team. Be my press secretary.'

'Are you serious?'

'Sure. Jump the barricade.' He imagines himself as a latter-day Cromwell. 'We can carve out our own destiny. Together we can build a new nation out of the ashes of the old.'

He's stiff as a flagpole.

She guffaws and casts the sheet aside. 'Come to bed, you crazy man.'

# 13

# Home turf

When Lee chaired the first meeting of his Policy Priorities team, just a few weeks ago, there were only five other participants: his campaign manager Denzel, his fellow Red Wall MPs Daamini Dhatta, Trevor Cooper and Chantal Carny, and Alan Mitchell, a twice-failed leadership contender who was formerly the Secretary of State for getting the fuck out of Europe pronto. Lee's single direction was for them to come up with wonderful ideas. As a troubled child, who found a natural fit on Outward Bound exercises, he was taught expeditionary learning principles that included 'wonderful ideas'. That one stuck with him. It's what he's always expected of those in power. It has fuelled his disappointment in so-called 'leaders', be they generals or politicians.

He has pledged to be different.

Now, sitting in Nan's front room in the constituency and putting to one side the whooping and yelling from the impromptu family football match going on in the close outside, he surveys the whiteboards and flipcharts covering Cabinet appointments, first hundred days initiatives and pressing legislation; the heat maps of enemies, friends and the unaffiliated in the Commons, his Party and the country; and a GANT chart of carefully shaped media opportunities.

Nothing unusual there – it's the content that's blistering.

That and the size of the team: now they spill out of the room, into the kitchen where Nan is cutting the crusts off sandwiches and halfway up the stairs. And you can see by the expressions on their faces that they're true believers. No one can say that they haven't approached the task with verve and determination. Particularly if by wonderful you mean a scorched-earth policy: burn it all down and rebuild from the foundations up. He could quibble with some of the suggestions, tinker at the edges a little, but there's no doubt that it's a stab at the kind of wholesale change the public are clamouring for; on that basis alone, he's content to light the fuse, stand back and watch the fireworks.

He smiles beneficently. 'Let's do it.'

Lee catches up with Denzel after the session. They stand with their backs to Nan's garage doors, two former fighting men in shirts and ties having a confab over a cigarette at the touchline of a football match that ranges all around the houses.

There are thirty or so people playing football, mostly nephews and nieces, some cousins and half-brothers and half-sisters, a few local orphans and strays, a trio of campaign kids and a couple of the better-behaved Noble Boys. And let's not forget Bala in a pair of eye-catching gold shorts and a diamante tiara. She is quick with the ball, weaving in and out of the flowerbeds and cars, and darting across the tarmac circle at the centre of the close. She passes readily and shouts words of encouragement to her teammates. She's undoubtedly captain material.

'I'm impressed,' Lee says. 'We have a coherent plan of action.'

Denzel acknowledges the compliment with a nod. 'It was your nan that used to say: "You only get one chance, make the most of it."'

'Nan was right.'

As one of the strays, Denzel had spent a lot of time here in the close when he was a teenager.

Salamanca Close has five detached red-brick houses protected by a horseshoe of barbed steel railings, hidden by artfully placed shrubs, and a single access road leading in and out. It was his late dad's idea, once he'd 'acquired' sufficient money to exit the council estate, to buy up the whole close and fill it with trusted relatives, calling it both a fortress-redoubt and a springboard to the wider world. It's also one of the few places that they can be confident is free of surveillance. Lee is confident that the Investigatory Powers

Commissioner's Office wouldn't sign off on an intrusive surveillance warrant on him, but those around him seem to be fair game for MI5's watchers.

'Amanda Chappell came to see me in the dark hours last night.'

Denzel doesn't look surprised. 'Did you accept the offer?'

'I did.'

Denzel shrugs. 'So what's there to say?'

'I asked where the *kompromat* came from.'

'What did Amanda say to that?'

'Best I didn't know.'

'And?'

The ball is being fought over around the back of Auntie Dee's house and everyone has piled in, even the goalies. Lee and Denzel are effectively alone.

'Come on, Denzel,' Lee says with a sigh. 'Don't make me pick you up and shake you.'

Denzel blinks. He can tell that Lee is serious. 'You met the source at Wolfhanger. She said she wants what you want, boss. A new man in the Kremlin.'

'I don't know what to think about that,' Lee says, chewing his lip. 'I really don't.'

Bala sprints out from behind Dad's third wife Busaba's house, with the rest of the pack trying to catch her. An open shot: the ball slams into the garage door.

Goal!

Bala screams and does a victory lap with her arms in the air and her teammates pursuing her. It all ends in a pile on Uncle Terry's front lawn.

He glances back at Nan's front door. She is standing there watching. She looks across at him and nods.

That's all the affirmation he needs.

Bala extracts herself and runs over to Lee, launching herself into his arms. He lifts her up with her legs scissored around his waist and kisses her. He's conscious of cheering and a wolf-whistle or several from the big boy cousins and the Noble Boys.

'I love it,' Bala says, when they eventually disengage.

A press team staffer sticks her head out of one of his nan's upstairs windows and says, 'Fabian's on the television.'

Lee puts Bala down.

'Shall we?' They go inside with Denzel following. The crowd parts for them, and they find themselves in front of the television. Fabian Pees is standing with his pregnant wife and six children at the head of the driveway to his substantial ancestral pile. Bala's hand finds Lee's and grips it tight. Glancing around, he sees Amanda Chappell watching from over by the window.

'I have decided that it is in the best interest of my country for me to put aside my ambition to lead this Party at this time,' Fabian says to the assembled press pack. 'Instead I shall offer my support to my esteemed colleague Nigel Featherstone.'

'Cunt!' Denzel says.

'Only Nigel can bind together the fractured elements of this country,' Fabian says. 'He is a steady hand in uncertain waters. Thank you.'

Everyone's phones are ringing except Lee's. Bala has whipped one out of her shorts. It's tiny: the sort that you buy on Amazon for prisoners.

'The Party has confirmed that the ballot papers will go out to the national membership in the morning,' Denzel tells him with his phone clamped to his ear. 'We can press go on the get-out-the-vote campaign and the social media blitz.'

'Do it,' Lee says.

'The BBC has requested a one-on-one interview with Alice Preen tomorrow night on *Spotlight*,' Bala tells him.

*Spotlight*'s Alice Preen is basking in the recent glory of publicly eviscerating a hapless member of the Royal Family. Lee thinks destroying Windsors is a bit like shooting fish in a barrel: noisy but too easy to constitute a genuine field sport.

'Bring it on.'

# 14

## God's covenant

Jude and Yulia visit the MMK, the modern art museum near Frankfurt's old town plaza, while they are waiting for flight connections. The first brush-past of their illicit liaison was in London's Tate Modern and it seems somehow fitting that they should part in similar circumstances.

The MMK has a large pop art collection with some of Warhol's iconic Americana: a hundred red-and-white Campbell's soup cans, thirty-five blue Jackie Kennedys, ten green car crashes. Jude isn't a fan. He gets the argument about the democratisation of mass production, but artistically they leave him cold.

'If he had been Russian, it would have been endless nicotine-coloured Kalashnikovs and sepia-toned Brezhnevs,' Yulia says, mournfully.

'I might have preferred that,' Jude replies.

He likes the colour field paintings, particularly *First Coming* by Morris Louis, the parallel stripes of pure colour arranged side by side on white canvas. He's an avowed atheist but there is something about the painting that conveys the ancient mystery of the rainbow. God's pledge to never destroy all life on Earth again: *I do set my bow in the cloud, and it shall be for a token of a covenant between me and the earth.*

The human race is evidently incapable of such a commitment.

'I'm struggling to understand how my husband managed to keep what he was doing a secret from me,' Yulia admits.

Jude reaches out and puts his arm around her shoulders, resisting the urge to observe that perhaps she was too busy keeping secrets from her husband to notice the ones he was keeping from her. 'He was acting under orders.'

'From a made-up directorate!'

'From the president.'

'You know what the worst thing is? I can believe it. Come on.'

They leave the museum and walk arm in arm beside the river along the Eyssenstrasse.

'I knew that my husband was desperate to ingratiate himself with the president and his circle,' Yulia says. 'But I hadn't realised how far he was prepared to go. It is a regrettable feature of our diminutive president that he is nothing if he does not have enemies to measure himself against, and always he must have the means to humiliate and destroy them. His biggest fear is the loss of those means.' She shakes her head in frustration. 'I saw it myself in Germany before the wall came down. He was here with the foreign intelligence directorate, ostensibly as a liaison officer with the Stasi, but in fact nurturing armed anti-capitalist groups like the Baader-Meinhof. Nobody could have predicted that he would one day be president. But he was astute. He could see what was coming. The Soviet Union was on the brink of collapse. For him, it was a race against time to smuggle black cash out via front companies in the West and use it to sustain networks of illegals and maintain operations capable of disrupting and destabilising the West – disinformation, assassination, sabotage – even after the collapse.' She stops and grips the lapels of Jude's coat. 'You understand what is happening? He can see his own end coming. That is what Grom is, his response to the sword of Damocles hanging over him, his threat to those who would usurp him. He's damaged because of what has happened, Grom going public in this way, but he's never going to give up his networks of illegals entirely. Without them he believes that he is naked.'

'Then we had better hope that there are no further attacks.'

'There hasn't been a single act of industrial sabotage or terrorism since Sizewell that could be attributed to Guy Fowle,' Yulia says. 'Not one! Maybe he's finished?'

Jude shakes his head. 'He'll never be finished.'

'So what is he waiting for?'

'I don't know.'

★   ★   ★

They go their separate ways in the Departures hall at the airport. Yulia is heading east to Moscow from where they have agreed she will pursue the hacker Khmer Bear and the mysterious Thirteenth Directorate and Jude will return to London to rejoin the hunt for Guy Fowle. He'd prefer to go with her but as she points out, he's unlikely to receive a welcome reception in Russia.

'My darling,' she says at the gate, before giving him a farewell kiss on the cheek, 'our president is not a forgiving man and you're too pretty for our prisons.'

'Be careful,' he urges her. 'Don't take any unnecessary risks.'

She smiles.

An hour later he boards a flight for Heathrow.

As the plane crosses the English Channel Jude looks down from his window seat at a huge offshore wind farm and beyond it the Thames Estuary. They follow the meandering glide of the river into London, flying over the Thames Barrier and the Chicago spires of Canary Wharf. The drawbridge is up on Tower Bridge. He spots the burnt hulk of the Gherkin, the skyscraper destroyed in an incendiary attack on a nearby synagogue. The widespread rioting and looting that followed the failure of London's banking systems prevented the Fire Brigade from saving the building. It's not the only building that burned to the ground. The streets have been cleared of broken glass and abandoned cars but the damage is visible from the air as blackened spaces scattered like patches of mould across the city.

There has been so little time for reflection in recent weeks. Staring out at it, he is reminded how close London came to catastrophe. But for the sacrifice of an entire nuclear accident response team, the out-of-control reactor at Sizewell would have exploded, releasing a lethal cloud of radioactive ash across the city. Their actions meant the Grom attacks killed thousands instead of hundreds of thousands, even millions.

Jude's last memory of Fowle is of almost dying at Sizewell: rolling, hooked together, down a mud bank into rushing water. Jude's claw knife twisting between Fowle's ribs and Fowle's blade a searing pain in Jude's side. He remembers Fowle's teeth bared like fangs in the dark and turbulent water, and a spinning corona of blood surrounding his head. Then they struck something on the bottom and lost their grip on each other. Jude was carried away on the current and for a few brief moments gave in to its seductive embrace, before striking out for the surface. By the time he dragged himself out of the water onto a reed bed, Fowle was gone.

More than two weeks later, Fowle is still at large and with him he has the notebook that he used to transcribe the attacks from the Grom app before the phone was destroyed. Nobody except Fowle knows what is in the notebook, how many more nuclear reactor or oil terminal attacks. How many other critical elements of what ties the country together have been infiltrated by sleeper agents waiting to be activated. What Jude has observed is that Grom has a logic of its own, a violent, inexorable pressure towards a fearful reckoning.

They are all just waiting for the next attack.

# 15

# Sanjay is home

There is an unmarked police car parked in the cul-de-sac at the entrance to the converted warehouse in Shoreditch where Jude lives, along with a team of snipers on the adjacent rooftop. As he approaches the car, one of the plainclothes officers gets out.

'The owner of the property has returned,' she says.

'Sanjay?'

'Yes, Mr Kumar is inside.'

'You're sure it's him?'

She gives him a look familiar to those who know Sanjay. He is not an easy man to impersonate.

'Yes. He's not alone.'

From the expression on her face, it seems that Jude is in for a surprise.

Jude finds his younger sister Tamar sitting at the kitchen counter-top, eating something out of a cardboard pot with a wooden spoon. She is wearing a man's shirt and by the looks of it little else.

He puts his bag down on the floor.

'What are you doing here?'

She rolls her eyes and on cue Sanjay saunters bare-chested out of his bedroom wearing unzipped black leather trousers. There is a vape that looks like an extra-long USB stick poking out of the side of his mouth and he looks as lean as ever, his torso all hard lines.

'There you are, man,' he says. 'I was worried about you.'

Jude opens his mouth and then closes it again. He can't decide whether to be outraged or not. Eventually he settles on, 'When did you get here?'

'Today, man. This morning, in fact, though I've only just been let in; I spent five hours in a police station. They stripped me naked and tickled my prostate. Scraped the fur off the inside of my cheek. It's okay, though. They were achingly polite about it. I tried calling you, but you must have changed all your numbers again. Luckily Tamar came to my rescue. Didn't you, babe?'

He's never known anyone call Tamar *babe*. It seems an act of extreme folly: tantamount to poking a tarantula with a stick. He believes that she's broken limbs for less.

'Sure,' she purrs and licks her spoon.

'Talking of DNA,' Sanjay says, 'maybe you can ask your colleagues if they have a match on their secret database, maybe they know who my father is?'

The whole fatherless *shtick* has been a staple of Sanjay's for years.

'You don't really want to know,' Jude tells him.

'It's some security you've got,' Sanjay continues, unperturbed, 'don't get me wrong, I'm grateful for it. I saw the state London is in on the way in from the airport. You guys really haven't been looking after the place.'

Jude is nonplussed. 'I thought you were . . .'

'In some tropical paradise filming size-zero models in lingerie?' Sanjay finishes for him. 'I quit and a couple of days later the show was cancelled. Associations with socialite sex traffickers and fat-shaming executives meant that the allure of pristine white sand and a warm turquoise ocean lost its lustre. Plus, I found out that the tropical island survives on subsidised gas from Russia, in return for which they give international recognition to any chunks that Russia bites out of its neighbours. It doesn't matter how far you go, how good the weather is, every fucker is up to no good. I would have come back earlier but there were no planes landing.' He wanders over to the window. There are still four bullets lodged in the floor-to ceiling ballistic glass and a spall about the size of a dinner plate around each one, from when Fowle tried to kill Jude after Sizewell.

'I'm sorry about the window,' Jude tells him.

'Shit worked!'

Not long after he bought the top floor of the un-renovated warehouse and he was living a hand-to-mouth existence as an up-and-coming film director, Sanjay had directed a promotional film for a cash-strapped security start-up specialising in ballistic glass and taken payment in their Protect Life range.

'You're lucky it wasn't a larger calibre,' Tamar says.

'Right!' Sanjay rolls his eyes and winks at Jude. 'I love a room full of Lyons.'

'I'll pack my stuff and get out of your hair,' Jude says.

'The spare room's yours, mate.'

'I think it's safer for you if I move out.'

'Don't be ridiculous. You want to take off and leave your little sister and me without any protection from a psychopathic madman?' Jude wants to say that Tamar's perfectly capable of protecting herself, but Sanjay is in full theatrical mode. 'She took a bullet for you, man. I've seen the wound.'

'It was a piece of shrapnel.'

'And that makes it okay?'

Jude looks at Tamar, who shrugs as if to say, *he's your idiot and your responsibility.*

'Are you back for long?' Jude asks.

'I don't know. It depends.' He pads over to the kitchen area, opens the fridge, and examines its meagre contents. 'Most of all we need food.'

'You can order a delivery,' Jude says. 'The police will bring it to the door.'

'That's too weird. What's this?' He looks back with his nose in a repurposed jam jar and says, 'This kimchi is really good.'

'A friend of mine made it. She's dead now.'

'I'm really sorry,' Sanjay says. Then he gets a familiar expression on his face. 'Are you saving it?'

'No.'

'We should build a meal around it, man. She deserves that, right? There's still some of that ramen stock in the freezer that took me like twenty hours to make. You can go pick up some belly pork from Boat People and greenery from those beardy guys in Roots and Fruits.'

'Let's do that,' Jude says, because the idea of a meal does seem like a fitting tribute to Gretchen, who made it. And realistically, he's not going anywhere. The thought of good food and good company, maybe forgetting about Fowle for a few hours, is comforting.

'I'll put some Bolly on ice,' Sanjay says, popping a fresh nicotine capsule out of a blister pack and slotting it into his vape. 'Why don't you invite someone, so that there are four of us? Tamar says that there's some journalist who you keep failing to close the deal with.'

'Is that right?' Jude says to Tamar, who shrugs. 'As I recall, the last time that you met Kirsty you warned me not to mix personal and professional.'

'We're all bored of waiting for you to connect.' She scowls at Sanjay. 'Can't you go back to your room? I have things to discuss with my brother.'

'It's my home!'

They both look at him. 'We could move out and take our security with us,' Tamar says. 'And leave you for Fowle.'

'It's your security as well now? This is a home invasion. I've been cuckooed!'

'Trust me,' she tells him. 'You have not been cuckooed. If you had, I'd have shit on the rug by now and taken a hammer to your pretentious fucking coffee machine.'

That's the Tamar that Jude recognises. Sanjay looks at Jude as if he expects him to do something about her. When nothing is forthcoming, he shakes his head at being so badly let down and goes off to his bedroom.

'He's my best friend,' Jude says, accusingly.

'He's your only friend,' Tamar says. 'And stop being petulant. Go and phone Kirsty.'

He's about to refuse but then thinks that if he doesn't see her now, there's a chance he might never see her again.

# 16

# Ramen for Gretchen

Jude isn't sure if Kirsty will accept the invitation. Instead of calling her he texts, which by his line of reasoning leaves her room to casually decline without feeling any pressure. After all, she was there in the apartment when Fowle took shots at them from a nearby rooftop and if not for the armoured glass, she would be dead. Maybe she has had enough of the place and by extension him. It's not the first time she has almost died beside him.

He misjudges her. She texts right back:

> A simple dinner? You can cook? How did I not know this? I'll be there.
> Sanjay's back. He's the cook. I'll send a car
> I can walk!
> Not safe.
> Ok.
> My sister is here
> Which one?
> The scary one
> I'm coming

Thus, he finds himself standing on the landing ninety minutes later, awkward, and unsure of what to do with his hands as if perhaps he should stand to attention, while the lift rises to the top floor with her in it.

'What put you in a good mood?' she says, when the doors open. Because suddenly he's beaming and although the answer is *you did*, he doesn't say it.

'Thank you for coming.'

'Hard to tell with the mysteriously acquired suntan but I think you're actually blushing.'

Under her coat, she's wearing a short-sleeved, ankle-length leopard-print dress that is in equal parts demure and sexy, and brandishing a bottle of red wine in each hand. She is by any measure a woman to delight in. He takes the bottles and follows her into the apartment.

'This is Kirsty,' he says.

Sanjay shakes her hand mock-formally and Tamar waves nonchalantly from the couch. She's now wearing a pair of Sanjay's jeans and a Ramones T-shirt.

'Are you going to do something about those?' Kirsty asks, walking over to look at the bullets. Ever since it happened, Jude has been trying not to think about how much it's going to cost him to replace the window.

'I've decided to keep them,' Sanjay tells them from the kitchen island, where he is stirring a pot full of broth. 'They make for an interesting talking point. And they clearly embarrass my secret-agent friend.'

Jude sighs and carries the bottles over to the island, where a bottle of Sicilian Carricante is on ice. He's persuaded Sanjay that given current circumstances champagne is inappropriate.

'Plus!' Sanjay says with a finger in the air for emphasis. 'They hide the crispy gherkin, which is good for my performance anxiety.'

'There's someone on the rooftop with a gun,' Kirsty says.

'He's on our side,' Tamar says.

'Our side?' she replies, to remind Tamar and her brother of the difference in their occupations. They are keepers of secrets and she's an investigative journalist who uncovers them.

'He's there to stop Fowle from having another go at us,' Jude says, filling a wine glass and handing it to her.

'And is that why I got driven here in an armoured vehicle and why you have people following me everywhere I go?' Kirsty responds.

Jude pours himself a glass. 'I couldn't possibly comment.'

Sanjay points his vape at him. 'You're stalking her?'

'I'm prepared to accept that protecting me doesn't amount to harassment,' she says.

'That's very gracious of you,' Sanjay says. 'But don't let his charm blind you to his more authoritarian tendencies. He can change his colours so fast you can never really tell who he is.'

She lifts her eyebrows at Jude. 'Something smells good.'

'Are you hungry?' Jude asks.

'Famished!'

'The Lyons are feasting on the forbidden swine,' Sanjay adds gleefully.

'We're not exactly observant,' Jude admits.

'Jude's a rule-breaker,' Sanjay says and throws out his arms in an operatic gesture. 'A maverick spy.'

'You couldn't be more embarrassing if you tried,' Jude tells him.

'Did they give you your double-O badge yet?'

'That was never an actual thing.'

'Of course not!' Sanjay says, an expression of mock horror on his face. 'Because who would come up with a system that rated people by the number of people they have killed?'

'Are you always like this when you're together?' Kirsty asks.

'Always!' Sanjay says, gleefully.

'Always,' Jude says, cutting a plump slab of slow-roasted pork belly into half-inch-thick slices. Beside him, Sanjay places the slices in a frying pan on the gas hob to bronze them.

Tamar gets up and joins them. She dips a finger in the broth and dabs it on her tongue. 'That's tasty.'

'How did you two meet?' Sanjay asks as he tips four eggs into a saucepan of water that he has brought to a gentle simmer.

'His sister invited me to dinner,' Kirsty replies.

'Not me,' Tamar protests, 'his other sister, Hannah.'

'The properly socialised one,' Jude says.

'She seemed to think that we'd get on,' Kirsty says.

'Did you?' Sanjay asks.

'I thought so but then he disappeared. Given his line of work I assumed he was dead.'

'I was overseas,' Jude protests.

'Very rude,' Sanjay says, wagging a finger at him.

'Have you spoken to Hannah?' Kirsty asks Jude.

He looks apologetic. 'Not since before . . .'

'. . . your mysterious overseas adventure?'

'Yes.'

'You guys finish sentences for each other?' Sanjay says.

'I've seen Hannah and the Lyon cubs,' Tamar says. Everyone looks surprised. She bristles indignantly. 'I can do family too.'

'I bet you can't name your nieces,' Jude says.

'I can do better than that, I can give you the latest information on Mee the rabbit's recent wedding to Teddy.'

Jude is a veteran of his niece's soft toy soap opera. 'Mee is already married to soft toy T-Rex. I have the video evidence. Hannah filmed the ceremony.'

'That's where you're wrong,' Tamar says, squaring up to him. 'It didn't work out. Did you know that it's her third marriage? The first was to Mr Moving-arms-and-legs Teddy. Apparently, although he seems nice when you first get to know him, he didn't treat her very well and has been consigned to a cupboard.'

'What happened with T-Rex?' Jude asks.

'Apparently, T-Rex needed to go out to roar as he is a dinosaur. And she couldn't go with him because she is a rabbit. It all seems to have ended amicably. T-Rex came to the wedding. Mee and Teddy have been best friends for so long and she realised that they couldn't just stay friends any longer.'

Sanjay is beaming.

'I'm impressed,' Jude admits.

Kirsty is nodding in agreement.

'Can we eat?' Tamar demands.

They watch as Sanjay divides the meaty broth between four large soup bowls and adds shredded roast pork, steamed spring greens and sushi rice, poached eggs, and the belly slices. He tucks a square sheet of seaweed into the side of each bowl like a handkerchief. Finally, he adds a tablespoon of Gretchen's kimchi, and scatters a mix of finely chopped spring onions and coriander leaves as garnish.

He carries the bowls carefully, one at a time, across to the table.

'It looks great,' Kirsty says.

They sit and before they eat, they raise a glass to Gretchen and the two protection officers who died alongside her in her allotment. Gretchen's not the only one of his colleagues to have died in recent weeks. Rosanna Bevan, who ran the MI5 team hunting for Fowle, died in the marsh at Sizewell, leaving behind a husband and a baby. Then there are the police officers, many of whose names he does not know, who died in the battles at Woolwich, Barking, Borough and Sizewell.

'May their memory be as a blessing,' Jude says.

He can't help reflecting on what more he might have done to avoid their deaths. He feels his hand squeezed and realises that Kirsty has reached across the table. She smiles reassuringly. He feels embarrassed. He picks up a fork and spoon.

'This is delicious,' Tamar says.

She's right: it's lip-smacking, gelatinous, and savoury.

'What do you make of Lee Chapeaux?' Sanjay asks. 'I saw footage of him tearing off his shirt outside Westminster Tube after the attack there. Very manly! He was a combat medic right, in the SAS?'

'Yes,' Jude says.

Lee Chapeaux had not been in the chamber of the House of Commons when Fowle attacked; instead he'd been in his office in neighbouring Portcullis House. In the aftermath of the attack, much had been made of his refusal to be escorted to safety. Instead, he'd insisted on heading towards the gunfire and used strips of his shirt as dressings to pack gunshot wounds on Westminster Green.

'Just because he did something brave and bare-chested doesn't make him fit to be Prime Minister,' Kirsty says.

'I hear he's wildly popular,' Sanjay says.

'With some sections of the public, maybe,' Kirsty says. 'But his party's demographic is against him. He frightens the hell out of them.'

'All it would take is one more attack and the alternative might seem even more frightening,' Tamar says.

'That's true,' Kirsty concedes.

'We're lucky we have you guys to keep us safe,' Sanjay says, raising his glass to Jude and Tamar.

Watching his friend, Jude feels the same overwhelming sense of anger and powerlessness that gripped him as he flew into Central Africa. He can't bear the thought of losing these people who are so dear to him. But it's too much to ask of him to keep them safe. It's impossible. It takes all his effort not to clench his teeth or tighten his hands into fists.

After dinner, he accompanies Kirsty down to the waiting car.

'I can't kiss you,' she tells him, out on the cobbles. 'Because there are snipers watching and besides, bad things happen afterwards.' The first time they kissed it was just days before Fowle attacked the Houses of Parliament and the second time it was just before Fowle escaped from Woolwich Crown Court. On both occasions people died. 'I know that there isn't an actual causal link,' she adds. 'It's just bad luck.'

Either bad luck or that bad things happen to him as a matter of course, he thinks, and any intimacy will inevitably be punctuated by violent events. He shouldn't have invited her tonight. And then she kisses him on the mouth with her lips parted. It's surprising and wonderful, somewhere between coy and crude, more powerful for his not having done anything to deserve it.

It carries with it the giddy promise of passion and romance.

When she releases him, the smile has returned to his face.

'Good night.'

# 17

# A brute bearing flowers

Yulia pays for a suite on the twentieth floor of the Ukraina on an oxbow bend of the Moskva River. It's the tallest of 'Stalin's high-rises', the baroque skyscrapers built after the patriotic war, and reinvented as a luxury hotel. On arrival, she decides that she isn't going to do the rounds of *Kremlin kleptocrats* like the last time she was in Moscow or report to SVR headquarters in the forest at Yasenevo.

Instead, because life feels too *fin-de-siècle* to bother with austerity, she maxes out her credit card in the boutiques of the Arbat buying a brand-new wardrobe to replace her Africa wear. It is only a short taxi ride from the hotel, but she spots that the metro stations are closed and sees dark vans full of Special Purpose Police in the side streets. Outside the shops, gangs of workmen are unloading pallets of chipboard to cover the windows ahead of planned demonstrations. On their way back the driver makes a detour south along the river to avoid a roadblock.

Back at the hotel, she has a Thai massage in the Wellness Club and allows the in-house dermatologist to inject a little hyaluronic filler to smooth the lines around her mouth and plump her cheeks. She eats salmon kulebyaka with smoked sour cream on the mezzanine at Matryoshka and retires to her room at ten p.m.

Let them come to her.

It's just after eleven and she is lying on the bed in Olivia von Halle pyjamas decorated with black Siamese cats that are fresh out of tissue paper, and she is watching the latest international news. Mashenka is giving up at least some of what she knows. In Washington and New York, the FBI have arrested fifteen suspected illegals embedded in key infrastructure – power, water, telecommunications, and transport – and are searching for a motorcycle courier who is believed to be carrying enough malware to catapult the entire eastern seaboard back to a pre-industrial era. The arrested illegals all look so ordinary. Some of them have children who have known no other life.

In London, the police have launched an inquiry after the only illegal who surrendered under the government's much-derided amnesty scheme died under suspicious circumstances within an hour of handing himself in.

Here in Moscow, the foreign news channels are reporting planned mass demonstrations against the president's rule, but there's no reference to it on domestic news, which seems fixated on the ongoing story of the triplets born to a Siberian tiger at Moscow Zoo. They are now six weeks old. She imagines that the demonstrations will be the usual brutal business of clashes and arbitrary arrests, a cat-and-mouse game conducted with bricks and batons that swells and roams, rages, and burns, with no clear winner. It is a truism that the strictness of Russian law is compensated by the lack of adherence to it. What worries her more is that the president has not been seen in public for several weeks.

There is a knock on the door.

She switches off the television and puts on a matching dressing gown. Opening the door, she finds Alexei the General standing in the corridor holding a bunch of bright blue sage from his garden. She almost laughs out loud. There were times – long ago –when she'd jumped into bed with him for less.

'May I?'

He was always courteous around women. He could be a brute too, though. She firmly believes the often-repeated story that he beat a man to death with a gold bar during the storming of the presidential palace in Kabul in December '79. He offers her the sage. She takes it with grace and lets him in. He moves slowly and purposefully over to the sofa. He's like a bear – not like the CGI ones that the hackers favour as their avatars, but the real thing with blunt and brutal features, powerful and dangerous even in old age.

She opens a couple of ten-year-old Ararat miniatures from the minibar, pours the brandy into glasses and adds a cube of ice to each.

'Your wife told me that you had been arrested,' she says, passing him a glass. His wife Svetlana is a malicious liar but something about the bitterness in her voice had made Yulia believe her.

He stares into the glass, which is dwarfed by his huge, gnarled hands that have spots the colour of old meat and black dirt under the nails. 'I was.'

'And now?'

He looks up at her. He might be old, but his eyes are still beautiful. 'They reinstated me in my old position.'

They've put him back in charge of the operations department of Directorate S, one of the more secretive units of the Foreign Intelligence Service. She considers this news and says, 'You could have sent a car for me. Or a helicopter.'

'I could have,' he concedes with a wry smile.

Not an easy job, she thinks, being put in charge of Illegal Intelligence when every non-Russian intelligence agency in the world is ferociously hunting for illegals. They've given him command of the witches in the time of a witch hunt. She wonders if he has gone mad. If so, it's a clear-eyed sort of madness and not at all what you'd expect of a man in his eighties.

He takes his phone out of his pocket, switches it off with one of his massive thumbs and puts it down on the coffee table. He gestures for her to do the same. She wonders how he manages to type. *Maybe he just growls, and a virtual assistant obeys.* He gets up, goes over to the bathroom, and invites her in. She sits on the toilet seat with her brandy, and he closes the door behind them. The first time he made love to her it was in the women's bathrooms at the Red Banner Academy. She was the only female cadet, and he was a legendary spymaster of the KGB's First Chief Directorate, the predecessor of the modern SVR, the epitome of duty and loyalty to motherland, and nearly thirty years her senior. She remembers him filling her with bruising fingers that looked better suited to strangling. Now she watches him use the same blunt fingers with Russia's elemental black earth under the nails to open the taps and switch on the shower. He sits on the edge of the ceramic bath and although it creaks it does not break.

He leans through the steam towards her and says in a low voice, 'Dmitri Troshev, the chief executive of PMC Valkyrie, died of a heart attack two days ago in the Lubyanka.'

*Damn it!*

'Who killed him?' she demands.

'The president is covering his tracks.'

'What can you tell me about the GRU's Thirteenth Directorate?'

'The Thirteenth has been erased.'

'What does that mean?'

'You were in Dresden before the Wall came down. It was a different century but it's the same thing now. All the evidence is being destroyed.' Yulia remembers the fires burning night and day as the man who would be president burned the KGB's entire East German archive as the Wall came down – communications, contacts, networks – he burned so much stuff the furnace burst. 'To save embarrassment, and that is the one truly unforgivable sin, to publicly embarrass him, the president has decreed that the Thirteenth and anyone associated with it never existed.'

'But if it did?'

'I'd say it was a hybrid, a mix of public muscle and private enterprise intended to circumvent the usual sloth and careerism to maximise the financial return for all involved.'

'Who ran it?'

'Solokov.'

'The billionaire? He seems like an unlikely head for a military intelligence agency.'

'You need money to make money, Yulia. You of all people should know that.'

'Where is he?'

'His helicopter went missing on the way to Penal Colony No. 7 at Segezha.'

'Damn!'

'They flew too close to the sun. None of these fools ever expected to use Grom. Our president, who spends too much time at the far end of a long table, dreamed up the idea of an app that could, at the press of a button, destroy the infrastructure of western nations. He was happy to throw money at the project and Troshev and Solokov were happy to take it. It was a scam from the start.'

'But somebody built it.'

'Yes, that's the tragedy of it. Valkyrie recruited the hackers, who approached the task with relish and imagination. And the GRU created a network of illegals embedded in key utilities in the West. They stocked the safe houses and caches of weapons. Your dumb husband imagined it was real and Guy Fowle made it so.'

'And what about the illegals?'

'They are in an impossible situation. They watch the news like us. Who are they supposed to believe – that they are the agents of the president's will or the tools of Fowle's vengeance? We have no means of identifying or communicating with them and therefore no means of bringing them in from the cold.'

'We need to track down the hackers and find the server with the Grom database on it,' Yulia tells him. 'We have a clue. A computer at a Valkyrie unit location in the Donbass and a hacker named Khmer Bear. We must go there.'

He laughs. 'You're asking a lot. The president may not be pleased if he finds out.'

She rests her hand on his forearm. 'Nevertheless, we must do it. There has never been a more dangerous time than now.'

'I could never refuse you,' he says, begrudgingly. He stands up and looks down at her. 'Don't leave the hotel again and don't use your phone. It's not going to be safe on the streets tomorrow. And the Ministry of Justice has been instructed to add you to the foreign agents list, which means you are already at risk of arrest and imprisonment.'

'That's ridiculous.'

'There is the small matter of accounting for a million dollars from embassy funds that you claim to have spent on freeing a Russian national held hostage in Africa.'

'It's not my fault that she defected.'

'Better to have left her in the jungle, I think. I'll be in touch.'

# 18

# The narrow-boat summit

Early the following morning, Chuka Odechukwu is waiting in the cul-de-sac beneath Sanjay's apartment in black-and-yellow Lycra shorts and running shoes. It's not the first time that Jude has gone for a run with him, although the last time Chuka was an ambitious lawyer at the Cabinet Office and now he's the head of MI6. There is a female protection officer standing behind him in pink-and-black Lycra with a matching bum bag that presumably contains her gun.

'Shall we?' Chuka says, though of course there is no choice.

They run north on the pavement through Hoxton with an unmarked police car following at a discreet distance. It's well before rush hour and the streets are practically empty. The protection officer runs just behind them, glancing left and right and over their shoulders, like she's shepherding them.

'I've been talking to Doctor de Leij,' Chuka tells Jude as he swerves around a litter bin.

Helena de Leij is Jude's shrink. It's not the most promising way for his new boss to have opened a conversation with him.

'She told me you were advised eleven months ago that sharing a residence with Sanjay Kumar posed a significant risk of compromising your cover.'

'I didn't know he was going to come home,' Jude protests in what is, frankly, not the best defence.

Chuka shakes his head. 'The maverick spy?'

'You've bugged my home.'

'It's not your home. It's his home. We're vetting him.'

They cross the Regent's Canal and double back onto the towpath, where there is a male protection officer waiting by the water. He sets off as soon as he sees them. Glancing back, Jude sees that another has joined them and is jogging along about thirty metres behind them. There's something about the canal, Jude thinks, the lack of cameras and curious neighbours that appeals to Chuka's sense of the clandestine. They run west past an outdoor café with a whiff of early-morning bacon and under a bridge. Beyond it, the canal runs behind a housing estate and Chuka lengthens his stride.

'Let's go.'

They sprint, feet pounding the pathway.

After two more bridges, Chuka slows to a jog and then a brisk walk. He's barely out of breath. 'Why has Yulia Ermolaeva gone to Moscow?'

Jude takes several large breaths before replying. 'She's on the trail of the Thirteenth Directorate and the Protean Bears.'

'You believe that?'

Jude's face is flushed. 'I do.'

'Have you heard from her?'

'No. But it may not be safe or prudent for her to call.'

'Let's hope you're right.'

Chuka ducks under a weeping willow and crosses a small bridge and then darts right into a concealed basin with a collection of canal boats in it. A protection officer is standing at the entrance to a gangway leading to one of the boats.

'The principal is on his way,' the officer informs him.

'Thanks,' Chuka replies. He runs down the gangway, jumps aboard the boat and climbs down through the hatch into the living quarters with Jude following. The long narrow space has a row of wooden cabinets on one side with a white Belfast sink. On the other there is a banquette booth with a counter and just enough room for two people to sit facing each other on upholstered benches. Behind it, there is a wood-burning stove and beyond that, standing in front of a bookcase that serves as a partition to a bed in the prow, is the nation's chief mole hunter, Evan Calthorp, the sour-faced head of the Security Service, MI5. The prospect of a network of illegals embedded in the infrastructure of the country is to Calthorp what a nest of rats is to a terrier.

Jude nods to him and Calthorp purses his small, mean mouth.

'Sit,' Chuka says, gesturing at the nearest bench. Jude obeys and Chuka squeezes into the space opposite him.

'This is a brush-past,' Chuka says. 'The politician wants to meet you and hear what you have to say.'

'Right,' Jude says.

'Just remember that we're not politicians. We don't have to entertain strong and settled opinions.'

'Understood,' Jude replies, although he thinks Chuka must be one of the most politically minded people he has ever encountered.

There is a loud thud and the boat shifts slightly on its mooring. Chuka slides out from the bench, gesturing for Jude to stay where he is. The visitor drops through the hatch into a boxer's stance and makes eye contact with each of them in turn.

'Mr Chapeaux.' Chuka greets the candidate in a placatory manner.

They are four tense men in a cramped space: three spooks and a combative politician who looks short on sleep and like his first instinct is to punch.

'This is Mr Lyon.'

Lee nods and slides onto the bench that Chuka just vacated. He stares intently at Jude across the narrow counter.

'You took out that suicide bomber outside Parliament with a headshot. And you fought Fowle in hand-to-hand combat at Sizewell.' He tips his head slightly. 'I can't tell if you're brave or foolhardy.'

'Mr Lyon is motivated by a desire to protect our country,' Chuka says, with his back to the sink.

Lee sticks out his chin. 'Is that right?'

'I do my job,' Jude replies, staring back at him. 'You were with Fowle at Hereford?'

'I was just an ordinary trooper, and he was an officer in special operations,' Lee replies. 'I don't think that he ever spoke to me.'

Jude has found it hard to get anything intelligible out of people that were at Hereford when Fowle was there playing the role of enemy on SAS exercises, working to a term of reference that majored on 'challenging plans, policies and assumptions' and often manifested itself as fiendishly complex ambushes. The reaction he got was such that he wouldn't have been surprised if they'd crossed themselves or spat on the ground when Fowle's name was mentioned. 'But you must have formed an opinion?'

'I remember somebody saying that you wouldn't want him to "actually" be an enemy,' Lee adds.

'He scares people. The sort of people that don't usually admit to fear.'

'But not you?'

'He scares me,' Jude admits.

Lee grins as if he has scored a point. 'My man Chuka here thinks you're going to persuade me that the Russians aren't a clear and present danger?'

'They're dangerous,' Jude replies. 'Particularly if poorly handled.'

'I'm not in the business of appeasement, Mr Jude Lyon. I'll take whatever action is in my power to defend this country.'

'I don't think that the Russian government is in control of the situation,' Jude tells him. 'I believe that elements of the Russian intelligence services have been co-opted by a combination of big business and organised crime. There's no doubt that building Grom was a belligerent act, but the Russian president did not press the buttons that launched the attacks.'

'And you believe this because, according to Chuka, you have a contact in the Russian SVR?'

'That's right. She's tracking Grom back to its source to uncover the identity of illegals and prevent any further attacks.'

'That's what she has told you?'

'I believe her.'

'She's a credible source,' Chuka adds. 'She acted as a trusted intermediary with the Russian president in the build-up to the Sizewell incident.'

'Could she do that again?' Lee asks.

Chuka shrugs. 'The president is not taking calls.'

Lee continues to stare at Jude, whether in disbelief or deep thought it's impossible to tell. Jude keeps his mouth shut. He's not sure what to make of this man who may become the next Prime Minister. He is instinctively suspicious of populists – of anyone who seeks to fan the flames of division. But there is something compelling about Lee, a force of personality that would fill a stadium and is almost overwhelming in this narrow space.

'Will there be further attacks?'

'We can't make that assurance,' Chuka says.

'I'm asking Jude.'

'Yes,' Jude replies without hesitation. 'Unless we find Fowle and stop him.'

Lee nods grimly and slides out of the booth. He pauses at the steps leading out of the hatch and looks back at Calthorp. 'Don't think I'm not aware that you've got surveillance on my people.'

When he is gone, Chuka sighs. He glances at Calthorp. 'Don't tell me that's true.'

Calthorp scowls. 'The biologist E. O. Wilson said that if Hamadryas baboons had nuclear weapons they'd destroy the world in a week. Lee is surrounded by a circus of misfits and degenerates, any one of whom could be a Russian illegal.'

# 19

# Helena and the glyphs

Jude is alone with his shrink in a room at Vauxhall Cross but for once she doesn't want to talk about him. The walls and blinds of the room, which is accessible only via a cypher-locked door, are a not-quite shade of white intended to promote calm and concentration, and there are life-size images of eight naked women pinned to the walls.

Fowle's chosen ones: a select group – as much collaborators as victims – that were permanently marked by him. Each image is a collage of photos – breasts, belly, abdomen, buttocks, and thighs – made of multiple and contrasting viewpoints that have been fitted together to form a whole, which makes Jude, ever the art historian, think of David Hockney's 'cubist' portraits of the 1980s – as interpreted by a sociopath with a gruesome fetish.

'Scarification is a means of transforming both the appearance and the texture of the skin,' Helena de Leij explains. He can imagine the level of excitement this new project will provoke on the encrypted message group that he's heard shares conjecture about her. She is wearing a yellow SIS visitor's pass and standing in front of a collage of Katherine Fowle, Guy Fowle's sister, the first in the sequence. 'The dermis and epidermis are cut, resulting in wounds that create raised scars or keloids that form due to an increased amount of collagen. Fowle often used an inert substance, either wood ash or clay, to pack the wounds. They heal over the packing creating these distinctive ridgelines.'

The tip of Helena's silver pen traces a braided ring, almost but not quite a circle, made of multiple overlapping and interwoven cuts, that surrounds Katherine's navel. Beneath the ring, a yoke of stippled lines rises from her pubis and over her hipbones before flaring across her buttocks. Radial scars surround her nipples. Jude can see why Helena's fitted each collage together like this. It's the only way to see the designs that Fowle has carved in their flesh in their entirety. There is something hypnotic about them – the whorls and spirals, glyphs, and sigils – that defies easy interpretation. To Jude, they are as mysterious and sinister as Rorschach inkblots. In very different circumstances, they might be considered eerily beautiful.

In Belmarsh Prison, Jude had told Fowle that he wanted to understand him. In response, Fowle had warned that it would lead down a path that he might not be able to handle.

'The earliest evidence of scarification dates to the Palaeolithic era more than ten thousand years ago,' Helena says. 'Archaeologists have uncovered statues and rock paintings of fertility goddesses with similar scarification.'

'It's about fertility?'

'I certainly believe that there is a sexual element to it. In the bloodletting, he is eroticising the women's bodies, increasing his own sexual attraction, and enhancing his sexual pleasure. However, I don't believe that's the primary purpose of the scarring. I think that they are a form of writing that conveys meaning.'

'Katherine said that he had put a demon inside her.' Jude vividly remembers her in the prison, pressing her scarred torso against the security glass and screaming at her brother to get it out of her.

'Fowle convinces his victims that the symbols have a power all their own,' Helena says.

'What does Candida say?'

Candida Taunton is the only survivor that they know of; all the other victims are dead.

'In one of her more lucid moments, she described it as magic. She told me that it was impossible to say whether she existed separate to the demon inside her. She certainly believes that Guy is the only one who can control the magic. That's how he exerts authority over them.' Helena crosses over to the composite of Zeina Hussein, the suicide bomber that Jude shot dead in Parliament Square before she could blow herself up. 'The

anthropologist Lévi-Strauss described the body as a surface waiting for the imprint of culture. In Ray Bradbury's short story *The
Illustrated Man* the circus man's tattoos predict the future.' She
looks back at him. 'Are you okay?'

He's staring at the puckered pale hole in the centre of Zeina's
forehead and he's back in Parliament Square during the attack.
Her thumb on the red button connected to her martyr's vest and
his forefinger squeezing the trigger of his pistol.

Helena puts her hand on his cheek and says calmly, 'Look at the
table.'

He turns and stares at the table: the bottles of water in the
middle with notepads and glasses at each place as if it would be
perfectly normal to have a meeting surrounded by such harrow-
ing images.

'Breathe slowly and deeply. Fill your diaphragm.'

In and out, in and out.

'You think that there is information in the designs?' he asks after
a couple more breaths.

'There are similarities between the composition and the shapes
of the designs,' Helena says. 'It's impossible to know the meaning
of individual symbols without access to Guy Fowle. And even if
we did have him in custody, it's unlikely that he would share their
true meaning. But it is possible to recognise patterns. Are you
okay to continue?'

'Yes.'

She leads him to the other side of the room and a body that he
does not recognise. Her pen follows the line of the ring of scars
around the woman's navel. 'This resembles an *ensō*, a symbol used
in Japanese calligraphy and usually applied with ink and a brush.
The *ensō* may be open or closed. When the circle is closed it repre-
sents perfection, but when the circle is open like this it suggests
that the work is incomplete. Unfinished. From the door clockwise,
I have arranged them chronologically. In each case the women
have a similar *ensō* around their navel. Katherine Fowle is the first.
The first marks on her skin appear to date back to her early teens.
The next two victims are contemporaries of Guy's at university.

Both privately educated and from wealthy families. They died in a joint suicide pact after emptying their savings accounts. In the letter that they left behind, they claimed to have demons inside them. Guy was in their social circle, but he wasn't questioned.

'The fourth victim is Maili McEwan. She was first marked in her teens, but I believe that the *ensō* was completed in her early twenties when she was a student at Glasgow School of Art. She grew up on the same Hebridean island as Guy and she gave birth to one of several children of his that we know about. Her medical records suggest that she suffered from regular bouts of depression and anxiety. She committed suicide and her mother raised the child.

'This is the fifth victim, Rebecca Page, who worked at the National Archive in Kew. We believe that she shredded his army personnel file, and methodically destroyed or deleted any reference to him in the public records. She died of asphyxia due to hanging. At the time, Thames Valley Police treated her death as unexplained. The sixth victim was an administrator in the regimental headquarters of 22 SAS in Hereford when Guy was running a red-team unit there. Again, I think she conspired to delete any mention of him. She died in a house fire. Then we have Candida Taunton. She's unusual in that we have what are effectively two separate pieces of work: the original design he marked on her before he went to Iraq and the supplementary marks that he made recently, which form a sort of postscript. You can see the differences in the prominence of the scars. After her is Zeina Hussein. There are eight victims.'

'That we know of,' Jude says, aware that she's holding something back.

Helena nods. 'Exactly. I called in a favour at the Jackson Lab in Cambridge and borrowed some computational power usually reserved for protein folding.'

'And?'

'The algorithm identified a variation in the pattern in the open tails of the *ensō*, a Fibonacci sequence of increasing complexity, such as that found in an uncurling fern. And there's a gap in it.

Which means that there is a symbol missing in the sequence.' She points at the wall between the composite of Candida Taunton and the one of Zeina Hussein. 'Here.'

Jude stares at the space between the two women. 'When he was in Iraq or Syria, he marked someone else.'

She nods. 'You need to find out if she's still alive. If she is, she may lead you to him.'

He heads for the door.

'Jude,' she calls after him. 'Be careful. Do the breathing.'

'Of course, I'm sure breathing is the answer to everything.'

# 20

# The Sheikh's granddaughter

Jude sits in the empty incident room of the Situation Awareness Group surrounded by a swathe of empty desks. The SAG is an autonomous suite of offices with its own Echelon server in a utilitarian tower block on Albert Embankment. First set up as a fall-back if its ostentatious green-and-gold neighbour at Vauxhall Cross came under attack, it has more recently served as a launch pad for the kind of Active Measures operations that the Pure Intelligence gatherers of MI6 regard as reckless interference. Working in a building adjacent to HQ but not in it suits the nonconformist streak in Jude, the desire for self-sufficiency and privacy, but makes him equally aware of how easy it would be for the Service to wash their hands of him.

There is one desk that still looks occupied: half a dozen orchids in cache pots; a screen covered in yellow Post-it notes and the message light on the phone flashing. It's Gretchen's workstation.

Even in death, she demands thoroughness. He has found only one key-word reference that links Guy Fowle to a woman in the trawl of Iraqi phone networks by the US National Security Agency covering the period after Fowle left the UK and joined al-Qaeda in Iraq. It is a conversation between two suspected senior al-Qaeda commanders, one located in the mountainous area north of the refinery town of Beiji in Salah al-Din province and the other in the city of Fallujah in Anbar province. They are disagreeing over what to do about a fellow commander referred to as *al-Gharib* – the Stranger – Guy Fowle's nom de guerre in Iraq. Without seeking permission, the Stranger had summarily executed a member of al-Qaeda in Anbar and taken the dead man's wife as his bride. The commander in Anbar says that he wants to arrest the Stranger and strip him of his power before he kills any more of the believers. The commander in Salah al-Din advises caution and expresses his concern over how the woman's grandfather will respond.

The Anbar commander says, 'The grandfather brought this on himself.'

Jude has read the transcript before. That was before he had identified the Stranger as Guy Fowle. This time, he closes the file containing the transcript, puts his headphones on and listens to the raw intercept in the original Arabic. He realises immediately from their tone of voice that the two men are more worried about telling the woman's grandfather about her fate than they are about the execution.

They refer to the grandfather twice. The first time the Salah al-Din commander uses the Arabic word *jid*, literally grandfather. But the second time, rather than using the word for father, the Anbar commander uses the phrase *walrajul eeajuz*, the term for an old man.

Jude feels a shiver of excitement.

The Old Man.

The Old Man, commonly referred to in intercepts as the *Sheikh al-Jabal* or more simply the *Sheikh*, was one of the Black Flags, the twelve battle-hardened leaders who crossed into Syria from Iraq to establish the Caliphate, the Islamic State, which at its height covered an area larger than the United Kingdom.

Jude enters *Sheikh al-Jabal + granddaughter* in the system search function.

*Access denied.*

*Refer to Security Department.*

Twenty minutes later he is back in HQ, standing in front of a desk on the executive floor.

'What do you want?' Charles Feist, the Service's embittered Head of Middle East Security, demands.

'Why is the *Sheikh al-Jabal*'s file locked?' Jude demands.

'It's closed to tourists and troublemakers,' Feist replies. 'Uncontrolled access poses a threat to Service security.'

'I'm not interested in raking through the rights and wrongs of the past,' Jude says.

Feist was a loyal acolyte of Queen Bee, Chuka's disgraced predecessor as Chief of MI6. He sits in the camp that believes the tens of millions of dollars she paid in protection money from a secret contingency fund to the *Sheikh al-Jabal* was money well spent to protect against Guy Fowle. By extension, he blames Jude for deposing her. It's sad really, Feist's loyalty to Queen Bee. He had been a favourite of hers for a while and a potential successor, but it was said that she'd cooled to him after his wife ejected him from the family home for going on a six-month-long extra-marital rampage in Istanbul.

'What are you interested in, then?' Feist demands, sourly.

'I think that the Old Man, the *Sheikh al-Jabal*, had a granddaughter.'

'They breed,' Feist says. 'What do you expect?'

'If I'm right, Guy Fowle was in a relationship with her.'

Feist folds his arms and leans back in his chair. 'Go on.'

'Fowle was the Old Man's secret weapon, his means of attacking the far enemy. We know they planned the Westminster attack together. After the Basra Ambush, the Old Man moved him around Iraq, keeping him hidden. I think we should assume that he was doing the same with his granddaughter. It's not unreasonable to suggest they might have spent time together in isolation.'

'You're clutching at straws. Most people in this building believe that Fowle was so badly wounded at Sizewell that he found himself a quiet corner to curl up and die in. He just hasn't been found yet.'

'I don't believe that. And neither do you. Are you going to help me, or do you want me to give Chuka a call and tell him you're being obstructive?'

Feist folds as Jude knew he would. 'All right,' he says.

They both know he's vulnerable. Chuka's still in his first hundred days and according to rumour has his sights set on a sweeping management restructure, a cleaning of the stables.

'According to our friends in Riyadh there is a granddaughter, an Iraqi national by the name of Alysha al-Sabbah,' Feist says.

'Her parents were killed in the nineties, in one of Saddam's purges. You remember Saddam? Makes you feel nostalgic for the smack of strong government. She was just a baby when her parents died and she is, as far as anyone can tell, the only living heir to a fortune that is vast or non-existent depending on whether you believe her grandfather was a terrorist mastermind or a figment of our over-heated imagination.'

'What do the Iraqis believe?'

'That Fowle emptied her grandfather's crypto accounts before he killed him and left her in the lurch.'

'How do they know that?'

'They've got her locked up.'

Jude is astonished. 'She's in custody?'

'Yes. In one of their nasty overcrowded prisons. Did you know that they're legally entitled to lock up women in lieu of male relatives? The law also says you can detain someone for as long as you want for crimes that include the death penalty. And everything in Iraq ends in the death penalty. All of which adds up to one inescapable conclusion: if she wasn't broke, she would have paid her way out of prison by now.'

## 21

# The road to *Jahannam*

Arriving at Baghdad International Airport at dawn, Jude takes a bus out to the checkpoint at the airport perimeter where two police SUVs with spinning blue lights are waiting. A sharp-faced Iraqi in a shiny suit with a narrow tie is standing beside them. He introduces himself as Mustafa and says he's from the Prime Minister's office, which identifies him as an officer in the National Security Service, one of Iraq's complex web of competing intelligence agencies that answer to individuals in different corners of government.

'Get in,' Mustafa says, grinning as he opens a rear passenger door of the lead vehicle. His teeth have brown stains on them that suggest childhood deprivation.

The two policemen in the front are wearing helmets and khaki-coloured body armour and in addition to their handguns there is a Kalashnikov with a foldaway stock in the passenger foot well. There is a strong smell of male sweat.

'Are you tired? Do you want to rest?' Mustafa says. 'I can take you to a hotel.'

'No,' Jude replies. 'Please take me to Alysha al-Sabbah.'

There was a time when the eight-mile stretch of highway into town was known as Route Irish. That was back when the Americans were nominally in control and this was one of the most dangerous journeys on Earth, a terrifying void that sucked in Iraq's tormented impulses: roadside bombs, suicide bombers, drive-by shootings . . . at least one attack a day. Not any more. The median is no longer strewn with trash, and city workers have dug up the stumps of the shredded, shrapnel-studded palms of Jude's memory and replaced them with new ones. The cynic in him wonders what sins the beautification hides.

'It is not possible to find Alysha al-Sabbah,' Mustafa tells him. 'Not straight away.'

'What do you mean?'

'She is not in prison any more.'

'Why not?'

'She was released by the courts and sent to one of the camps.'

In Jude's experience, the Iraqi courts are far more likely to hand out a death sentence to Islamic State fighters and their sympathisers than release them. He also knows that asking questions about how the courts work is a dangerous business that can get you killed. As for her destination, there are tens of thousands of displaced people in camps spread across the country.

'When was she released?'

'Four weeks ago, or maybe six.'

Jude curses Feist for his arrogance and complacency. Alysha al-Sabbah could be anywhere by now. 'Do you know which camp? Are you sure that she is there?'

'Yes. Of course she is there. We will go there. When you have rested.'

'No, let's go there now.'

'It is far.'

'So let's go.'

'Everything will be okay. Don't worry.'

'We go there now,' Jude says, firmly.

Mustafa looks offended but nods eventually. 'As you wish. As you request.' His face takes on a sly cast. 'I have the prosecutor's file.'

'Can I see it?'

'It is five thousand dollars.'

Of course it is. Jude is familiar enough with Iraq to have come with plenty of slush-fund cash. He hands over five thousand in hundred-dollar bills and Mustafa hands him a manila folder wrapped in a red ribbon. Opening it, Jude sees that there are stamped copies of a Civil ID card, a nationality certificate, a G-series passport issued in 2007 and a double-page entry in the local family registry, all in the name of Alysha al-Sabbah. Beneath them is a black-and-white mugshot with her hair scraped back from her face, which he memorises. And beneath that, there are photos from the medical examination that followed her arrest that confirm Helena's theory that Fowle marked another woman. Jude has seen enough of Fowle's handiwork not to want to linger over them. It is only going to make him feel compromised and unclean.

He sees enough to know that Alysha is one of Fowle's chosen ones.

'Where are you from?' Mustafa asks.

'London,' Jude replies.

'Sizewell!'

Mustafa laughs and spreads his hands to signify an explosion.

They drive west on Route One. At times, the road is fast and the cars and pick-ups weave in and out of the lanes to pass lumbering trucks and buses. Close to the cities there are epic traffic jams, the vehicles jockeying for position and spilling off the tarmac onto the sand to get ahead. They drive through checkpoints manned by the Iraqi army and those manned by irregulars from the Popular Mobilization Forces, the Shiite militias that helped to defeat Islamic State but are viewed by many, in this predominantly Sunni province, as an occupying force. They cross the Euphrates at Fallujah and again at Ramadi.

'There are a million people missing in Iraq,' Mustafa says. 'It's very difficult to find one person.'

'We have to try.'

When they eventually arrive at the camp, they find that it has been flattened. Leaving the cars by the roadside, Jude stumbles across the chewed-up ground through clouds of black diesel smoke in the wake of a bulldozer. All that remains of the camp is rubbish and tattered all-weather sheeting being shunted into a pile by the dozer blade. Beyond a flattened chain-link fence at the perimeter, Jude sees a solitary tent. Beside it there is a pile of scavenged plastic and a toddler who is being watched with predatory interest by several dogs.

When he calls out, a woman replies from inside the tent. She is a widow and an amputee and there are four more children with her, all of them under ten years old. Jude squats at the tent's entrance to talk to her. She is sitting on a threadbare cushion with her prosthetic leg lying beside her. She tells him that all the families except hers have been loaded onto buses and sent back to their villages. She explains without conviction that there was no room for her or her children on the buses. It's left hanging in the air – the likelihood that she was left behind because of her missing limb.

'I thought Iraq was a big place,' the woman says, 'but now it is small. There is no place for us.'

Jude thanks her and gives her a bundle of hundred-dollar bills. She stares at him as if she is frightened of what he might demand in return. He hurries back to the vehicle.

'These people are outcasts,' Mustafa tells him casually. 'If the people back in their villages see someone who was with Daesh they will kill them, just like that.'

'We better get after them,' Jude says.

'Tomorrow,' Mustafa says.

'Now!'

'You are a foolish man.'

Jude gives him another five thousand dollars.

An hour later they are stopped at a checkpoint of the Hashd al-Shaabi militia of the PMF. There is a starved-looking man kneeling in the dust beside a Humvee with his hands tied behind his back. A masked militiaman is standing over him with a Kalashnikov but when he sees their vehicles he saunters over and reaches into the window to shake Mustafa's hand.

Mustafa explains that they are looking for someone and asks him if any of the buses have come this way. He does not mention Alysha al-Sabbah by name or refer to the village that she comes from. The militiaman confirms that several buses have come this way heading for different destinations. He gestures with the rifle at the kneeling man who was taken off one of the buses.

'Daesh,' he says, contemptuously.

As they drive away, Jude looks over his shoulder through the rear window as the militiamen drag their prisoner into a shipping container. He does not rate his chances of survival.

They cross the Euphrates again and head north-west, driving across a parched landscape towards the Syrian border.

After an hour or so, they turn off the highway onto a rutted dirt track. In the distance there is a village of flat-roofed houses and a scattering of greyish palm trees. A column of dust indicates a convoy of vehicles driving out of the village towards them. As they converge, Jude sees that there is a Humvee at the head of the convoy with a bus behind it. The men in the Humvee are wearing balaclavas and the bus is empty.

Jude swears under his breath.

There isn't an obvious centre to the village or any communal space. The houses are surrounded by high walls and give a forbidding impression.

'This is where the Old Man was born,' Mustafa says, 'back when Iraq was a kingdom. The people here gave him their loyalty but later during the Awakening they turned against him.'

They park beside a metal door set into a twelve-foot-high wall. Mustafa gets out and bangs on the door with the heel of his palm. No one answers. After several more attempts, Mustafa moves on to the next compound with Jude following and bangs on another door.

There is something ferocious about the silence. No voices, no music, no indication that anyone is living until the door opens and a woman steps out and points. Beside him, Mustafa raises his nose to the air like a wolf catching the scent of something injured and vulnerable. Jude breaks into a run. He runs down a narrow path between two high walls and past the rubble of a collapsed house and sprawl of trash. He can see large black birds circling beyond a stand of palms.

He heads towards them with a sense of foreboding.

Beyond the trees, an elderly woman is kneeling beside a shallow pit that is full of bodies. She has pulled a young girl's corpse partway out of the pit and is cradling her head.

The first vulture has landed and is goose-stepping towards the pit with its hooked beak moving back and forth. Jude yells and the bird hops away and takes flight. He looks down at the corpses of women and children lying face down in the pit. Someone has made a desultory effort to cover them in earth.

He jumps into the pit. They have only recently been killed and their limbs are still loose. He lifts one up by the shoulders and blood runs out of the holes in her chest. It's not Alysha. He checks another. He does not touch the children. The old woman is staring at him. Soon it is too much, and he gives up.

He sits beside the grave, covered in blood and dirt, and feels the tears roll down his cheeks.

When he looks up, he sees that Mustafa is watching him.

'It will be dark soon.'

'Where is she?' Jude shouts at him.

Mustafa shrugs and walks away.

'Who are you looking for?' the old woman asks.

'Alysha al-Sabbah.'

'Are you the Stranger?'

'No.'

'She will not die here,' says the woman. 'It is not written. She will die in a place and at a time of her choosing.'

After several deep breaths, Jude climbs to his feet and heads in the direction of the car.

'Let's go.'

It's an unnerving journey back, past the monstrous shadows of stationary trucks and the windborne sparks of roadside fires. At the checkpoints, the militiamen are nervous and shout at them. Mustafa argues and each time they are allowed reluctantly to pass. At one point, children run out of the darkness to throw rocks at them and later someone fires a burst of gunfire at them, the tracer-like red dots whipping across the windscreen.

They reach Baghdad in the early hours of the morning and head straight to the airport.

## 22

# Tremors

While Alysha is sleeping, Guy's trembling fingers trace the elaborate geometry of the mandala that he carved in her skin with scalpel and compass needle when she was seventeen.

That was Iraq. They were being hunted and they never slept in the same bed twice. She was the granddaughter of the *Sheikh al-Jabal,* one of very few humans that he has ever considered his equal, and he was *al-Gharib* – the Stranger – responsible for murdering twenty-five British crusaders in a complex ambush in Basra. Also, he had recently killed her husband, a hothead from Fallujah with a large and vengeful family.

They were outlaws.

Each night when he cut her, he licked the wounds, the taste of her blood like copper coins on the tongue. Then he whispered into the flesh. She knew what he was doing and welcomed it, putting a fierce piece of him inside her. Afterwards he rubbed acacia ash into the cuts to raise the welts.

Her body has changed in the intervening years. Her hips have broadened, her waist narrowed, her breasts have new weight. The scars have swollen.

They are as pale as driftwood.

He feels the desire for her rising from his core.

The mandala is mesmerising in its beauty and blinding in its complexity: a microcosm of the destructive power of the cosmos waiting to be unleashed on the earth. He can feel the heat of the demon that he trapped in the mandala. It has grown ravenous during the years of its incarceration.

Its mouth is as wide as a tunnel.

★　　★　　★

Guy knows that the tyrant Saddam executed Alysha's parents for an unrecorded sleight not long after she was born, and her grandfather looked after her as a child. They were exiles, finding refuge where they could, in the ungoverned parts of the world. She told him that she spent much of her childhood in Afghanistan. The Old Man had little interest in providing her with a conventional upbringing, allowing her to sit unseen while he met with his fellow exiles and they spoke of God's will, of near and far enemies, of revolution and justice, and violent martyrdom.

She boasted that she learned one of the skills of a predator – being quiet around prey – while watching from the shadows. She also taught herself the use of weapons. The first man she killed was a Russian conscript, a pitiful creature who had been held captive by the Afghans for more than a decade, first for pleasure and later because he learned to make tea in the traditional way. She described the fierce emotion that coursed through her when he glimpsed the sharpened edge of the blade in her hand in the final moment before she slit his throat. She was fourteen. There were plenty of others after that. Too many to count, she claimed.

He remembers the first time that he saw her, across the floor of an Iraqi cave. They were both silent and watchful. Both interlopers, despised and feared in equal measure. She was the most striking woman that he had ever seen. Her aura burned like nuclear fission.

She was already married to a man with a gift for violence. He had many of the more banal characteristics of a lesser, undisciplined sociopath: a fast talker with a less-than-fifty-word vocabulary and an allergy to adverbs, a tendency to malapropism and self-contradiction. He might have been fine fighting and fucking on prehistoric grasslands, but he hadn't sufficiently learned the patterns or protocols to infiltrate human society. Guy despised him for his inability to camouflage himself.

'I like an early kill,' he told Guy. 'A dead Shiite puts me in a good mood all day.'

To give him some reptile credit, he could react to threats in a fraction of the time it took the ungifted, but still he wasn't fast enough.

'Mood is worthless without intelligence,' Guy told him before he killed him. He left his corpse to shrivel down to bones and cheap leather in the desert air.

The territory wasn't large enough for two of their kind.

Their brief time as outlaws ended abruptly when the Old Man betrayed him.

He sent fifty men in the dead of night to seize Guy and it was not too many. They surrounded the house and killed the dogs. The silence in the moments before they broke in alerted him. He had time to roll off the bed and grab his rifle. Alysha was almost as fast. The suicide bombers that stood guard for them ran out into the street and detonated their cargo, breaking the first wave. They held off successive waves for three hours. When they had no more ammunition they fought with knives. Then they punched and kicked. Alysha tore a chunk of a man's face off with her teeth. Eventually they were subdued.

The Old Man's men separated them.

They did not see each other for several years. Later, when the gypsies were guarding Guy in the mountains, she was able to bribe them to allow her to visit him. By then he was already planning his attack on London. The Old Man had revealed to him that he planned to send him against the far enemy.

Alysha pleaded with him to take her with him when the time came.

He agreed.

He lied. He has never had any room for sentiment. He killed the Old Man and stole his crypto. He travelled to London with another woman, a former police officer named Zeina Hussein, who was more suited to the task. After Belmarsh he teamed up with another former lover, Candida Taunton.

It was only after Sizewell, when he was grievously wounded, when it was no longer possible to disguise the effects of the disease that had been slowly crippling him, that he reached out to Alysha. He left a message in the drafts box of an email messaging service and waited for a response. A lawyer from Irbil responded. Guy made the necessary payment and secured her release from prison. From Iraq, she travelled to Dubai, where she collected a cigar-shaped vacuum flask from a Russian scientist and brought it to Scotland.

A man dressed as a chauffeur drove her from Edinburgh Airport to the south side of Glasgow, where she met Grigor, who drove her the rest of the way. Several vehicle switches later they were reunited.

Guy's cryptocurrency holdings have doubled in value in a matter of weeks. He's as rich as Croesus but he's indifferent to his wealth.

Alysha has shown him how to move the money just as her grandfather and his financier, the Kuwaiti Wahab Mutairi, taught her. Using the information written in his notebook, she has co-opted the GRU's means of communication and left chalk marks on anonymous street furniture. She has made additional payments to those illegals whose active cooperation or ongoing silence is a matter of priority. And to the organised crime syndicates that are the source of their weapons and matériel. She has travelled to London and other cities for him. She has prepared the ground for his last chance at mass destruction.

His balance is impaired. He's lost his sense of smell and his ability to read people's auras. Only regular injections of apomorphine get his aching limbs moving. He has reached the unwelcome realisation that his time as a top predator is coming to an end. How does this happen?

To be defeated out of the blue and without a battle.

Alysha wakes to find that Guy has left her.

Reluctantly, she leaves the warmth of the bed. The stone floor is cold beneath her feet. She stands shivering in the window and looks out over the dark shadows of the mountain, the glassy loch, and the huge trees. They are giant redwoods. She has only ever seen them before in a *National Geographic* magazine.

It's raining. Fine, almost imperceptible beads of water cover everything. She has never known anything like it.

Then she sees him.

Guy is moving across the steep slope above the tower with his back to her. His progress across the rocks and scree is slow and careful. A hunter checking his traps: he does this every morning after shooting up.

She goes back to bed and waits for him to return. He does not know that she knows. Grigor let it slip. After an hour, she hears the whisper of his feet on the curve of the staircase. He stands in the room. She wonders if he is fighting the urge to kill her.

He looks away. The spell is broken.

'Have they found us?' she asks, stretching like a cat.

'Not yet,' he says. Ignoring the tremors, he reaches out and strokes the curve of the *ensō* that surrounds her navel. 'It is my finest work.'

'Tonight, you can finish it.'

A violent reckoning is coming. She accepts that. She does not fear death. She chooses it. She has prepared for it all her life.

# 23

# The Red October

Alexei and Yulia cross into Belarus in a convoy of ten black Mercedes saloons from Zaslon, a special operations unit of the SVR. At the border, Yulia stares out through armoured glass at rain falling from a slate-grey sky. Beside her, Alexei opens his eyes and grunts sceptically at the sign proclaiming a *Year of National Unity*. He snored like a lion through the entire flight and all the way to the border in the car and she has been grateful for her earplugs.

They pass a line of men and women stretching out of view behind a corrugated-iron shed. Most are carrying bags full of agricultural produce to sell in Russia. The same box-shaped nylon bags, in blue-and-white and red-and-white check, found across the former Soviet Union. Yulia remembers her mother sponging them down every evening. In those times, when plastic was so rare, the clothes lines in the communal areas always had rows of bags of varying sizes and thicknesses hanging on them.

Alexei has received word that the demoralised remnants of the Prizrak – Ghost – Unit of PMC Valkyrie abandoned their positions in the Donbass after the organisation was declared an illegal formation and have set up camp in the ruin of the Red October smelting plant here in Belarus. When she asks what they will do when they reach the plant, Alexei scowls.

'We will seize it.'

For a man who has spent his entire professional career manipulating hidden levers, it's surprising to Yulia that Alexei has retained what seems like a naïve and sentimental attachment to the full-frontal assault. She's heard it called *bychit*, literally to behave like a bull – the feeling you get from hitting something very hard with your head. She wonders if it's a product of age and running out of time.

There are many miles of primeval forest to drive through first.

After two hours they pass an ambushed convoy pushed to the side of the road, the rusting hulks of Msta self-propelled howitzers spray-painted in the white-and-red of the resistance, a testament to the crushing failure of the president's ambition. She had watched the same tracked artillery flatten Grozny back in 1999 in the Second Chechen War when the doctrine of bombarding cities and killing civilians was born. She had been there on the trail of foreign jihadis back when they were considered a nuisance rather than an existential risk. Her husband Valery had also been there, though in his case it was about settling old scores – killing as many Chechens as he could in revenge for the humiliation of the first war when his unit was annihilated. In his cups, Valery would often speak freely of how the dead from the Grozny Road visited him in the night.

She wonders what role his guilt for surviving played in his enthusiastic participation in building Grom.

At midnight, the convoy races between canyon-like slopes that radiate outwards from the defunct smelting works, the pulverised rock sparkling with trace metals so that it appears as if they are driving through a projection of the Milky Way.

They rattle across a metal bridge over iridescent-orange water and the convoy disperses, the vehicles spreading out to encircle the plant.

The casting house is a vast shoebox a dozen storeys high with a forest of blackened smokestacks and a superstructure of rusty gantries and staircases. They stop beside a line of decrepit-looking buses parked in front of one of the loading bays. There is a frayed red carpet and a rope line that leads to a doorway. Beside it, armed Valkyrie contractors are gathered around a fire in an oil drum.

'Yulia and I will go in alone,' Alexei tells Timofey, the head of the Zaslon unit, whose muscular physique and square jaw wouldn't be out of place on a Soviet poster. He looks unhappy at the idea.

'After ten minutes come and get us. And kill anybody who gets in your way.'

'Of course, General,' Timofey says.

They get out of the car and walk together towards the fire; a bearded man in a tactical vest with the Valkyrie orc-skull patch on his shoulder greets them. He is holding a torch the size of a baton.

'Please follow me.'

He leads them up the red carpet and into the building, following a pathway between huge pieces of machinery – conveyors, rollers, and presses – the torch a lozenge of light on the rough concrete floor, picking out scattered ingots and piles of filings. Somewhere in the darkness a generator is throbbing.

Unnerved, Yulia spits on the ground for luck, like her mother used to do.

They turn a corner and arrive at a floodlit checkpoint. A man and a woman in hooded black parkas are standing beyond a metal detector.

Yulia goes first, putting her phone in a pink basket and stepping through the detector. She raises her arms, and the woman runs her hands under her coat and down her legs. She is thorough but not at all rough. They make eye contact while Yulia's arms are being patted and she senses that the woman has something to say but will not do so in front of her colleagues.

When it's Alexei's turn to go through the metal detector he empties his pockets, which include a telescopic baton and a bone-handled pocketknife. The man confiscates them.

'I want those back.'

'Of course,' the thin man says. 'Please, this way.'

He escorts them past a row of huge rotary furnaces like ancient cauldrons and into a large space with a bonfire and a dining table.

'Here you are, at last. General,' says a man in a white suit. His grey hair is boastfully long and there is a dark line around the gums of his front teeth. Sitting beside him is a red-eyed, shaven-headed man who Yulia recognises as Mikhail Metelkin, the commander of the Ghost Unit. He is wearing a T-shirt with the folkloric *Kolovrat* wheel beloved of Heinrich Himmler on it. The irony is not lost on Yulia that the hired guns that the president uses for the brutal 'de-Nazification' of his neighbours themselves worship at the altar of neo-Nazism. The man in white raises his glass. 'And welcome to you too, Ms Yulia Ermolaeva. Your reputations precede you. I am Timur. We are blessed by your presence. Please join us. I am almost finished with my business. Isn't that right, Mehmet?'

A tall man with a bushy black moustache, who is sitting on the other side of Timur, stands up. 'I will check the merchandise,' he says, casting a suspicious look at Alexei and Yulia.

'Of course, take your time,' Timur says with a wave of the hand. He smiles at Alexei. 'Please sit.'

The table is covered in a half-eaten meal: plates of shashlik and cheese, stacks of black bread, jars of pickles and bottles of wine and vodka. Two women dressed for a nightclub vacate their chairs to make room, but Alexei does not sit. He presses his knuckles into the white tablecloth and sticks out his chin.

'Give me the bear,' he says.

Timur raises an eyebrow to his dinner guests. 'General, please, we haven't even begun the negotiation.'

'I'm not here to buy her.'

'You think you can seize her?' Timur tuts and waves an admonishing finger. 'I had heard you were a brute, General, but no one told me that you were disrespectful.' He switches his attention to Yulia. 'Please, Yulia Ermolaeva, sit. Have a drink.' Bored of posturing men, she sits in one of the vacated seats. Alexei shoots her an angry look but then grunts and sits beside her. Timur pours clear liquid from a flask into four shot glasses and passes two of them across the table. 'I think it's fair to say that the imagination and artistry of the Protean Bears has taken us all by surprise. Add to that the mystery of their intentions. Can you be sure that they align with those of the Russian state? Are the bears really your friends? Yes, I can see why you are worried. *Budeem zdarovye!*'

To our health.

Alexei downs the shot and Yulia follows suit. It's *chacha*, vodka made from the residue of winemaking. Timur practically purrs in approval. Metelkin downs his and wipes his face with his eyes half closed.

Looking across the fire, Yulia realises that there are rows of silent women in the space beyond it. As many as a hundred she guesses, sitting two metres apart from each other on the concrete. Mehmet is walking along the first row with four armed minders. While she watches, he stops and squats down in front of a young woman. It's far away for Yulia to hear what he says. Beside him, a man scans a barcode on the woman's wristband.

Timur sees what she's looking at and smiles. 'The people here have always used migration as a survival strategy. You can make more money as a nanny or a construction worker in Russia than you can as a teacher or doctor here.'

'And as a sex worker?' she asks.

'There is plenty of demand for workers in agriculture, construction, and the domestic services. And yes, the sex industry.'

'You're a slaver.'

'I'm a trader. People here have been offering their labour overseas for five hundred years. Since the time of the Khans. But you should know this already. Your agency has often used my routes as a pipeline for moving people. I have been a valuable partner to the SVR.'

Alexei grunts impatiently. 'What do you want?'

'It's obvious that the answers that you are looking for are not available in Moscow or you would not be here. Ipso facto, the bear is very valuable. Knowing this, my friend Mikhail brought him to me.' He grips Metelkin by the shoulder. 'Now I have the bear; therefore, you must negotiate with me.'

'Where's your sense of national duty?'

Timur laughs. 'I swore an oath to the Soviet Union more than thirty years ago. I never swore an oath to its impecunious bastards. No matter how hard the little man in the Kremlin tries, what is broken cannot be put back together again.'

She watches Alexei with his head down, eyebrows up and eyes wide open. She knows what's coming.

*Bychit.*

*Crack, crack, crack.*

The sound of gunfire is startling.

Alexei grabs Timur's hand and grips it tightly. With his other hand, he sweeps the bottle of *chacha* out of the ice bucket and smashes it over Timur's head.

The lights go out.

More gunfire echoing amongst the machinery and off the walls. Somebody close by screaming. Yulia is on the floor with Alexei and her face is wet.

A few moments later a string of flash-bangs go off, lighting up the whole factory as if someone was using an arc welder. The ricochets all around make it difficult to locate the source of fire.

She watches drifting dust motes. Someone picks her up with apparent ease and carries her through the smoke and out into the cold night air, amazingly without banging her against anything.

'Are you hurt?' Alexei mouths or perhaps he is shouting, and she is deaf. She's not sure. She can't feel any injuries. It's not as if being in a building during an assault is a unique or historic experience. She's done this before and recently. She knows what injury feels like.

'I'm fine,' she says. She is pleasantly surprised to discover when she tastes it that the liquid covering her is *chacha* and not blood. Alexei is smiling. He is a very reassuring bear. She wonders if her coat is ruined.

## 24

# The brave mole

Yulia's ability to sniff out a mole is as acute as ever.

She finds the woman that searched her corralled with the surviving members of Timur's gang in one corner of the casting house. They exchange a look and Yulia moves on. Rather than single her out, Yulia instructs the local police to do a 'sort-and-sieve', separating the detainees by gender and then age, moving them about the casting house in ever smaller groups until she can be extracted without drawing attention.

Now they are sitting in the back of one of the Zaslon Mercedes. The woman's name is Oksana, and she works for an anti-slavery network.

'You stink of *chacha*,' she says.

'Bring me coffee,' Yulia tells the driver, who gets out and heads towards a group of men standing by their cars. Oksana fidgets beside her. There are dark circles under her eyes and the roots of her hair are growing out, the straw-coloured dye falling in lank waves from her temples to her shoulders. 'You are either fool-hardy or extremely brave.'

'I don't have anything left to be frightened of,' Oksana replies. She has prison tattoos on her fingers and her nails are bitten to the quick.

The driver returns. Yulia rolls the window down as far as the armoured glass will go, which is only about six inches, and accepts a vacuum flask through the gap.

'Take a walk,' she tells him.

They pass the lid of the flask back and forth, sipping at the bitter, steaming coffee.

'Where were the women being trafficked to?'

'Most of them were heading for Russia to work bottling and packing vodka from black market stills. Some of them were heading for a Turkish brothel. From there they might end up in Germany or even China.'

'Where will they go now?'

'We've set up a reception centre on the outskirts of the city and we pay the police a finder's fee to take them there. It discourages them from selling the women back to the traffickers.'

'And from there?'

'Some of them will have been sold by their parents so they may not want to go home.'

'Is that what happened to you?'

'What do you want?' Oksana demands, defiantly.

Yulia sighs. 'I'm looking for someone. A hacker named Khmer Bear. Can you help me with that?'

'Timur has a place he likes to keep quiet. It's an old dacha near the woods. I can drop you a pin.'

'Thank you.'

'What will happen to Timur now? Will he be free to get back to business?'

'No,' Yulia replies more fiercely than she expected. She opens the car door. 'He will not.'

A Zaslon team member escorts her through the casting house. Someone has got the generator going again but it doesn't fully muffle the sound of Timur screaming. She steps over the body of Mikhail Metelkin and several other Valkyrie contractors before catching sight of Timur hanging head down like a bat, at the end of a length of rope. Someone has pushed him out of the observation window of a control room, its lights blazing in the darkness.

She climbs the metal staircase that leads to the control room, passing within a few feet of Timur, who is slowly rotating. One of the Zaslon agents opens the door for her, and she finds Alexei sitting at the edge of the window, surrounded by broken glass with his pocketknife in his hand.

'I should have gagged him before kicking him out,' Alexei grumbles.

'I know where the bear is,' she tells him.

'Then we don't need him.'

She recalls her commitment to Oksana just minutes ago. 'We don't.'

Alexei cuts the rope. Timur falls thirty feet, hitting the concrete floor like a sack – a satisfying thump.

They go down the stairs past his corpse.

Timur's dacha is hidden in a forest of birches at the end of a long gravel drive, a single-storey Soviet-era house, painted in stippled green-and-white camouflage making it deliberately hard to see from the ground and air. By the time they arrive, the guards have fled.

Alexei marches up the steps into the dacha at the head of the Zaslon team.

'Find the bear!'

He advances across an expanse of parquet towards the embers of a fire in a brick hearth while the team fan out and start searching. He picks up a poker and jabs the fire, shunting a stray log into the centre.

After fifteen minutes, Timofey returns. 'She was in a crate in the cellar.'

Two of his men carry a limp body to an armchair in front of the fire.

Yulia goes over to the chair while Alexei tosses more logs on the fire. Pine sap hisses, steams, and burns. Yulia kneels and parts the woman's lank black hair. Her face is filthy and there is a rank, animal smell coming off her.

'Can you hear me?'

'Yes,' she croaks.

'Where are the Grom servers?'

'Franz Josef Land.'

The closed military archipelago in the Arctic Ocean that is the northernmost part of Russia and less than a thousand kilometres from the North Pole – not top of Yulia's bucket list of destinations to visit before she dies.

She sighs. 'I'm going to need a warmer coat.'

# 25

# Crash and burn

Lee has always preferred to barge into any interview with the perspective that he's already lost the job. It gives him a kind of loose-limbed freedom of action. Knowing he's doomed, he can bob and weave, and strike at will. He is currently cooking under the hyper-real glare of studio lights in New Broadcasting House with the cameras aimed at him like wire-guided anti-tank missiles, and a coating of powder on his face like war paint.

Opposite him, the enemy: an alumnus of Cheltenham Ladies' and Brasenose with lush honey-blonde hair and spray-tan legs that are as shiny as conkers. She is speaking to camera with casual confidence:

'The final say is with Party members but the decision being made will profoundly affect us all. It's firmly in the public interest for audiences to hear from the next Prime Minister. Tonight, we interview the second of the two contenders.' She turns her crafty, fox-like face on him. 'Lee Chapeaux, welcome to *Spotlight*.'

'Thank you, Alice.' He smiles warmly and lets the words run like water from his mouth. 'We've been through a testing time. We've had our backs to the wall. My rival has been scribbling IOUs since the London attacks, promising to sort everything out at some mysterious point in the future but delivering absolutely nothing. He's a symptom of something rotten: a "Whitehall knows best" culture, which is a cancer in the system.' He bypasses Alice and speaks direct to the camera. 'I'm saying the time has come to make good on the promises. It's time to reward the bravery of our nurses and doctors, our police and fire officers, and our armed forces. For too long we have undervalued the very people that bind this great country together and give it backbone. For too long we've been walked all over by Russian oligarchs with dirty money. They've snatched up our land and pushed house prices through the roof.'

He bats away the questions about how he's going to pay for the public sector pay rises that he's proposing. It's not rocket science: interest rates are low, public borrowing is cheap and he's going to issue Patriot Bonds. He announces his intention to create Britcoin, a new government digital currency, allowing people access to a free, safe, universal means of payment that is guaranteed by the full faith of the state, not a fallible bank; plus, his intention to seize unexplained wealth from oligarchs, including those using shell companies in overseas territories, and to plough it into the health service. On immigration and law and order, he is, as they say, cut and dried: behave and you're welcome; misbehave and you're going to end up banged up or deported. He wishes the porridge wogs good fortune (he doesn't use those actual words, of course. He acknowledges the Scots' right to self-determination. Many divorced couples get on fine, etc.). He professes love for his copious nephews and nieces, which confirms that although he's childless, he comes from fecund northern stock. He admits that he's been single for quite some time but – making clear he doesn't want to jinx it – he is hopeful of imminent change. Alice lands a couple of flesh wounds. He confesses to some ill-considered comments in the past, borderline racism and misogyny, but puts them down to locker room banter and the irreverent humour of the fighting man. He's apologised and been humbled. He's learned salutary lessons from the strong-willed men and women around him.

'I'm not a perfect person,' he tells Alice. 'I don't pretend to be. I know when to seek advice. But I also know when to make decisions: life-or-death decisions. I've learned the hard way.'

'One of the central planks of your platform is re-armament,' Alice says. 'Do you intend to send our armed forces into harm's way?'

'Let me be clear, I'm not interested in fighting small wars,' he tells her, emphatically. 'I did my time in Afghanistan. One of my best muckers bled out in my arms in Sangin. I saw what it cost us in blood and treasure. Frankly, the less those people see of us the better for them and us. This is not about that. It's not about expeditionary wars. This is about preserving our way of life. We came close to total annihilation at Sizewell. A radioactive country!' He pauses to let the viewers fill in the gap with their own fears. 'Never again can we let ourselves be vulnerable to foreign attack on our own soil. We need the means to attack and deter. Look at how underpowered we are. We need destroyers and tanks and helicopter gunships. Our naval ships are herbivores without the teeth to attack. Our jets are overpriced and irreplaceable. Our tanks have so much bolt-on armour they waddle like fatsos.'

'You have said before that the greatest threat to our security is Russia, do you still believe that?'

'How could I not? Remember, I was here in London when my opponent Nigel went AWOL, and the Cabinet fled the city. When the BBC ran to Manchester and Glasgow. When only the brave women and men of the emergency services remained, and Russian agents very nearly obliterated everything.'

'How do you respond to the Russian president's claim that the attacks were the fault of anarchist hackers who teamed up with Guy Fowle, a British terrorist?'

'Just words, isn't it? We all know what happened. Russian sleeper agents, so-called illegals, ran amok.'

'Last night Nigel Featherstone, when he was sitting where you are now, told us he has a personal guarantee from the Russian president that he has neutralised the hackers and there will be no more attacks.'

Lee rolls his eyes. 'Who does he think he is? Neville Chamberlain? One cosy chat with a man who murders his political opponents and sponsors terrorist attacks abroad and Nigel thinks we can trust him. Look at how Nigel got spurned by NATO on Article Five. It's just one more example of the wilful naïvety of our political establishment who won't stand up for what's right.'

'Are you accusing the Foreign Secretary of naïvety?'

'I don't have to.' And despite the extensive coaching that he's received, he can't resist widening his smile to show his shark-like grin. 'It's obvious to everyone. Let me be clear, I'm accusing him of being a danger to this nation. If he is not prepared to recognise the real and present danger posed to our country by Russia and prepare for it properly, he is risking British lives. If he becomes Prime Minister, I warn you now, we are not safe in our beds.'

'That's very intemperate language from someone who hopes to move into No. 10 Downing Street. But of course, you are no stranger to reckless rhetoric. We've been looking through your social media accounts, including at some posts that have been recently deleted. In a tweet that followed the attack on the North London oil terminal you threatened to lock up all foreign workers.'

Lee shrugs. 'We have to be prepared to take the action required to meet the threat.'

'Are you seriously advocating imprisonment for anyone who wasn't born here?'

'I didn't say that.'

'Yes, you did, in that tweet, which was deleted just before your leadership campaign was launched.' Alice is looking like all her Christmases arrived at once. 'Changing your position to try to win votes, isn't that exactly the kind of hypocrisy you accuse your opponents of?'

Lee is outraged. *Who the hell does she think she is?* 'I'm no hypocrite.'

'Then what are you?'

'All right,' he says, with his chin out. 'I *am* going to detain foreign workers.'

Alice recoils. 'Pardon me?'

'I will use anti-terrorism legislation to remove them from their positions and take them somewhere secure where they can be processed. It's a temporary measure determined by extraordinary circumstances. We must feel safer, knowing that they won't . . .' He catches himself, knowing that it's better left unsaid, that in the minds of many of those at home it goes to all manner of fears about what an illegal might do.

It's Alice's turn to be outraged. 'You're talking about locking people up who live and work here legally, pay taxes and contribute to our economy, against whom you have no evidence of wrongdoing, simply based on their nationality?'

'When ordinary people can't feel safe it's time to change the law, which is why I will seek emergency legislation to increase the amount of time that terror suspects can be held on remand.'

'You'll be challenged in the courts.'

'As is right and proper.' And with that, he switches from aggressor to reasonable man. 'They will be treated fairly.' He lifts his head and smiles at the camera, letting his self-confidence communicate itself to the viewers. He is real and genuine and straight-talking.

'I will keep you safe.'

I'm right, his smile tells them. Not just in this but in everything.

Which is not how the early editions of the tabloids report it:

*Car Crash!*

The broadsheets aren't any kinder. The left-leaning press lauds Alice Preen as a protector of the nation. On the right, an editorial in the establishment's favourite morning paper describes the greatest threat to the country as a thinly disguised authoritarian in populist clothing.

# 26

# Sweet salt Śárkarã

Gustavo Montes is passionate about sugar.

He has the chemical composition of sucrose, a disaccharide of glucose and fructose, tattooed on his forearm for anyone to see. His last girlfriend said that it looked like two fat men with tiny heads holding hands. She had not been convinced that he would ever realise his ambition to quit his job at the refinery and start up a business making bespoke high-quality rum from Otaheite 'sweet gold' cane.

More fool her.

He's a cryptocurrency millionaire.

'Lock 'em up? I ask you, what was that terrible man Chapeaux thinking?'

Gustavo is standing in the office looking out at the Thames, and Julie from Human Resources is rolling her eyes and assuring him that there are no plans to suspend him.

'Of course, sugar is not exactly critical infrastructure,' she says, wistfully. 'Though try going without for a day is what I say.'

She's the sort of size and shape that gives sucrose a bad name.

'Is that all?' he asks. 'I need to get back to the control room.'

A consignment of raw cane sugar has arrived by sea from the Caribbean and there's no time to waste.

'Bless, dear, I know how hard-working you are,' she says. 'I just wanted you to know that you have the full backing of the management. You are critical to us! And it doesn't matter if Russia and Cuba were friends years and years ago, if anyone so much as looks at you funny, I expect you to let me know the minute it happens and there'll be hell to pay.'

'Thank you,' he says. 'But I don't think that will be necessary.'

There's little point correcting her. He's not Cuban. He's Venezuelan. And what of it? Warriors don't wear national uniforms any more.

Leaving the administrative block, he walks back towards his domain: the East London Sugar House, the largest refinery in Europe, where purified syrup is concentrated to super-saturation and repeatedly crystallised in huge steel vats, producing a million tonnes of refined sugar a year.

After the North London oil terminal exploded in the first wave of Grom attacks, Gustavo had visited an internet café used by migrant workers in Newham. He'd logged on to an encrypted email account hosted on servers in Switzerland that had never sent or received an email on the internet and consulted the drafts box to see if he had been left a message. All that was there was the quarterly update with the latest automatically generated proverbs to use as passwords.

No indication that he was being activated.

He remembers feeling disappointed. But feeling sure that his time would come.

On the day after the banking system crashed, and the ATMs and chip-and-pin failed, he'd returned to Newham and found another internet café that was open despite the chaos. In exchange for cash, he'd bought himself fifteen minutes online and found a single email in the drafts box with a one-word heading:

Стой!

A cease-and-desist order issued from the *Aquarium*, the headquarters of the GRU.

And the minute he read it he felt the bitterness of a life wasted. What was the point of it all: the brutal training, the lies that he'd told and the sacrifices that he had made?

He walked home with his head down.

Days passed. People got sick and the hospitals struggled to cope. Sizewell came close to a meltdown. At work, he went through the motions.

He almost missed it: a distinctive chalk mark on the side of a dark green fibre-broadband cabinet on the route back to his flat. The fall-back signal for when the internet is compromised or no longer functioning.

He felt a rush of excitement.

He hurried home and then five minutes later, he went out on his bike. Stopping by a low wall in Greenwich, he extracted a brick and recovered an envelope from behind it. Inside there was a card with an email address and a password. He memorised both and set fire to the card. Again, he travelled to Newham, visiting a third internet café. This time, when Gustavo logged on to the new account, he found two unsent emails in the drafts box: the first was a thirty-four-digit numeric key to a cryptocurrency account with a value of one million dollars. The second was a notification of a further nineteen million in escrow to be released on completion of his mission. You had to admire the thinking behind it. A million is *bueno*, but not quite enough to retire on, particularly if you are going to have to take life-long and extraordinary measures to keep your identity and location hidden. Twenty million, however, is ¡*muy bien!*

He'd thought about it for twenty-four hours. Going about his business as usual but with his chest doing flips. He realised that the messages were from Guy Fowle and not a *doverenniye litsa*, a custodian of the Grom network. Who else could it be? But so what if it was Fowle? The mission was the same. But the financial reward was greater. More in keeping with the sacrifices that he'd made. This way he really could set up the distillery of his dreams.

Twenty-four hours later he'd logged on again from a fourth location and left a new message in the drafts box of the account.

One word only

*Da.* Yes.

Then he waited. Nothing happened. He began to wonder if Fowle had given up. He heard nothing more from the *Aquarium*. When he saw the news about the arrests in America and the angry denials from Moscow, he began to consider a unilateral extraction. He had a million dollars, which wasn't so bad. There were no emotional attachments to keep him in London.

And then, just after midnight, a woman called him on his mobile from an unknown number and they exchanged passwords.

*'Still waters are inhabited by devils.'*

*'If you're scared of wolves, don't go in the woods.'*

*'Better to be the right hand of the devil than in his path.'*

He waited thirty minutes and then rode his bike to Greenwich. This time there was a USB stick in an envelope behind the loose brick in the low wall.

He felt the exhilaration of activation: an operation underway, a task nearing completion.

In the control room, Gustavo sits at the horseshoe-shaped console and checks the levels. Carefully, he reaches under the console for his ankle and retrieves the USB from his sock. He slides it into a port – counts thirty seconds under his breath – then ejects it and slides it back into his sock.

Job done. Payload delivered.

Once, that might have been enough to earn him an audience in the Kremlin and a medal from the president. In secret of course, these kinds of activities could not be acknowledged. How much more satisfying than that to be a multi-millionaire.

At the end of his shift, he hands over to the night supervisor.

He takes his time to change from his work clothes into his cycling gear, conscious that he will never return. He rides his bike to St Pancras, where he boards the Eurostar for Brussels Midi, arriving just over two hours later. He collects a passport in a different name from a storage locker and heads to the airport, where he boards the first of several flights.

All is not well in the Sugar House.

As the sugar crystals are ground into smaller and smaller particles, and as the surface area increases, the number of collisions between the molecules on the surface of the particles and the oxygen molecules in the air also increases. Soon the air is filled with highly volatile dust. Usually, the exhaust systems would extract the dust and if for any reason the system failed, the refinery would automatically shut down. However, the custom-ised DarkMatter malware that Gustavo inserted in the system switches off the exhaust and tricks the control system into think-ing it's still working. No alarm sounds in the control room.

The fog of sugar dust thickens overnight.

Collisions like pinballs.

Not long after sunrise, a spark.

The accumulated dust acts like gunpowder. The refinery explodes. The blast wave sweeps outwards across London City Airport. A passenger plane coming in to land is flipped on its back and thrown into Royal Albert Dock. Houses and apartment blocks are flattened across Silvertown and North Woolwich. The rotating floodgates of the Thames Barrier are jammed in place and the London Internet Exchange, one of the vertebrae of the global internet network, burns to the ground.

A few hours later, Nigel Featherstone, who returned from Russia brandishing a personal guarantee of no further attacks, pulls out of the leadership race.

# 27

# Now the hard part begins

'This is your moment,' Bala tells Lee, in the wings with her eyes shining. 'When you are leader, you are briefly – too briefly – unassailable. Seize it, my love. Grab everything you can.'

On the stage the joint chair of the backbench 1922 Committee, who looks old enough to have survived the Blitz, is making the announcement to a packed room of MPs. She is urging them to rally around the new leader and be kinder than they were to his predecessor.

Lee bounds up to the lectern and kisses the old dear on the cheek, feeling the tremor of excitement in her frail and bony shoulders. He stands before the crowd with his hands out and his palms raised, absorbing the applause like Pharaoh or Freddie Mercury. At the first hint of a pause, he jabs his hand out in a Brecon point (a whole-hand chopping gesture beloved of British soldiers) and tells them straight that he's not interested in their kindness. He demands their obedience.

'The time for self-doubt is over,' he tells them. 'Now is the time for action.'

He jumps off the stage, landing with his knees bent and his feet together like a true-born paratrooper, and strides out to face whatever the world can throw at him. From Party HQ, he is driven in an armoured Jaguar Sentinel that still bears the hallmark of his famously temperamental predecessor.

'The old PM was no stranger to rage, sir,' Roger, the head of his newly inherited protection detail, tells him as Lee prods an inquisitive finger in one of the holes stabbed in the seat fabric with a sharpie.

'Don't call me *sir*,' Lee tells him.

'Boss?'

'That'll do nicely.'

They sweep through the gates of Buckingham Palace. Lee brushes the Monarch's hand with lips that gorged that morning on Bala's lady-baton and is invited with a minimum of fuss to form a government.

*Will do, Your Majesty!*

Back down The Mall and through the Admiralty Arch. A right turn for the seat of power. They advance slowly through a boisterous thicket of jubilant Noble Boys to the Whitehall barricade, where a Challenger tank reverses to let them through.

They sweep through the gates at Downing Street just as the heavy lectern is being dragged out onto the street towards the media pen. The purpose-built conference centre at No. 9 is out of action over concerns about the Russian contractors who built it. It's back to open-air briefings in front of the famous door, which as far as Lee is concerned is just as it should be. There's a small crowd waiting to walk in behind him: the bright young things of his campaign team, a couple of the more presentable Noble Boys, Denzel looking sharper than ever in a three-piece Harris-tweed suit and Bala upstaging them all in an electric-blue sari. He winks at her as he strides up to the lectern.

'This is me,' he says, palms raised, momentarily blinded by camera flash, 'unvarnished and unspun.'

A roar goes up on Trafalgar Square where Ezra's paid for a huge live screen.

Rising on the balls of his feet, Lee gives the hacks both barrels: decreased waiting times, increased minimum wage, a new deal for frontline health workers and the firefighters, more police, Britcoin and Patriot Bonds, zero tolerance for foreign interference, selective internment, re-armament, and a new age of confidence on the world stage.

On the news, it's described as a bravura performance.

'Thank you.' He waves and turns, bouncing up to the door with his hand raised to bang the lion's head doorknocker. *Let me in, little piggies!* He doesn't get the chance. The uniformed custodian whisks the door open and everyone inside is clapping. He swings his head from left to right with his jaw out. The most senior civil servant, the Cabinet Secretary, is there on the black-and-white tiles doing a two-step with a spotted handkerchief spilling out of the breast pocket of his suit jacket, and the rest of the No. 10 staff line the walls of the entrance hall and the corridor beyond. He grins and motions for Lee to go on in.

And then he's in the PM's seat in the Cabinet Room, where he remains the centre of attention as he's receiving a series of brief- ings on everything from the ministerial appointments process to his living arrangements to the state of the damaged reactor at Sizewell. They are about half an hour in when he is told without warning that the US president is on the line. The Cabinet Secretary ushers him into a side office, where he takes the call. Later when he is recounting the story to Bala in the upstairs flat, he will strug- gle to remember what was said – something about the enduring relationship, positive noises about the provision of additional advanced weapons systems to the Baltic states, a carrier group to the high north and a threat to suppress Russia's raw commodity prices – gas and grain – that must be balanced against the risk of it driving the Russians further into China's sphere of influence, and to cap it all a baseball anecdote.

After the US president it's back in the Cabinet Room and he's learning the protocols for urgent decisions and the nuclear release policy and every twenty minutes or so he must take a call from some world leader or other with the notable exception of the Russian president, whose Ambassador to the UK has expressed public surprise on social media at the lack of democratic process in Lee's appointment.

After the briefings, it's into a high-octane HR session with his transition team that some in the left-wing press will condemn as a 'coup-in-all-but-name' and those on the right will froth enthusias- tically over for days. He gets rid of a total of twelve permanent secretaries, replacing them with candidates from the Civil Service Commission's list who have been personally vetted by Denzel. He sacks the six most senior Cabinet ministers – Exchequer, Foreign,

Home, Health, Education and Defence – walking them in and out of No. 10 in a matter of minutes. Their replacements are whisked in the Horse Guards entrance and made a one-time offer, take it or leave it, that they only employ personal staff nominated by Denzel and agreed by Lee. All agree and are allowed to process triumphantly out the front door. To Daamini Dhatta, the chair of his campaign committee, he gives the job of Deputy Prime Minister, on standby 24/7 to take over if Grom makes a casualty of him.

The most diverse Cabinet in British history: *Tick!*

Then he appoints his private staff team: chief of staff, communications, policy unit, and the political and constituency secretaries. As promised, he appoints Bala his press secretary and head of story development.

That done, he stands down the Noble Boys.

'Back to your homes, lads. The battle is won. It's time to seek solace in the arms of your loved ones. And if the nation is threatened again, I know that you will be ready to answer the call.'

There'll be some grumbling, a few broken windows perhaps, but he knows them well enough to be confident that they'll comply.

After that, in search of a more professional class of fighting chap, he phones Chantal Carny, who has just been given Defence and made a nuclear deputy, and tells her to get back to Downing Street pronto and drag the Chief of the Defence Staff along with her. The CDS is exactly the kind of entitled tosser regurgitated by the English private school system that Lee spent most of his army career dodging. He orders him to prepare 3 Div., the Iron Division, the UK's land warfare contribution to NATO's Allied Rapid Reaction Corps, immediately for deployment. In response, the CDS adopts a pained expression and explains to Lee that of the fewer than two hundred tanks in the army cupboard, barely three dozen work. And twelve of them are defending key installations, including the two parked outside Lee's new home. When pressed, the CDS concedes that no one looked after the tanks while the army was away fighting Mr Blair's wars in Iraq and Afghanistan. He's sorry to say that deployment of a fully armoured division would take a minimum of six months and that realistically the best he can do at a couple of months' notice is an armoured battle group of a thousand men, forty-five or so armoured infantry vehicles and a couple of dozen Challenger tanks. Add to that a dozen or so Typhoons and perhaps a dozen F35 Lightnings if Lee's happy with the aircraft carriers reverting to people carriers again.

'Get on with the planning,' Lee tells him. 'And I want 16 Air Assault on immediate standby. You're still capable of throwing paratroopers out of planes, aren't you?'

'As I'm sure you are aware, much of our rapid response capability is defending key installations including nuclear power stations and there is the matter of the losses that we suffered at Sizewell.'

Lee gives him his best shit-eating grin. 'Now, General, I'm sure that I've read something by you about the importance of the ability to plan, coordinate and execute decision-making in complex operational environments. I've given you mission command, are you saying that you're not up to it?'

The CDS reddens. 'I must tell you, Prime Minister, that for too long our defence was built on flawed assumptions including the protective power of the United States, European solidarity, our own technological superiority, and the absence of a direct threat to the British Isles. The Americans became increasingly quixotic. The Europeans effectively disarmed. That dynamic is changing as they wake up to the Russian threat, but we remain under-armed and under-prepared. We do have the world's most advanced weapons, but we don't have very many of them and they're fiendishly difficult to service. Sustained combat of any form would be difficult for us. We'd quickly run out of bombs, missiles, and projectiles. As for the threat, I hardly have to tell you that it is here on home turf and not overseas. Frankly speaking and taking into consideration our concerns about the mental health of the Russian president, I am very wary of starting World War Three.'

'In case you hadn't noticed, General, we are effectively at war. If we don't respond in strength and make it clear that there will be consequences for Russia if they continue to attack us, then they aren't going to stop. I want troops ready to go. And if you can't organise that, then I suggest you consider your position.'

'I was appointed by the Monarch, Prime Minister.'

'And your replacement will be too.'

Lee holds his gaze until the General looks away.

'I will do as you wish, Prime Minister,' he says.

'You will!' He waves his arm at Chantal. 'Keep an eye on him. No backsliding.'

'Of course, Prime Minister,' she says, cool as a cucumber.

'Good girl.'

'I thought that went well,' he tells the Cabinet Secretary, who has been spared for now.

'Yes, Prime Minister.'

'Cheer up,' Lee tells him.

After tea and biscuits, he chairs a meeting of the intelligence chiefs: MI6, MI5, and GCHQ, the Chair of the Joint Intelligence Committee, and the National Security Adviser; also there, Trevor Cooper, the first Home Secretary born to Windrush immigrants.

After Lee has informed them of his intention to ramp up the pressure on Russia, he demands a list of non-UK citizens working in critical infrastructure. The look he gives them should leave them in no doubt that their jobs are on the line. Evan Calthorp, who has had his fingers flat on the table like a frog, slides a buff file across the table towards him. 'Here's one we made earlier, Prime Minister.'

'Good.' It's nice to see the grumpy fucker delivering something tangible. Lee slides it across to the Cabinet Secretary. 'I want this actioned immediately. Denzel has a short list of ready-to-go service providers to run the camps. Now, what about Guy Fowle? What's being done to find him?'

Embarrassed silence.

'We have one lead,' Chuka Odechukwu says. Another buff folder slides across the table towards him, 'a suspected accomplice to Fowle who was recently released from an Iraqi prison. Facial recognition software suggests that she entered the UK at Edinburgh Airport on a UK passport. She is Alysha al-Sabbah, the granddaughter of one of the founders of the Islamic State. We haven't released her photograph yet.'

Lee lifts the cover of the folder and looks down at the screen grab with the date-and-time stamp on the lower left-hand corner of the image. He feels a strange out-of-body sense of dislocation. There has always been a well-hidden part of him that is frightened of what he might do or what he might become. He is looking at a photograph of the woman that he met in Ezra's study at Wolfhanger, whose *kompromat* helped put him here in this seat. It doesn't take the brains of an archbishop to realise that makes him Guy Fowle's bitch.

'Let's keep this close hold,' Lee tells them. 'If we go public, we risk her going to ground.'

# 28

# Rare beasts

Back in a suite at the Ukraina in Moscow, Yulia catches up with the news from London: the terrorist attack that caused a passenger jet to crash at City Airport, killing all on board, is being blamed by the British press on a Russian-trained saboteur; and a new more belligerent Prime Minister has taken up residence in Downing Street without facing the electorate or his own Party membership.

NATO remains divided and has not yet reached consensus on an Article Five response. The BBC shows Lee Chapeaux pledging to send troops to support British allies on the Russian border. A pledge welcomed in Eastern Europe but causing disquiet amongst many of Britain's more traditional European allies. Calling the deployment an unacceptable threat to the security of the Russian Federation, the Russian president has ordered a 'snap military exercise' deploying the 1st Guards Tank Army to Russia's western border. Later in the bulletin, she watches the anchor of Russia's Channel One News delivering an on-screen polemic, cautioning the British to be careful in their response to a domestic calamity of their own making and warning that Russia is perfectly capable of turning the British Isles into radioactive ashes.

The United States has yet to publicly pronounce, seemingly preoccupied with the ongoing hunt for illegals on the home front, but a carrier strike group led by the USS *George H. W. Bush* has sailed from its home port in Norfolk, Virginia, for an undisclosed location and sources close to the White House are suggesting that the US president is considering even tougher sanctions.

Add to this the information obtained from Khmer Bear after she was pulled out of a basement crate. She claims to have been in recent communication with Fowle, providing up-to-date information that discredited one of the candidates for British Prime Minister; and that the so-called North Atlantic version of Grom stolen by Fowle includes Russia on its drop-down menu of infrastructure attacks. The addition of the Russia option was conceived by the Protean Bears as a failsafe in case the Kremlin ever acted against them. It's startling treachery. So treacherous that Alexei has ruled that it should remain a secret until such time as they have verified whether it is true.

It seems to Yulia that whereas before she was standing on the edge of an abyss, she is now over it and falling. And so, she must learn to fly.

Officers of the Federalnaya Sluzhba Okhrany, the Federal Protective Service, arrive at midnight and pack the corridor outside her room. She counts a dozen of them, as indistinguishable as Agents in *The Matrix*, dressed in matching black suits and Nike Air Force 1 trainers, crisp white shirts, shiny black earpieces, and skinny black ties.

'Are you coming in?' she asks, holding her dressing gown together at the neck.

One of them, at a guess a woman, steps inside and Yulia closes the door on the rest of them.

'*Grazdhanka,*' the agent says, using the formal term for citizen, which usually precedes an arrest. 'You must come with us.'

On balance, she preferred it when the president's people called her *Baba Yaga* – the terror of the forest – at least it conveyed a measure of respect.

'Am I dressing for the indoors or the outdoors?' she asks, considering the contents of the wardrobe. If there is no prospect of returning alive, she would prefer to look her best.

'The outdoors.'

So, it's a ditch in the forest.

She chooses warm clothes intended for an Arctic expedition, which she lays out on the bed: high-waisted woollen trousers, a long-sleeve silk vest and a black roll-neck cashmere sweater, and to go over it all one of Ksenia Chilingarova's Arctic Explorer parkas.

'Are you going to watch me undress?' she asks.

'Yes.'

Fair enough. If she had a weapon, she might have been tempted to conceal it.

They drive a hundred kilometres west on the M9 to Volokolamsk in a convoy of matt-black Range Rovers with blue LED lights flashing. It feels to Yulia like an overly ostentatious way to make someone disappear. But when they arrive at the Centre for Rare Animal Species Reproduction, she realises that she is mistaken. She is here for an audience not an execution.

The president is alone inside a glass-walled enclosure, playing with a trio of Siberian tiger cubs while the Patriarch of Moscow and a phalanx of black-robed orthodox priests wearing brimless black stovepipe hats stand with their faces pressed to the glass. She takes off her parka and allows herself to be frisked while wondering why the president's inner circle, his heads of intelligence agencies, and the security council, aren't with him. Is it better to have poor information than no information? Can he really be this isolated? One of the agents escorts her through a door and down a damp concrete tunnel to a steel gate, which opens on the enclosure.

'Come and sit down, Yulia Ermolaeva,' the president says in his unprepossessing voice. He is wearing a linen *rubakha,* a collarless peasant's shirt, and loose-cut *shtany* trousers. She kneels in the straw beside him and one of the triplets climbs in her lap and swipes at her hair with its paw. She flips it over and scratches its tummy until it purrs. It is the male cub. Like a puppy, he has paws that are too large for his body.

'I understand that your trip to Belarus was informative and that you wish to continue your investigation?'

'That's right.'

He pulls a cub over his shoulder and tips her into the straw. She springs back at him, and he wrestles with her before tipping her back into the straw again. She bounces up and chases her sister around the enclosure.

'What is your assessment of this young new British Prime Minister?' he asks, his eyes never leaving the cubs.

'Politics is volatile there now,' she explains, continuing to scratch the cub in her lap. She almost says, 'As it is here', but controls herself. 'The terrorist attacks have made ordinary people angry and uncertain. They want the reassurance of a wartime leader.'

'Why is he threatening to send thousands of troops to our borders?'

'It's a political gesture. A piece of theatre. Nothing more.'

'Is that what he believes?'

'He believes that Russia has played a role in the attacks on his country. He feels that he has no choice but to make a show of force.'

'Russia is a besieged castle surrounded by enemies,' the president says, with conviction – it is a phrase that she has heard him use before. 'Our historic lands have been occupied. We have no choice but to fight back.'

He's a believer. She's never thought of him as a kleptocrat. Even the palace he's building on the Black Sea feels more like a mausoleum than a house. He genuinely thinks he's the right person to protect the Russian state. The corruption that exists in the system is a function of the task rather than its end goal. The function is to protect the state from any challenges brought against it. Of course, it attracts people who are there for the money but that is a second-order concern for the president.

'I don't believe that the British Prime Minister wants a war,' she says.

'Is that what your friend in MI6 believes.'

'Yes, it is.' She pauses, fearful of provoking him. He is such a ridiculously prickly man. 'But if Guy Fowle continues to utilise Russian assets to commit atrocities on British soil, then I am afraid that events may run out of control.'

'You have my permission to continue with your investigation,' he tells her. 'If you can prevent further attacks, do so. But be careful, I will not countenance an admission of guilt or the sharing of secrets. Anyone who threatens my country, and my people, must know that my response will be immediate and lead to consequences never seen before in history. If there is no Russia, there is no need for this planet.'

The two sisters dive into his lap, and he tucks one under each arm and shakes them while they screech in delight.

# 29

# On Blackheath

They meet at the bandstand on the edge of the Wilderness, Jude approaching from the Naval College at Greenwich, which was damaged in the sugar refinery explosion, and Evan Calthorp from the Village to the south, which seems a surprisingly pleasant place for him to live. A rebuke to the Whitehall rumour that he sleeps in a coffin in the damp cellars beneath Thames House. As if to add to the impression of endearing Englishness, Calthorp has a dog of uncertain ancestry: a jet-black mongrel with waves of tufted hair like opposing tides and a ruff that runs the length of its back.

None of which changes the fact that he's a cunt.

'Have you found Alysha al-Sabbah yet?' Jude asks. In his experience, it's a good idea to get a jab in first.

'Not yet.' Calthorp's tone is relaxed, which Jude finds unnerving. Calthorp is never relaxed. The dog sniffs at Jude's pockets for treats and lopes away, unimpressed.

Calthorp tips his head. 'Shall we?'

They head south across the grass with the dog ranging here and there. Calthorp seems happy to walk in silence. He must want something.

'Is it true that it's a plague pit?' Jude asks, eventually. For Blackheath read Black Death: two hundred acres of unrecorded bodies dumped in vast pits in the fourteenth century with a strict prohibition on digging foundations ever since, for fear of what might be released. Urban planning determined by disease.

'That's a myth,' Calthorp replies, with the briefest curl of the lip. 'Though the plague plays a part in a more pertinent association.'

This is more like it. 'Go on.'

'The heath was a rallying point for the Peasants' Revolt.' The dog returns and sits expectantly. Calthorp feeds it a morsel from his pocket, and it springs away again. 'A lesson in the perils of rebellion,' he muses. 'In the aftermath of the plague, the Kentish rebels camped here before moving into the city and running amok, capturing the Tower, killing the Chancellor, and burning the law courts. Fearing for his life, the king granted their demands and agreed to abolish serfdom.

'For a moment it seemed that the rebels had succeeded,' Calthorp says. 'But the Mayor of London murdered Wat Tyler, and the king persuaded the rebels to return to their homes. As soon as they'd gone, he rescinded the abolition. As a revolution it failed miserably.' He stops and the dog raises its head from whatever it is sniffing to look back at him. 'The outcome of rebellion cannot be assured.'

'And yet it's on your mind,' Jude says.

'Yulia Ermolaeva asserts that a hacker working for Guy Fowle tampered with the process to select a Prime Minister.'

'That's what she was told,' Jude confirms.

'It was by any measure a flawed and unaccountable process and the victor is manifestly unfit for the role. Now I am led to believe that he was Fowle's preferred candidate.'

'Yes.'

'In receipt of this knowledge, I am forced to consider what it means and what can be done. I must consider how best to ensure that the nation is in safe hands. Any attempt to remove a serving Prime Minister is uncertain and fraught with risk. Despite his flaws, perhaps because of them, Lee is popular across the country. I believe that neither Parliament nor the people would take kindly to a coup.'

It's strange, Jude has always considered the head of the Security Service to be more of a zealot than a pragmatist, but he sees that he is wrong. How else could Calthorp have achieved high office other than by making accommodation with political realities?

'You 're not sure whether the PM is aware of Fowle's tampering,' Jude guesses.

Calthorp acknowledges the truth of this with a quick nod of the head. 'And I have no idea what Fowle wants.'

'He doesn't want anything,' Jude replies. 'He doesn't believe in anything. He's in this for the violence.'

'You don't think he wants to start a war with Russia?'

'Quite possibly, but I don't think that's his primary motivation.'

'Well, what is it?'

'He feels wronged.'

'We all feel wronged.' Calthorp sighs.

'He won't be happy until he's punished everyone that he holds responsible for every indignity that he has ever suffered.'

'I preferred it when we had rational enemies,' Calthorp says, bitterly. 'Nowadays they are all nihilists.'

'What do you plan to do?'

'The Prime Minister is interested in you.'

Jude is mystified. 'I don't know why.'

'He's read about you, and he's met you. He can put a face to a name. Perhaps because you have survived where others have not, he respects you. We know that it's what makes you of interest to Fowle and his associates.'

'You're calling the PM an associate of Fowle?'

'That would be precipitate. I need to know more before I make any such accusation. I've spoken to Chuka, and we've agreed to attach you to Specialist Operations at the Met to help with the hunt for Guy Fowle and Alysha al-Sabbah. I mentioned it to the Prime Minister in our most recent conversation and he seemed interested in your perspective. My sense is that he may reach out to you.'

'You want me to spy on him?'

'You know my view on the circus of clowns that he surrounds himself with. The more I investigate them, the more inconsistencies I uncover; any one of them could be an agent of Fowle.' He grips Jude's upper arm. 'Find out what you can.'

# 30

## Maggie Thatcher eyes

Lee is driven in convoy from Parliament's temporary new home at Olympia having completed his first Prime Minister's Question Time, the weekly punch-up that passes for scrutiny in this green and pleasant land. Thanks to some late-night swotting and Bala playing the Leader of the Opposition in fetching silk pyjamas (while remaining two sword-lengths apart as per parliamentary tradition), he went in studs-up from the start, sweeping aside the Opposition's cod outrage and asserting his authority upon the restive chamber. He demonstrated his command of a range of topics across government policy and was decisive in his response to the East London terror attack. The first internment camp, a former RAF base in Norfolk, is now officially open for business and 16 Air Assault Brigade are on standby to deploy to defend one of Russia's closest neighbours. He shed a mocking tear at the box-faced Opposition leader's claim that Lee was a cross-dresser who'd stolen his Party's clothes (the non-repressive anti-poverty element of the wardrobe, obviously) and reassured him that it meant his messy, ungovernable Party wouldn't be entirely forgotten by history.

'You knocked them out of the park,' Bala tells him from the seat beside him. Later, the parliamentary sketch writers will gleefully seize on the fact that several times during his performance he glanced up at his glamorous press secretary in the public gallery.

'Maybe I can do this after all,' he says.

She grins. 'No doubt about it.'

He grips her hand tightly.

It's a shame to see the lack of a Royal Standard flying outside Buckingham Palace. The building and its grounds have been judged too large a space to defend and the Monarch's now sheltering at Windsor. They sweep through the entrance to the outer cordon at Wellington Barracks, drive past lines of emergency vehicles on Birdcage Walk and the anchor point of the surveillance blimp that used to float above Kabul and now monitors Whitehall.

They enter Parliament Square, where the Fire Brigade's recovery and decontamination operation is ongoing in the asbestos-choked halls of Westminster and the rubble-clogged shaft of the underground station. At the inner barricade, the tank scoots back to let them through and in no time, they sweep through the gates of Downing Street to No. 10.

Lee and Bala part ways on the ground floor and he heads to the study, where Denzel is standing by the fireplace beneath the portrait of Margaret Thatcher. The former PM has a somewhat sceptical expression on her face as if, despite his performance at PMQs, she's still reserving judgement.

'That went well,' Denzel tells him. 'You're carrying the Party with you.'

'It helps that the other lot are weak and divided.'

'That's how we like them,' Denzel says. He pauses. 'I've had Amanda Chappell bending my ear. More than once. Ezra's ego is bruised. You didn't warn him that you were going to disband the Noble Boys. And he is wondering when he is going to get an invite for supper. He seems intent on choosing your wallpaper.'

'Ezra's got fuck all to complain about and no he can't choose my wallpaper. He's just been given the internment camps to run and he can staff them with the Noble Boys, For that reason alone he needs to keep his distance. As for that witch Amanda, you tell her that she's lucky she's not been squished in a tunnel like Princess Di.'

They have reached an agreement over the meeting with the Arab woman at Wolfhanger, which is that it never happened.

'Ezra's bodyguard Tito has gone on an extended and well-remunerated sabbatical in the Philippines with instructions to remain off-grid for the foreseeable.'

'That's good.'

'And I can manage Ezra and Amanda until things settle down.'

They were in tricky situations together in Afghanistan that they did not expect to survive and yet, through sheer bloody-minded persistence, they'd come out alive. Hang on tight had always been their motto. As the Cold War sage George Kennan once said, 'Heroism is endurance for one moment more'.

'I don't know what I'd do without you,' Lee says.

And, hey presto! His private cellphone rings – an unknown number on Telegram. He's been expecting it. Why go to all the trouble of putting him here if you're not going to make use of it?

'You really should stop using that, Prime Minister,' Denzel rebukes him from across the room.

Lee nods and accepts the call. 'Who is this?'

A voice, familiar from Hereford, in his ear: 'You know who it is.'

Lee pivots and gestures for Denzel to leave the room. He gets a disappointed look in response.

'I thought you'd forgotten that I exist,' Lee says when they are alone, trying to sound more cheerful than he feels.

'I never forget,' Guy tells him. 'You know that.'

'Yeah.'

'You've only recently become interesting.'

'Yeah.'

'Or should I say I've only recently made you interesting.'

Lee's damned if he's going to thank him.

Guy continues, 'As you know, I don't like loose ends. Now that I've got you where I want you, I don't want anyone interfering. And so, I've done you a favour.'

'What's that?'

Lee has a strong suspicion that he's not going to like the answer.

'I killed your grotesque friend Ezra Gullet and his trophy wife. And his hatchet woman Amanda Chappell.' Lee's immediate thought is that it could be worse. He's grateful to Ezra for the support, of course, but the tycoon was never going to be anything but a liability once Lee had made it into Downing Street. And he won't mourn Amanda. 'I arranged them in a pile in Ezra's study and set fire to them. You're too late for the people, but if you're quick and dial 999 you might save Wolfhanger.' Lee won't be making that call. He catches Thatcher's eye and resolves to remove the annoying bloody painting. After a pause, Guy says, 'It's time for you to do something for me.'

'Such as?'

'I want Jude Lyon.'

Again, it could be worse. 'And if I do what you want, what then?'

'I let you stay in No. 10.'

# 31

# The worst Prime Minister

After the call, Lee throws open the door. Taken by surprise, he almost lashes out. There is a small man, with twinkly eyes, shiny shoes and a tight-fitting double-breasted suit, staring intently up at him.

'Prime Minister,' the man says with an unctuous smile while briskly shaking Lee's hand. It's hard to be sure but he looks to be in his sixties or early seventies, 'I am Sir Francis, your historical adviser. Strictly speaking, I'm the adviser to the address and not the incumbent. But the building does not seek my counsel, ha, ha, ha. This is our first session and so I thought that we might start with the main staircase and work our way down. Shall we?'

Lee remembers something from the early-morning diary briefing about a tour. Mostly he remembers wanting to climb back in bed with Bala and sleep several more hours. Whatever it is, it's got to be better than reading the contents of red boxes.

'Lead the way.'

A few minutes later, they stand side by side at the cast-iron balustrade at the top of the main U-shaped staircase, which is flooded with light from a south-facing window. The stairs rise from the ground floor with two parallel flights connected by a half-landing between each floor. The walls are lined with modestly sized photographs and engravings of previous Prime Ministers.

'A lot of ghosts here,' Sir Francis says and looks up at him. 'I feel like Piglet next to Pooh, ha, ha, ha.'

Staring down, with his fists gripping the mahogany handrail, Lee wonders how many of his predecessors have been tempted to throw themselves over the railings. It looks far enough down to break your neck.

'You'll go there when you're done,' Sir Francis says, pointing to a photograph of his predecessor by the door to his flat. 'He's the eighth to die in office, God rest his tarnished soul. And all the others get moved down one to make room.'

'And what happens when they reach the bottom?'

'Very good question,' Sir Francis says, 'very good. We haven't got there yet. Now tell me what you want to know? Anything you like! Most people ask about Churchill and his somewhat irregular working habits, the bath-time dictation, and the soap suds. But I live to be surprised.'

'Who was the worst Prime Minister?'

'Ha, ha, ha. Very good question! Well done, you. I think we'll get on famously. The worst! It's hard to choose, frankly. Many would say Lord North who lost America. He filled the house with children though. Come on, let's have a look.' Sir Francis steps nimbly down the stairs with Lee following. 'Gordon was super intelligent but awkward and not at home with people. Then there's Jim Callaghan. Crisis! What crisis? Did his best but the country was ungovernable.' He taps their likenesses as he passes, his fingernails shiny as pearls. 'Anthony Eden scuppered a distinguished career with his hare-brained seizure of the Suez Canal. Neville Chamberlain, the appeaser, who was well intentioned but so terribly wrong. A bit like Nigel Featherstone, your recent rival, ha, ha, ha.' He turns ninety degrees on a landing and continues his descent, tapping the portraits as he goes. 'Arthur Balfour took a confident Party and split it asunder. Then there's Wellington, a military man like you, a hero, and a conqueror, but an appallingly bad Prime Minister. He refused to live here. And wouldn't give ordinary people the vote.' He stops by an engraving of a man holding a paper 'One of my favourites, Spencer Perceval, his premiership was characterised by political infighting, weak government, and rioters on the streets. He's the only Prime Minister to have been assassinated. A member of the public who was angry at not having his letters answered shot him dead in the lobby of the Commons. Ha, ha, ha. I always say to my new Prime Ministers ignore your mail at your peril.'

'And the shortest-serving Prime Minister?' Lee asks, glumly.

Sir Francis skips back up a few steps and taps a black-and-white engraving of a man who is leaning against a Roman column. 'George Canning, one hundred and nineteen days.' He winks conspiratorially. 'He's the one to beat.'

Lee wonders if Guy Fowle will let him serve that long. It seems unlikely.

'Lee?'

He turns to find Bala standing on the landing above him looking uber-glam in a sequined evening dress that is slit to the thigh, and his darker thoughts are immediately pushed aside.

'Ms Bhatt!' Sir Francis glows. 'Welcome to Downing Street. You look radiant!' He skips up several steps. 'May I kiss your hand?' Bala looks askance but holds out her hand. Sir Francis gives it a dainty peck. 'I hope that you are both very happy here.'

'Darling, the people from *Hello* magazine are waiting,' she says, once she's retrieved her hand.

'*Hello*, indeed! Then I mustn't keep you,' Sir Francis says. 'Until next time!' He waves farewell and slips through a door that Lee hasn't noticed before.

'Who was that? Bala asks.

'I'm not sure. I thought I was tripping.'

'No time for that,' Bala says. 'You're about to come out of the closet.'

# 32

# The pied piper

The hunt for Fowle continues.

The police and the security services have utilised every tool at their disposal: search warrants, seizure of assets, surveillance, roadblocks, and a mass-market media campaign. More than two thousand people have been arrested in an operation that has targeted national and international organised crime groups, neo-Nazis, revolutionary workers, Islamist extremists, and para-militaries of Irish Republican and Loyalist persuasion – anywhere in the undergrowth that Fowle might find refuge or acquire weapons.

And yet he remains at large. The arrested have been reluctantly released. And an atmosphere of paranoia prevails.

Newly attached to the Metropolitan Police and licensed to carry a weapon on home turf by direction of the Home Secretary, Jude is standing with his back to the wall at the side of a packed briefing room at New Scotland Yard. There are plenty of familiar faces in attendance. His sister Tamar is beside him, along with his shrink Helena de Leij, who is waiting to go on stage. Jemima Connick, the Metropolitan Police Commissioner, is sitting in the front row with the Permanent Secretary of the Home Office on one side and the National Coordinator for Counter Terrorism on the other, and around them, in a protective wall, are her uniformed heads of Commands: Counter Terrorism, Protection, Security, Covert, Specialist Firearms, and Serious and Organised Crime. The Mayor's Office, the Cabinet Office, the Firearms Targeting Centre, Border Force, and Ballistics Intelligence Service all have repre-sentatives wearing their names and organisational acronyms on badges on their lapels. The seats at the back of the room are reserved for espiocrats without badges, including representatives of America's multitude of covert intelligence agencies.

John Nganga, a detective chief inspector from Counter Terrorism Command, and a fellow veteran of Sizewell, who Jude admires for his calmness in all things, is standing at the lectern. An image of Guy Fowle in a police uniform, hurdling the vehicle barriers outside the Houses of Parliament, fills the screen behind him.

'Guy Fowle has first-world military skills, access to an extensive network of illegals and an extremely large war chest,' Nganga tells them. 'He has already proven that he is capable of coordinating complex attacks that threaten the integrity of the British state.' He advances through a slide deck of shattered landscapes: the charred maw of Westminster underground station, the fireball of the London oil terminal explosion, a barricaded Central London hospital with patients spilling out into the streets, the orgiastic rioting that followed the breakdown of the banking system, mosques and synagogues ablaze, the wreckage of the capital's super-transformers that supplied the city's electricity, ambushed police convoys in Bermondsey and Sizewell, and the most recent, a passenger jet floating upside down in the River Thames. 'The destruction of London City Airport and the surrounding area demonstrates that Fowle is alive and that his campaign is ongoing. We remain extremely vulnerable. We believe that he is spending money to subvert the Kremlin's "recall" of GRU sleeper agents and to buy the silence of those criminal elements that we know have already provided him with weapons and matériel.' He flicks through images of launch tubes and handgrips recovered from Sizewell and a block of flats in Barking. 'The sugar refinery explosion teaches us not to be narrow in our definition of infrastructure. It also reinforces the point that the illegals are not a homogenous group. We should not expect them to come from any one nationality or region.' The chief suspect, Venezuelan operations supervisor Gustavo Montes, smiles at the room from under a hard hat with a dancing sugar cube on it. 'They may have detailed backstories that have enabled them to pass extensive vetting procedures.' The next image is of Inspector Charles Fletcher of the Civil Nuclear Constabulary, who killed the operations room staff at Sizewell and inserted the malware that very nearly caused a nuclear reactor explosion. 'We cannot be sure that there are not more like Fletcher, even in this audience.' He pauses and a ripple of disquiet travels across the room. 'I cannot stress enough that if we expect the next attack to look like the last one, we will not succeed in stopping it.'

Next up is a genial American from the Embassy in chinos and a blazer who speaks for the clandestine cousins at the back of the room. The suspicion on the British side is that the Americans have learned more than they are willing to share from Mashenka Alfyorova, so-called Angry Bear. Why? For the very reason that John Nganga has highlighted and an editorial in the *Washington Post* has trumpeted: like a dilapidated stately home riddled with ravenous moths, the British establishment is suspected to be awash with Russian illegals.

'The debriefing of Maria Alfyorova, aka Angry Bear, continues,' the American informs them. 'Unfortunately, our preliminary conclusion is that, except for Guy Fowle, no living individual knows the full range of options for attack on the Grom App, not the software developers who designed the operating system, the individual GRU officers responsible for the sleeper agents, not the hackers who built the worms and phages to knock out specific industrial control systems, and certainly not anyone in a position of authority in the Kremlin. Ms Alfyorova's testimony includes the assertion that the UK variant of Grom includes a group of illegals that constitute an armed GRU stay-behind team.' He glances in Jude's direction. 'If this is the case and Fowle has made payment for their continued service, then he not only has access to the embedded illegals but also a capacity to initiate kinetic operations out with the current target sets on the Grom menu. That's it. Thank you.'

The American steps away from the lectern, having told them what they already know, and Helena comes forward to take his place. She picks up the remote and the screen behind her is filled with Alysha al-Sabbah's face, a prison mugshot from Iraq with her hair scraped back and her headscarf pulled down.

'Guy Fowle is not an ordinary sociopath,' she says. 'They do not usually have long careers. You have heard about his skills, his connections and capabilities, and his money. What you should also understand is that he is an enchanter, a pied piper – those closest to Fowle will do anything for him, up to and including blowing themselves up. And they are marked by that commitment. The image that you are about to see is an illustration of that.' She presses the remote and the room flinches. Taken from Iraqi medical records, a picture of Alysha's naked body with her nipples and pubis pixelated, and a whirling vortex of scars radiating outwards from them. 'Alysha al-Sabbah allowed, probably encouraged, Guy Fowle to do this to her. She is in thrall to him just as Zeina Hussein was.' She presses the remote and again you can feel the disquiet in the room. An image of Zeina in the middle of Westminster Square with her arms flung out and her finger on the trigger of her suicide vest. Jude realises that it must have been taken from the helicopter that was hovering above them in the final seconds before he shot her. 'I have no doubt that if she had not been killed, Zeina would have detonated the vest.' Jude takes a deep breath and Helena presses the remote. The next image is nearly a month old. Alysha al-Sabbah is removing her sunglasses at passport control in Edinburgh Airport. 'Alysha is here. She is equally committed. She will not hesitate to kill for Guy Fowle or sacrifice her life for him. She will be one of those nearest to him. If she is not physically with him then she will be doing his bidding. And if you can find her, she will lead you to him.'

Jemima Connick gets up from her front-row seat and turns to face the room.

'Let's find Fowle, people. By whatever means.'

As the room is emptying, Helena comes over to Jude. She searches his face. 'Are you all right?'

He nods.

She touches his forearm. 'You had to stop Zeina.'

'I know.'

There's something that I want to tell you.' She steers him to the back of the room where no one else can hear. 'As I said to the crowd, true sociopaths don't usually have long careers. I can't prove this, so I'm not going to share it widely, but I think that Guy may have Parkinson's disease. The motor symptoms are hard to distinguish from the effects of the acute use and withdrawal from heroin, but I've been studying the video footage from when he was in prison at Belmarsh and I think that he may have reached the point where he can't hide it any more.'

'And if he does have Parkinson's?'

'It's a degenerative condition and as the disease progresses the symptoms intensify. He'll be feeling cornered with nothing to lose. He is likely to be as careless with his own life as he is with others. That will make him very dangerous.'

Jude's black-taped work phone rings, an unknown number. He gives Helena an apologetic look and answers it.

'Mr Lyon.'

'Yes?'

'This is the Downing Street switchboard. Standby.' He hears a click and then a familiar voice. 'Jude?'

'Prime Minister,' he replies.

'Can you come over?'

'Of course.' He replies without thinking, without reflecting on Calthorp's unwelcome request that he spy on the Prime Minister. But once he's said it, there's no other option but to go. Besides, Lee has already ended the call.

Helena purses her lips. 'You have a new friend?'

'Not exactly.'

'He is very charismatic.'

'If you'll excuse me.'

She laughs. 'You better run along then.'

# 33

# Bo staffs in the White Room

From New Scotland Yard, Jude takes the long way round via Parliament Square, passing a queue of tipper trucks waiting to carry rubble excavated from the underground station through the outer cordon. It's still not clear when the trains will start running again.

He sees the blimp overhead. He has always thought that they look both ridiculous and menacing, like Pink Floyd's inflatable pigs. The windows of the Red Lion pub are boarded up and there are military police standing beside the tank parked at the entrance to the inner barricade. All this for Fowle. And is it enough? He's still trying to process Helena's claim that Parkinson's may make Fowle even more dangerous.

He shows his Service ID and is allowed through. There has always been something sombre about Whitehall but without pedestrians or traffic it feels even more like a memorial to generations of the dead.

*With a pig floating above it.*

He shows his ID again to an armed officer of the Diplomatic Protection Group at the gates to Downing Street. He goes in through a wicket gate wide enough for a single person and into the security hut. Along with his wallet, belt, shoes, and keys he adds three mobile phones, each one marked by different coloured tape, to the tray for scanning and proceeds through the metal detector.

Inside the perimeter, he walks across the street, catching a brief glimpse of the resident cat as he approaches No. 10. The polished black door opens before he can touch it. In the entrance hall, a custodian takes his phones and gives him a chit. There is a young woman from the garden floor wearing a lanyard, waiting for him on the black-and-white tiles at the edge of a Persian rug. There is a portrait in oils of Sir Robert Walpole, the first Prime Minister, behind her.

'This way please, Mr Lyon.'

She leads him down a corridor, through an anteroom at the entrance to the Cabinet Room and turns right into the Private Secretary's office. It is a wood-panelled room with a high ceiling and a view of the gardens. There is a large desk with the PM's Principal Private Secretary (PPS), Jonathan Guest, sitting behind it. Everything is calm and quiet. The woman points to a chair with its back to the wall and suggests that he sits down.

'The Prime Minister will be with you shortly.'

'Thank you.'

He sits with his knees together and his fists on them because that seems fitting.

After twenty-five minutes, a door behind the PPS opens and the Prime Minister strides in, filling the room. Jude jumps to his feet. Lee Chapeaux has his arm out for a hand grab and then moves in for a shoulder bump. He pounds Jude on the back with his free hand.

'Good man,' he says and steps back to look Jude up and down. He seems genuinely pleased. 'I'm sorry to have kept you waiting.'

'It's no problem.'

'A dear friend of mine died along with his wife, and one of his employees. I've been talking to his daughter. She's understandably upset.'

Jude has read about the mysterious deaths of the Gullets and Amanda Chappell.

'I'm sorry to hear that,' he says.

'Come on.'

Lee leads him out through an adjacent room with four secretaries in it and past a staircase at the entrance to the corridor that connects to the Cabinet Office.

'It's like a bloody labyrinth. A Tardis: bigger on the inside than it looks on the outside.' They join a back stair that connects the garden rooms in the basement with the staterooms on the first floor. It's a miniature of the main staircase, with switchbacks and landings. Lee takes the stairs two at a time. 'For the first couple of days, I kept trying to open doors that weren't really doors, just looked like them. Who would do that?'

'John Soane,' Jude tells him, keeping pace with him. 'He was brought in at the end of the eighteenth century to give the state-rooms an imperial makeover. He had a thing for symmetry. Hence the fake doors.'

Lee raises an eyebrow that suggests he's impressed. 'I'm more of an asymmetry guy,' he says with a hint of self-mocking. There's something very open about Lee. Despite himself, Jude is warming to him.

At the top of the stairs Lee turns into a room with an oval-shaped dining table.

'There was a journalist with you when Fowle tried to assassinate you, Kirsty McIntyre was her name?'

'Yes.'

'She's not a big fan of mine, I suspect,' Lee says, opening a door to the official drawing room, the Pillard Room, which Jude recognises from Prime Ministerial briefings.

'I think that she's reserving judgement.'

'Is she all right? It's an unnerving experience being shot at. Of course, you know that.' Lee crosses the room and stops in front of a door. 'Relationships are precious. It doesn't matter how difficult it is, how much opposition you face, if the spark is there you should go for it.'

'I think I will,' Jude says.

Lee smiles and opens the door. They enter a smaller drawing room that is flooded with light. It has been turned into a space for competitive martial arts, the furniture removed and replaced with a tatami mat on the floor.

'A room for meeting foreign heads of state,' Lee explains. Jude spots two Turners on the wall, including a late masterpiece. When he looks back, Lee is grinning wolfishly. 'I sent a picture of the mat to the judoka in the Kremlin along with an invitation. I thought he might like a match. You know, throw, pin, and choke. We're different weight classes, of course. I would have to go easy on him. No need to embarrass the chap.'

'I don't think that the president likes to be embarrassed.'

'That's what everyone tells me. Should I let him win?'

'I think that's advice beyond my pay grade,' Jude tells him.

'Carrot and stick,' Lee says, undoing his tie. 'That's my approach to diplomacy. Behave and you get a kiss. Misbehave and you get the fist. Are you okay to spar?'

Jude considers the two six-foot bamboo staffs lying parallel to each other at the centre of the mat and wonders if he can refuse.

'You sparred with Fowle at Sizewell,' Lee says, removing his cufflinks, 'am I right?'

'In those circumstances, I didn't have any choice.'

Out of ammunition, Jude had been forced to use his rifle as a staff against Fowle's sword.

Lee laughs. 'You're being modest.'

At Jude's first weapons lesson titled *kitchen kubodu*, in a jungle camp on the Indonesian island of Sunda, his teacher, Master Sumaryono, had laid out a bucket, an iron, a frying pan, a kitchen knife, a jerry-can, and a broom on a woven mat.

'The chances are that you will not have your weapon of choice handy when you need it most,' Sumaryono told them. 'But all around you there are weapons, you must learn how to recognise them.'

He told them to choose a weapon, pair off and take their places in the sand arena for the first round. At the end of each round, they swapped weapons. By sunset, they all understood the superior reach of the broom handle, the so-called king of weapons.

'I'm impossible to embarrass,' Lee says, stripping off his shirt. He picks up two pairs of Kendo *kote* gloves from an armchair in the corner of the room and hands a pair to Jude. 'Come on, it'll be fun.'

'Okay,' Jude says, reluctantly.

A couple of minutes later, they step barefoot and bare-chested onto the mat and pick up their weapons, holding them in both hands.

'Ready?'

Lee opens with a blitz attack, leaping forward with both feet, a sudden right-to-left strike with the tip of the staff aimed at Jude's temple. Lee's front foot hits the ground just as the strike lands, his full momentum behind it. Jude only just blocks it, his staff a *wall*, perpendicular to the strike. Lee follows with an intense barrage of strikes intended to quickly overcome him, which Jude manages to block, stationary at first and then retreating.

He counter-strikes a *fleche* using the heel of the staff to strip Lee's lead hand from the staff and follows through with a strike aimed at the pocket of the neck. Lee only just evades it. Jude drops the tip and strips away Lee's remaining hand, knocking the staff to the mat. He follows through with the heel of the staff, stopping just inches short of the exposed left side of Lee's neck.

They pause, slick with sweat, panting.

'You're good,' Lee concedes, when he's caught his breath. He puts his foot on the fallen staff, rolls it back onto his instep and then kicks it up into his hands. 'Tell me what Fowle is going to do, worst case?'

'It will be a complex attack,' Jude says, in the ready position. 'A volley of coordinated assaults, some designed to sow confusion or deflect attention from the real target. And whatever that is, it will be high profile and high impact.'

'Will I be the target?'

'Both previous attacks have been targeted at London,' Jude replies. 'So, you should consider it a serious risk.' He sees something in Lee's face that gives him pause. Does the PM know something that has not been revealed? 'With Fowle it's often personal. The attacks are motivated by a sense of grievance. Does he have a reason to consider you an adversary?'

'Not that I know of.'

'You didn't cross him at Hereford?'

'No.'

Lee launches another full-frontal assault. Jude drops his lead foot back, leaving his left side open. As expected, Lee reacts with a right-handed attack, which Jude counters by stepping forward in a wall block. He follows with a heel strike to the head, which Lee only just ducks. Pressing his advantage, Jude performs a hooking disarm, striking at the neck and stripping the hand. Again, Lee loses his grip on his staff.

Jude steps onto Lee's lead foot, pinning it to the ground, and thrusts forward and down, striking Lee's shoulder as he falls back onto the mat.

Jude steps back.

Lee climbs to his feet with a rueful expression on his face.

'I walked into that.'

'You did.'

Jude watches him take off his gloves. It seems that combat is over for now. No anger. No histrionics. Maybe he really can't be embarrassed.

'What are Fowle's principal weaknesses?' Lee asks.

Jude doesn't hesitate. 'The people around him.'

'Alysha al-Sabbah?'

'Yes.'

'You're hunting her?'

'We are.'

'What else?'

'That sense of grievance.'

'That's it?'

*And just maybe, he's losing his powers.* 'He may not care if he dies.'

Lee looks thoughtful. 'Come on, I'll walk you out.'

They get dressed and Lee leads Jude down the main staircase past the Prime Ministers from Lee's immediate predecessor all the way back to Walpole. At the bottom, beside the huge wooden globe, Lee pulls him in for another shoulder bump.

Despite himself, Jude likes him.

Outside the famous black door, he calls Kirsty on his red-taped phone. She answers just before it's about to go to voicemail.

'To what do I owe the honour?' she asks, dryly.

'I'd like to see you.'

He decides it's best not to reveal that the Prime Minister has played a role in prompting him to make the call.

'I have clams,' she says.

'I like clams.'

'I guess that's decided, then.'

'What time?'

'Seven thirty but be ten to fifteen minutes late.'

'Why?'

She laughs. 'Because that's what regular, normal people do, spy man.'

# 34

# Clams and candlelight

Jude's there, in a side street off Brick Lane, at seven thirty sharp but rather than announce his presence and suffer the inevitable mockery, he gets in the back of a nondescript white van that is parked with a view of the entrance to her red-brick apartment block.

'My money is on you having Thai tonight,' one of the watchers tells him, eyeing the tissue-wrapped bottle in Jude's hand.

'Oh, yes?' Jude says.

'She was out thirty minutes ago. Assuming she's got fish sauce in the larder and maybe a tablespoon of sugar, I think I know what you have got coming.'

'He reckons he's a chef,' the other watcher says, rolling his eyes.

'What about the emergency exit?' Jude says, looking up at the building.

The first watcher nods at a gallery of windows on one of the wall-mounted screens including a live stream from several CCTV cameras pointed at the building's access points. 'It's covered.'

'We've got this,' the second watcher says in a reassuring tone. 'Enjoy your dinner.'

Jude wishes that he felt their confidence. But experience has taught him that anyone who falls within the orbit of Guy Fowle's attention is in harm's way.

'Thanks,' Jude says and leaves them to it.

After Kirsty's buzzed him in, he walks up several flights of stairs and along a landing that overlooks a central courtyard, and up a discreet back stair that is open to the sky and lined with well-tended plants in terracotta pots. It turns back on itself and delivers him to one of two rooftop flats. He's been here once before, on the day that Guy Fowle broke out of Belmarsh Prison. He remembers thinking then that there was something sequestered about its location that made him wonder if she shared the same urge to privacy that he did.

He knocks on the door.

She opens it with a smile on her face and brandishes her watch. 'Well done, Jude Lyon.'

She is wearing an empire-line mini-dress that whirls like a dervish as she turns. He follows her inside. Much is as he remembers it: there is a forest of copper pots hanging from the ceiling and rows of spices in labelled jam jars with red-and-white chequered lids on shelves that climb the walls. Hatched-steel handles stand proud of a wooden knife block and there are magnets on the fridge that chart a road trip across the USA. On the wall there's a portrait of Black Agnes, a fourteenth-century Countess of Dunbar. Judging by Kirsty's welcome, he's likely to receive a better reception than the English army that laid siege to Agnes's castle. He sees the clams in a bowl of water in the sink, a wok on the gas hob and a rice steamer on the countertop. The watcher appears to have been right: on the chopping board there is a bushel of Thai basil, birds-eye chillies chopped into thin strips, and several chopped garlic cloves.

Kirsty pours two glasses of a pale Provence rosé.

He stands glass in hand beneath the arch that separates the kitchen from the living room. The sofa has been pushed back and a small square table and two wooden chairs have been placed where there was a coffee table before. The table has a white tablecloth and has been set for two, with mismatched vintage-looking crockery and cutlery.

'How was your day?' she asks.

A loaded question to ask someone in his line of work. He shrugs. 'I had a fight with the Prime Minister.'

She gives him an evaluating look from the sink. 'A divergence of views?'

'No, we tried to hurt each other with sticks.'

'Are you serious?'

'He's put a fighting mat down in one of the staterooms at Downing Street and he's challenged the Russian president to a bout.'

'I feel the world has taken an odd turn,' Kirsty says. 'And it's never been truer that we get the politicians we deserve. What do you make of Lee?'

'I can see what people find attractive in him,' Jude says.

She raises an eyebrow. 'Sounds like a budding bromance.'

'I wouldn't exactly call it that.'

'And how was my day?' she asks, archly.

'Other than a shopping expedition you didn't leave the house, so I'm guessing you were making calls.'

'I've been trying to track down members of the special forces unit that Fowle commanded at Hereford, but the Ministry of Defence are being obstructive.'

'To be fair to them, Fowle did a thorough job of erasing its existence. The records in the MOD's personnel centre were destroyed. It's hard to find anyone alive who'll talk about it.'

She is watching him. 'What about Staff Sergeant Thomas Flynn? He was injured in an "accident" on the Hereford training area.'

'Yes,' Jude admits. 'He was badly burned when an IED detonated. He claims that it was punishment for publicly questioning one of Fowle's orders. He's traumatised. I doubt that he will speak to you.'

'But he spoke to you?'

'He told me that he wasn't worried about Fowle coming after him, that as far as Fowle was concerned he was finished business.'

'But you and I are unfinished business?'

'Yes.'

'How long is this going to go on for?'

'Until Fowle is captured or killed.'

The rice steamer starts to whistle.

'Let's eat,' she says, brightly.

He admires the way that she can change the subject and put concern for herself to one side. She puts on a canvas apron from the back of the front door and lights the burner under the wok, turning it up high. She taps the clams as you would mussels, before adding them to a steel bowl. Next a glug of bright yellow rapeseed oil in the wok. She flicks the garlic and chilli off the board into the sizzling oil, stirs them and then adds the clams. She keeps moving them around the wok as the juice runs out of them.

'So are Sanjay and your sister Tamar an item?'

'Apparently.'

'You seem sceptical?'

'They're quite different.'

'So are we.'

'That's different.'

They both smile. He watches as she adds fish sauce and sugar, and a tablespoon of an unctuous red-and-black chilli paste. After a few more minutes she adds the shredded leaves, gives the clams a final stir and tips them into a serving bowl. She carries it over to the table, trailing the scent of the Thai basil. The white rice goes in another bowl and is fluffed with a fork before serving.

They sit opposite each other, and she spoons rice and clams into the shallow bowls in front of him while he refills their glasses.

'This looks so good,' he says. The thumb-nail sized clams are succulent and briny, fiery and sweet at the same time. 'Wonderful.'

She smiles, enjoying the compliment. They eat in silence for a few minutes, building a mound of empty shells in a bowl between them. He can't remember a meal that he enjoyed more.

'So, what are we going to do about us?' Kirsty asks, eventually.

'I've been giving it some thought,' he admits.

'Any conclusions?'

'Yes.'

'I'm all ears?'

'I'd like you to be my girlfriend.'

She giggles. 'I don't think I've been asked that since school.' She laughs until she cries and then has to press her face into her napkin. It's infectious and Jude finds himself laughing with her. Abruptly, she puts the napkin down and asks, 'Have you obtained the necessary permissions from your employer?'

'I thought that would be presumptuous.'

'Bloody right, it would.'

And they are laughing again.

'Dessert?' she asks, at the next pause.

'I'm full,' he says.

'Not that kind of dessert . . .'

She stands up and offers her hand. He takes it and she leads him to the bedroom. He stops in the doorway, and she looks back at him.

'What is it?'

'You should close the curtains.'

'Because they are watching?'

'Please.'

She lets go of his hand and he watches as she pulls the curtains together and moves around the bedroom, lighting a trio of candles in brass candlesticks on the mantelpiece and one each on the bedside tables.

'I've put in a freedom of information inquiry into the cost of protecting me,' she says, facing him. 'Do you think I'll learn how much it's costing the state to have you in my bedroom?' She unzips her dress and lets it fall to her feet. She is naked beneath it. 'Either way, we should make the most of it, don't you think?'

'Definitely.'

She grabs his belt and pushes him towards the bed. He sweeps his shirt over his head and falls back on the covers. They are both grinning. She grips the ends of his trouser legs and pulls. She flings them behind her and straddles him, her face filled with mischief.

# 35

# Subterranea Britannica

It's close to midnight and Bala is staring out through the bay window of her ground-floor office, which gives her a view of the now-deserted press pen on the far side of Downing Street. The tsunami of attention that she was expecting in the wake of her gender reveal has not materialised and the news at ten had been all about lead elements of Britain's Rapid Reaction Force – 16 Air Assault Brigade – arriving in Latvia, and the national hunt for the terrorist Guy Fowle. As predicted, the press descended on her hometown of Durban like a ravenous horde, but came away with little more than the testimony of a couple of wistful ex-suitors and that of a former fellow volunteer at an AIDS hospice, a video from a local TV station of her cooking the local *bunny chow* curry, a wholesome beauty pageant portrait and a somewhat more risqué image of her tucked in Daisy Duke shorts at Durban's Gunfire Tactical shooting range above the title: S*ilver medallist in the Lady Junior category*. She has a stern but thoughtful father who says he respects the decisions that she has made in her life and is proud to call her daughter, and a loving and supportive mother. In the press, she is driven but down-to-earth, sassy but with a heart, and best of all lacking any kind of axe to grind. Even the TERFs are holding fire for now. If there is a lesson there, she thinks, it's that it's a mistake to second-guess the British public. You never know what they'll take in their stride. As the presenter of *Woman's Hour*, a woman notorious in her previous job for eating politicians alive, whispered to her with conspiratorial glee just before they went on air, 'The listeners are entirely unshockable.'

There's a knock on the door.

'Come.'

The door opens and she finds herself staring at Lee and the building's foppish historian, Sir Francis. They are grinning like schoolboys and can barely stand still. She glimpses Denzel behind them, lurking in the corridor like he always does. There is so much work still to do and she doubts that Lee has even made a start on the night's mountain of red boxes. She sighs. 'What is it?'

'*Descende, audax viator, et terrestre centrum attinges,*' Sir Francis says, with a theatrical flourish.

'That's Latin for we're going underground,' Lee says.

'Not quite, but almost, ha, ha, ha. I was telling the Prime Minister that beneath its surface Whitehall possesses rich strata of hidden but still-in-use passages, ducts, and tubes. And he said, show me! How could I refuse?'

'Do you want my permission?'

'We want you to come with us,' Lee says. He points at the News Channel on the TV in the corner. 'Ignore the braying sheep.'

There's something brittle and nervy about him that she has only rarely glimpsed before. She knows that he's worried about the deployment of troops.

'Please, Miss Bhatt.' Sir Francis has his hands pressed together, appealing to her better nature. 'It would be my honour to show you our subterranean delights.'

Perhaps this is the kind of temporary distraction that Lee needs. 'Very well.'

Sir Francis twinkles. 'Follow me.'

They walk down a carpeted corridor and through a door that she hasn't noticed before, along another corridor past a window looking out on a grassy quadrangle, through another door and down a flight of stairs to a steel door.

Sir Francis brandishes a key. 'The Ordnance Survey may have scoured every inch of this land above ground, but the underworld remains a mystery.'

He opens the door and beyond there is a lift and a door marked emergency exit. They go through the door onto a balcony above a dimly lit concrete shaft with a staircase leading downwards, where it is too dark to see the bottom.

'What's down there?' Lee asks, leaning over the railing.

'After peering into the mouth of a cave,' Sir Francis replies, 'Leonardo da Vinci once wrote, *"Two contrary emotions arose in me, fear and desire – fear of the threatening, dark cavern, and desire to see whether there were any marvellous things in it."*'

'How deep is it?' Bala asks.

'About seventy feet,' Sir Francis replies. 'Shall we?'

As they descend the metal lattice stairs, Bala is glad that she's wearing flats and not heels. She also notices that it gets warmer the deeper they go.

'No need for central heating down here,' Sir Francis says.

At the bottom there is an eight-foot-wide tunnel with cast-iron ribs and cladding that smells of engine oil. Thick bundles of cables are strung along the walls and suspended from the ceiling. They follow the tunnel to the junction with a larger, well-lit tunnel with several smaller tunnels running off it.

'This is the Q tunnel,' Sir Francis says, 'the inner sanctum of the state-in-hiding. It runs south from Trafalgar Square, the length of Whitehall, a dogleg along Broad Sanctuary, and down to the World War II Fire Control Centre on Horseferry Road. It used to connect to twenty-five miles of tunnels excavated by the Post Office under the city. It is said that after a particularly congenial Christmas party a civil servant once walked from here to Bethnal Green entirely underground and emerged on a traffic island in the middle of the public highway.'

'What's the point of them?' Bala asks.

'Very good question, Miss Bala. Originally the tunnels provided a wartime link for telephone communications but then the system was enlarged in the fifties and sixties so that officials could take cover in the event of nuclear war.'

'Why bother?' Bala asks. She's never really understood why anyone would want to survive a nuclear war and the winter that would follow.

Sir Francis looks surprised. 'You have got to have someone to organise the survivors, haven't you?'

'I'm not sure that they would be the right people for such circumstances,' Denzel says.

Again, Sir Francis looks surprised. 'That hadn't really occurred to me. You are the most interesting people.'

'Keep talking,' Lee urges him.

'Of course, I was going to say that there are three bunkers known as citadels accessible via the Q tunnel. The one known to the public is the Cabinet War Rooms that were used by Churchill. The ground floor of the Treasury buildings was filled with concrete to a depth of seventeen feet, turning it into a protective cover for the bunker beneath. There used to be an underground telephone line directly from there to Selfridges. Not, as you might think, so the great man could order luxury goods during Luftwaffe bombardment – ha, ha, ha – but because the basement at Selfridges was the only one large enough to house the eighty tons of equipment necessary to encrypt a trans-Atlantic conversation with Roosevelt.' He points north up the Q tunnel. 'The next tunnel on the right leads to the Ministry of Defence's Pindar Complex, named for the Greek poet whose house was the only one left standing when the Macedonians ran amok in Thebes. It's the closest and that's where you'll go if the nukes fly, ha, ha, ha. The third, the Admiralty Citadel, is on a western spur beneath the ivy-clad monstrosity at the east end of The Mall. It's a bit late in the evening for patrols but usually there are a couple of chaps with guns in a golf buggy.'

'What about access points?' Denzel asks.

'It's now sealed at either end but there are several points of entry, including via Downing Street and the Cabinet Office. And at the north end of Whitehall, there is an entrance at the old Telephone Exchange on Craig's Court.'

'I think that we should get back,' Bala says, hugging Lee's chest, 'before we're missed.'

'Agreed,' he says. 'And thank you, Sir Francis.'

'Please, don't mention it.'

# 36

## County lines

Jude is woken at six by one of his phones thrumming on the bedside table. A message from his sister Tamar:

I'm outside.

Kirsty stirs and turns over without waking. Jude slips quietly out of bed and goes over to the window. Parting the curtains, he looks down onto the street, where he sees Tamar standing astride her Triumph Thunderbird.

He texts back.

On my way

Five minutes later, after leaving a hastily written note to Kirsty beside the kettle, he lets himself out of her flat.

'Congratulations,' Tamar says, handing him a spare helmet.

'Thank you, where are we going?'

'London Heliport.'

He climbs on behind her and she guns the engine and they're off, heading south over Tower Bridge to Elephant and Castle, through Lambeth and along the south bank of the Thames, past MI6 headquarters and Battersea Park, to the heliport where a police Eurocopter is waiting.

They run across the tarmac apron and climb aboard just as the rotors begin to turn.

Ninety minutes later, Jude is in an observation room in a police station in Northampton staring through one-way glass at an eleven-year-old, one of six under-age mules who were swept up in a night raid on a local trap house.

There are visible ligature marks on the boy's neck and a bruise in the shape of a hand on his throat. According to the medical report following his arrest, there are burns and bruises all over his body. His name is William though he goes by Billy and there's no record of him being enrolled in a school or receiving any kind of education for the last two years. The only up-to-date records are of him as a suspect or an offender in twenty-nine police reports, although he has never been brought before the courts, due to lack of evidence or victims not wishing to press charges.

Before she went in Tamar had told Jude that the police believe there are as many as thirty thousand minors like Billy caught up in county lines in England and Wales. It's a staggering and shaming number: enough to make Jude wonder if the nation's security is worth risking his life for.

'These kids just fall off the map,' she said, 'and, in most cases, the local council doesn't give a shit.'

What kind of society are we?

Now Billy is fidgeting in a plastic seat beside a duty solicitor and in the corner of the room there is an appropriate adult. Tamar is sitting opposite Billy and beside her there is a police constable named Dawn, from the local force, who was on the night raid. She opens the interview.

'I want you to tell Detective Inspector Lyon about the rucksack that you were given to carry with you from London.'

He mumbles.

'You need to speak up, Billy,' Dawn says, 'or we can't help you.'

'It was heavy.'

'Heavier than the usual you carry?'

He nods.

'Not cash or wraps?'

He shakes his head.

'And you looked inside? It's very important, Billy, Inspector Lyon is trying to prevent a terrorist attack.'

He looks helplessly at his solicitor, who nods.

'I unzipped it,' Billy admits.

'And what did you see?'

'I was curious. I didn't know what was in it.'

'Tell us, Billy?'

'Weapon parts.'

'What kind of weapon?'

'G36C ultra-short assault rifle.'

'How could you tell that?' Tamar asks.

Billy shrugs. It's evident that every gamer his age knows: 'Modern Warfare. You build it via the gunsmith from a Holger 26 base weapon. You have to get to tier fifteen to unlock the Holger.' He shrugs again. 'But you don't need to be max weapon rank.'

He explains that the mules delivered twelve G36C carbines broken down in parts. They made two trips each, from London to Northampton on the train. In between they stayed in the trap house and played video games. Dawn asks him about the handover. He explains how the other kids in the house were told to stay in one room before the big man with the broken nose and the white hair came. Billy was the only one to see him and the only one to hear his Scottish accent. The man from Scotland didn't step inside or touch anything other than the two black bags, each one with the parts for six carbines. He was wearing blue gloves and he lifted the bags like they weighed nothing, even though he looked as old as Billy's grandpa. Billy didn't see where he went. He closed the door like he was told to.

'What did he say to you?'

Billy shivers. 'If you speak a word of this, I'll kill you and your mum.'

'You're very brave,' Dawn reassures him.

After a pause, Tamar leans forward in her chair and asks him about the man who gave him the bag in London and the instructions. Suddenly, he looks small and frightened. His leg is shaking furiously.

'We can get you on a rehab programme and then back into school,' Dawn says in a soothing voice. 'I spoke to your mum before we had this chat and she's agreed to have you back. We're going to move you both somewhere nice so you can start over again. We can do that for you because this is important, and we really need you to be completely honest with us. Do you understand, Billy?'

Billy nods.

'Go on then,' Tamar urges him.

He speaks the name of a South London-based drug dealer.

Shpend Murati.

'Thank you, Billy,' Tamar says. 'Dawn here is going to take you to an artist who is going to do a drawing of the Scottish man based on your description to help us identify him. Then we're going to get you back with your mum.'

Twenty minutes later, Tamar joins Jude in the observation room. She looks pissed off.

'Tell me about Shpend Murati?' Jude asks.

'Albanian,' she replies. 'He came over here as a kid at the time of the Kosovo War. Now he's an enforcer in a South London OCG that answers to the Mafia Shqiptare.' They both know that Fowle has used the Albanian crime syndicate as a source of weapons before. 'They're like the Sicilian mafia used to be, clannish, secretive, quick to take insult and even quicker to use violence. Under any other circumstances, I'd have Shpend lifted and rattled until the coins fell out of his pockets but I'm reliably informed that he skipped the country a couple of days ago.'

'With more than coins?'

'Oh yes, another recipient of Fowle's crypto largesse: British Airways business class from Heathrow. No more Wizz Air for . . . wait for it . . . the big Shpend-er.' Neither of them laughs. After a pause, Tamar says, 'Billy saw large green pelican cases in a lockup when he went to collect the gun parts.'

'Larger calibre weapons?'

They both know that Guy Fowle purchased Russian-made rocket launchers with armour-piercing and incendiary warheads from the Albanians before.

Jude calls Yulia. She answers immediately.

'There's something else you can help me with,' he tells her.

'Go on.'

'I need leverage against the Mafia Shqiptare. I'm pretty sure that you had a hand in creating them.'

She seems on the point of scolding him for the accusation but, after a deep breath, decides against it. 'There were close links during the Hoxha years,' she concedes instead, 'and afterwards too, when the clans rose to prominence and spread across Europe. I will make some calls and get back to you.'

'Something fast and dirty, and I don't give a damn about breaking a few eggs.'

'I understand.'

He waits five minutes and then calls Chuka. 'I'm going to need advance ministerial sign-off on an unlawful operation.'

'How unlawful?'

'I'll try to keep it within bounds.'

Chuka sighs. 'I'll speak to the Prime Minister. He understands expediency and necessity.'

'Thank you.'

He ends the call. There's nothing else to do but wait for Yulia to call back. Tamar is watching him with a hard-to-read expression on her face.

All he had ever wanted was to defend courtesy and tolerance and fair play, the qualities that he attributes to his home country. Fowle had taken that and twisted it, warping his natural caution into something violent and desperate.

# 37

# The silk

Kirsty's landline rings just after she's popped the cork on a bottle of white. After all, she's in a celebratory mood. She can still feel the imprint of Jude's hands on her breasts, thighs, and buttocks. If it's her dad, she's not going to be able to resist telling him, in a serious tone, that an eligible man has made her an attractive proposition. And if C or the crown or whoever agrees, they shall officially be an item. If it's Hannah, she will delight in describing to his sister the night's gymnastics in graphic detail and how she found it to be such an agreeable experience that she intends to repeat it as soon as possible.

'Is this Miss Kirsty McIntyre?' The sort of booming Anglo-Scots voice that ought to dominate an Edinburgh courtroom and it turns out does. The caller introduces himself as Alexander Ledmuir QC, silk for the government's Investigatory Powers Tribunal examining MI6's role in the extrajudicial rendition of Nasruddin al-Raqqah, and by extension, the events that led to the Westminster attack.

'It's Ms actually.'

'Of course it is,' he says, indulgently. 'The Tribunal is committed to recording a thorough and accurate account of what happened to Mr al-Raqqah and his wife and child, and I must salute you for very diligent investigative work in the case of Nasruddin, the so-called "voice of the Stranger". As you know the family are now safe in this country and the government has indicated that it is prepared to pay adequate compensation to them. Can you come to Edinburgh for a consultation? I'd like to talk about Mr al-Raqqah's time in Greece. I'm particularly interested in your recollection of a conversation on a hilltop encampment between Mr al-Raqqah and Mr Jude Lyon, an officer in the intelligence services. What promises and undertakings might have been made?'

She remembers kissing Jude on the hilltop. A promise of sorts and one now fulfilled. It was mid-morning and she had already had a couple of glasses of ouzo. It seemed like the only proportionate response to the injustice of the situation. And Jude, bless him, had persuaded Chuka Odechukwu, then of the very same Investigatory Powers Tribunal, to offer Nasruddin resettlement and witness protection in return for testimony against Fowle.

'We'll arrange your travel and your costs, of course,' Alexander Ledmuir tells her. 'I would be most terribly grateful if you came.'

'When?'

'The sooner the better, so that your memory of the details is fresh: how about tomorrow? Can you come here? These things are better done in person. I'll get my assistant to call you.'

She agrees. Why not?

Two minutes after he's off the phone a woman with an English accent and an efficient manner calls and takes her details. A business-class plane ticket from London City to Edinburgh Airport arrives in her inbox fifteen minutes later.

With a second glass of wine in hand, she googles Alexander Ledmuir: he looks the part. He played rugby for Scotland's under-21s while at Edinburgh University before practising law. There are pictures of him at work in a suit and gown, and at ease in the casual wear of his caste: corduroy trousers, a Tattersall shirt and a navy cardigan. He can afford to get his eyes lasered, but he wears reading glasses, presumably for the additional gravitas he believes that they afford him in the courtroom. He wants to talk to her about Jude. She wonders if she should have refused or declared an interest.

*Now she's sleeping with the enemy.*

Of course not! If Jude is dedicated to the cause of national secrecy, then Kirsty should equally hold fast to transparency and truth.

She wants to text him, but pride stays her hand.

★   ★   ★

A black cab from Edinburgh Airport drops her at an address in the New Town just after eleven the following morning. Kirsty stands on the slope of the street above a layer of *haar* – sea fog that has rolled in off the Firth and swallowed the north side of the city. She stares up at the elegant double-fronted Georgian townhouse. As her research the night before suggested, the law has been kind to Alexander Ledmuir. She goes up the steps and knocks on the door.

She waits.

She hears footsteps and a woman in a plain black dress with a high collar, swept-back hair and a severe expression opens the door. She is wearing white gloves and she looks like a meido – a sinister housekeeper from an Anime cartoon. Kirsty stifles a giggle, and the woman makes a face that suggests Kirsty might have farted.

'Kirsty McIntyre for Alexander Ledmuir.'

The meido steps back to allow her to enter.

The hallway has black and white marble tiles and a grand staircase lit by a cupola in the ceiling. It seems Ledmuir has a surprising eye for contemporary Scottish art: there is a hyper-real nude on the wall that looks part carcass and part Old Master.

The meido passes her, moving with the grace of a ballerina. She is very beautiful – Middle Eastern heritage, at a guess. Kirsty follows to a door behind the staircase, which opens onto a study with a garden view. A white-haired man rises from a desk. He is very tall and built like a prop forward, with a fetchingly brutish broken nose. He smiles warmly. Under other circumstances she might have found it reassuring but he is not the Alexander Ledmuir of the web, and he is wearing blue nitrile gloves.

'Please,' the man says, with a glint of amusement in his eyes, 'sit down. I'm sure this is a surprise for you.'

She scans the bookshelves. They look too neat. Unread. It comes as a sudden revelation: she's in a show house. Someone has borrowed it.

'There you are,' the man says, looking over her shoulder.

She turns to see Guy Fowle standing in the doorway. She hasn't seen him in the flesh since Woolwich just before the tear gas grenades came spiralling across the courtroom and the machine-gun opened fire.

'Hello, Kirsty,' he says.

## 38

# Franz Josef Land

There is a huge twin-turbine heavy-lift helicopter waiting for them at an airstrip on the outskirts of Moscow. Yulia has added a fleece-lined cap with earmuffs, waterproof trousers, and silk gloves with woollen overmitts to her Arctic wardrobe.

They walk across the runway and up a ramp broad enough for an armoured personnel carrier into the cargo hold, squeezing between two auxiliary fuel tanks that take up most of the space and into a small passenger area beyond. Yulia has spent far more time on helicopters recently than she would like and the thought of being on one that is carrying this much fuel is, frankly, alarming.

She buckles herself into a seat behind the cockpit, puts on a pair of matt-grey steel headphones and stares out the nearest porthole window as the rotor blades begin to slowly turn. Alexei returns from talking to the pilots and buckles in beside her.

'How far is it?' she asks with her finger on the Pressel switch.

'Three thousand kilometres,' he replies, curtly.

It seems like an extraordinarily long way. As the turbines roar and they lift clumsily off the ground – as ungainly as Dumbo's first flight – she reaches out and grips Alexei's arm tightly, seeking reassurance in his solidity. He smiles indulgently at her. She stifles the sudden urge to swear at him.

*Poshyol Nahui*. Fuck off!

The chopper climbs rapidly and turns north-east.

After five tedious hours, they touch down at an airstrip in a vast boreal forest. Alexei suggests a leg stretch and they walk down the ramp and across the runway to the dark edge of the trees. There's a cold wind blowing, and Yulia puts up the hood on her fur-lined parka. A fuel truck drives up to the helicopter and its hose is connected to the tank.

'Is anyone expecting us at our destination?' she asks.

'There is a base for long-range bombers at Nagurskoye that has declared a no-fly zone around it.'

'Does that mean we are going to get shot down?'

'*Ya ne znayu.*' I don't know.

She can't tell if he's joking.

'The pilot will tell them that we are a high-level delegation from the Kremlin,' Alexei adds as he pisses on the grass. 'If the frontier guards show up, you'll have to dumb down a little. Do you think you can manage that?'

She doesn't bother replying. Instead, she pulls down her waterproofs, woollen trousers and silk long johns, and squats down to pee beside him.

As soon as the tank is full, the chopper takes off again.

Against her better judgement, Yulia allows herself to be lulled into sleep by the chopper's vibration. When she wakes a couple of hours later, they are flying in darkness. The pilot flicks on the searchlight and its beam illuminates the barren tundra below, the dark lakes and peat bogs. The next time he flicks it on they are approaching a snow-covered ridge. They cross the ridgeline, and they are flying over water, following a river that extends like a tongue towards the ocean. Soon there is nothing but water beneath them.

At some point in the hours that follow, she sees what she thinks are the running lights of a ship far below. She has never felt so far from the world that she knows.

As the sun rises, the helicopter flies towards a pair of gleaming white icebergs on the very northern edge of the Barents Sea. Closer in, they are revealed as rocky outcrops capped by ice. The pilot steers them through the gap between the two islands and emerging, they ascend to see an archipelago spread out before them, a panorama of charcoal-grey islands, shining white ice and black water.

They head towards one of the larger glacier-covered islands. The surface of the ice is scored with rivers of intense blue water and dark holes where the water is tunnelling down to bedrock. At the far end of the island there is an exposed mountain slope with the remains of a radio dome cracked open like an eggshell just below its summit. As they fly over the mountain top, Yulia sees that it is all that remains of a collapsed volcano. Beneath her, the C-shaped curve of a steep-sided cliff offers the shelter of a natural harbour.

'*Svalka*,' the pilot tells them over the intercom.

A smouldering junkyard.

In the lee of the cliff, there is a scorched expanse of ships of all shapes and sizes visible through swirling gusts of oily smoke. Yulia sees the wreckage of battleships, tankers, cruise liners, passenger ferries, and trawlers leaning together in a slush of solidifying ice and thinks that it's just the kind of lair you'd expect the bears to operate from. On the outer edge, a fuel line burns like a monstrous candle and she wonders what size of reservoir must be feeding it and whether it might be about to explode. They fly towards the centre, which is dominated by the hulk of a huge icebreaker, its superstructure damaged by fire. Beyond it there is a gaping hole with ragged edges that looks like it was caused by an explosion and threatens to break the makeshift raft of ships asunder.

'What happened?' Yulia asks.

'By the look of it, a missile strike,' the pilot replies.

He lands them on a blackened bull's-eye on the icebreaker's helipad beside what looks like a functioning helicopter with its rotors tied down. When the ramp is lowered, the Arctic wind snatches out hours of accumulated warmth in seconds. The cold is stunning and Yulia gasps. Her teeth start involuntarily chattering. She pulls on her gloves and follows Alexei down the ramp into a crosswind that scours her face with soot and ice particles. At the bottom of the ramp, a man stands with his back to the wind. His fur-trimmed parka hood is up and he looks out through an aperture that is only a few inches wide. Whatever he says to Alexei, Yulia does not hear it because of the noise of the wind and the rotors. Alexei nods and they follow the man down a metal staircase from the helipad to the deck.

They cross the deck and descend a staircase that has been welded onto the outside of the ship's hull and leads down to a huge submarine. There is a waist-thick cable running alongside the stairs, presumably there to carry power from the submarine's reactor to the decommissioned icebreaker. Looking out across the frozen harbour at ships canted together at different heights, she sees that they were once connected by a maze of cables and walkways rising and descending between the different levels, many of them now broken or bent out of shape.

Climbing down a ladder from the fin, through two circular watertight hatches, into the submarine's hull, Yulia is slammed by a wall of heat. Stepping clear of the ladder she unzips her parka and pulls off her gloves.

The man who met them on the helipad shakes her hand. His skin is cool and dry to the touch, like holding a snake.

'I am Dima.' He has a certain watchful presence. 'This way.'

They follow him along a narrow corridor through two sets of oval bulkhead doors to the control room.

The billionaire Oleg Solokov is sitting in the officer of the deck's seat surrounded by what looks like a mix of security and engineering staff. He is wearing a Flecktarn camouflage smock, and his unkempt beard makes him look less like a Romanov emperor than it does in the photos of him in celebrity magazines. In real life, there's a stretched look of fatigue around his eyes.

'Dima, you have brought visitors. How lovely.' He takes a swig from a silver hip flask and gestures at them. 'Welcome to the Shark, the global fucking cockpit of Protean Bears' hacking operation. You have met Dima, my head of security, and here beside me is Boris, my head of engineering.'

Boris gives them a world-weary look. It's Yulia's first time in a nuclear sub and she's struck by how antiquated it looks, with its banks of box-like buttons, hooded screens, and switches in sockets.

'I thought that you are a fugitive?' Alexei says. He is too tall for the space, and he looks like his forehead is about to collide with something.

'I'm trying to fix this,' Solokov says, grimly.

'Does the president know that you are here?' Yulia asks.

'How can he know when he refuses to acknowledge that this place exists?' Solokov retorts. 'Or that we've been ass-fucked by a gaggle of punk rockers. Fucking bears!'

'Where are they now?'

'Who knows? They've gone. My guess is they took a helicopter and fucked off over the pole before the missiles struck.'

'They knew the missiles were coming?'

'Put it this way, the Protean Bears exceeded the parameters of the design specification that they were given. So yes, I think it is possible that they are inside our decision cycle. They scrammed the reactor before they left. For all I know the fuckers launched the missiles themselves to cover their tracks.'

'You got the reactor going again,' Alexei observes.

'Thanks to Boris. Yes. First thing I did was fly an engineering team in.'

'What about the servers?' Yulia demands.

'The servers are on the icebreaker. Now they look like burnt toast. Terabytes of toast, *suka, blyad*!'

Yulia stares at him. 'Everything is lost?'

'There is an access team flying in from St Petersburg. They are due in a couple of hours. Maybe they can recover something. Maybe not. Maybe they will get here before the low. Maybe not.'

'Low?'

Solokov laughs at her. 'Low is what they call a polar hurricane. Didn't you look at the weather forecast?'

She glances at Alexei, who only grunts.

'I want breakfast,' she says.

'In that you are lucky,' Solokov says. 'I brought my own chef.'

# 39

## *Svalka*

Dima escorts them to the galley, where he tells them that they must eat at least six thousand calories a day to combat the cold and watches until he is satisfied that they have helped themselves to enough food before escorting them to the officers' mess.

On the screen in the mess, the approaching storm has the appearance of a tropical hurricane with dense thunderclouds surrounding an eye.

'Did you know this was coming?' Yulia asks.

Alexei only grunts.

'We're going to get stuck here, aren't we?'

'For a couple of days, maximum.'

There doesn't seem any point in being angry. 'If we stay too long, we will soon be as plump as seals.' She has a mug of coffee and a plate piled high with pillowy *syrniki* fresh from the pan – sweet, cheesy pancakes covered in berries and a large dollop of sour cream. Alexei has an even larger stack of pancakes. 'It could be worse, I suppose.'

'Who knows what may yet happen,' Alexei says. 'Maybe the president will fire more missiles at us.'

'Let's hope not,' Dima says and excuses himself.

Soon after they have finished eating, Solokov joins them in the mess and pours himself a coffee. Yulia stacks the plates and shifts along the bench to make room for him.

'I liked your husband,' Solokov tells her as if he is bestowing a favour. He smells of drink.

'Most people hated him,' she replies. She certainly did, for most of their marriage.

'He was a patriot.'

Alexei scowls across the table. 'Is that why you built Grom, out of a surfeit of patriotism?'

'You know the existential threat that we face,' Solokov replies. 'By my count, there have been thirty revolutions in the last twenty years. Chaos on the streets of foreign capitals stage-managed to cause the overthrow of our friends and allies. From Damascus to the Maidan, the hand of outside powers reaches in to control the people, making anarchy and terrorism. You think that we won't be next? Do I have to point out to you that there are mobs on the streets of Moscow and St Petersburg and a dozen other cities?'

Yulia sneers. 'And so you gave the keys to the armoury to a bunch of terrorist anarchists?'

Solokov blinks at her. When you're that rich you probably forget what it's like to have women talk back at you, she thinks.

'What choice did we have?' he says, in a wounded tone. He has not lost that peculiarly Russian faculty for using one's own short-comings as an excuse for intemperate actions. 'Our early warning systems are decrepit. Our tanks and helicopters are easy meat for NATO missiles. Our soldiers are ill-disciplined and unmotivated. We tried to fix it: we spent billions on defence, but the money was stolen. The United States and its allies continue to threaten Russia directly and indirectly. Only in electronic warfare do we have capabilities that can defeat our enemy's advantages.'

'But the outcome of your endeavour is that a psychopath now has the capability to break nations,' Yulia says. 'Grom is an idiot bomb, you have to be stupid to want one.'

'Is Fowle really our enemy?' Solokov says. 'He hates the British. Let him.'

'More stupidity,' Yulia snaps. 'Fowle is everyone's enemy.'

'If you have any hope of recovering your favoured status with the president,' Alexei tells Solokov, 'you had better hope that the British find Fowle.'

Later that morning the access team arrives from Murmansk and Dima takes them and their equipment straight from the helipad down into the hold of the icebreaker where the servers are housed.

After lunch, and more calories, Yulia climbs the fin and goes out on the surface navigation bridge with the Iridium phone. She stands on the anechoic rubber and stares up at the icebreaker's hull rising far above her like a wall, marked here and there with gnomic graffiti. It acts as a windbreak, but further out across the ships, the wind is rising, shaking superstructure, whipping ice into the air.

The sky is as dark as a bruise.

She calls Jude. He answers immediately.

'Where are you?' she asks.

'Istanbul.'

'I see.' It feels like a lifetime ago but it's only a few weeks since they were sharing a bed in Istanbul. 'The information that I gave you was useful?'

'I'm about to find out.'

'Don't do anything that you'll regret later,' she urges him. 'Remember your Nietzsche, darling: whoever fights monsters should see to it that in the process he does not become one.'

'And you?' Jude says, after a painful pause. 'Where are you now?'

'In the high Arctic,' she says. 'We've found the servers, but they are badly damaged. There is a team here trying to recover the data.'

'What about the bears?'

She can hear the tiredness and frustration in his voice.

'They've gone.'

'Damn!'

'I'll let you know as soon as I have anything to share.'

'Take care,' he says and ends the call.

She stares up at the sheer metal of the icebreaker's hull and sees Dima and the access team hurrying down the staircase towards her. It is swaying precariously in the wind. While she has been talking, the sky has turned completely white.

On the far side of the raft of ships, a crane topples.

# 40

# Monster time

Jude strolls down the hill from the Galata Tower in a navy-blue single-breasted suit and an open-necked white shirt. His shoes are polished and his gun in its shoulder holster is compact enough not to affect the hang of the suit.

He is arm in arm with an athletic Londoner by the name of Bethanie in an off-the-shoulder skater dress. She is easily as tall as he is in flat shoes. They step off the kerb in front of an armoured Mercedes saloon that contains two minders and cross the cobbled street. Their destination is a discreet restaurant with a narrow steel-glass frontage.

Inside, Jude gives a name that provokes a welcoming smile, and they are escorted past tightly packed tables and down a brick passage alongside the kitchen into an ancient stone vault with an arched ceiling. There are three tables: two other couples have also paid for the privilege of candle-lit intimacy.

They order the set menu and a bottle of Öküzgözü, a full-bodied red wine made from a native grape variety that grows on the Anatolian Plateau.

The target is at the next table. Flutura – *Butterfly* in Albanian – is taking yet another selfie – collagen-plumped lips in a pout with a painted eyebrow raised – as if nothing could *ever* surprise her. They have been tracking her by her postings all afternoon: from bed to gym to *hammam* to make-up to dinner.

The waiter fills their wine glasses from a decanter.

'It's delicious,' Bethanie says, taking the merest sip.

A series of mezze plates are delivered and described: hummus with marinated grilled mushrooms, fish pâté with cabbage sprouts, spinach borani, veal liver with sumac, grilled octopus and a dish called *too hot to handle*.

'Please eat,' Jude says, and Bethanie obliges enthusiastically. He read her personnel file on the flight over: foster care, military police and then the Met, serving as a firearms officer with the diplomatic protection group before volunteering for special operations.

Unlike Bethanie, Flutura eats almost nothing. Lorik is staring across the table at her with a rapt expression. He's two years younger than her, the spoilt and priapic youngest son of a doting father who also happens to be a *Krye* – boss – in the Mafia Shqiptare.

Jude would dearly love to knock back several glasses of wine to prepare him for what is to come but that way cowardice lies. Ruthlessness requires a clear head. He calls for the bill when Lorik does, and they rise from their seats in unison.

Jude smiles indulgently and motions for the other couple to go out before them. He follows with Bethanie at his shoulder. As they step out into the street, one of the minders gets out of the Mercedes and holds open the rear passenger door.

It's an ambush.

Taff, striding down the road towards them, flings a flash-bang stun grenade into the back of the car as Smudge, approaching from the opposite direction, fires a taser at the minder. Beside Jude, Bethanie has swept a gun out from beneath her skirt and is pointing it at Lorik's head. Taff kicks the door shut as the minder hits the cobbles in a spasm and the grenade goes off inside the car, shivering it on its axles.

Two black vans have blocked the road.

Smudge pulls a hood over Lorik's head and propels him into the van, where he plasticuffs his wrists and ankles. Jude and Bethanie climb in after them and Taff follows, pulling the sliding door closed behind him.

The van accelerates away across the cobbles, leaving Flutura standing, eyebrow raised, in the middle of the street.

Taff and Smudge haul Lorik up onto a bench seat in the back of the bouncing van and Jude, who is holding on by a hanging strap, takes a phone from his pocket. He presses the screen and holds it out to the cloth-covered head in front of him.

'Say hello to your dad.'

A gravelly voice answers on the speaker, '*Pershendetje?*'

'Lorik?'

'Papa!'

Jude slaps Lorik hard across the face and speaks into the phone: 'I have your son, Lorik. In ten minutes, I'm going to kneecap him. Ten minutes after that, I'll shoot him in the other knee. Then it will be his wrists and his ankles, the full six-pack, all at ten-minute intervals.'

'What do you want?' the man asks, in English.

'A list of all the weapons that you have delivered to Guy Fowle.'

The Krye considers the demand. 'I need time.'

'You don't have time.'

Jude hands the phone to Bethanie. Ignoring the dismay on her face, he draws his gun and presses the muzzle down firmly against the patella in Lorik's right knee, partly to stop his own hand shaking.

Lorik starts sobbing. 'Papa, please!'

'You do this; you are a dead man,' the Krye says.

'And your son will be a cripple. Nine minutes.' Jude nods to Bethanie. 'Cut the connection.'

She does as she's told.

Jude turns his back on Lorik and staggers to the front of the van, which is still rattling across cobbles, and collides with the plywood partition that separates them from the driver. It's like an oven inside and the sweat is running off his forehead. He wipes it away with the sleeve of the hand that has the gun in it. He grimaces with gritted teeth. It feels like he's in a tailspin and the brakes have failed. Any minute, he might explode.

He wishes no one could see him like this.

With less than two minutes left, Bethanie bumps against him, her mouth inches away from his.

'You're not going to?' she says.

'Try me.'

'By what authority?'

'The Prime Minister's written instruction.'

She is appalled. 'That doesn't make it right.'

The van bounces off the cobbles onto tarmac and speeds up. They are heading out towards the airport, where a plane is waiting.

Jude turns and staggers back to Lorik, pressing the gun down into the top of his knee while Taff and Smudge hold him down.

'There are four bones in the knee,' he says, 'patella, femur, tibia and fibula. They'll splinter like matchsticks. The bullet will pulp the meniscus and the ligaments. You'll limp for the rest of your life. And that's just the beginning. You don't want me to tell you about the ankles: each one's a ball of bones, ligaments, and tendons. And then there's the wrists.' He lets his head drop. He's counting the seconds. He shouts over his shoulder: 'Call the number!'

Furious now, Bethanie obeys and holds the phone out to Jude.

'Are you there?'

'I'm here,' the man says. 'I need more time.'

'You have less than thirty seconds.'

'My people are working on it.'

'I don't give a shit!'

'Please, Papa!' Lorik sobs. 'Please!'

Jude scrunches up his face and presses down harder with the barrel. He starts counting down from ten. Lorik is screaming and his father is shouting. And so is Bethanie. It's all just noise in comparison with this ugly, ugly choice. It's a mirror for him to see his worst self, the darkness inside him.

'Three . . . two . . .'

He knows that he will be replaying this moment in his head for the rest of his life.

'One.'

Explosive noise.

Jude squeezes the trigger. The bullet narrowly misses the front of Lorik's kneecap and punches a hole through the floor of the van. Convinced he's been kneecapped, Lorik is screaming.

'I'm sending the inventory,' his father shouts in desperation. 'I'm sending it.'

Jude stumbles away. He's not sure whether he deliberately missed or not.

'He's sent a screenshot of a document,' Bethanie says. She's panting with relief. 'It's a list of weapons.'

'Stop the van!' Jude yells, banging on the partition. He slumps down onto the floor.

They pull over to the side of the road. Taff slides the door open and Smudge kicks Lorik out. He tumbles out onto the verge and rolls down a grassy embankment. They unload their guns and throw them after him.

'Give me the phone,' Jude says. She hands it over. He looks at the inventory list, a bespoke mix of modern Russian, European and American weapons:

12 x H&K G36C 5.56mm assault rifle
12 x Glock 17 9mm pistol
24 x M84 stun grenade
24 x AN-M8 smoke grenade
8 x M14 TH3 thermite grenade
4 x RPG 30 'Kryuk' one-shot anti-tank weapon
4 x MRO-A one-shot thermobaric weapon
24 x M2 Selectable Lightweight Attack Munition (SLAM)
2 x M20 20 lb Demolition Charge Assembly
2 x GShG-7.62 Minigun

'What does that tell you?' she asks.

'An up to twelve-person assault team,' he replies, 'equipped with explosive charges, and thermite and thermobaric weapons intended for breaching buildings and destroying matériel. The anti-tank weapons have tandem shaped charges designed to counter the reactive armour and active protection systems fitted on Challenger tanks. And the short-barrelled rifles are for close-quarter battle. They are standard issue for Met Police specialist firearms units.'

# 41

# Five-a-side by the Cenotaph

'That is a very grumpy bear,' Lee concedes.

He is sitting at the head of the table in Briefing Room A considering the disposition of Russian troops on the digital map on the screen in front of him. The 1st Guards Tank Army has been reinforced by the 6th Combined Arms Army from St Petersburg, which has deployed to assembly areas in Opochka and Velikje Luki, near to Latvia's eastern border. The 76th Guards Air Assault Division, veterans of the president's wars in the Caucasus and Ukraine, has left its base in Pskov and is moving through Belarus towards Latvia's southern border.

'You did poke it with a stick,' Denzel says.

'I did.'

The lead story on Russia's Channel One evening news bulletin, broadcast on one of the screens, showed tanks advancing and salvoes of rockets being fired with the president taking charge of it all from an underground war room.

Denzel sniffs. 'Rather a small stick.'

'Indeed.'

Lee has a lightly armed and equipped airborne brigade of around six thousand troops on the ground. What tanks and armoured fighting vehicles the army could muster at short notice are transiting the Kiel Canal on commercially hired roll-on/roll-off ferries and until they arrive his ground forces are vulnerable. If they arrive that is! Between them and Latvia is the Russian Baltic Fleet in Kaliningrad with some nippy little corvettes armed with cruise anti-ship missiles that would make short work of the ferries.

Thus far, his calls for assistance from his so-called allies in

NATO have gone largely unanswered. Only the Danes – there is still some Viking juice in them – have pledged support.

He leans back in his chair and rubs his eyes.

When he opens them again, he looks across the room at Darren, the head of the redcap close protection team that is now guarding him. Like the rest of his team, Darren is wearing camouflage and the distinctive scarlet-red Royal Military Police (RMP) beret. The redcap team replaced the SO1 team after the revelation that Fowle and a team of illegals might come masquerading as a police firearms unit. 'What was that film with a handful of buff Greeks defending the Hot Gates against a horde of pervy Persians?'

Darren is quick to answer, '*300*?'

'That's it! That's the vibe I'm getting.'

'Prime Minister!' The CDS looks like he's about to have a brain embolism.

Lee winks at him. 'I think we need a political solution.'

The CDS is nodding. 'Yes, Prime Minister. Please.'

'Right,' he says, clapping his hands. 'Let's go play football.'

Denzel grins. 'Yes, boss.'

Lee chooses Bala, Denzel, his PPS Jonathan Guest, and finally Darren, the head of his new protection detail, to fill the goal. They are playing against a team from Defence led by Chantal Carny in a red Adidas Original tracksuit with her permanent secretary in goal. CDS has cried off, Denzel says he's probably lying somewhere with a cold flannel on his head.

The cordoned stretch of Whitehall is their pitch and unlike at home in Salamanca Crescent, there are rules to adhere to: five-a-side with red-and-white traffic cones for goal posts and the Cabinet Secretary as referee. From the centre, you can see the tanks blocking the road at either end. Supporters turn out from either side of the road. The burly statue of Bill Slim, the soldier's soldier, scowls at him from his plinth.

Despite his reluctance the Cabinet Secretary proves to be an assiduous referee and it soon becomes clear that cheating will not be tolerated. No matter that the Prime Minister is most often the guilty party.

He can't help himself.

At half time, Lee's team is two goals down after a couple of penalty shots. When they are changing sides, he spots Evan Calthorp standing, sombre as an undertaker, on the pavement outside the Cabinet Office. Lee waves to him and Calthorp scowls.

Bala saves the day, scoring two impressive goals: one a shot with the instep from the other side of the pitch and the other with the outside of the foot that curves the ball around the charging goalie. She also sets up the winning goal with a tricky-looking back heel, stepping over the ball and propelling it to Lee, who kicks it through the cones.

The crowd erupts.

Lee chases Bala all the way down to Parliament Square and around the tank and back up Whitehall as far as the northern barricade, with his redcaps in hot pursuit. Then she stops and leaps into his arms when he reaches her.

She kisses him hungrily while they spin around.

'I love you,' he tells her, breathlessly.

'Don't be daft!'

'Marry me.' He blurts it out and she pummels him with her fists until he lets her go. 'At least, think about it!'

She runs to her teammates without looking back. He strips off his top and saunters bare-chested over to Calthorp, who steps off the pavement and walks with him out of range of any eavesdroppers.

'How are you, Evan?'

'I'm very well, Prime Minister.'

'And to what do I owe the honour?'

'You were part of the special projects team at Hereford?'

He sighs. 'You know I was. And so was Denzel.'

'Does the name Thomas Flynn mean anything to you?'

As it has done throughout Lee's career as both a soldier and a politician, his father's insistence that honesty must always be weighed against the damage it might cause guides his response.

'No.'

Calthorp wrinkles his nose as if he can smell something unpleasant. 'That's strange. He was also at Hereford in special projects. I'm sure that you overlapped.'

'What's this about?' Lee demands.

'Flynn died earlier today, in a fire in a cottage in Wales.'

'I'm sorry to hear that but I fail to see what it has to do with me?'

'Flynn served with Guy Fowle in his red-team unit and was badly injured in a range accident that he blamed on Fowle.'

An event not easily forgotten.

Lee had been there when the incendiary device went off at Pontrilas Ranges and witnessed Tommy's head burning like an immense candle. It was a warning. Tommy had foolishly dared to question one of Guy's orders and was punished for it. After that, the rest of the team, Lee and Denzel included, did as they were told.

'Hence, I don't know him. I had nothing to do with Fowle's red team.'

'He was something of a recluse,' Calthorp says. 'He didn't watch the news or keep up with people from the regiment. When Jude Lyon interviewed Flynn, he was insistent that Fowle wouldn't come after him. He said he had been punished enough. Now he's dead. It made me wonder what had changed to make Fowle go after him.'

'Fowle doesn't need a reason to kill people. And you're sure it wasn't suicide?'

Calthorp eyes him sceptically. 'Before he died, Flynn left a message on the phone of a constable who keeps an eye on him. He said that he had recognised someone from Hereford and wanted to talk about it.'

'Did he say who?'

'No.'

Lee's face is impassive but inside he is rejoicing.

'Flynn didn't have a television, but he did have a radio,' Calthorp says. 'I had a look at the BBC schedule. He made the call five minutes after the end of a Radio 4 profile of you.'

'I don't answer to Guy Fowle,' Lee tells him. 'And I'm not a Russian spy.'

Calthorp looks unconvinced. 'Thank you for the reassurance.'

'If I was you, I'd be checking the loyalty of those tank crews.'

'Why is that?'

'Because the only thing that's ever destroyed a Challenger 2 tank was another Challenger 2 tank.'

Lee walks back towards Downing Street and Denzel falls into step beside him.

'What did Calthorp want?'

'Tommy Flynn is dead.'

'Did he talk?'

Tommy was the only remaining person who could have credibly connected them to Guy Fowle.

'Before he died? No. Calthorp is just fishing.'

## 42

# In the vertical launch tube

The submarine's canteen is empty except for the young men and women of the access team, who are sitting in a small group at one of the tables. They are leaning into each other over the remains of food and drink on their trays, engaged in low, intense conversation. They stop talking when they catch sight of Yulia approaching.

She pulls up a plastic chair and sits, introducing herself as an aide to General Alexei Baranov of the Sluzhba Vneshney Razvedki. She senses wariness rather than hostility. A young woman in black coveralls with a ring in her nose and bolts in her eyebrows leans forward and shakes her hand.

'I am Care Bear.'

She is at least twenty years younger than Yulia. 'You're bears?'

'Not Protean ones,' a young man answers, a little too readily.

'That's not strictly true,' Care Bear says. 'I was once.'

Smart move, not to try to hide that, Yulia thinks. She warms to the young woman. 'Do you have an actual name?'

'You can call me Natasha.'

'Thank you, Natasha. Perhaps you can tell me where your former colleagues have gone?'

Natasha shakes her head. 'The collective was always careful to have multiple means of exit.'

'And how much do you know about Grom?'

Natasha hesitates before answering. 'We follow the news. We are aware of what happened in London.'

'I need to know if there are going to be any more attacks,' Yulia says to the table.

'Perhaps you can answer a question that we have?' asks the young man who spoke before.

'If I can.'

'Who knows we're here?'

'Hardly anyone, I imagine,' she replies.

'So, this isn't an approved operation?'

She decides not to mention her encounter with the president, the patriarch and the tiger cubs. 'The presence of the General changes the dynamic.'

'Will we get paid?' another man asks.

'I suppose that depends on what it is that you can do?'

'We made a preliminary inspection of the servers,' Natasha explains. 'They were very badly damaged in the fire that followed the missile strike. However, the platters that contain the data are made of glass that can endure temperatures up to 1,500 degrees centigrade. Which means some of the data may be recoverable.'

'So, recover it! If you do that, I promise you will get paid.'

'We can't do anything until the storm passes.'

Despite its multiple pressure hulls, the submarine creaks like some ancient wooden schooner trapped in pack ice. There's no signal on Yulia's satellite phone and it's too dangerous to go outside to find one.

Jude will have to manage on his own until the storm passes.

Dima escorts her to a single-bunk room in the officers' quarters, between ones occupied by Alexei and the pilot of the helicopter she arrived on.

'The president may not say so, but he is pleased with your progress,' Dima tells her, standing in the doorway. 'He thanks you for your service.'

She wonders if Dima is KGB, GRU or FSO, or maybe even a member of the president's personal entourage.

'And what about Solokov?'

'He is coming to the end of his usefulness,' Dima says and pulls the curtain closed.

She undresses and puts on her pyjamas. Lying flat on the narrow bunk and staring at the grim institutional paint on the walls, she finds that she cannot settle. There's too much metal and weather pressing down on her. Eventually she decides to go for a walk. She puts on her dressing gown and goes out into the passage.

She looks left and right, chooses left and heads that way.

She finds Natasha sitting in a sleeping bag at the bottom of a thirty-foot vertical shaft designed to hold one of the nuclear missiles. She has her back to the curve of the tube and a laptop on her knees; a shifting mosaic of data lights up her face.

'Couldn't sleep?' Natasha asks.

'Can I join you?'

'Of course.' She closes the laptop as Yulia climbs in beside her.

'I have a question,' Yulia says.

'Go ahead.'

'If the Protean Bears are so obsessed with security, why did they allow you to leave?'

'My father is the Chief of Staff of the Siberian Military District.'

'General Yevkurov?'

'Yes.'

'I see.' It's hard to believe that a talentless ogre like Yevkurov could produce a woman like Natasha.

'We are not close,' Natasha says. 'In fact, you could say that we are diametrically opposed. I think that it appealed to Chilly Bear to have the anarchist daughter of a reactionary general in the collective. At that time, our manifesto was to expose wrongdoing and corruption, not to give one side a military advantage over another.' She sighs. 'But it was obvious from the start that exploiting vulnerabilities in control systems had huge weaponisation potential. We were too good at what we did to escape attention. I saw the way it was going and was able to extricate myself before the state co-opted the collective. I promised my father that I would behave and in return he protected me. Until now.'

'And what do you know of Grom?'

'Only what I have heard. But I know Chilly Bear and how he works. He has the idiosyncratic characteristics of a founder. Even in its design, Grom will have employed tradecraft: a cell-like structure designed to encourage innovation and initiative at the local level, so that no one, except for Chilly himself, will have had a clear picture of the overall capability of the weapon.'

'And Chilly is nowhere to be found.'

'I think that just about every global ransomware attack for the last three years has informed the design and reach of Grom,' Natasha says. 'The bears got rich on ransom pay-outs but the point of it all was to probe vulnerabilities. Always probing. They cripple a pipeline. It's not just some local pipeline. It's the jugular. They corrupt software supply chains to managed service providers. It's the nation's nervous system. They knock out point-of-sale tills and self-service checkouts in supermarket chains. It's the gut. This is a new kind of warfare deep in the enemy's territory.'

'And not just in the enemy's territory,' Yulia says.

'What do you mean?'

'I was told that the Protean Bears may have created an insurance policy against the Kremlin to safeguard them from any attack.'

Natasha looks sceptical. 'If they did, it didn't work.'

'I don't think anyone expected it all to unravel so fast.'

'And what form does this insurance policy take?'

'I don't know.'

Back in the officers' quarters, Yulia knocks on the door of Alexei's bunk.

'Come in.'

He is sitting on the edge of the bed in a pair of striped pyjamas that make him look like a convict. Standing in front of him, she is at eye level with him.

'Svetlana told me that I was a fool to accept this job,' he says.

Much as she dislikes Alexei's wife, Yulia feels she has a point. 'Why did you accept it?'

'It was either that or murder her. Besides, I hoped I might see you again.'

She cups his face in her hands and fights back the tears.

'You foolish man,' she says, fondly.

She kisses him. He responds gently and with the manners of a bygone era. She has always thought that he kissed like the hero in a classic movie, with none of the brash urgency of younger gener-ations. She can feel the pull of him in her breasts and the tops of her thighs. With him, she will never feel that she is too much woman. When she eventually releases him, he offers her his hand. She smiles and bites down hard on his index finger until she feels a shudder all the way up his arm. Then she kisses the red tooth marks on his flesh.

'I've missed you,' he says. He buries his face in her neck and kisses her there, and she clasps his battered boulder of a head in her hands.

Back in her bunk, she dreams of being trapped beneath the ice and sinking into the depths.

No light. No sound. No air.

She wakes suddenly to the sound of Solokov shouting at Dima out in the passageway.

'*Otvali, mudak, blyad!*'

She slips out of her bed and pulls the curtain back half an inch. Solokov is drunk and demanding to use the satellite phone. He is refusing to believe Dima's explanation that it's not working because of the storm. Eventually, Dima tires of it and slaps Oleg so hard that he bounces off a steel bulkhead and falls to the ground. Dima kicks him twice for good measure and she can swear that she hears ribs break. As he lies on the ground whimpering, it is clear to Yulia that any residue of power and influence has left him.

She closes the curtain and goes back to bed. She listens to the sound of the submarine's ventilation fans whirring and Alexei snoring next door and the occasional sob from the oligarch. Eventually Dima moves on.

She does not venture out to help.

# 43

# Woman on a chain

Although the steel chain attached to her ankle prevents Kirsty from reaching the windows, she can get close enough to see something of her surroundings when the view is not obscured by rain.

On one side she can see a distant ridgeline with steep slopes crowded with trees rising to exposed peaks and high waterfalls like tiny white ribbons. On the other side the view of a near-vertical scree slope that is much closer is partially obscured by the dark green foliage of a giant redwood.

As far as she can tell, she is on the top floor of a medieval tower. Its walls and ceiling are lined with silvery, aluminised tarpaulin that makes it feel like the inside of a tent and the only access is via a spiral staircase set into the stone floor.

She has no idea how she got here.

The room has a wooden bed fitted together with dowels so that there is nothing metal to use on the padlock that attaches the steel shackle at her ankle to the length of chain that is bolted to the floor. There is a camera high up on one of the walls, so she assumes that someone somewhere is watching. She cannot tell whether it is possible to step out of the arc of its coverage at the end of the chain.

For clothes, she has a pair of leggings and a shapeless sweat-shirt, and thick socks, which are a blessing given how cold the flagstones are. There is a kapok-filled pillow and two rough tweed blankets. She wraps one of the blankets around her waist while she pisses in the plastic bucket that was left for that purpose.

Not long after, she hears metal cleats ringing on the stone steps and watches the large man with the broken nose and the booming voice emerge head-and-shoulders first from the floor below. He is wearing a wool sweater with a hole in one elbow and a pair of threadbare cords. He is carrying a plastic tray with a brown paper bag, a cardboard carton and a paper cup.

'Breakfast time,' he tells her jovially from the top of the stairs. 'First, bring your waste here.'

She picks up the bucket by its plastic handle and carries it out to the end of the chain.

'Good. Now go back and sit on the bed and don't move until I say so.'

She complies. The man puts the tray down on the flagstones and picks up the bucket, which he moves out of her reach.

'Eat,' he says.

Kirsty walks back to the end of the chain for the tray. It seems like a lot of rigmarole for what turns out to be a rubbery-looking croissant, a carton of barely warm porridge with a cardboard spoon, and not much more than a mouthful of orange juice.

'You'll not catch scurvy while you're in my care,' he says when she takes a sip of the juice.

'That's very reassuring,' she replies, slurring her words slightly. Does he fancy himself a comedian? From the close attention he pays, she assumes that whatever the strong sedative is that they are giving her it is in the juice. She eats the croissant and the porridge. She can only manage small mouthfuls and swallowing is an effort. When she's finished, she says, 'What's your name?'

'You can call me Grigor,' he replies.

'Are you an illegal?'

'Heavens, no!' he scoffs. 'Do I look like a Russian? No, no, I go back much further than that. Bring me the tray.'

He steps back out of reach as she walks towards him with the tray and he doesn't pick it up until she is back on the bed. It's hard to see how she is any kind of threat given how out of it she is feeling. But he's right that the chain is the only weapon that she has.

She watches Grigor leave, chuckling to himself as he goes down the stairs with her waste, presumably because she thought he might be a Russian.

The rain comes on and there's nothing to be seen outside the windows. The chain is too noisy and the shackle too uncomfortable for her to find much solace in walking back and forth. Instead, she spreads out one of the blankets as a yoga mat and tries to do a sun salutation. Her head starts spinning very quickly and she topples out of a warrior onto the flagstones. Whatever they have dosed her with, it's playing havoc with her balance.

Through the fog in her mind, she tries to understand what's going on and what it means. She is alive. They have not harmed her or threatened her. They don't seem in any hurry to get information from her. It suggests that they have a plan for her. She finds a desperate, clutching-at-straws kind of comfort in the thought that things rarely go according to plan.

She wakes in the middle of the night to find the meido in silhouette in one of the window embrasures.

'Why are you here?'

It seems like a ridiculous question for a kidnapper to ask.

'I don't know,' Kirsty replies, although it seems clear to her that she is the bait in a trap.

'What is your relationship with Guy?'

Her sense of jeopardy increases. Does the woman see her as some kind of rival?

'I've never met him.'

'Don't lie to me! Lift your shirt.'

'Excuse me?'

Kirsty is blinded by sudden torchlight. 'Show me!'

Then she gets it. Fowle's relationship with his female accomplices and their devotion to him has been raked over by the media with voyeuristic zeal. The meido wants to know if Guy has marked her.

She rolls up her sweatshirt, showing her stomach and breasts. 'Happy?'

The torch goes off. The meido is silent in the darkness.

'Where is Guy?' Kirsty asks, eventually.

'He's away on business.'

Business seems an odd word to describe the wanton destruction that Guy causes wherever he goes. 'Is he coming back?'

'Of course he is coming back.'

'Are you sure?'

The meido leaps up and Kirsty curls instinctively into a ball, expecting to be beaten. But nothing happens. When she opens her eyes again, she finds that the meido has gone as silently as she arrived.

It feels like a very strange encounter but then she knows that Guy exerts a disturbing and destructive compulsion over those in his orbit. With Fowle, Kirsty has always had a sense that his deep and visceral need for vengeance, for settling scores – against his family, the institutions that treated him with suspicion and loathing, or any individual who thwarted him – has acted as a subconscious brake on his capacity to wreak larger or more apocalyptic destruction. It is a perverse and horrifying notion, and maybe even wishful thinking, but she wonders if perhaps the world is safer while she is a prisoner and Guy is concentrating on killing Jude.

That night she drifts in and out of sleep and listens to a rainstorm beating the surface of nearby water. There is a strange and mournful beauty to the sound. More than anything, she hopes that Jude is prepared for what is coming.

# 44

## Visiting the troops

Lee corkscrews into Lielvārde air base with a grin on his face from eighteen thousand feet.

At the bottom of the spiral, rather than the leisurely landing at three degrees of a commercial flight, the press pack, who boarded at Brize Norton without knowing their destination, are treated to a stomach-clenching sixty-degree drop, the C130 pilot pulling up at the last moment so that the landing gear, rather than the nose, hits the runway first. As soon as the wheels thump down, the spoilers open wide, and the plane is in full reverse to use as little of the runway as possible.

It's just after three a.m. local time and Lee is here to visit the troops in a navy flak jacket with Prime Minister stencilled on it. He bounces exuberantly down the steps near the nose with Bala in athleisure wear just behind him and receives a crisp, moonlit salute from the brigade commander before shaking hands.

How they must hate saluting a former corporal. He can't resist winking at Bala whenever it happens.

'This way, Prime Minister,' the brigade commander says.

They jog over to a waiting Chinook with its rotors spinning, while the journalists are herded down the plane's vomit-slicked ramp with much hilarity by soldiers wielding fluorescent batons, and across the frosty runway and up the waiting helicopter's ramp.

Moments later, the Chinook lifts off and ferries them east, to where the paras have taken over a Latvian Defence Force bunker complex on the Russian border.

Bala has warned him that he's going to get stick in the press for wagging the dog, creating a diversion from the nation's grievous problems – load shedding, internet fucked, staff shortages caused by internment, and worst of all, Fowle on the loose. But with Calthorp sniffing around and the usual *Telegraph*ful of fatuous generals asking *why are we in Latvia?* he feels the need to slap his cock on the table for all to see.

They touch down in a field beside the silhouette of an abandoned nine-storey apartment block where the commanding officer (CO) of 1 PARA is waiting alongside his regimental sergeant major (RSM). They salute Lee and lead him through ankle-deep mud to a stand of birches that disguises the entrance to the trenches.

They go down concrete steps, the press directed into an underground bunker while Lee is escorted along the duckboards at the bottom of a trench. It's very dark; the only light from red-lensed torches. They pass a soldier and beyond him a line of people huddled against the wall of trench.

'Stop,' Lee says and holds his hand out to the RSM. 'Give me your torch.'

He shines it on the nearest person, a man of indeterminate age in a dirty tracksuit and flip flops, squatting on the ground. He has unmistakably grizzled features: a jutting chin and enormous hands.

'*Salaam Aleikum,*' Lee greets him. '*Sanga yaast? Kha yaast?*'

The man replies in Pashto with his hand on his chest: '*Shokor day, zhowandy oose.*'

Rather than light someone up as he would like to or better still batter the fuck out of them, Lee points the torch at his feet and asks in a controlled manner, 'Why are there Afghans in my trench?'

'They're migrants, Prime Minister,' the RSM explains. 'The Russians send them over every night. It spooked the shit out of us the first time it happened, excuse my language. I thought I was back in Sangin and under attack. They were lucky they didn't get slotted.'

Lee shakes his head. 'Fuck's sake!'

'They're no trouble. We give them a cup of tea and some scran, and hand them over to the Latvian police in the morning.'

'Get them out of the way,' Lee says, 'I don't want the journos seeing them.'

'Yes, sir.'

They escort Lee along the trench to where a sentry is watching through a Scout Sniper periscope with a night-vision adapter. He hands Lee the periscope.

'At the closest point, they're two hundred metres away, Prime Minister,' the CO explains. 'You can see the line of the trench-top.'

'Migrants aside, it's been quiet since we arrived,' the brigade commander adds, 'which suggests that the Russians are trying to avoid a confrontation.'

Lee leans against the sandbag wall and steadies the periscope before putting his eye to the scope. It's a desolate and muddy wasteland with splintered trees and arcs of barbed wire in mono-chrome green. It takes a few moments to locate the other side's trenches. Almost immediately he does, he spots the long neck and ghoulish eye of a periscope staring back at him.

'I guess they're curious,' Lee says.

'As we all are, Prime Minister,' the brigade commander says.

'Don't worry,' Lee says without taking his eye off the scope. 'I have a plan.'

'We look forward to understanding your intent, Prime Minister.'

'Bala, darling, could you send up the cameraman,' he says.

'Of course, Prime Minister.'

He takes his eyes off the scope and sees where the brigade commander's torch is pointing, at the swing of Bala's hips in skinny cargo pants as she heads off down the trench.

'You're a dirty perve, Brigadier.'

'Sorry, Prime Minister.'

'She does have a peach of an arse,' Lee concedes. 'Don't worry, we'll have you back home in time for Christmas.' He lowers his voice so that just the two of them can hear. 'In the meantime, stick to your script or I'll fuck your career faster than you can call me a faggot.'

'Yes, Prime Minister.'

The press is pooling footage from a single cameraman who films Lee conferring in the darkness with his senior officers and staring through the periscope across no man's land, before walking thoughtfully down a trench, reflecting on the sacrifice of the fighting man. Next on the agenda, Lee serves egg banjos to the troops in a cramped but well-lit bunker, avoids the photographic landmine of eating one himself, and demands a show of hands from all those who've been on a boozy stag weekend in Riga.

At least half the room raise their hands. Everyone is grinning.

'That's what we're defending, lads!'

He delivers a speech in which he explains that the British Army's presence on the line of contact is not a belligerent act but rather an act of solidarity with the hard-pressed Latvian people, fellow NATO members who have been as egregiously fucked as the Brits. What he actually says is that 'like the British, the Latvians have been grievously harmed by the actions of a reckless Russian president who has developed in Grom an unconventional weapon of mass destruction that is a huge, huge liability to the whole security of the world. It's very important to show our allies here that we're in with them for the long haul and we are giving them the strategic resilience they need.'

After the speech, he smiles indulgently while the squaddies (men and women) line up for selfies with Bala and then enters a command bunker where he gives five minutes each to the correspondents from Sky, ITN, Channel 4 News and the BBC.

First up, a grouchy diva from Sky quotes a former Chief of the Defence Staff who asserts that British forces are being used for political ends with no clear military objective and the embittered former Defence Secretary, who he's only just banished to the backbenches, who warns that Lee risks a nuclear war that will cause global destruction not seen since the dinosaur-killing meteorite.

Lee sticks his chin out. 'I'm defending our national pride, standing up to aggression as any self-respecting British person should and telling the Russians that we won't stand for it.'

He delivers the same trenchant message to each of them in turn and then announces it's time to skedaddle. They fly back to RAF Brize Norton, touching down in time for breakfast and brag rags.

'Brag rags?' Bala asks.

He rolls his eyes. 'Medals, darling.'

# 45

# Taking the bait

A firearms officer wearing a name badge with *Bains* on it meets Jude on the front steps of the Edinburgh townhouse. Jude's come straight from the airport in the same clothes that he was wearing when he left Istanbul.

'I'm really sorry,' she says.

The news had hit him like a roundhouse punch with the full force of a body behind it. He was already reeling from Istanbul and the realisation of what he came close to doing. Now he's in danger of coming completely unstuck.

'Are you sure that you're up to this?'

'Please.'

'The house has been on the market for six months and in the meantime the owner rents it out for TV and film shoots,' Bains explains as she takes him inside. 'On the day that Ms McIntyre disappeared, the house was on loan to a Glasgow-based production company. I've spoken with them and they've confirmed that there was a scheduled pause in filming that day and the house was empty.'

Jude follows her down the cold, quiet hall past an unsettling Jenny Saville painting and through to the book-lined study. A door leads out onto a patio and lawn screened by high walls.

'They entered and exited through the back gate,' Bains tells him.

Partially hidden between two mature rhododendrons there is a wrought-iron gate that leads to a communal garden of several acres, which is accessible only to the affluent key-holders who live on the crescent. It must be one of the most expensive residential addresses in Edinburgh. There was a time when he was a student here that the presence of such gardens in the city provoked the class warrior in him. It's the first time that he has thought of them as sinister.

*No ...*

'We have casts of footprints for three different shoe sizes,' Bains says, 'most likely two men and a woman. And the tyre marks of a wheelbarrow, which we believe they used to transport Ms McIntyre.'

'Fingerprints?'

He is speaking like an automaton. She shakes her head, 'No. We're still waiting on fibres, etc.'

'Did the neighbours see anything?'

'No.'

It's hardly surprising. It's the sort of place where people zealously guard their privacy.

'What was she doing here?'

'She spoke to her editor in the morning and told him that she was travelling to Edinburgh to meet with a lawyer named Alexander Ledmuir from the Investigatory Powers Tribunal to discuss the case of Nasruddin al-Raqqah. We know from the browser history on her laptop that she researched him on the night before she travelled.'

He knows that working journalists take risks and there are only so many precautions you can take. He had given the police her password from the cockpit of the Gulfstream jet flying him back from Turkey, allowing them to break into her laptop. No one asked him how he came to memorise it. The answer is instinctively, by observing her fingers moving on the keyboard. Not out of any specific desire to spy on her. It's just a dirty habit: the pornography of espionage.

'Have you spoken to Ledmuir?' he asks.

'Yes. He was planning to talk to Ms McIntyre in the coming weeks but knows nothing of a scheduled meeting and has a solid alibi for the time of the incident. He was in court.'

'Where was the surveillance?'

'She was followed to City Airport and observed boarding a flight for Edinburgh. The unit didn't have the authorisation to leave London.'

Simon Conway

'What about her phone?'

'Someone took a hammer to the handset and we found the SIM card fried in the microwave.'

'Cameras?'

'We have footage from a security camera on one of the houses with a partial view of the entrance on the far side of the gardens. It captured a man in a hoodie pushing a tarp-covered wheelbarrow up a plank into the back of a van that was marked in the livery of the landscape company that tends the gardens. The van was located in Sighthill three hours after the incident. It was torched.'

Jude walks across the grass to the gate.

'Do you have the key?' he asks.

'Yes, of course.' She hands it to him from her pocket.

He unlocks the gate and steps through into the verdant garden beyond. It's as if he has descended a staircase and brought the silence of the house with him. Pathways curve away and disappear between shrubs that are glistening with raindrops. He follows one and it opens out into a hidden lawn that is a bright, mossy green. A narrow rut on one edge of the lawn is all that marks the wheelbarrow's passing. Through a curtain of trees, he glimpses the iron palisade that surrounds the garden and keeps the public out.

He imagines Kirsty curled up under a tarpaulin in the wheelbarrow, unconscious perhaps but alive. He's sure of that. Fowle wouldn't have gone to this trouble if he simply wanted to kill her. He has a purpose for her in mind. Jude recognises with grim certainty that Fowle is going to use her as the bait in a trap.

A trap intended for him.

# 46

# On the beach

Kirsty is sitting on the bed staring at the flagstones when she hears Grigor's brogues on the stone steps. It is getting harder and harder to think straight. He is holding a set of handcuffs.

'Put these on and I'll undo your chain,' he tells her. 'And then you can go outside.'

She shuffles to the end of the chain and holds out her wrists. He cuffs her and then tells her to sit down on the floor and put her legs out in front of her. She does as she is told. He takes the key out of his right pocket.

'Were you one of Guy's teachers?' she asks, trying with only limited success to wiggle her toes.

'I was much more than that.' He kneels and undoes the padlock that secures the shackle at her ankle. She wants to kick him in the face, but she can't summon the energy. Besides, his face looks immune to further damage.

'But you knew him when he was young?'

He gets up and pulls her up after him. He points at the staircase, 'After you.'

The steps are uneven, some tall and some short, which makes no sense until she realises that they were designed so that anyone familiar with the fortifications could move quickly and surely, but for an attacker moving in the narrow space it was a deliberate hazard. Twice she almost falls but Grigor's hand on her shoulder stops her. On the first landing there is a closed wooden door concealing the rooms beyond. On the second, the door is ajar, and she glimpses a table with two large multi-barrelled guns on it. On the third, the door is closed but she can hear a man speaking. It doesn't sound like Guy. At the bottom, the stairs end in a hallway and a rectangle of light. A double-layer of doors stands open: a medieval-looking grille as an inner cage and a hefty wooden outer door with iron straps and studs.

There is a pile of muddy wellington boots in green and black in the hall and a wooden chair.

'Sit.'

Grigor rummages in the pile and finds one that seems to satisfy him. 'I didn't care for your depiction of Guy in the newspaper,' he tells her as he fits the boot on her. 'I thought that it was rather one-dimensional.'

'Surely that's the point,' she replies, 'sociopaths are one-dimensional.'

'That's so reductive and, if I may so, beneath a journalist of your talent. You should really try to be more open-minded. Then you might see the purpose and design in his actions. The majesty. Does that fit? Close enough? It'll do.'

Majesty? Again, she feels the urge to kick him. She doubts that a boot would be any more effective than her bare foot. He searches for the matching boot.

'What did you teach him?'

Grigor laughs. 'Biology and chemistry.'

'Was he a star pupil?'

'I was the family doctor.' He pauses. 'Before I gave up medicine.'

She flinches at two gunshots fired in quick succession.

'The answer to that will have to wait,' Grigor says, putting the other boot on her. 'You have an appointment.'

'Am I about to be executed?'

'Not unless you are very badly behaved. You are far more valuable to Guy alive.' He gestures towards the doorway. 'Shall we?'

Outside, the air feels thicker, bluebottles buzz and it smells of redwood: spicy and earthy, and almost dusty because not much rain makes it to the bottom of these giants. The tower is surrounded by a grove of them, rising like rockets from a thin screed of moss. They look old enough to have been grown from the original Californian seeds brought back by expeditionary botanists in the

Victorian era. Beyond the trees and a narrow strip of grass, there is a hard barrier formed by a mad scribble of brambles at least six feet high.

'Go on.'

She walks unsteadily out from under the canopy and looks up at the sky where a plane must have recently been because there's a white seam across the blue. Grigor points her towards a narrow path between the brambles, leading to what she thinks must be the loch.

'I presume you know what happened to Andrew Arbuthnot,' she says, in a deliberately conversational tone, as she walks down the path between the brambles. It's a close, moist passage with a string of muddy puddles. In places, the brambles loop across like trip wires and she's forced to step over them or duck under them.

Arbuthnot had been the English teacher at one of a string of private schools that Guy attended during his difficult adolescence before he learned to disguise his true nature. Guy had sheltered in Arbuthnot's East London house after breaking out of Belmarsh Prison. Arbuthnot's diaries, which were recovered from the house after his death, had included a lengthy treatise on the beauty of violence. 'You know that Guy killed him and his lover with a heroin overdose?'

'I'm not the slightest bit concerned about what might happen to me,' Grigor calls out ahead of him, 'if that's what you are worried about.'

She stops abruptly and watches a cloud of midges circle slowly upwards in a spiral. In front of her feet is what looks like a strip of freshly turned earth, a narrow trench no more than six inches wide that has been dug across the path and filled in afterwards. Looking right, she sees a larger area of turned earth cut in the brambles beside her.

'It's not armed yet,' Grigor tells her. He winks. 'Even so, try not to tread on the pressure plates.'

She steps across the mound of earth and four more at random intervals.

She looks over her shoulder and asks, 'What was he like? As a child, I mean?'

He smiles indulgently. 'He was extraordinary. I delivered him with my own hands. On the way home, I saw a double rainbow from the car.'

The path opens out onto a beach of grey pebbles and a tideline of kelp, branches, and scuffed plastic at the edge of a wide loch. In the distance on the opposite shore, far beneath a ridgeline, there is a fishing village: a cluster of whitewashed buildings with slate roofs arranged around a church.

'The flame that burns twice as bright burns half as long,' he says, sadly.

'What does that mean?'

'She's waiting for you.'

Over to the right, the meido is standing on a grassy promontory, holding an over-and-under shotgun. She is wearing an oversized waxed jacket with bulging pockets and knee-high neoprene boots. They walk across the pebbles towards her.

'Pull!' she shouts.

The voice-activated trap fires a fluorescent orange clay out over the water.

She fires.

The limestone clay is pulverised by steel pellets.

'Kill,' Grigor calls out approvingly.

'My grandfather's plan for Guy was always for him to take the battle to the *far enemy*,' the meido says, when they are in earshot. 'In that Guy succeeded but not yet to the extent that he wishes.'

'I don't know who you are,' Kirsty says, watching her load the shotgun with shells from her pockets.

'I am Alysha al-Sabbah, Guy's wife.'

Kirsty can't recall mention of a wife in the court documents or any of the other source material. The words are out of her mouth before she can check herself, 'I didn't know that he had a wife.'

Alysha turns and points the loaded gun at her. 'Don't assume that just because Guy wants you alive I do too.'

Alarmed, Grigor takes a step away from her. Clearly, his understanding of what constitutes bad behaviour significantly differs from Alysha's.

The barrels are like two black holes. Kirsty curses her big mouth.

'I meant no offence,' she says, thinking that to die in a fit of someone else's petulance would be an ignominious way to end, particularly if that someone had suicidally appalling taste in men.

Alysha shouts: 'Pull!'

The clay shoots out across the water at a different angle to the last. Alysha spins and fires the second barrel.

Misses.

'Bird away,' Grigor says.

Abruptly, Alysha cracks open the shotgun, ejecting the spent cartridges, and Kirsty sees a glimpse of the deep reservoir of anger inside her.

'Who is Jude Lyon?'

'A foreign intelligence officer.'

'Why does Guy hate him so much?'

'He prevented Guy from destroying London.'

'Guy should thank him. London was too small a target. Now he has a much greater ambition.'

'Which is?'

'There are too many people in this world: ugly, inferior people in every country. To Guy, they are like cattle queuing to be slaughtered.'

'He wants to kill everyone? How?'

Her eyes narrow. 'Let's go in.'

They head back up the path towards the tower: Kirsty in the front, then Alysha with the gun pointing at her and Grigor bringing up the rear. Back in the tower, Kirsty sits in the wooden chair with the handcuffs in her lap. Grigor helps her out of her boots.

'Take her back upstairs,' Alysha says, taking off her jacket.

'Of course,' Grigor says and motions for Kirsty to precede him up the stairs.

Reaching the top floor, she gets close enough to one of the windows to see the approach to the tower on the landward side. Beyond the redwoods, amongst knee-high grass there is a field of dilapidated caravans crowded together against the persecution of the weather. And beyond the field, there is a strip of tangled forest between the mountainside and the sea with a single-track road cutting through it. She's fairly certain that she's somewhere in Argyll on the west coast of Scotland and she may even have stayed in one of the caravans as a child. If they are where she thinks they are, this must be familiar terrain. Guy was born on an island less than fifty miles away.

'Get down on the floor.'

She sits and puts out her legs.

'Where is Guy?' she asks.

'I don't know why you are so eager for him to return,' Grigor says, reattaching the manacle to her ankle. 'If he comes, he'll have Jude hot on his trail. How do you rate your chances of survival in those circumstances?'

'How do you rate yours?'

Grigor smiles, wearily. 'I'm like a bad penny. I'll always survive.'

'Why did you give up being a doctor?'

'It gave me up really. There were a few misunderstandings.'

'Because of Guy? What did you mean when you said the flame burns half as long? Is Guy sick? What's the matter with him?'

Ignoring the question, he removes the handcuffs. 'There you go. You can get up now.'

'There's nowhere to go,' she says. She wants to see Jude more than anything, but she prays that he does not come.

# 47

# Rest and be thankful

Jude's phone vibrates. It's his sister Hannah. She's angry and upset about Kirsty.

'I should never have introduced you.'

'It's on me,' he admits. 'I let my feelings for Kirsty cloud my judgement.'

His phone vibrates again: a call from an unknown number that has been forwarded from a phone he has kept charged since Guy Fowle tried to assassinate him.

'I have another call.'

Hannah is indignant. 'Don't hang up on me!'

He ends the call and accepts the incoming one.

'Are we alone?'

By the sound of it, Guy is standing outside somewhere. Jude can hear the wind and what sounds like passing traffic in the background.

'No.' He doesn't see any point in lying. The phone that Guy is calling has been cloned since right after he first contacted Jude on it. 'Do you have her?'

'Do you want me to cut something off and send it to you as proof.'

'No.'

'Well then, you'll have to take my word for it. Kirsty McIntyre is alive and in my hands.'

'What do you want?'

He laughs and cuts the connection.

Forty-five minutes later Jude is sitting beside the Chief Constable of Police Scotland in a conference room on the Crime Campus in

Gartcosh along with his sister Tamar, the Assistant Chief Constable who commands organised crime and counter terrorism and two fresh-faced officers from Border Policing and the Fugitive Unit who look barely out of their teens.

There are two large screens on the walls: one has an interactive real-time map of the county of Argyll, and the head and shoulders of the Prime Minister dominate the other. He's wearing a hooded sweatshirt and looks like an assassin from a video game but, on reflection, it strikes Jude that the person he most closely resembles is Guy Fowle in the surveillance capture images during the attacks on London.

It is a strange and unsettling association.

Beneath the PM, in gallery view, are a row of functionaries in business suits or uniform with their cameras on: the Cabinet Secretary, a minister from the Scottish government, the heads of MI5 and MI6, a commissioner from the counter terrorism operations centre in London, the head of counter terrorism for the army, the Director Special Forces, and a representative of the National CBRN Centre, which is tasked with protecting against chemical, biological, radiological and nuclear threats. There are others with their cameras off, Americans presumably, anonymous in person at the last briefing but now with indecipherable acronyms for names.

A detective inspector named Gallagher is delivering the briefing beside the map of Argyll. 'Cellphone triangulation put Guy Fowle on the A83 at the Rest and Be Thankful at the time of his call with Mr Lyon,' Gallagher tells them. On the map a red data point marks the summit of the high pass – the Rest and Be Thankful – that leads west through the Arrochar Alps to the Knapdale and Kintyre peninsulas, and the islands of the Inner Hebrides. 'A convoy system is being used through the pass due to recent rock falls so that we were able to close the traffic eastbound almost immediately. We have also closed the roads north to the Highlands.' He uses a red laser pointer to indicate checkpoints at the northern end of Loch Awe and on the road to Oban. 'And set up roving checkpoints on the A roads across the rest of the county. We've notified the ferries, the principal port harbourmasters at

Campbeltown, Rothesay and Oban, and the area managers for Argyll. We've also put out a warning to all fishing vessels on Marine channel 70. However, there are more than forty council-owned piers and slipways across Argyll, many of them unmanned, and countless privately owned ones. If he's heading to the islands, we may not be able to intercept him before he gets there.'

'What measures are you taking to prevent a terrorist attack?' Lee asks.

'In terms of threat mitigation measures, we've requested reinforcement of the commando squadrons at Faslane and the nuclear warhead storage facility at Coulport in case that is his target and Fowle doubles back across Loch Long,' the Chief Constable explains. 'But to cover the entire county I need more ground, sea and air assets, Prime Minister.'

'And you'll get them,' Lee says. 'We're pulling troops off leave and mobilising reserves.'

'If Fowle keeps going in his current direction there is no critical infrastructure,' the commissioner from London tells them. 'There are no major oil or gas lines. The power generation is hydro and wind, and destruction of those facilities doesn't present a significant risk to the population. In terms of transmission lines there are three 132 kV power circuits and two 220 kV subsea circuits; if he knocks those out, there will be a localised effect on the national grid, but we can compensate. None of the trans-Atlantic internet cables come ashore on the Argyll coast. There are multiple routes for the Highlands and Islands submarine cable systems but again cutting them will have a mostly localised effect.'

'But a very real effect,' the Scottish government minister protests.

'It's a trap,' Jude says.

The Chief Constable looks sideways at him. 'Elaborate?'

'Fowle was born in Argyll. It's familiar ground. He's using the call as a lure to reel us in.'

'We've had his father's house under surveillance since Fowle escaped from Belmarsh,' the Assistant Chief Constable says, 'and I'm sending more firearms officers.'

'That's too obvious a destination,' Jude says.

'So where is he leading us?' Lee asks.

'Somewhere of his own choosing, where he can utilise the weapons that he purchased from the Albanians to the greatest effect.'

'Who does he have with him?' Lee asks.

'We know of at least two accomplices,' Gallagher replies, 'Alysha al-Sabbah.' He clicks and the map on the wall is replaced with the photo of her at immigration at Edinburgh Airport. 'And a man that we have not yet identified.' He clicks again. This time an artist's impression of the Scottish man who collected the guns from Billy at the trap house – it looks like a Peter Howson portrait, bulky and over-masculinised.

'That's Grigor Muir,' the Chief Constable says, to general surprise. 'A disgraced doctor turned chemist with a talent for cooking MDMA. He grew up in Argyll. He was released from the top end at Barlinnie a couple of years ago. They'll give you a recent photo.'

'Plus, Fowle may have the support of any number of Russian illegals,' the commissioner adds.

Gallagher's phone buzzes and he glances down at the screen.

'They've found the car that Fowle was travelling in,' he tells them. 'It was abandoned by the pier at Lochgoilhead.'

'That's it,' the commissioner says, 'he's doubling back for the nukes.'

Jude is not so sure. It seems as likely to be a feint.

'Get the missiles out to sea where they are beyond reach,' Lee says, 'and flood the ground with troops. Throw everything at it. Apply overwhelming force. I want Fowle captured and killed.'

Overwhelming force does not sound like something that Kirsty will survive.

# 48

# At the head of the crooked loch

The police helicopter flies over the naval base at Faslane, where a Vanguard submarine is being hastily prepared for launch.

Looking out the left side as they cross the Roseneath Peninsula, Jude spots the reinforced bunkers at the armament depot at Coulport on the eastern shore of Loch Long, where the submarine will take on its cargo of Trident warheads before being escorted out to sea by a rapidly assembling naval task force.

They head up a crooked sleeve of water with forested slopes on either side that rise to rocky peaks that look almost close enough to touch. Jude is acutely aware that they make an easy target and Fowle is a master of nasty surprises.

After a nerve-wracking couple of minutes, the chopper reaches the loch's head, banks, and sweeps over a chalet park, looking for somewhere to land, coming down on a school playing field at the water's edge. Jude and Tamar run out from beneath the spinning rotors and join the incident commander who is coordinating the response from a vantage point on the roof of the school.

Most of the village has already been evacuated. Just a few stragglers are being escorted out through the cordon by police officers. Bomb disposal are there, and a wheelbarrow robot is trundling towards the pier-side car park where Fowle's abandoned car was discovered.

Jude looks up at the surrounding peaks again with a nagging feeling that they are being watched.

'You think he's up there?' Tamar asks, from beside him.

'Maybe.'

They are just as exposed: easily within range of a sniper rifle from an elevated position amongst the rocks.

'Why?'

'Because he wants to see what we do.'

He's trying not to consider the possibility that they may find Kirsty's body in the boot of the car. They listen to a succession of shotgun blasts as the wheelbarrow brackets the car, shooting out the door locks and windows and popping the boot open. Jude waits, controlling his breathing, while it investigates with the three-fingered gripper and the cameras mounted on its telescopic arm.

Nothing.

She's not inside.

Tamar grips his upper arm tightly.

Satisfied that there is no obvious explosive device, an EOD tech in a bomb suit sets off on the lonely walk to the car.

Jude's work phone vibrates. An unknown number. He answers and a now familiar voice says: 'Jude?'

'Yes, Prime Minister.'

'Is there any recent news of Ms McIntyre?'

'No.'

'You can't blame yourself for the kidnapping,' Lee tells him. 'That's on Fowle, not you. Guilt is paralysing. It's a mind killer. You can't give in to it.'

'I understand.'

'What about Guy Fowle?'

'Nothing.'

'Do you think that he's heading for the nukes?'

'No,' Jude says. 'I think its misdirection.'

The EOD tech at the car gives the 'all-clear' over the intercom and the white-suited police forensics team walk out to join him.

'So where is he?'

'I don't know. I think that I should go and speak to the father.'

'Earlier today, you said that Guy wouldn't go there. What's changed?'

'Nothing's changed but if anyone has an idea where he is hiding, it might be the father.'

'That sounds sensible. Keep me informed. And good luck, Jude.'

'Thank you.'

Lee ends the call. Tamar is watching him.

'Do you trust him?' she asks.

'I don't know,' he admits.

'Do you think that the father will agree to speak to us?'

'There's only one way to find out.'

'The helicopter is ours to use,' Tamar tells him.

Jude does not relish the prospect of such an exposed take-off but what choice is there if they hope to get to the island before nightfall?

'Let's go,' he says.

Tamar follows him back out onto the playing field where the pilot is waiting.

Soon the rotors are turning, and they lift off, climbing above the mountains and heading west.

# 49

# Breothadh

As it flies over the water and approaches the forested eastern coast of the island, the helicopter descends, crossing the rocky shoreline at the Breothadh Estate and keeping just above the treetops. In a clearing, Jude spots the charred and roofless hulk of the castle where Guy was born and, out on a promontory, the run-down coach house and stables that his family moved into after the fire.

The helicopter tilts and turns to the left, flying over the police barricade at the entrance to the estate and following the coast past a succession of wooded inlets. They put down on a vivid green lawn beside a distillery with white-painted maltings towers and a Trojan armed response vehicle in the car park. A police sergeant meets them as they run out from beneath the rotors and introduces himself as Campbell.

'This way, ma'am,' he tells Tamar and gives Jude a wary look.

It's a ten-minute drive to Breothadh along a single-track tarmac road that climbs and descends through the ancient forest of sessile oaks and downy birches. They park behind a van with blacked-out windows and walk towards the two patrol cars that are blocking the entrance to the estate. Beyond them are two granite gateposts topped with whale vertebrae and a rutted track leading towards the castle.

'He hasn't allowed us on the property since the original search warrant turned up nothing of interest,' Campbell tells them. 'He's got himself a fancy Edinburgh lawyer who's claiming harassment. His firearms certificate was revoked and the legally held weapons were confiscated but I'll wager that he's got more guns buried somewhere on the property. Do you want an escort?'

'I don't think that we should go in heavy,' Jude advises.

Campbell looks to Tamar for confirmation. She nods.

'Can you take the post?'

Jude agrees and is handed a red Royal Mail pouch with a clear plastic window that is stuffed full of letters.

'He gets fan mail now,' Campbell says, shaking his head. 'There's no accounting for taste.'

'Shall we?' Jude says.

Tamar nods. They step between the cars and head down the track between beech trees in autumnal orange. It's as verdant and mossy as Jude remembers. The track opens out abruptly on an area of overgrown parkland, dotted with gnarled trees like witches' fingers and the ruin of the castle. There was a time when ruling a clan meant defending yourself from outsiders, but it was his own son that had set fire to Angus Fowle's home. The last time he was here Angus Fowle told him that Guy had 'Satan in him'.

They continue to follow the track past a collection of mature exotics: giant redwoods, monkey-puzzles, and Douglas firs. On a promontory overlooking the sea there is a muddy courtyard that has stone buildings on three sides and two Land Rovers up on blocks. There's no sign of the wolfhound that was here before. When he eventually appears, Angus Fowle looks even more skeletal and pinched than Jude remembers: his frayed and faded Barbour jacket looks several sizes too large for him. The police sergeant was right about one thing, Angus has a shotgun, which he is not quite pointing at them.

'My name is Jude Lyon. We met here before, Mr Fowle. When your daughter Katherine was alive.' Hearing her name, he seems to get even smaller and meaner. 'May we speak with you?'

He grunts and turns his back on them, heading back inside. He leaves the door open, which Jude takes as permission. He goes in with Tamar following. It's colder inside than outside and there is mildew climbing the walls of the narrow hall that leads from the kitchen to the living room. Everything smells of damp and garbage and chimney soot. Angus is sitting beside a peat fire in a filthy armchair with stacks of dirty plates surrounding it. Jude sees that the shotgun is propped against the wall but within reach. Angus gestures impatiently at Jude, who gives him the pouch full of mail.

They stand and watch while Angus rifles through his mail, throwing most of it on the fire unopened.

'Have you heard from Guy?' Jude asks.

'No.'

'We believe that he is in Argyll,' Tamar says.

'He won't come here,' Angus replies. 'I used to think that he would. That he wanted to cut my throat. But he prefers a life sentence. It's the same with that bitch that weaned him. He prefers to let us suffer. You know how much hate mail I get?' He pauses to peer at a mauve letter with a handwritten address in a looping style. He sniffs it.

'It's not all hate mail,' Tamar observes.

Angus flings it into the fire. 'Mad cows.'

'If Guy's not coming here, then where is he going?' Jude asks.

'How would I know?'

'Are there any places that you went on holiday as a family?' Tamar asks.

Angus sneers at her. 'You think we had holidays?'

'What about with the school?'

Angus frowns. 'Maybe. There was a place. Speak to Margot McEwan.'

Tamar shows him a prison photograph of Grigor Muir, which provokes mocking laughter.

'Mucking around behind my back! The fool puffed himself up with the notion that he was Guy's father. But when I invited him to look in the crib, he practically pissed himself with terror.' Angus's face takes on a sly cast. 'They said the same of the emperor Augustus, the first Roman to be made a god in his own lifetime, that anyone who approached the nursery was seized with terror. Maybe that's why you're doing such a miserable job of trying to catch my son, Mr Jew Lyon. He's beyond your limited understanding.'

'I think that we've used up enough of your time,' Tamar says, grimly.

'Yes. Get out of my house.'

★   ★   ★

The retired primary school teacher Margot McEwan lives several streets back from the town's pier in a recently built crescent of houses on the edge of the moor. The gardens are unleavened by trees or landscaping and seem stark and unfinished in the rain.

'I'm not sure what I was expecting of a serial killer's father,' Tamar says, as they are walking up the path to the front door.

'Monsters beget monsters,' Jude says.

'We turned out all right.'

'Did we?' he wonders. She's always quick to defend their father, the suicide.

'Let's park that for another time,' Tamar says before she rings the doorbell.

A white-haired woman answers the door and looks them up and down and at the police car that brought them.

'You'll be from the government, then?'

'Yes,' Tamar says, showing her warrant card. Margot looks unimpressed.

'Angus Fowle suggested that we talk to you,' Jude says.

She replies with a staple of Scottish disdain. 'Is that right?'

'Can we come in?' Tamar asks.

'Take your shoes off,' she tells them.

It's a furnace inside and they take off coats and jumpers in addition to their shoes while Margot watches.

'This way.'

They follow her into a comfortable-looking sitting room that has a gas fire going in addition to the central heating. Margot sits in an armchair, apparently unaffected by the heat, while Jude and Tamar sit sweating side by side on the sofa.

She does not wait to be asked a question and issues a statement: 'Guy was at the primary school here until he was nine when it was agreed with his parents that he should be transferred to a school away from the island. As I am sure that you are aware, he was an extremely difficult child. It was less a question of teaching him than of managing the disruption that he caused. We did not know then what he would become.'

'Did you ever take him to the mainland on a school trip?' Jude asks.

'Why do you ask?'

'We think he may be using somewhere in Argyll as a hideout.'

She takes her time to answer. 'There was a campground on private land in the Knapdale Forest that was used by schools in the county. We used to take the primary five and six kids there every year. They learned to put up tents and build fires. It was supposed to promote self-sufficiency and initiative. It was closed after a boy from another school drowned when a jetty collapsed. I believe that the owner went to prison. And yes, Guy was a witness, which means he probably was involved. Though we didn't suspect him at the time.'

They hear the door open, and someone calls out, 'Hey, Gran.'

A young woman in her early twenties enters the room and perches on the arm of her grandmother's chair. Her gaze is watchful and guarded, and her resemblance to Guy Fowle is uncanny.

'This is my granddaughter Eve,' Margot says with a hint of defiance.

'Is he coming?' Eve asks. It's hard to judge from her expression what emotions the prospect of his return provokes in her.

'I don't think so,' Jude says, when he has recovered sufficiently from the realisation that she must be one of Guy's children. 'But we think that he is somewhere in Argyll. Somewhere secluded that is well known to him.'

'We don't know anything about that, do we, Eve?' Margot says, firmly.

Fowle's daughter stares at the carpet and shakes her head.

'I think that you should leave,' Margot says.

Looking back from the police car, Jude sees Margot watching them from the living room window.

They check into a hotel overlooking the harbour and eat in a quiet corner of the bar. It's off season and the place is almost empty. They are nursing locally distilled Scotch in exhausted silence when Eve enters the bar.

She comes straight over and sits at their table.

'I'm sorry about earlier,' she says. 'Gran doesn't like me to talk about my father.'

'It's okay,' Tamar tells her.

'I was thinking about what you said. When I was little, my mum told me that she used to meet my father on the mainland, in a castle surrounded by punchy trees.'

'Punchy trees?'

Eve shrugs. 'I don't even know what it means.'

# 50

# Juliet in the graveyard

Kirsty wakes from foreboding dreams to the sound of a car and the crunch of gravel at the base of the tower. She hears a door slam and indistinct voices.

He's barefoot, so she doesn't hear him on the stairs. Unlike a vampire of old, Fowle doesn't have to wait to be invited in. One moment she is alone and the next he's there in the darkness, owning the room. Watching him move, her skin crawls.

'Jude is searching for you,' he tells her from over by one of the windows, which now have a curtain of camouflage netting in front of them. 'He's getting closer all the time.'

'He won't walk into a trap,' she says.

He glances back at her, his eyes shining like black pearls in the moonlight. As a child, she read tales about predators paralysing their prey with a stare. Now she knows how it feels.

The cruel lines of his face sharpen when he smiles. 'For you, he will.'

He's probably right, duty and obligation will propel Jude open-eyed into the jaws of the trap that Fowle has laid.

She falls asleep to a drizzle and wakes to a downpour. The roof is alive with the assault of water. Despite the noise, she can hear shouting.

It sounds like Alysha.

The next time she wakes, Fowle is naked on the end of her bed, his lupine face alive with dancing shadows. By rights, her first instinct ought to be to scream and get as far away from him as her chain will allow, but her limbs are so heavy. What's the point? At least he's showing no physical signs of arousal. Then there's the matter of her interest in the Moleskine notebook that is open in his trembling hands. She has written about the notebook, after learning about it from a source within the police investigation. She described it as a measure of Fowle's effectiveness as a guerrilla fighter that his plans are entirely analogue and a measure of the deadliness of the Grom app that it only took a couple of days of notetaking for him to record sufficient information to destroy the building blocks of First World democracy that so many take for granted. As for the tremors, she's only now beginning to consider what they might mean.

'What's next?' she asks him.

He looks up at her and smiles. 'Don't worry, you'll be right at the heart of it.'

'Are you dying?'

He grimaces. 'Who told you that?'

'Guy!'

Alysha is standing at the top of the stairs, also naked. Kirsty sees the elaborate designs carved in her skin. She read about the scarring in the published extract of the autopsy report of Zeina Hussein, and it was front-page news in the tabloids, but this is the first time she's seen Guy's handiwork for real. It's horrifying that any woman should allow herself to be so disfigured.

Guy closes the notebook and gets up off the bed. He smiles indulgently at Kirsty and runs a shaky finger down the inside of her calf before following Alysha down the stairs.

She feels hands touching, grabbing, and gripping. She is lifted to a seated position on the bed and her head lolls forward. It feels incredibly heavy. Too much bloody orange juice. She opens her eyes. With an effort, she looks up. There is a tripod-mounted camera pointing at her from the foot of the bed. Fowle is standing behind it and watching her with an amused expression on his face.

She's pretty sure that she's not looking her best for the camera.

Whatever they have given her, it's very strong. Her arms feel as bendy as Mr Tickle's. She lets her head roll around to the left and watches as Alysha slides her hand through the armhole of a vest that is as bulky as a lifejacket. *Is there a boat trip ahead?* She lets her head fall back, her eyes travelling across the silver folds of the ceiling as it rolls around to the right, to where Grigor is holding her wrist and manoeuvring her other arm through the hole.

Behind him, she sees that the very large multi-barrelled gun that was on the table downstairs is now mounted on a tripod over by the window. It's fed by a belt of ammunition from a coffin-sized box on the flagstones. She's relieved that it's pointing out through the camouflage netting and not at her. The bullets are so large they look like they could cut her in half.

'Breathe in!' Grigor gives her a quick wink before he tugs the zip upwards, and it feels like she's being squeezed into a corset. When he's done, he ties her hands behind her back and steps back looking satisfied. 'There you are.'

She looks down at her chest: complicated wiring links a row of bulky pouches together and rubber-coated cables loop under her arms, and snake away across the floor.

It's a suicide vest.

*Not good. Not good at all.*

If there's an upside to being so off her head, it must be that she is less scared than she ought to be. She knows the havoc that Fowle has wrought using suicide bombers as proxies in London. She should be terrified.

She looks up. Grigor is holding a whiteboard with writing on it in big letters and Alysha is standing behind the camera.

'Say the words on the board into the camera lens,' Grigor tells her.

She tries to focus. Some gobbledygook.

'Drink . . .' she says, slurring the words.

'You've given her too much,' Fowle says from somewhere out of sight. He sounds angry. There is some more talking, but she can't distinguish the words. Time passes. She has the sense that something is going to happen.

'Kirsty!'

She opens her eyes and gets a bucketful of icy water in the face.

'Read the words,' Grigor says, flinging the bucket away.

The red light on the camera is on and her whole body is shuddering with cold. She opens her mouth as the first line slides into focus. It's some bloody riddle. 'What does that even mean?'

'Just read it.'

'I am chaos,' she says. 'You may not be interested in me, but I am interested in you.'

The second line is short: 'I am zero.'

Then she reads the final line. Of course, it's from Shakespeare – Juliet stabbing herself. *Do they think that she's just a girl?* Fowle is such a bloody drama queen. He's like the Prime Minister, in that. They're peas in a pod. Christ, she thinks, they're in cahoots.

Guy Fowle and Lee Chapeaux working together. *How did she not see it before?* It's a profoundly depressing thought. Jude doesn't stand a chance. Weighed down by the vest, she speaks the words:

'This is thy sheath; there rust and let me die.'

# 51

# Deep fake

After two days under the surface, Yulia and Alexei climb back up the ladder through the submarine's sail and go out onto the bridge.

Startling cold.

The junkyard is transformed. Everything is covered in a thick layer of snow. It blunts and softens shapes, so it's impossible to tell what has toppled, ripped away, sunk, or simply been buried.

Yulia's Iridium vibrates as it locates a satellite. There are no missed calls from Jude, which is not what she expected. Rather than call him now, she decides to wait until after she has heard what the access team has found. They are already over on the icebreaker. They left when the wind speed dropped sufficiently to allow a person to stand up without being blown over.

'I want to marry you,' Alexei tells Yulia, with his head tilted down and his ice-crusted eyebrows raised. Only Alexei could make a proposal look like the prelude to a head-butt.

'You are already married.'

'I'll divorce Svetlana.'

'You promised me that a very long time ago.'

'Now I am ready.'

She sighs. She remembers her grandmother telling her that there was no fool like an old fool. 'Maybe we should save the world first?'

He gives her a disgruntled look and she softens, leaning into his shoulder and kissing his cheek. 'I will give full consideration to your offer.'

He growls contentedly. How simple he is to please. There was a time when she would have married him without hesitation.

★   ★   ★

They climb the creaking metal staircase slowly and carefully to the top, where Yulia, an avowed atheist, gives thanks to God for it not collapsing.

'Follow me,' Alexei says.

The servers are in an echoing hangar space beneath the deck, which is reached by a companionway and a succession of passageways, doors and hatches that Alexei navigates by means of torchlight and a sketch map drawn for him by Dima. Arriving, Alexei stares at the tableau in front of him as if it is an unfathomable pagan ritual.

Two metres tall, resembling a grove of charred stumps after a forest fire, the stacks stand at the centre of a floodlit circle. Beneath them are grilled plates that give access to a root system of electronics, refrigeration circuits and fibre-optic connections that have melted in the heat. Members of the access team in white coveralls are using tools to carefully prise open the stacks and remove the magnetic plates inside.

Yulia steps over power cables snaking across the deck from the submarine and joins Natasha, who is sitting in front of a triptych of screens that are mounted on top of the shockproof boxes they came in. Dima is standing at her shoulder, watching impassively.

'We are transplanting the least damaged platters into new hard drives,' Natasha explains, 'and using tailored recovery software to try to read the bits.'

The screens in front of her are running with data, turning her body into a bright patchwork of flickering graphics.

'Bits?' Yulia asks.

'Zeros and ones.'

'I see,' Yulia says. 'And what have you found?'

'We've partially recovered a data log of encrypted communications sent and received in the weeks before the reactor was scrammed, and the servers shut down. There is a spike in activity that correlates to the acceptance-testing phase of the Grom app with a further spike when Guy Fowle took possession of it, as you would expect. The communications were automatically routed through a series of data exchanges to disguise their origin; however, we have been able to trace many of them to a single IP address in the UK that ceased operating at the time that the phone containing the app was destroyed.'

'Are you able to break the encryption?' Yulia asks.

'Not yet. We think many of them are messages to deep cover assets. However, there are some larger and more sophisticated data packets that relate to artificial neural network architectures including auto-encoders and generative adversarial networks that will interest you.'

Yulia sighs. 'Please explain.'

'Historically, if you wanted to fool a monitoring system into thinking that everything was normal when in fact it wasn't, you would replace the contemporary data with a recurring loop of historical data, but the systems are so sophisticated now that they can spot repetition. A more complex algorithm using deep learning is required to take the historical footage and alter it before feeding it back into the system. That's what was using up the bandwidth.'

'I still don't follow.'

'In layman's terms, Grom sent out a sequence of deep fake data including personal ID logins, video footage, air-pressure sensor readings, aerosol sample analysis and sewage-water testing results over a three-day period from a laboratory in eastern Siberia to the Federal Medical and Biological Agency in Moscow.'

Yulia's mind is racing. 'Three days in which anything could have happened?'

'Yes.'

'What do you know about the lab?'

'Like Vector, which stores smallpox, it's registered here in Russia and with the International Science and Technology Centre in Kazakhstan as a Biosafety Level 4 lab. Level 4 is the highest level of biosafety precautions and is for work with pathogens for which there are no available vaccines or treatments.'

'*Ty che, blyad?*' Alexei growls. What the fuck?

It seems that Natasha has uncovered the Protean Bears' insurance policy against the Kremlin.

'We need to get back in the helicopter,' Yulia says with a sinking feeling. She is heartily sick of trusting her life to precarious tin cans.

'I'm coming with you,' Dima says.

Later, before they board the helicopter, she speaks to Jude, who tells her that Kirsty has been abducted. She has never known him so angry. He sounds wrathful and relentless on the phone, determined to burn anyone who stands in his way. He tells her with a monomaniac's fervour that his best hope is that Fowle is keeping Kirsty alive to draw him into a trap. There is nothing she can say that will reassure him, but she tells him that rushing headlong into an ambush is in nobody's best interests.

'My darling, if you get yourself killed you won't help her or us.'

She can tell that he's not listening. And he barely seems to register the gravity of her discovery.

'I'll call you from the lab when I know more,' she tells him and ends the call.

# 52

# Cell culture

Guy leaves the tower and walks out from under the foliage of the redwoods, feeling the relief of voluntary movement in his restless legs. He goes along a dirt track, past a pit filled with the rusting skeletons of several Land Rovers and a stand of reddish Scots pines. He crosses a prefabricated steel Bailey bridge over a river of fast-running water from the mountain, noting with some satisfaction that the demolition charges are not discernible to the naked eye. After the bridge, the track leads along the foot of the scree-slope, turning into a windless passage between walls of black rock. Deep ruts caused by a heavy vehicle lead to the mouth of a tunnel, which opens into a spacious chamber. Entering, he switches on a torch. The walls of the chamber rise to a vault thirty feet above and are covered in murals known as the Dark Friends that were painted in the nineties by a girl from the islands named Maili, a horror-comic fan with a pleasing interest in apocalyptic scenarios.

In the eighteenth century, the cave contained a copper still built to feed Glasgow's voracious thirst for unlicensed whisky, so-called 'Argyll water'. The smugglers used to transport the whisky from illicit stills hidden throughout Argyll to the port of Troon and, from there, overland to the city. The wreckage of the antique still is in a corner.

He walks past a humming 34 kVA diesel generator and a DAF truck with a flatbed and a Hiab crane towards a modified shipping container in one corner of the chamber, where the ceiling is lower. The container has an externally mounted ventilation unit that is connected to a row of oxygen cylinders. There is a steel door cut in the side at one end with a short staircase leading to it. Guy

236

climbs the stairs. Opening the door, he is silhouetted by ultra-violet light.

He feels the positive air pressure on his face and listens to the soft hum of HEPA filters cleaning the air. He steps inside and closes the door behind him. He is standing in a small stainless-steel vestibule with an airlock system leading to the rest of the container. In front of him there are two black police CBRN suits hanging on a garment rail and a row of gas masks with particulate air-filters on a shelf. The waterproof, fire-retardant suits have a chemical, biological, radiological, and nuclear capability and are strengthened with a Kevlar blend. They are unissued surplus purchased by Grigor from a website called Uniform. Fowle puts one on and clips a radio to his belt. He puts on a mask and pulls the hood up. He uses black gaffer tape to seal the elasticated cuffs at his ankles and wrists.

Satisfied, Guy spins the wheel and opens the outer airlock door. It is tiny inside, room for one only. He waits for the air to change. When the red light turns green, he spins the dogs on the inner door and steps into the small laboratory where Grigor is at work. He is up to his elbows in a sterile cabinet beneath a hood with a continuous whooshing exhaust. Around him are the tools of cell culture: a bench-top refrigerator containing dishes of animal tissue and growth medium, a temperature-controlled incubator, and a centrifuge for removing debris. All of them are covered in Post-it notes scrawled with prompts from the NHS standards on microbiology investigations. Guy watches over his shoulder as Grigor uses a spatula to transfer a small dollop of grey matter from a Petri dish to a stainless-steel aerosol can with a narrow neck. Next, he attaches a steel nozzle cap to the open top of the can.

He glances up at Guy, owl-eyed through the mask.

Guy nods.

Grigor takes the can carefully out of the safety cabinet and puts it on a crimping rack that resembles a bench-mounted corkscrew. He locks the can under the collet and pulls the handle down to seal it. Then he reaches down to the air compressor at his feet and switches it on. The needle on the right-hand gauge climbs to 140 psi and then automatically shuts off. Grigor picks up the pistol-grip nozzle and switches the dial on the left-hand gauge up to 95 psi, feeding air from the reservoir tank into the hose. He sets the sawn-off valve stem on the end of the pistol grip against the can's nozzle and presses the trigger. The can quickly fills with compressed air.

Finally, Grigor attaches a spray head to the can and offers it to Guy.

They leave the cave and walk back along the track, Guy gripping the aerosol like a relay baton. Alysha is waiting for them at the base of the tower wearing a matching CBRN suit and gas mask. She follows as he climbs the steps to the top of the tower where Kirsty is spread-eagled on the bed. The suicide vest has been removed and she is now tied to the bedposts with cable ties.

'For you this is a step change up from the suicide vest,' he tells her, though he's not sure if she can hear him through the mask.

She can barely manage a whisper. 'I fuckin' hate sci-fi.'

He chuckles. 'There is nothing extraordinary or fictional about death on a massive scale. The plague of Justinian in the sixth century killed 50 million people, half the world's population. The Black Death killed 200 million people in the fourteenth century. Smallpox killed 300 million in the twentieth century.'

He nods to Grigor, who goes around behind her and cups the back of her head in his gloves.

'You will not be forgotten.' He points the nozzle at her.

It shakes in his hands.

'I'm not looking for a legacy, pal.'

She struggles frantically.

He's pleased that she can hear him, after all. She deserves to know her fate. He presses down and sprays her face. She closes her eyes and mouth and attempts to look away, but Grigor's huge hands are gripping her head and twisting it back.

A cloud of vapour engulfs her.

Guy steps back while Grigor puts a gas mask over her head.

Now, she is zero – ready to be unleashed.

# 53

# The punchy trees

The jetty has long gone and the clubhouse that was at the centre of the campground has been flattened and replaced with an architect-designed house with larch cladding and a sod roof. Inside it has a wall of triple-glazed glass that looks out across the sea loch and the spine of a dark mountain on the opposite shore.

'We bought the site at auction,' the owner explains with a sweeping gesture that takes in the view of the water. He introduces himself as Christophe. He's barefoot and mannered with curly grey hair and a coral necklace. Jude can feel the warmth of the under-floor heating through the soles of his shoes. 'All we knew was that it had been derelict for more than twenty years. We saw an opportunity to build the house that we dreamed of. We didn't find out about the boy that drowned until later.' He shrugs. 'I don't know what we would have done if we'd known. She came here, the mother I mean, once a year, on the anniversary of his death. We think that she had been coming since it happened. She just wanted to stand down at the shoreline. Of course, we let her. We tried to behave sensitively. Then she stopped. I don't know why.'

'Do you have any outbuildings?' Tamar asks.

He shakes his head. 'No, we knocked everything down and we burned all the old canvas.'

'We'd like to fly a drone over the property.'

'Of course, you must.'

'Thank you.'

He raises his eyebrows at them. 'Do you think that Guy Fowle drowned the boy?'

'Why do you ask that?' Tamar asks.

He shrugs. 'Every unexplained death around here is now being attributed to Fowle. The locals believe that he started young. Fowle was here on a school trip when the boy died, it may have been his first murder . . .?'

'We don't know that.' For all his confidence, there is something dislikeable about Christophe. He keeps saying *we* but there's no sign of anyone else in the house. There's only one pair of wellingtons by the door.

'I'm not being ghoulish,' he responds, defensively. 'Or trying to profit from what happened. In fact, a man came here. He said that he was researching a book on Fowle, and he wanted to know about what happened. He seemed rather unsavoury, thuggish even, so I refused to speak with him.'

'Did he tell you his name?'

'He left a card. Shall I fetch it for you?'

'Please,' Tamar says.

They watch him pad across the room and through a door into what looks like a small recording studio. Tamar sighs. Jude goes over to the glass and stands beside a tripod-mounted telescope with an optical tube that looks large enough to house a warhead. He stares across the mile-wide stretch of water at the narrow strip of habitable land beneath the barren scree slopes of the mountains. It looks like a precarious existence. There are no villages as such but there are houses dotted along the shore that must be connected by a road, although he can see no traffic moving. After the last visible house there is a forested gap and then a grove of extremely tall, dark trees cupped by a mountain. After them, the shoreline runs out and is replaced by a sheer cliff that follows the promontory to its end.

Jude frowns. It's there on the tip of his tongue. He just can't bring it to mind right now.

He changes the declination of the telescope so that it is on the horizontal and swivels it so that it is pointing at the distant grove of trees. Looking through the eyepiece, he adjusts the focus. The tall trees with their distinctive rust-red bark and lush green foliage leap into view. They are in a natural bowl in the side of the mountain. Almost hidden at the centre of the grove, he sees a stone tower.

'Punchy trees!'

'What?' Tamar says.

Jude looks up at her. 'The bark of giant redwoods is soft. You can punch it.'

'What are you doing?' Christophe demands from the doorway, with a card in his hand.

Jude points across the water. 'Who owns that place?'

'I don't know. It's been derelict for years.'

Tamar shows him a prison photo of Grigor Muir. 'Is that the man who came to see you?'

'Yes,' Chris says, 'that's him.'

Jude is already out the door, striding towards the police officers standing by their Trojan BMW and pointing across the water. 'Take us there.'

Jude is agitated, his knees trembling and his fingers beating staccato on his thighs as they drive down a single-track road full of potholes with lichen-covered trees on one side and a rocky shoreline strewn with kelp on the other.

They pull over into a passing place to allow a postal van to pass but encounter no other traffic. Jude feels the heightened consciousness of someone who may be driving towards a battle. He needs the weapons from the lock box in the boot of the car, but he can't risk alerting the police officers to the potential danger. He needs them to deliver him as close as possible to the tower.

His phone vibrates. A video with an accompanying text:

Watch this

He's suddenly cold, his blood pressure dropping even before he holds out the phone so that Tamar can also see.

'Go on,' she says, gripping his upper arm.

He presses play.

Kirsty is soaking wet in a suicide vest. Behind her there is a silvery foil backdrop and Jude imagines Fowle just out of view. It's unbearable, watching her struggle to focus and slurring her words.

'Pull over.'

He stumbles out of the car and down on to the beach, where he throws up what little food there is in his stomach. Dry heaves. Afterwards, he straightens up and wills himself to concentrate on deep breathing. Filling his belly and chest. In for a count of four and out for six.

Four more full deep breaths.

He turns and looks back at Tamar. Whatever it is that she sees in his face, he can tell that it scares the hell out of her, as it should. She should be terrified.

'Let's go,' he says.

She raises her arm. He sees that she is pointing a taser at him. 'You're not going anywhere.'

'Don't be ridiculous!'

'It's a trap.'

'I know that. I need to get in there before this place turns into a circus and a lot more people die, including Kirsty.'

'It's you I care about. I'm sorry, Jude.'

She fires.

Five excruciating seconds of contractions and then a stumble; he falls to his knees.

Tamar moves around behind him and cuffs his wrists.

# 54

# Decision point

'I know you! You were intent on charging in there,' Tamar says as she unlocks the handcuffs. Jude strides across the Forestry Commission car park towards a command trailer, shaking the blood back into his wrists. It's more than two hours since he was tasered and he's still feeling nauseous. Tamar catches up with him as they pass a Royal Engineer search team from 33 EOD who have finished checking the site and are packing up their equipment. 'You're no use to anyone, least of all Kirsty, if you get yourself killed in a pointless act of bravado.'

Ignoring her, he nods to one of the guards at the foot of the steps to the trailer, who moves aside to let them enter. Inside, Major General Giles Munro, the skull-faced Director Special Forces, is standing in front of a collage of Ordnance Survey maps, title plans, satellite and orthomosaic drone images and other telemetry with one of his squadron commanders from Hereford beside him.

'Hello, Jude.'

'If you go in there hard, Kirsty is likely to die,' Jude tells him, walking to the map. He sees that the tower is named in the Land Registry as Feall-Fholach and according to the boundary positions covers a hundred and twenty acres of forest, open parkland, and mountainside. It is the southernmost property on the western shore of a barren and rocky promontory like the spine of a lizard that reaches down into the Firth of Clyde on one side and a sea loch on the other. He sees that there is only one route in: a single-tracked B road on the western side that rises and dips with the contour lines, hugging the shoreline at the base of the mountain. It cuts through a narrow strip of old-growth forest and ends at the tower.

'Sit down, Jude,' Munro replies, calmly. They know each other well. Munro commanded Jude in Helmand a decade before. 'I'd like your perspective. Tea?'

Tamar nods but Jude shakes his head impatiently.

'Corporal Calderwood!'

A soldier sticks his head through a hatch.

'One tea, please, for the detective inspector.'

'Aye, boss.'

They sit at a fold-down table. Calderwood brings Tamar a milky tea in a cardboard cup and three sugar sachets, which she shakes into it.

'It's a cul-de-sac that ends in a sheer cliff,' Munro tells them. 'We've blocked the entrance to the sea loch on the west side with Royal Marine patrol boats from Faslane and we've dropped unattended ground sensors on the ridgeline above the tower to the east. We control the key terrain.'

'There's no escape route,' Jude says. 'That's not like Fowle. Are you sure he's there?'

'We have some initial data from a Watchkeeper drone operating at high altitude. The thickness of the walls and the roof of the tower mean that we can't distinguish individuals; however, passive infra-red imaging suggests the presence of a diffuse heat source spread across the top two floors of the building. Somebody is at home.'

'And expecting us to come calling . . .'

'Ground-penetrating radar and 3D laser scanning have identified areas of freshly turned soil and buried objects on the verge of the approach road from the north, on the path leading in from the beach, and beside a metal bridge behind the tower. We suspect that these contain explosive devices.'

'Fowle is adept at canalising forces into choke points,' Jude tells him. 'By closing off the only viable approach routes he is channelling you into pe-prepared kill zones.'

'I understand the threat he poses,' Munro replies. 'And the weapons that he is armed with.'

Jude points to pale lines on a Lidar scan that lead over the bridge and into a narrow re-entrant in the mountain. 'Those are tyre tracks?'

'The Registry records the location of a cave large enough for several vehicles,' Munro acknowledges. 'You should also know that the property has been owned by a limited holding company in the Caymans since the late 1990s when, as you know, Fowle was based in Hereford. We can't prove it yet, but I think we must assume that either Fowle or one of his followers owns it.'

'Which gives him a further five years before he left for Iraq to have prepped the site,' Jude says.

'Yes.'

'Fuck,' Tamar says.

'Fuck indeed,' Munro replies. 'You will therefore understand why I am reluctant to commit to an assault.'

Jude bristles. 'I can feel a *but* coming . . .'

'The Prime Minister is understandably eager to establish whether Guy Fowle, and your friend Kirsty McIntyre, are on the site. We have significant military assets committed in Argyll, both here and at Faslane. Add to that the forces deployed in Latvia and our losses at Sizewell, and we're beginning to look thin on the ground in London and the rest of the country.'

'Which is probably what Fowle intended,' Tamar says.

'Yes.' He looks at Jude. 'Has Fowle been in touch with you?'

'Not since he sent me the video,' Jude replies.

'Cellphone towers are sparse here so it's difficult to triangulate but I'm told that the video was sent from this general area.'

'But not necessarily by Fowle,' Tamar says.

'Fowle or someone who has the phone that he has been using to communicate with you,' Munro acknowledges. 'Either way, I'm under orders to find out.'

'I'll speak to the Prime Minister,' Jude says, getting to his feet again.

Munro gives him an evaluating look. 'He sounded like his mind was made up when I spoke to him.' He pauses before speaking again. 'I know you're both as equally bone-headed as each other.'

'We'll see.'

Jude leaves the trailer and walks over to the far side of the car park, phone in hand.

Lee answers on the third ring. 'Jude?'

'Prime Minister.'

'How are you? Don't give me a bullshit answer.'

The question unmoors Jude. He's in pieces. The only reason that Kirsty might still be alive is that she has not yet fulfilled her role in his debasement.

'You can't order an assault.'

'We don't have the luxury of time necessary for a siege,' Lee replies. 'I need to know if Fowle is there. Because if he's not there, he's probably here.'

'It's a trap,' Jude tells him. 'An ambush.'

'You know the only answer to an ambush,' Lee tells him, sadly. 'You need to fight through it.'

'People will die.'

'I know that, Jude,' he says, solemnly. 'That's the burden of command.'

'Let me go in there,' Jude tells him. 'It's me that Fowle wants, not Kirsty.'

'Absolutely not. Giles Munro has orders to keep you under close observation. If you stray from your assigned role he will detain you, by force if necessary. That's it. I'm sorry, Jude, but my mind is made up.'

Lee ends the call.

Tamar is watching him. 'I'm going back to London,' she says. 'I've done everything I can to stop you making a fool of yourself. It's up to you now.'

He nods. He won't meet her eyes.

# 55

# Lee the Confessor

Lee is standing at the ironing board in boxer briefs with jumping Santa Clauses on them. There is something about his uncharacteristic stillness, the absence of strut and martial hand puppetry, that makes Bala, who is sitting at the breakfast bar, look up from her laptop.

He looks desperately sad, like a lost child.

'What is it, darling?'

He glances at her and then out beyond the dark mass of the Downing Street garden towards the floodlights at Horse Guards Parade where the helicopter gunship is parked.

'Tonight, I watched a video sent by Fowle of a young woman in a suicide vest, who looked out of her mind, reading out a threat.'

'I'm sorry.'

'By rights, I shouldn't be here.'

She sighs. She's not unfamiliar with soothing fragile men. 'If it's a mandate you want, call a general election. Darling, you've got Guy Fowle cornered in Scotland. Just catch him or kill him. Then we are assured a victory.'

'Fowle's the problem.'

He has her attention. He clearly wants to unload his conscience. She closes her laptop. 'How is he the problem?'

'He put me here.'

'Explain.'

'I don't want to lie to you. Not ever.'

'We all have secrets. I've kept one for most of my professional life.'

'That's different,' he says.

'Is it?'

'Guy Fowle cleared the path. He provided the financial information that caused Fabian Pees to pull out of the race and he timed the destruction of the sugar refinery so that Nigel Featherstone would withdraw, leaving me unopposed.'

'Are you sure?'

'Guy called me afterwards to congratulate me.'

'Who else knows?'

'Ezra and Amanda are dead, killed by Guy. Only Denzel. I'd trust him with my life.'

'There's no danger of it getting out?'

'Fowle is good at covering his tracks.' He stares at the ceiling. Bala has observed that high office has a habit of ageing men before their time and Lee is no exception. The lines on his forehead and around his eyes are deeper than even a week ago, as if he is being scoured by the tide of responsibility. 'I served under Fowle at Hereford. Not for long, mind, just a few weeks. Under different circumstances I'd have been termed a battlefield casualty replacement. I don't think he thought much of me. I was even louder then.' He smiles ruefully and her heart melts. 'I was posted soon after. But now he thinks I owe him my entire career.'

'What does he want?'

'To destroy the country, but from me all he wanted was the means to punish Jude Lyon.'

'That's it?'

'I gave him the details of Jude's friend, Kirsty McIntyre. I watched her delivering her final words tonight.'

'Oh, no.'

'It's my fault. I don't think I'll ever sleep again.'

'Every Prime Minister faces a moment when his mettle is tested,' she tells him. 'This is no different to any number of situations faced by your predecessors in Downing Street. It doesn't matter how you got here; everybody makes compromises on their way to the top. What matters is what you do while you're here in No. 10. When you have the power. I've told you before that you don't get long. You need to hold your nerve and do what you promised me.' She smiles encouragingly. 'The chance to carve out our own destiny: to build a new nation out of the ashes of the old.'

He laughs. 'I was cunt-struck. I'd have promised you anything.'

'I don't have a cunt, darling. Not yet.'

He winces. 'I'm sorry.'

She jumps down off the stool and walks over to stand before him. 'You're a strong leader, Lee, decisive and assured. People believe in you, and they trust you. Don't shake your head at me. The polling says so. The country is amid a crisis that it has never faced before, and the people are relying on you to steer them through it unscathed. They need your full attention.'

He nods his head, thinking about it. 'You're right. I can't give up now. Not until the country is safe again.'

'That's more like it. The Lee I know and love.'

'You win.'

'You need to issue orders that Fowle is killed and not captured. It makes perfect sense. Alive, he's a magnet for every apocalyptic conspiracy nut on the planet. Tell them to dump his body in the ocean like they did with bin Laden. After that you're in the clear.' She cups his balls in her hand and gently squeezes. 'Remember Fowle doesn't have you by the short and curlies, I do.'

He grins. 'You really should marry me.'

'You're too impulsive,' she tells him. 'It's a political vulnerability.'

'It's a proposal!' He claps his hands together. 'I can get them to open the registry office. It's a matter of national importance. We could do it tonight!'

She laughs. 'I'll think about it.'

# 56

# The assault

Just after one a.m., an unregistered mobile phone is switched on at Feall-Fholach on the Argyll coast and its transceiver automatically begins searching for the nearest cell tower. Instead, it is captured by a digital receiver system on board the circling Watchkeeper drone, which is jamming all other receivers. The drone is immediately able to use the control link as a listening device, recording anything in the vicinity of the phone. Within seconds, voice analysis is comparing the audio with samples on the GCHQ servers.

Giles Munro grips Jude's shoulder and he opens his eyes and sits up in the chair that he has been sleeping in. Munro hands him headphones and watches while he listens to the recording. He doesn't need voice analysis to recognise that it is Guy Fowle: he's talking quietly to another person but there's tautness in his voice that Jude hasn't heard before.

'I've waited long enough. If he doesn't come by morning, I'm going to activate Grom.'

'What does than even mean?'

It's Kirsty. Her voice is slurred and hard to understand but it's her. Defiant as ever. At least she is alive and for that Jude gives thanks. He hears footsteps on stone flagstones. When Fowle next speaks, he is further from the phone. 'Maybe I'll let you live long enough to witness it.'

'We can prevent Fowle sending an activation message by phone,' Munro says, 'but he may have other means of mobilising illegals. I need to inform the Prime Minister.'

Seconds later, the drone intercepts a text message intended for Jude and forwards it to him:

I'm waiting. Come alone.

Thirty minutes later, Munro sits down beside Jude and says, 'The Prime Minister has given the order. We're going in.'

The phosphors in Jude's night-vision goggles give the ancient forest an eerie green glow.

He is moving through the trees with the squadron command group and a tactical air control team. Just ahead of them is an extended line of black-clad SAS troopers who are advancing slowly and painstakingly through the thick undergrowth of bracken, briars, and mossy stones towards the tower. The infra-red lasers on their assault rifles flick left and right, and up and down, as they search for potential targets. Jude is carrying an assault rifle and has a pistol in a holster on his thigh. He's wearing a Kevlar vest with an anti-stab layer and over it a tactical vest with pouches stuffed with extra magazines and flash-bang stun grenades.

'No one goes in there unarmed,' Munro had told him, before giving the order to issue him the weapons. 'We don't carry baggage.'

In addition to the command net in his left ear, Jude has a live feed from the phone inside the tower relayed by the drone in his right ear. There has been no audible activity in the tower since Fowle threatened to activate Grom.

Abruptly, the line stops and Jude crouches beneath an oak draped in ferns.

The Watchkeeper drone is flying high enough to be inaudible and the other mixed air assets including an Apache helicopter gunship, a Typhoon multi-role combat jet and a fresh-out-of-its-wrapping Wedgetail early warning aircraft are somewhere out over the Irish Sea. In addition to the two troops of SAS approaching through the forest, a troop from the Special Boat Service is swimming across the sea loch and the third SAS troop, with the squadron's best snipers, has climbed the ridgeline five hundred metres above them to provide fire support.

Jude has received an assurance from Munro that every effort will be made to preserve Kirsty's life but given that their orders are to kill and not capture Fowle, he's not setting much store by it.

The squadron commander whispers into his throat mic and the soldiers commence their advance through the trees. They are all painfully conscious of Guy Fowle's talent for ambush and equally conscious that if there are casualties, the only extraction will be lengthy, overland and on foot. In Basra in 2004, Fowle initiated an undetectable bomb under a helicopter full of casualties at take-off, killing everyone inside it.

No one wants a repeat of Basra, except Fowle.

They stop just short of the edge of the treeline. Ahead of them is a meadow with an obstacle course of static caravans raised on blocks, creating hard-edged shadows amid the glow-in-the-dark grass. Beyond the caravans is the towering grove of redwoods like black sentinels guarding the medieval five-storey tower.

They all know that the next step is likely to provoke a response.

Jude feels a searing clarity: all his senses prickling, attuned to the faintest sounds and smells, the dampness of the moss and the branches above him soughing in the breeze.

You rarely live more fiercely than in the moments before combat.

Munro orders the advance.

The point man rises. A forward air controller makes to follow but Jude puts out his hand and stops him. The trooper steps out into the meadow.

It's like tripping an invisible wire.

Thunderous noise.

Jude's goggles are washed with bright light.

A chainsaw roar as a minigun in the tower scythes right to left along the treeline and back again. Foliage and wood splinters rain down on their heads. A second minigun aimed at the shoreline opens fire. In Jude's right ear, he can hear shell casings cascading onto flagstones.

A flare shoots high into the sky and explodes into a blinding white star that drifts across the forest.

Jude flips his goggles up. His fears are realised as the assault force returns fire, tracer converging on the top-floor window of the tower from multiple sources: the edge of the forest, the sniper positions on the mountain and the SBS troop on the shore.

The chances of Kirsty surviving are fast diminishing.

He crawls forward across jumbled rocks, snaking his hips and dragging himself on his elbows, to the edge of the treeline where he finds the point man, who has miraculously survived, clinging to the ground beneath the relentless fire.

'Wait,' Munro tells them. He's counting on the rate of fire of the multi-barrelled guns– several thousand rounds a minute – exerting a limit. There can only be so much ammunition in the tower. After four minutes the guns stop firing.

'Ceasefire,' Munro commands.

In the eerie calm that follows, the only sound is the electric whirr of the empty guns sweeping back and forth and the occasional pop of a flare fired from inside the tower.

A quick headcount reveals that there are no casualties.

'Move!'

Jude shrugs off the blanket of debris. Troopers rise from beneath the shredded trees either side of him and advance at a crouch across the meadow into the caravan park.

Moments later, the first IED explodes: a blast wave of sound. A caravan is propelled into the air and crashes down in pieces. Fragments whistle overhead. Jude doesn't understand how the aerial surveillance can have missed so much metal.

'This is Two Zero Alpha; Sunray is down. Sunray is down.'

The squadron commander is a casualty.

'Two Zero Alpha, you now have command,' Munro says.

Over the command net, he hears that 33A, the squadron sergeant major, is also dead, and through the trees, he sees shadows flitting across the moonlit spaces between the caravans. They are still advancing.

A burst of laughter from inside the tower.

Two other caravans detonate in quick succession.

Almost overwhelmed by a sense of jeopardy, Jude takes several deep breaths. He must rescue Kirsty before the tower is completely destroyed. He sprints across the silvery, moonlit grass with his heart pumping and his skin burning.

# 57

# The burning tower

Jude reaches the nearest caravan alive. Edging forward in the darkness with his fingers running along the caravan's lower rim, he eventually finds what he's looking for: an infra-red motion sensor covering a choke point between two caravans. He traces the wiring that runs from it under the caravan and uses the multi-tool from his belt to cut it.

He advances to the corner, crouches and risks a swift glance through the drifting smoke. By flare light, he can see the ragged edges of a crater surrounded by debris. Beside the crater, a trooper is lying on his back with his mouth open but no sound coming out. Jude waits for the flare to go out and dashes over to the casualty, dropping to the ground beside him. Jude's hands slide through spurting arterial blood into a deep hole in the man's thigh. He pulls a plastic pouch out of the trooper's tac-vest and tears it open, removing the haemostatic bandage. He presses the gauze firmly against the wound for sixty seconds while the blood-clotting agent takes effect. He then stabs the trooper in the other thigh with one of his morphine auto-injectors and holds him until he feels the drug take hold. He flips down his night-vision goggles and looks left and right through the tubes. To his right, he sees a soldier on one knee with a launch tube on his shoulder. The missile streaks out of the tube and detonates against the top floor of the tower.

Cursing, Jude springs up and runs past the crater, veering away from an inviting gap between two caravans for fear of activating another sensor. Instead, he rolls under the caravan and crabs side-ways past fertiliser bags full of pottery shards that Fowle has used to create non-detectable fragments for the IEDs.

When Jude comes out the other side, he sees that the top of the tower is in flames. Moments later, a missile fired from the shoreline hits the third floor and the machine-gun stops firing. In one ear, he can hear Munro ordering an assault team to breach the tower. In the other, he can hear Kirsty screaming. There is another explosion somewhere to his left. Pottery shards puncture the side of the caravan and clods of earth rain down on him.

He gets up and runs around the back of a caravan and over to a redwood, its soft, fibrous bark embedded with pottery like a votive offering. He reaches it just as a four-person assault team reach the doorway at the base of the tower. He watches the team leader attach a charge to the hinges, insert the detonator in the end cap and spool out the firing cable as he slides away from the door with his back to the tower. When they are all clear, the team leader crouches down, pulls the safety pin out and presses the firing button.

The blast bounces the door inwards against the iron grille behind it and then outwards onto the gravel. The assaulters lean in from both sides, post grenades through the grill and get clear again. Jude sees the flash and the cloud of smoke that rolls out of the tower. He can hear movement in his right ear.

Two grenades drop out of a second-floor window and bounce off the ground in different directions. Jude ducks back into cover behind the redwood.

Two explosions in quick succession.

Seconds later, Jude is joined by the three surviving members of the assault team. One of them has multiple wounds on his torso and arms. While he's being treated, the team leader takes more shaped charges out of his pack. They'll need them to blow the grille to gain access to the building.

'Come on, Jude,' Fowle says in Jude's ear. 'I'm waiting for you.'

Two more grenades go off, closer to the redwood. Down on the shoreline, there is a much larger explosion. Over the radio, he learns that the SBS team has used a Bangalore torpedo to blow a path through the thickets of brambles.

'I have to get in there,' Jude shouts, tapping his chest and pointing at the tower.

The team leader nods and speaks into his throat mike, enunciating each word with precision for the air control team because he can't hear his own voice.

They leave the wounded trooper propped against the tree and the team leader switches the magazine on his rifle for a fresh one. Jude checks the pins on his grenades and heels the magazine on his rifle with his hand to check it is seated properly. He hears the thump of helicopter blades. The team leader counts off his fingers: five, four, three, two, one . . .

An Apache gunship skims above the surface of the lock and one after another, two missiles flash from beneath its stunted wings, striking the windows on the first and second floors. The team leader runs towards the gate with Jude following and attaches the charges to the hinges while Jude empties a magazine into the darkness of the hallway, and they are both showered with fragments of rock from above. The team leader grabs Jude by the collar and drags him to one side.

He pulls the pin and presses the button. The gate crashes inwards. They post grenades in after it.

Two dull thumps.

Fowle is laughing in Jude's ear.

The team leader fires a burst into the dust and heads. Jude follows, sliding along a wall, stumbling over a pile of wellington boots and finding the spiral staircase by falling into it.

Something is tumbling down the stairs towards him. A grenade bounces over his head and out of sight. He scrambles upwards, trying to get above it and around the curve.

The grenade explodes. More dust. His eyes are raw with grit but thanks to the goggles he can still see.

If Kirsty is still alive, she's somewhere close. He pulls a flash-bang out of his vest, removes the pin, and lobs it up and around the curve of the stair onto the next landing. After the flash and an ear-splitting bang, he charges upwards.

The door to the first-floor room is open and Fowle is staggering backwards, flash-blinded and disorientated. Jude hits him in the face with the butt of his rifle. He hits him again, in the mouth.

Smashed ivory. He hits him again, driving him into the well of a window. Fowle stumbles and trips. Dropping his rifle on its sling, Jude grabs Fowle's legs and tips him up and out the window.

Except Fowle is still laughing.

Jude spins around. There's no one else there, just tangled sleeping bags and scattered clothing covered in rock dust, piles of unused grenades in the embrasures.

'Come on, little piggy!'

He heads back to the stairs and climbs another storey with his rifle raised, throwing a flash-bang ahead of him. The second floor is a makeshift kitchen, a strip of it from the window surround to the far wall chewed up by cannon rounds. He can hear the hiss and pop of burning timber from higher up the tower.

He uses the last of his flash-bangs on the third floor. There is a gaping hole in the wall and rubble spread across the floor from the missile strikes. He climbs another storey, the smoke getting darker and thicker the higher he gets. He shifts his rifle behind him on its sling and draws his pistol.

Fowle is still laughing, just a few feet away.

He eases himself into the room, which is dominated by a four-poster bed. Reaching across the bed, he grabs a phone taped to a digital recorder with Fowle's laughter coming out of it. He throws it against the wall, smashing it, and the noise in his right ear goes quiet.

He climbs the final staircase with his eyes streaming and sticks his head just above the level of the floor. The rafters are on fire. It looks as if the roof may be about to collapse. Flipping up his goggles, he sees that there is a thin strip of air about a foot high with dense black smoke above it. He spots the legs of the bed and crawls towards it. Reaching it, he gropes above his head, patting the mattress, trying to find her. The bed is empty. Kirsty's not in the tower.

He crawls back and stumbles down the stairs, coughing. At some point an assault team passes him, coming the other way. At the bottom, he goes out through the shattered doorway and gasps for air. The prisoner is kneeling handcuffed on the gravel. His shirt is ripped revealing a stag's horns tattoo and there is a black cloth bag over his head.

Jude rips the bag off his head and flings it away.

His face is a mess. It's uncanny. It could almost be Fowle, but it is not.

'You are Jude Lyon,' the look-alike says with a mid-European accent and spits blood on the ground. He looks up and smiles triumphantly through a shark's maw of broken teeth.

'Where's Kirsty?' Jude demands.

There is a huge explosion from the mountainside.

# 58

## In the hole with the Dark Friends

When Jude reaches it, the approach to the Bailey bridge has been taped off because it's booby-trapped, and he is forced to wade across the river to reach the other side. The water is fast and freezing, reaching his chest when he is midway across. He is thankful for the rope line decorated with fluorescent glow-sticks that the engineer search team have rigged across the river, which is all that prevents him from being swept away.

He catches up with the troop shivering within sight of the entrance to the cave. It's still burning inside, smoke billowing into the narrow passage, and they're all bracing themselves for something to lunge out of it. The troop commander is waiting for orders. One of the soldiers passes a thermos lid down the line and Jude takes a sip of hot, sweet tea.

'It's colder than a witch's tit,' a trooper grumbles. Jude is shaking and his teeth are rattling. They need to get moving soon or they will start going down with hypothermia.

After another five minutes, the troop commander gets his orders and issues the command to mask up. They rise and walk in a staggered line towards the cave, hugging the sides of the passage, full of the dread of darkness. As soon as they enter, visibility in the chamber is down to just a few feet. The troop divides into four-man patrols but only one moves forward to reduce the risk of blue-on-blue in the dark and murky space. They advance with Jude just behind them.

It's warm as an oven, and the water steams off their clothes.

'A lot of kit here,' says the point man.

Through the smoke, his barrel-mounted torch lights up the blackened hulk of a truck with its rims sunk in pools of molten rubber and a generator with what looks like an oxygen cylinder embedded in it like a spear. Jude can hear the crackle of a fire at one end of the cave.

They continue forward.

A sudden shift: a jet of flame and a buckle of noise.

The blast lifts his feet off the ground. He falls through the air in a stinging cloud of debris. He crashes to earth and curls into a ball. His whole body is engulfed in a shudder of panic. He can't die yet. Not before he's found Kirsty and freed her. He scrambles up onto his hands and knees. He's disorientated and his ears are ringing. Nevertheless, he staggers to his feet and lifts the barrel of his rifle, its torch barely penetrating the smoke.

He moves forward to the back of the cave.

The smoke parts and a huge spider with red-and-black jointed legs and sparkling compound eyes rushes towards him out of the darkness. Unnerved, he very nearly opens fire. Then he understands that it is a mural, the shadows of its legs painted in matt black on the grey rock to give it the illusion of movement. He points his torch at the floor and reveals that he is standing on the edge of a dark hole like a creature's throat with a ramp like a tongue

*It's Hell Down Here* is written in fluorescent green paint on the wall beside the ramp.

He descends with his rifle up into the aim, emerging under a layer of smoke where he can see more clearly, and removes his gas mask. Edging forward, he sees the gleam of railway tracks ahead and realises that the ramp leads to a tunnel under the mountain, but to travel it he must walk into the pink-and-white tentacles and suckers of a massive deep-sea squid.

He glances back but there is no one there and he decides to continue alone. He follows the narrow-gauge track, sweeping the ground with the torch ahead of his steps, as the glistening tentacles seethe with life on the walls beside him. It's getting hotter and it stinks of ammonia. He squeezes between the wall and a wooden-decked railway trolley beneath the squid's unblinking eye. Next, there is a crab with vast pincers, and then he finds what he's looking for: a trip wire at ankle height that extends the width of the tunnel. In an alcove at one side there is a stake with a fuse attached and two lines of explosive detonating cord running from it down the stake and into the ground. He assumes the main charge is buried beneath his feet and large enough to bring down the roof and seal the tunnel. He takes the tape out of his tac-vest and cuts a length to wrap around the fuse and hold the pin in place.

He has just finished a single turn around the top of the fuse when he hears a whisper of movement and a second later hundreds of bats whistle around him and disappear down the tunnel while he holds as tightly as he can onto the pin with his eyes closed. He can feel his entire body trembling. When they are gone, he exhales and continues wrapping the fuse in tape until the pin is secure. Then he cuts the trip wire with his knife. It's not easy because his hands are still shaking. He snaps a glow-stick to release the light and leaves it at the entrance to the alcove.

He continues. He begins to despair of ever reaching the end of the tunnel.

Further in, the murals are monochrome as if the artist had run out of colours. White streaks of paint on chiselled black stone in an increasingly abstract style: a skull-faced ferryman on the River Styx, the three-headed dog Cerberus lazing outside the gates of Hell, and an army of walking skeletons.

Then nothing but dark rock.

The tracks go up a shallow incline and down again. The thought of the weight of rock above him is increasingly disturbing.

He wonders if Guy has lured him into a trap with no exit.

He finds one more trip wire and disables it as he did the first and marks it with another glow-stick. It is a long way before he gets a taste of the outside. At first, it's a faint whisper of cool air, fading for a moment, then returning, then fading. He can't tell if he's imagining it. Then he feels a gust of cold air on his face, and the tension flows out of him. Soon after, he hears water lapping against rock. He emerges at the back of a large sea cave and walks out onto a stone wharf that must have been used to load illicit whisky two hundred years before. He takes a deep breath, drawing in the briny air. Through the mouth of the cave, he can see moonlight outside on the Firth of Clyde.

His radio, no longer blocked by the mountain, crackles into life.

'Whisky Six November this is Zero, send locstat over?'

'I'm on the far side of the mountain,' Jude replies. He knows now how Guy made his getaway, taking Kirsty with him. 'Send a boat.'

This is not the end.

# 59

# The Institute of Ultra-Pure Biopreparations

They have flown all night across the churning velvet of the ocean to reach the Siberian mainland and as the sun rises, they approach a charred and steaming wasteland.

Zombie fires that survived the winter underground and burned out of control all summer have stripped away the thin layer of vegetation that covered the melting permafrost. Hundreds of millions of acres have been permanently destroyed. As they reach the coast, Yulia can smell the rising methane in the air. After several hours flying east, they enter a region where there are icy outcrops amongst the recently burned steppe as if, in places, the snow held out against the fire.

And then there is just snow and rock.

They spot the first polar bear soon after, running in the same direction, tracking their shadow onto an icy promontory locked in sea ice. By the time they catch sight of the institute, a concrete-and-glass structure with a circular tower and cube-like main building, there are three polar bears converging on the landing zone.

While they are still airborne, the pilot lowers the ramp. Frigid air rushes the length of the cargo hold. Yulia watches as human figures with guns spill out of the box-shaped all-terrain vehicles below and form a defensive perimeter.

Perchlorate flares shoot into the sky, combust and drift downwards on parachutes.

The pilot's voice crackles over the intercom, 'Prepare to move.'

Beside Yulia, Dima and Alexei are unbuckling their harnesses and she does the same.

The helicopter yaws right and touches down. Even above the noise of the rotors, Yulia can hear the air-raid sirens that are being used to scare off the bears.

Dima is out first, drawing a handgun, which she doubts is sufficient to stop a charging bear. Next is Alexei, who shambles past the
fuel tanks and down the ramp towards the nearest ATV with his
head held high as if daring a bear to take him on. There are bears
everywhere, Yulia thinks – fey hackers with an anarchist agenda, a
defiant spymaster with a burnished and bloody history, and now
even the common-or-garden variety with teeth and claws.

They reach the ATV and climb into the driver's compartment
just as a whole frozen side of beef is thrown out the back of its
cargo trailer as an offering. Dima slams the door behind them,
and the ATV sets off. It's impossible to speak above the snarling
roar of the diesel engines and the clatter of the tracks. Looking
back through the steel-caged windows, Yulia sees the helicopter
lift off and the polar bears fighting over the beef.

She wonders if the helicopter will ever come back.

She opens her coat and takes off her gloves.

Five minutes later, they approach the base of the tower. As they
come close, the driver hits the horn, and a steel shutter rises. They
drive down a concrete ramp into the brightly lit interior of an
underground parking area. From there, an elevator carries them
swiftly to the top floor.

Professor Grachyov, the institute's administrator, is standing by
the curved glass window on the far side of his office with his hands
clasped behind his back. He is a small man wearing raised heels on
his shoes.

'I hope that the bears did not cause you too much distress,'
Grachyov says with a brittle smile that reveals his gleaming white
dentures. 'The melting ice makes it harder for them to catch their
usual prey. Necessity has made scavengers of them and as a conse-
quence they have become interested in the institute.'

'We are interested in the institute,' Alexei says, crossing over to
sit in Grachyov's chair and spreading his hands on the administrator's leather-topped desk.

'It is not usual for us to have visitors from the security services,'
Grachyov says warily, his swept-back hair shining.

'Really?' Yulia says. 'I would have thought that security was your highest priority.'

'It is, but our defences are technological in nature. There's no requirement for, how can I put it, your sort of methods here.'

'Except when it comes to protecting yourself against bears,' Alexei says.

Grachyov smiles uncertainly. 'They are becoming a nuisance.'

'What do you do here?' Alexei demands.

'The institute was set up to study and prevent the spread of pathogens that have been dormant in the permafrost and are now being released because of the changing climate.'

'What sort of pathogens?' Yulia asks.

'Zoonotic ones,' Grachyov replies. 'Our particular speciality is Influenza A.'

'Go on,' she says.

'The Influenza A virus is primarily an enteric virus of birds and secondarily a respiratory virus of mammals. We are close to a site where waterfowl have begun their annual migration for tens of thousands of years. Some travel to North America and others as far as southern Asia, Africa, and Europe.'

'And you hold stocks of influenza here?' Yulia asks.

'That is correct.'

'Has any of it gone missing?'

'Of course not.' Grachyov laughs as if the very idea was ridiculous. 'We have immaculate procedures for record-keeping, stocktaking, accident notification and emergencies. Plus, we are part of an international network of laboratories that share real-time data. It is unfortunate that our chief researcher Dr Zhidkov is away, or he could explain his work in detail.'

'Where is he?' Alexei growls.

'He was granted compassionate leave. Tragically, his wife has cancer.'

'When was this?' Yulia demands.

'A month or so ago.'

'Have you spoken to him since?'

'No.'

'We need to see his personnel file,' Dima says.

'And we need to see inside your laboratory,' Yulia adds.

Grachyov is outraged. 'That's impossible. By what authority?'

'The president,' Dima says. 'He will speak with you in five minutes.'

# 60

# Victor has flu

Yulia strips naked behind a rubber curtain in a gleaming white locker room and places her clothes and jewellery in a plastic tray. She dresses in white scrubs and a white skullcap, and steps out barefoot from behind the curtain, holding the tray.

Without his heels Grachyov is the same height as her. It's just the two of them: Alexei has chosen to remain in the professor's office with Dima. His last words to her were, 'Try not to get infected.'

'Put your tray in one of the lockers,' Grachyov tells her. 'There is no need to lock it.'

'Are you sure about that?' Yulia says.

He blinks at her. His chat with the president has made him nervous. 'Are you ready?'

'Yes.'

'We will progress through Levels 1 to 4,' he explains with his hand on a steel door handle. 'When I open the door, you will feel resistance. The negative air pressure keeps anything on the inside from escaping.'

The room beyond is bathed in ultra-violet light and there are balled white socks in a bucket on a bench. Yulia steps inside and the door closes behind her with a soft sigh. She feels the pressure change in her ears. She copies Grachyov as he pinches his noses and exhales.

They put on the socks and go through another door into a shower room where they chalk their hands and put on gloves. Grachyov tapes her wrists and ankles before attending to his own. On a clothes rack on the far side of the room there is a row of bright yellow bio-hazard suits with full-face visors on hangers.

'The positive-pressure entry suits provide the highest level of protection against aerosol-transmitted agents including vapours, gases, mists, and particles,' Grachyov explains. He selects a size small for her from the rack. 'Put that on.'

This must be what it's like getting into a spacesuit, she thinks, as she steps into the legs and tugs the rest of the body up around her.

'You may have an extreme reaction to the claustrophobia that the suit induces,' Grachyov says, speaking to her through a built-in microphone, while he zips her closed. 'I've known women to scream.'

'And men?'

He will not meet her eye. 'Yes, men also. Turn around.' She can feel his hand running across the suit, looking for snags or tears. He steps back. 'You're fine. Follow me.'

They enter an airlock via a bulkhead door with a circular hatch that they close behind them. Grachyov advances and opens the far airlock door. They step into a corridor, where he attaches an air hose to Yulia's suit and hands her a pair of rubber boots to put on.

'You are now in Level 4.' She is experiencing a hot flush all over her body. Professor Grachyov walks slightly ahead of her. 'For the last three years, Dr Zhidkov was excavating a nearby burial site at a seasonal settlement occupied by Neolithic hunter-gatherers. He believed that he might have found one of the primordial sources of influenza.'

They go through a door into a long, rectangular room with one wall taken up by a bank of large steel drawers covered in a thin layer of frost. The professor walks over to one of the drawers and pulls it out. There is a blackened mummified corpse crouched on the steel tray.

'This is Victor, Dr Zhidkov's collaborator, so to speak. Victor's body was preserved in the permafrost for eight thousand years. The distinctive posture is common to the burial practices of various nomadic groups across the region. We believe that he was the last human formally buried here before the settlement was abandoned for good, although there are signs of mass cremation that date to around the same time.'

'How did he die?'

'Analysis of nasal swabs revealed five different strains of the influenza virus. When you have multiple strains that infect the same person, they may swap genes and become more virulent, a process known as recombination. One of the strains that Dr Zhidkov analysed killed five out of ten small mammals in animal testing. It's probably what killed Victor and the rest of his group. It was prioritised for further study.'

'And you have stocks of that virus here?'

'Of course.'

'Show me.'

'Very well.'

They go through another airlock into a containment room and through another airlock into a laboratory. Yulia watches as he taps the entry code in a wall-mounted refrigerator, which clicks open. He removes a Petri dish from a tray and carries it over to a sealed biosafety cabinet.

'Viruses are intracellular parasites that require living cells to replicate,' Grachyov explains. 'We grow them in an animal broth, and they form a lawn on the bottom of the dish.'

He uses a pipette to transfer a drop from the Petri dish to a glass slide. He places a second slide over the top and the liquid spreads between them. He inserts it under a microscope and looks at it, his face mask pressing up against the eyepieces of the micro-scope. He gets up and motions for Yulia to sit.

She leans forward.

'Can you see them?' Grachyov says, and she can hear the tremor of excitement in his voice.

Through the microscope the virions look like many-legged woodlice jostling for position.

'They are beautiful,' Grachyov says. 'Killers that are only forty-millionths of an inch long. The protein spikes that cover them are particularly adept at infecting and copying themselves in the human airway.'

'What does that mean?'

'It means that if it was released it would spread like the common cold and kill like Ebola.'

'You need to do an immediate stocktake.'

Grachyov winces. 'As I explained to the president, there is absolutely no way that something could go missing from here without it triggering an international alert.'

'Do it,' she says. 'Or I will have you fed to the polar bears.'

'There is no need to speak to me like that, Yulia Ermolaeva.'

'There is every need.'

Grachyov goes over to the refrigerator and takes out a tray of Petri dishes. He puts it down on a steel bench beside the cabinet.

'This is the cultured stock of the Zhidkov variant of Influenza A that is used for scientific investigation.'

'Is it your entire stock?'

'We have frozen pellets kept at minus 80 degrees. But they are inert.'

'Show me.'

He taps the entry code in a freezer, which clicks open. He takes out a test tube and holds it up to the light. He wipes away a coating of frost and frowns. It contains what Yulia immediately recognises as an animal-shaped piece of frozen fruit gum.

'What is that?' Grachyov says.

'It's a gummy bear.'

*Bears everywhere.*

There are test tubes with yellow, green, orange, and purple gummy bears in them. Grachyov looks sufficiently appalled that Yulia thinks he may not have been an accessory to the theft. He gives Yulia a desperate look. 'What are we going to do?'

The alarm goes off and the room is filled with noise and flashing red light. Panicking, Grachyov disconnects his air hose and runs for the exit.

Yulia hesitates and then follows him. She gets to the airlock just as he is pulling it closed. She squeezes through the gap. As soon as the door is locked the nozzles start spraying them with soapy decontaminant. It's like being trapped in a car wash, buffeted with the suds obscuring her visor, and then rinsed with pressurised water.

Grachyov opens the far airlock door, and they stumble out into the locker room and strip off the suits. They go through the door into the ultra-violet light room and out into the laboratory beyond.

Dima clubs Grachyov with the butt of his pistol and grabs Yulia by the arm. 'Hurry! We must leave. The president has ordered the destruction of the institute.'

The ATV accelerates up the ramp as the shutter is rising. Dima is at the wheel with his foot on the pedal and Yulia and Alexei are on the bench seat beside him. They burst out, briefly airborne before the churning tracks hit the snow. Yulia is thrown forward against the dashboard.

'What happened?' she demands once she has righted herself.

'Zhidkov is a traitor,' Alexei growls, above the roar of the engines.

'He obtained permission to take his wife for treatment at a specialist cancer hospital in Abu Dhabi,' Dima shouts. 'We think her medical records were faked. The immigration authorities have confirmed that they arrived in Abu Dhabi, but they didn't show up at the hospital. They spent one night at the hotel they were booked in and then disappeared.'

'When?'

'Three weeks ago.'

Yulia looks out the side window and sees that a polar bear is running alongside them.

'We're too late,' she says.

Alexei puts his arm around her, and she leans into an embrace with her eyes closed. It seems unlikely that they will manage to outrun whatever manner of fury the president has unleashed.

# 61

# The doppelganger

'It's like a Swiss cheese,' is how one of the troop commanders describes the mountain over the ship's radio, after his troop has completed their search of the tunnel complex. 'We've found a cave full of bones.'

'More of Fowle's victims,' Munro says. He's standing, grim-faced, beside Jude in the operations room of a Duke-class frigate patrolling Holy Loch. 'The police forensics team is on their way.'

The pilot of a helicopter searching the Firth of Clyde has nothing to report.

'They could be hundreds of miles away by now,' Jude says.

Munro nods.

The officer of the watch informs them that the doctor has finished her examination of the prisoner. 'You can speak to him if you wish.'

'Bring him to the canteen in twenty minutes,' Munro says. 'I need some coffee.' He looks across at Jude. 'Have a shower. You smell like a bonfire.'

Twenty minutes later, Jude joins Munro in the ship's canteen. He has showered and exchanged his torn clothing for navy coveralls.

There is a television on the wall; an early-morning news bulletin has images from a news helicopter of the burning tower and the news that Guy Fowle, Alysha al-Sabbah, Grigor Muir and Kirsty McIntyre remain at large. Jemima Connick makes an appeal to the public to anyone sighting them, to contact the police immediately. They are armed and extremely dangerous, and not to be approached. It bothers Jude that there is no attempt to explain Kirsty's status as a prisoner.

The canteen door opens, and two Royal Navy police escort the prisoner, in shackles and navy coveralls, to their table. He shuffles the last few steps and sits opposite them.

They are staring at a dead man.

His name is Thomas Fischer, and he is a German national of 'unknown fate' who was kidnapped in Baghdad in June 2004. No 'proof of life' call was made, or videos released, and after ten years his family had him declared legally dead.

'Hello, Jude,' he says.

On the table in front of him, Munro has the results from a portable DNA sequencer on a tablet.

'Hello, Thomas,' he says.

The policemen have their hands on his shoulders.

Fischer sneers. 'I don't recognise that name.'

'What do you want us to call you?' Munro asks.

'Guy.'

He's the same height and build, same facial structure – Jude assumes that he was used as a double in Iraq – but he lacks the raw menace of Fowle. It's possible to look him in his cultist eyes and not feel panicked. Nevertheless, there is something about him that makes the skin crawl. There are razor cuts, raw scratch-marks, and crude tattoos visible on his hands, wrists and forearms that look self-inflicted. The photos of him naked, taken when the ship's doctor processed him, show the marks are all over his body but particularly concentrated around his genitalia.

'If you're Guy,' Jude says, calmly. 'Then you must know all the secrets?'

Fischer taps the side of his bruised and broken nose. 'Guy knows where the skeletons are buried.'

Unpleasant and smug.

'We would be very interested to hear about that,' Jude says. 'But first maybe you can explain where you have come from?'

He giggles and spits blood on the floor. 'Is this a test? You know Guy was in Syria with the gypsies for years.'

'How did you get here? There's no record of you entering the UK.'

He shrugs. 'Guy was in the jungle, man. You know, in Calais. Then Guy gets the word in the drafts box that the team is getting back together and comes here.'

'The team?'

'You know, Alysha and the others.'

'Others?'

'There are always other disciples. People who believe in the cause.'

'What cause?'

'That there are too many people in this world. That you must destroy to create.'

'People like Grigor Muir?'

Fischer hesitates as if the name is unfamiliar to him. Jude shows him a photo on the tablet that was taken in Barlinnie Prison just before Muir was released.

'Yes, him,' he says, nodding vigorously. 'He's a believer.'

'And what about Russians?'

'Yeah, sure, they're new.'

'Where are they?' Giles demands.

He shakes his head in mock sorrow. 'I would love to tell you. But I can't. Operational security and all that stuff.'

'What about Kirsty McIntyre?' Jude asks.

'You should use my name if you want an answer.'

'Where is she, Guy?'

He nods in approval. 'Good question. Very good question. She has a very important role to play. History will not forget her.'

'What does that mean?'

Fischer tips his head to one side. 'Guy is grateful to you for introducing him to Kirsty and he has found an appropriate role for her. Her death will be a catalyst for change. She will make you proud.'

'You don't know where she is,' Jude says. 'Guy wouldn't trust you with that kind of information. You're nothing to him.'

'That's not true.'

'You've just spent more than a decade waiting for him while he was locked up and then he strides back into your life for a few weeks, and now you're about to get locked up again.'

275

'I had an important role to play.'

'Guy left you here for his own amusement. You added a couple of minutes extra entertainment while his voice recording did the work.'

'I'm the one that's laughing,' Fischer says. 'Just imagine what he's doing to your girlfriend now . . .'

Jude lunges across the table at Fischer as the police pull him away and Munro grabs Jude in a neck hold.

# 62

# Under the arches

Guy Fowle returns to London in the passenger seat of an anonymous white van with cloned plates and inner-city scuffmarks. Beside him at the wheel is the teuchter-giant Grigor Muir, disgraced medic and brazen cuckold to Angus Fowle, the laird of Breothadh. Guy is content to let Grigor take the credit for being his father: it puffs the deluded fool's pride and keeps him loyal.

Grigor is not his father. His aura is the wrong colour.

They come off the motorway south of Birmingham and change the plates.

There are fewer signs of damage in London than Guy would have liked: roadworks on the M1 repairing the crater caused by a truck bomb, a few boarded-up banks and the charred hulk of a mosque, a glimpse of the skeletal tip of the Gherkin at Bishopsgate before they turn east and head towards Bethnal Green. He wanted more. The city is a more challenging adversary than he anticipated. Its density, the proximity of industrial and residential terrain, the layers and inter-connectedness, the cheek-by-jowl living, the very qualities that caused the Grom attacks to be so effective, setting off cascades of knock-on effects, are also how the city can shift and realign its purpose, proving the resilience of its people, bouncing back from adversity.

Not this time.

There's a truly wild moment coming, a day of misrule.

Half the world dead.

Beyond Weavers Fields, they go through a tunnel under a railway viaduct and turn left into a narrow street with a twelve-foot-high brick wall on one side and rows of commercial units built into the arches on the other. The arch that Grigor hired for an entire year at a modest cost is located between an auto crash repair centre and a shop-fittings salesroom with a curved window full of naked, sexless costume dummies. The arch has a private front yard secured with barbed steel railings and a steel-mesh gate. Beyond the gate, the unit has two side-by-side entrances, one large enough for the van with a roller shutter and the other for pedestrian access. Grigor rolls down the window, opens a small metal flap on a free-standing pillar and presses a button. The gate opens and the van rolls forward into the yard. Grigor peers up at a camera above the shutter and waves. Seconds later it starts to roll up.

'I warn you, they're a dour bunch,' Grigor tells him as they drive into the enclosed arch and the shutter closes behind them. They park alongside a police van in Battenberg-pattern yellow-and-blue livery. The headlights reveal a second police van behind the first on the left and a line of three shipping containers down the other side of the space. There is an unrendered breezeblock wall at the back with a door in it. Near the wall is a folding table and chairs with a stack of black Pelican cases beside it.

Grigor switches off the lights and they wait in darkness for a few seconds before overhead strip lighting comes on and two four-person teams from GRU Spetznaz Unit 29155 emerge from the nearest container and stand in a line to greet him. He has memorised their real names, which are written along with their cover names and their biographies in his Moleskine notebook.

The four-person assault team is led by Anatoly, whose Hero of the Russian Federation award is only to be found inscribed on the memorial wall of the Far Eastern Military Command School. With him are Maksim and Yaroslav, who were blooded in the Donbass where they were known as 'little green twins', and the only woman, Vera, who infected a Bulgarian arms manufacturer with a neurotoxin in his bed. The four-person fire-support team is led by Sulim, whose Hero of the Federation inscription is on the memorial wall at Southern Military Command. With him are three Ossetians, Ukhsar, Dzantemir and Vano – veterans of conflicts in Chechnya and Georgia, from the now disbanded Special Battalion Vostok.

They are all graduates of the Russian Military Diplomatic Academy, known as the GRU Conservatory, where they were trained in foreign languages and dialects as part of overseas insertion and infiltration operations. They have manufactured identities, backstories and social networks that have stood up to scrutiny. For the last three years they have been working as illegals in the Metropolitan Police, National Air Traffic Services, Network Rail, the National Grid, the British Army, the Royal Navy, the London Fire Brigade, and Imperial College Healthcare NHS Trust. They have been English through and through. They have chosen to ignore the recall message sent to their inboxes by the GRU in favour of a more personal message from Guy Fowle that carries greater risk with the promise of much greater reward.

He gets out of the van and stands before them, an apex predator. He can feel the hunger and excitement, as if whatever appetite brought them here will soon be satisfied. They know that they might not survive – they've lived with that all their professional lives – but he has offered them wealth beyond their dreams. Better than a handshake from the president and a few scratches on a wall somewhere far from Moscow.

Behind him, Grigor opens the back door of the van and Alysha jumps out. She stands at Guy's side and immediately, predictably scowls at Vera.

'Where do you want her?' Grigor asks, lifting Kirsty, who is wearing a suit and a gas mask, from the back of the van. The twins take her out of Grigor's arms and carry her to one of the containers, which has been converted into a soundproof cell.

Guy is sitting in a folding chair under the arch surrounded by open Pelican cases with tandem-warhead anti-tank missiles and bunker-busting thermobaric weapons resting in foam inserts. On the folding table beside him, there is a pile of 25-gauge needles in sterile packaging, plus a 1ml syringe, a packet of gauze swabs and a bottle of rubbing alcohol. Within reach is a rubber-topped vial with 25ml of clear liquid: fifty doses of the vaccine.

There is an empty chair facing him and the Russians are lined up in front of it ready to receive their vaccinations.

Guy says, 'Who will step into my lair?'

'I'm first up,' Vera says in perfect Estuary English.

She sits and rolls up her sleeve. She's pretty in a hard-angled way, and taut as a gymnast. He tips the alcohol on a swab and leans forward, his knee between her thighs, pressing the swab to the hard muscle of her deltoid. She holds his gaze, even though she's been given the standard warning: *avoid direct eye contact, sudden movements, or antagonistic facial expressions.*

The bold ones don't listen. It excites him.

He leans across to the table, thigh to thigh, the weight of his penis pressing against Vera's knee. He breaks open the pack containing the first needle and despite the tremors, he manages to draw 0.5 ml of liquid into the narrow syringe and stab it in her arm.

She doesn't flinch.

'There,' he says, and leans back, while her hand slides across the inside of his thigh and the length of his penis, 'all done.'

He does the other seven Russians. They've been briefed that the vaccine will not reach full effectiveness for fourteen days. Once their job is done here today in London and the money is in their accounts, they need to get as far away from the city as possible.

It's a piece of theatre. Alysha is the only one of them who knows that the liquid in the vial is saline.

There is no vaccine.

# 63

# Smoking hole

Lee and Bala are chatting to the team from *Gardeners' Question Time* ahead of a special broadcast with a carefully vetted audience from the gardens at Downing Street.

'We have to give the impression that we are on top of the situation,' Bala told him that morning as she talked him through his diary before going off to deliver her daily briefing to the parliamentary lobby. 'That there is some relief from the general awfulness. And what could be more reassuring than *GQT*?'

The general awfulness being that Guy Fowle is on the loose and a significant proportion of the UK's military forces, that are not either in Latvia or on their way there (or generally malingering), have been tied up in a military operation that has been revealed as an elaborate but predictable ruse.

And he's the most likely next target.

He is telling the *GQT* team that his dad – *bless his soul* – grew dahlias and kept them on top of an electric storage heater until early June, which was the earliest they could be planted in their garden up north without the risk of frost damage.

'He used to call them riotous pops of colour.'

His dad also used to say, 'life goes on', but only when he was between wives and feeling fatalistic.

The Cabinet Secretary appears at Lee's shoulder with Darren, the head of his redcap close protection team. He is polite but firm. 'This way please, Prime Minister.'

He says goodbye to the very earnest gardeners and hopes he won't entirely wreck their planet during his tenure.

He is escorted swiftly through the garden rooms and up a flight of stairs, gathering the PPS Jonathan Guest and further redcaps as they go. They walk along the corridor to the door that separates Downing Street from the Cabinet Office. The Cabinet Secretary pauses with the key in his hand and says, 'There has been a very large explosion in Russia.'

He unlocks the door and shows Lee to Briefing Room A.

Chuka Odechukwu and Evan Calthorp are there along with the Defence Secretary, the National Security Adviser, and the Chief of the Defence Staff. There is a satellite map of a portion of the Siberian coastline on the big screen with a white plume of ash extending out across the dark ocean.

'The explosion was detected by infrasound detectors nearly two thousand kilometres away and ground-coupled acoustic waves were recorded at the international monitoring site at Norilsk in Russia and at US seismic stations along the Aleutian Arc,' the CDS tells them.

Lee is trying to get his head around the scale of the ash plume. It seems insignificant against the vastness of Russia. 'It's a nuke?'

'We're waiting for radionuclide data before we can say for sure but yes, it seems likely, Prime Minister.'

'Launched from where?'

'The missile fields at Kozelsk south-west of Moscow.'

'They bombed themselves?'

'It looks that way.'

'On purpose?'

'We believe so. The Americans have confirmed that there was a significant increase in the protection posture at Kozelsk in the ninety minutes before the launch. In which case it is deliberate violation of the Comprehensive Nuclear-Test-Ban Treaty, which includes all nuclear explosions.'

'What was the target?'

'A biological research institute specialising in prehistoric strains of the influenza virus,' the Cabinet Secretary explains. 'It is also the stated destination of Yulia Ermolaeva in her last call to Jude Lyon in which she revealed that she had uncovered inconsistencies in the biosecurity monitoring system at the institute.'

'At this point it's only conjecture, Prime Minister,' Chuka says, 'but if the Kremlin wanted to destroy evidence and prevent any further access to the site, then they have achieved that.'

'Evidence of what?' he demands.

'If it was proven that a deadly virus had leaked from a Russian lab, it could clearly cause a great deal of embarrassment to the Russian president,' the Cabinet Secretary adds.

'No shit, Sherlock!'

'Not to mention the potential loss of life and economic shock should it cause a global pandemic.'

'The electorate have been through enough,' Lee says.

'Absolutely, Prime Minister, however as you know, events are no respecter of the public mood. And pandemic is right at the top of your risk register.'

'Do we have any evidence that there has been a leak?' Lee demands.

'Not yet, no,' Chuka replies.

'How do we know that the Russians haven't solved the problem with their nuke? I don't suppose that flu stands much of a chance against radiation.' Lee pauses. 'I'm assuming it's more effective than bleach?'

Silence.

'Have you tried contacting Yulia Ermolaeva?' Lee asks.

'We have. To no avail. I think that we must face the probability that she perished in the explosion.'

'Does Jude know?'

'No.'

Lee leans back in his chair and exhales loudly. 'So, what do I do?'

'You must decide whether to close our borders and prepare to lock down the country,' the Cabinet Secretary says, 'the president of the United States will be making the same decision. And you must decide who else to warn.'

'Shouldn't we wait until we have proof?'

'Yes, Prime Minister, under normal circumstances that would be my advice, however if a deadly virus is out there somewhere, you can be sure that Guy Fowle is seeking to acquire it. We can only pray that he doesn't already have it in his possession. Might I suggest that you speak to the president while I convene the National Security Council?'

'I want my own team here now.'

'There is an issue with that,' Evan Calthorp says.

'What do you mean?'

'I mean that we have concerns about some of the people around you.'

'Are you serious?'

'I'm afraid so, Prime Minister.'

'And are you going to give me proof or more suspicion and conjecture?'

'You know as well as I do that Russian illegals working under deep cover have proven very hard to detect.'

'I knew it!' Lee jumps to his feet and points at Calthorp. 'Fake intelligence! Not another word from you!'

# 64

## *Scunnered*

Kirsty arches upwards from a wooden-framed bed, inhaling as she flexes her cable-tied wrists and ankles, exhaling as she sinks back onto the bare mattress.

*Purvottanasana*: a sort of half-arsed crab.

She is in total darkness inside a soundproof shipping container, which she hopes will play to her advantage. Grigor's not been paying close enough attention to her while she's drinking her orange juice. Since they arrived in London, he's been feeding her by torchlight, and she's been able to spit it out without swallowing. She's thirsty and she has a thumping headache and a dry throat, plus she's feeling slightly feverish, but for the first time since she was abducted, she has some clarity of thought and independent movement in her limbs.

She needs to escape and warn Jude. And do it without infecting anyone else with whatever they have given to her.

She's in a rhythm now, rising and falling, exerting more pressure with each inhalation. She can feel the strain on the vertical bars in the rails at either end of the bed and cable ties are cutting into her wrists and ankles. She rises again and the tenon holding one of the pine bars of the footboard to the bottom rail breaks.

*Yes!*

The bar pulls away from the mortise joint. She tugs on it and her right ankle is free. Lying still, she listens, her arms and legs prickling with sweat.

Nothing.

She rolls on her left hip and kicks out with her right heel, smacking the bar that her left ankle is attached to. She hits it twenty more times with her heel, ignoring the pain, and eventually the bar snaps. Her legs are free. She shimmies her arse up to the head-board, tucks her feet under her buttocks and pushes upwards into a crouch, tugging her hands behind her. The bed shakes. She crouches down again, forcing her heels into the gaps between bars, and pushes upwards again, feeling the whole bed straining. She gets into a fresh rhythm, squatting and lunging. The wood begins to splinter. With a final lunge the top rail of the headboard tears away. The bed sags and collapses.

She lies, limp as a rag, with her hands free. No one has come looking. The soundproofing worked.

She rises uncertainly to her feet, stumbles over to the nearest foam-clad wall, and steadies herself against it. It's like sponge. When she has rested for a few moments, she follows it to the doors at the end of the container and finds to her surprise that they are not locked. She pushes one open a short way, creating a wedge of light, and is grateful to whoever recently oiled the hinges. In the arch, only one of the overhead strip lights is on and she has a partial view across the varnished concrete floor of the back of a police van and the nose of the one behind. She can't see anyone, but she can hear casual voices from further back under the arch.

She sticks her head out and looks behind the door. The container is parallel to the wall and there is another container just in front of this one to create a neatly ordered space. She steps out into the narrow gap and carefully closes the door. If she can squeeze into the space between the wall and the side of the container in front of her, she hopes that she can travel the length of the arch without being spotted.

She creeps along the rear side of the container and stops. Through the wall she can hear the muffled sound of Alysha's voice.

She shivers. It's cold in the arch and she's feeling feverish. She continues moving as quietly as she can, telling herself not to hurry, until she reaches the end of the container.

Peeking around the corner she sees the side-by-side doors: the large vehicle entrance with a closed steel shutter and beside it the smaller steel door with a push pad exit device with a green latch beside it. If she can get through the door, she can get out into the street and shout 'fire!' which is what you're supposed to do if you want to guarantee that people rush to help rather than simply dismiss you as another street crazy.

She wipes the sweat from her forehead and realises that she's burning up. Her head is throbbing, and the shivering is getting worse.

It's now or never.

She stumbles across the space and presses the latch. The door swings open automatically, and she steps outside in the golden afternoon light. She is in a yard enclosed by barbed steel railings with a steel-mesh gate. On the far side of the gate, she watches a black cab pass by. She crosses the yard and presses her face between the railings.

There are two women walking alongside a twelve-foot-high wall on the other side of the road. They are wearing hijab and they are speaking to each other in what she thinks is Bengali.

She tries to shout but it comes out as a croak. One of the women glances in her direction and looks quickly away.

'There you are,' Grigor says, from behind her. He joins her at the railings and waves cheerily at the women, who ignore them. 'You made a helluva job of that bed.'

She can feel the tears running down her face.

'Don't be sad,' he tells her. 'You're destined for great things. Soon your picture will be on the news and the whole world will know your name.'

He takes her by the arm and guides her back to the door.

'What's the matter with me?' she asks him.

'A rare case of flu. A virulent strain harvested from the ice.'

'Why don't you have it?'

'I've been vaccinated,' he says, smugly. He pushes her through the door into the arch and back towards the container that she escaped from. 'I told you that I'm a survivor.'

# 65

# Slouching towards Downing Street

Alysha's flesh glistens with beads of sweat. The passion of the demon growing in the furls of the scars on her belly and breasts fills the container with its heat.

After years of sleep, its coming is at hand.

They are naked and surrounded by votive items: plastic-wrapped bars of plastic explosive, freezer bags full of ball-bearings, lassos of detonating cord, rolls of black gaffer tape, toggle switches, and a plastic matchbox-sized carton with detonators inside.

As a teenager in Iraq, she had a pact with her grandfather that they would not be taken alive, and they got into a rhythm of constructing fresh means of destruction every time they moved location. When she was on the run with Guy, they kept up the tradition, but the vests were for the zealous foot soldiers who provided their first line of defence.

She can build a suicide vest with her eyes closed and her mouth open.

It's never felt this real.

The hour approaches.

She pauses what's she's doing to watch Guy using a rolled paper cone to fill alternate pouches in their black police-issue chest rigs with steel ball-bearings. She loves the hard muscles and fibrous sinews of his beautiful, battle-hardened body. The history of conflict written on his skin: the tears and gouges, knobs and ridges, and the stag's horns tattoo rising from his lowest ribs and curling across the fused burls on his collarbones. The ball-bearings spilling across the mattress.

*He's beautiful and doomed.*

Into the empty pouches between the ball-bearings, he slides bars of explosive. It's satisfying to see how snugly everything fits. She closes her eyes and shares the afterimage of his skin with the demon in the dark with her. After a few moments, she opens her eyes again and returns her attention to cutting lengths of detonating cord with his K-Bar knife. She knots the cord that will connect the charges to the switches and wraps them in tape. She has always been deft with her hands. She is as accomplished a bomb maker as Guy. Soon all that will be left will be to slot the detonators into the pre-drilled holes in the plastic explosive.

She licks her lips, and the demon runs its tongue down the length of her spine. She shivers with lust. She needs Guy to touch her more than she needs to breathe.

'Make love to me.'

He looks up. She feels his eyes travel across her body – her engorged breasts and round demon-filled belly – and is delighted to see his penis rise like a Saxon sword – a *scramasax* – out of its nest of hair. In Iraq, in the evenings when they swapped words in their own languages, he'd told her that in Old English the word *wæpn* meant both sword and penis.

He is always horniest before battle.

He sets the vests and tools aside and lifts her parted legs down into the hollow at the centre of the mattress and penetrates the warm and wet of her.

He speaks Arabic to her: *tuqburnii.* You bury me.

She grips his lean, white jaw as he thrusts into her. As she comes, she hears the demon exhale in one long, loud moment and then Guy follows, roaring like some additional part of him has broken off inside her.

She is full of him. She loves him. She will die for him.

In flames.


They are lying beside each other, softly panting, when Grigor knocks on the container door.

'Boss?'

'What is it?'

'The prisoner tried to escape.'

He jumps up off the bed, strides naked across the space and throws open the door. 'Where is she?'

'Back in the container,' Grigor says, dull-eyed, staring at the floor. 'It was a mistake.'

Guy can see the sheen of sweat on his forehead. Neolithic death. 'How far did she get?'

'Outside in the yard, no further.'

'Did anyone see her?'

'Yes, two passing women; I engaged with them in a friendly manner.'

'We go now.'

A few minutes later, Alysha steps out of the container and walks past the watching Russians on parade. Like them, she is wearing a dark blue police CBRN suit, a close-fitting snood around her neck, needle-proof gloves, and black combat boots, but she is carrying an explosive chest rig.

Guy is waiting at a row of folding tables with weapons and equipment on them. At the first table, he helps her put on a Kevlar vest and then the suicide vest over the top of it. He attaches a padded nylon utility belt around her waist. The second table has guns on it. She loads and holsters a pistol and picks up a short-barrelled carbine, pulling the sling over her shoulders and pushing the gun around to the small of her back. She divides magazines of 9mm and 5.56mm ammunition between her pockets. At the third table she puts on a helmet and goggles and adds a respirator to a pouch on her hip.

Finally, Guy puts a lanyard around her neck with an RFID security pass loaded with a malware packet that will be used for exfiltration when the operation is complete.

On the floor beyond the tables there is a line of black holdalls filled with the larger weapons for the GRU fire support team: the anti-matériel and anti-tank weapons. Each one has a brown-paper tag with a name written on it in black marker pen.

The Russians are silent behind their masks and goggles, yearning to fight.

'Downing Street will be ours by dark,' Guy tells them. He smiles. 'Now.'

They grab their bags and carry them to the back of the second van.

Alysha is sitting between the twins in the front of the second van when Grigor brings Kirsty from a container. She looks delirious. He lifts her up into the plastic-lined cargo area of the first van and climbs in after her, pulling the door closed behind him.

The shutter rolls up and the steel-mesh gates swing open. Alysha pulls the snood up over her nose to disguise her face and they drive out onto the street.

# 66

## *Hic incepit pestis*

Jude is woken by a change in the speed and inclination of the helicopter as it makes a shallow dive. He tightens his grip on the rifle between his knees as they swing down to within a hundred feet of the roof of Buckingham Palace and the plane trees on The Mall. They land on Horse Guards Parade beside an Apache helicopter gunship. Two other helicopters carrying the remnants of the SAS squadron from Argyll land beside them.

Munro jumps out with Jude close behind him and they run at a crouch towards an air marshal holding two red fluorescent batons. Beside him there is an SAS captain named Hay, who salutes Munro and turns to Jude. 'Mr Lyon?'

'Yes.'

'The Prime Minister is expecting you. Follow me.'

Hay escorts them through the arch to Whitehall. They walk past a Challenger tank, which is parked outside Admiralty House, and Hay waves at the commander, who is sitting in his hatch with a mug in his hands. They enter the Cabinet Office through the mantrap airlock doors. It smells better than it did the last time Jude was here at the height of a citywide outbreak of cryptosporidiosis. He is taken past the Cabinet Secretary's office and parts ways with Munro, who heads towards the COBRA complex.

Jude is escorted down the corridor that leads to No. 10.

'I need your weapons and your ammunition,' Hay tells him. 'I'll keep them at COBRA for you.'

Jude hands over his assault rifle and pistol, and the chest rig, but keeps the Kevlar vest on.

'Go ahead.'

Jude knocks on the green baize door and a redcap opens it. He escorts Jude to the Principal Private Secretary's office.

'The Prime Minister will see you straight away,' Jonathan Guest says and takes him next door.

Lee is sitting surrounded by piles of papers at the Cabinet table. When he sees Jude, he springs to his feet and gives him a bear hug.

'I'm really sorry, mate.' He lets him go and looks him up and down. 'Did you join the Navy?'

Jude looks down at his coveralls. 'I need to change.'

'Sit down.' Lee steers him into a chair beside him and puts his hand on Jude's knee. 'There's more bad news, I'm afraid. We have lost touch with Yulia Ermolaeva, and we fear that she may have died in an explosion in the Russian Arctic.' Jude doesn't know what to say. He's been through so much with Yulia. She had seemed indestructible. 'It seems likely that she uncovered evidence of a leak at a Russian lab researching prehistoric strains of influenza. I've been advised to close the borders, but it may be too late. Guy Fowle may already have a sample. The virologists at Porton Down say that it would be relatively easy to set up a home laboratory using commercially available equipment to grow enough of the virus to cause a major outbreak that we would struggle to contain. The police are investigating anyone who has recently purchased the kind of equipment they'd need.'

'Kirsty said that she was zero.'

'Yeah, we saw that. Patient zero. It looks like Fowle intends to use her as a means of transmission. Like I said, I'm sorry.'

The door opens and Denzel sticks his head in.

'They're ready for you, Prime Minister.'

Lee nods. 'I'm speaking to the nation,' he tells Jude. 'We're locking down tonight.'

'What do you need me to do?'

'I need you to help me defend this place against Fowle. Come on.'

Denzel leads them up the central staircase to the landing where Bala is waiting. She kisses Lee and straightens his tie. 'This way.'

They enter the Pillard Room, where a desk has been placed perpendicular to the fireplace with a Union Flag either side of it. The desk faces a camera and lights on stands. Lee sits at the desk and waves away the make-up artist.

'They say that a taste for addressing the nation is as hard to give up as alcohol,' he tells Jude. 'But I don't get it. Frankly it's a chore.'

'As long as you need, Prime Minister,' the director says.

'I'm ready,' Lee says.

The director nods to the cameraman and the red light goes on. There is only one take. Lee stares directly into the camera with a solemn expression on his face and his fists side by side on the desk in front of him.

'Good evening. Guy Fowle is the biggest threat that this country has faced since the Second World War. I have learned that it is likely he is in possession of a deadly virus, an invisible killer with a devastating impact that he intends to release at any time. I am updating you on the immediate steps that we must take to prevent the virus spreading. This will require a huge national effort. If we fail, our health service will not be able to cope. There won't be enough ventilators, enough intensive care beds, enough doctors, or nurses. It is vital that we act to stop the spread of the virus. From right now, I am giving you a simple instruction: stay at home. I repeat, stay at home.' He pauses to let the viewers absorb the impact of his words. 'If you don't follow the rules, the police have the powers to enforce them through fines and dispersing gatherings. From now all shops selling non-essential goods and other premises including libraries, playgrounds and places of worship will close. All gatherings of more than two people in public are banned and all social events, including weddings, baptisms and other ceremonies, are cancelled. I know that you have been through so much already. I know the damage that this disruption will do. But until we catch Guy Fowle and prevent him from releasing the virus, we have no alternative. If we fail, many lives will sadly be lost. As you have in the past, so many times, you will rise to this challenge, and we will come through it stronger than ever. We will beat Guy Fowle. I urge you at this moment of national emergency to stay at home, protect our NHS and save lives.'

He waits for a moment and then exhales.

'That's it. Thank you, Prime Minister,' the director says.

'What time does it go out?'

'In just under an hour at six p.m.,' Bala says, consulting her watch. 'Across all channels, on TV and radio.'

'Good.'

A phone rings and Guest answers. He listens and nods.

'The National Air Traffic Services centre at Swanwick is reporting that the software at the London Terminal Control Centre has crashed,' he tells the Prime Minister. 'They've issued a ground stop at all London airports and are rerouting air traffic and increasing spaces between aircraft.'

It's begun, Jude thinks. Fowle's attack has begun.

# 67

# Rush hour

It's rush hour at the end of the working day and the streets and pavements are crowded with unsuspecting people with feeble, compliant auras. Guy believes that the hunter-gatherer with a flint blade and a basalt axe is the purest expression of what it is to be human. Ever since they abandoned the prehistoric grasslands, people have been nothing more than the cattle of stronger men. They have grown flabby and too numerous.

He is sitting in the cab of the first van, outside the Lyric theatre, waiting for the lights to change. All around him vehicles are idling in the dense traffic, polluting the planet. There are people every-where. Too many of them, they have overrun the place.

For a superior man, even one with a degenerative disease, it is an intolerable situation.

Beside him on the bench Anatoly and Vera are leaning forward, their auras pulsing with nervous anticipation. It is pleasing to him that he is reading auras so well again. The extent to which he underestimated both Jude Lyon and Lee Chapeaux has made him question his skill recently.

As they approach the turning for Great Windmill Street, Guy nods to Vera and she switches on the blue flashing lights. Rather than following the traffic signs around to the left, she drives straight down the bus-only lane to the traffic lights at the bottom of Shaftesbury Avenue and stops the van. She applies the handbrake, switches off the blue lights and turns on the flashing red lights that are only visible to the rear. Behind them, in the second police van, Alysha and the twins, Maksim and Yaroslav, do the same.

Anatoly gets out of the cab and walks around to the back to open the rear doors.

'Why do you hate him so much?' Vera asks.

'The Prime Minister?'

'Yes.'

'It's not the man,' he tells her. He is indifferent to Lee's fate. 'It's the institution.'

He despises government. It's a lie. There is no such thing as law or rights or freedom, there are no *a priori* principles, only spoils to be grabbed and adversaries to be killed.

'You're not going to blow yourself up,' Vera tells him, eyeing his vest. He decides that she's astute as well as attractive. And she's spotted that this may be her only opportunity. 'I want to go with you, afterwards.'

Why not? he thinks. Under normal circumstances he'd have grown tired of Alysha's possessiveness by now, her night-time rants. He'd be looking for a blank canvas to mark. Vera would be a fitting candidate. He reaches out and places his trembling fingers on her thigh. She parts her legs, and he slides his hand down between them into the wedge of her pubis. He does not look at her – he does not caress her, instead he grips her.

'I'll make sure you get through this,' he lies.

Despite her fierce desire otherwise, he thinks that she is unlikely to survive.

In the offside mirror, he watches Grigor guide Kirsty towards the pavement and sees Alysha watching from the van behind. Within ninety seconds, Anatoly is back in the cab. They are ready to go. Guy glimpses Grigor, head and shoulders above most of the crowd, walking towards the steps at the entrance to Piccadilly Circus underground station. It's only a matter of minutes before all hell breaks loose.

It's time to move.

'Give it some noise,' Fowle says into his radio.

With the sirens whooping and blue lights flashing, the vans nudge forward against the traffic coming in perpendicular from Regent Street. Cars shuffle backwards or forwards to make way for them. A car directly in their path mounts the pavement beneath Eros on his fountain. Vera drives through the gap with the second van following and heads west on Piccadilly because it's a warren of one-way streets.

'Turn the siren off.'

Very soon the whole area will be flooded with sirens, but until then they don't want to draw further attention. They turn left on St James's Street and head south, driving past White's, the gentlemen's club that Guy's father was thrown out of for gross moral turpitude, and beside it the Beretta shop where he bought Guy his first shotgun. They turn left again outside St James's Palace and drive the length of Pall Mall. At the entrance to Trafalgar Square, they pull up onto the pavement beside the portico on the north side of Canada House and park beneath a maple-leaf flag.

Vera switches off the lights.

A final pause, a glance at his wristwatch. 'Go.'

The twins jump out of the second van and go around to the back. By the time Guy joins them, the fire support team are lined up with the holdalls slung across their shoulders, ready to go. He nods and they walk east across Trafalgar Square, heading for the National Portrait Gallery.

He smiles at the assault team. 'Let's go pay the Prime Minister a visit.'

They walk as a squad down the west side of Trafalgar Square past Landseer's Lions at the foot of the column and the statue of the beheaded king, Charles I. A reminder, if such was needed, of the fragility of power. They cross in front of Admiralty Arch, entering Whitehall from the north end.

Before they reach the barricade, they take a left turn down an unremarkable cul-de-sac opposite the Trafalgar Theatre. At the end of a narrow channel barely wide enough for a car, Guy stands in front of a set of wooden doors in a stone portico with *Telephone Exchange* written on it.

He smiles up at the camera and presses the intercom. 'Still waters are inhabited by devils.'

The intercom crackles: 'A chicken is not really a bird and Poland is not really abroad.'

Guy winks at Anatoly. He is fond of the clumsily translated proverbs used by Grom. 'A bad dancer blames his testicles.'

He gets out his phone and taps the screen. He opens his crypto-currency wallet and activates a payment that's been held in escrow. It makes a satisfying whooshing noise to signify the transfer.

A few moments later, the doors click open. Twenty-five million dollars well spent.

They walk down a corridor lined with tiles to a door with a fire exit sign above it. Guy opens the door, and they go down a spiral staircase in a concrete shaft. At the bottom Guy opens a steel door and Sir Francis, the Downing Street historian, is waiting for them on the other side.

'You're a rich man,' Guy tells him.

'Yes, I am, ha, ha, ha.' He looks at his watch. 'You have eight minutes until the doors lock.'

# 68

# Day of misrule

On the way down No. 10's main staircase, Jonathan Guest explains that the London Terminal Control Centre handles traffic flying to or from London's airports and is one of the busiest airspaces in Europe, extending south and east to the borders of France and the Netherlands, west towards Bristol and north to near Birmingham.

The Cabinet Secretary is waiting for them on the ground floor. 'GCHQ believes that Swanwick has been attacked by DataSlay, one of the Grom malware variants. They are working on tailored countermeasures.'

They hurry down the corridor that leads to the Cabinet Office, Jude walking shoulder to shoulder with the Cabinet Secretary, a couple of steps behind the Prime Minister. The redcap stationed at the green baize door opens it for them. Lee knows that beneath the green cloth and brass tacks, there is a reinforced steel door.

On the far side, one of the control room staff from the COBRA complex is waiting. He calmly explains that an outbound train leaving King's Cross station has just run through a green signal that should have been red and collided with an inbound train from Scotland.

They arrive at COBRA in time to witness a live feed from a police helicopter hovering above King's Cross. Diesel fuel dispersed by the collision has ignited, engulfing the jumbled carriages in a fireball.

Lee stands and stares.

'Network Rail is reporting that their traffic management system is infected with malware,' Munro explains. 'They've lost control of signalling.'

'Send out a National Emergency Alert text,' Lee commands. Rather than taking his place at the head of the table, he strides the length of the room.

'The malware is spreading, Prime Minister,' the Secretary of State for Transport explains from the virtual gallery. 'We've lost control of airspace in the Scottish and Shanwick Oceanic regions, and we've lost military air control.'

'Nevertheless, we've scrambled two Typhoons from RAF Coningsby to patrol airspace over central London and we have a Rapier missile battery on the roof of Millbank tower,' the Chief of the Defence Staff adds from the gallery with the bare concrete walls of the Pindar Complex behind him.

'I'm not giving you carte blanche,' Lee tells him. 'You ask me before you shoot down any passenger planes.'

'Of course, Prime Minister.'

Jemima Connick, the Metropolitan Police Commissioner, appears in the gallery from New Scotland Yard and a head-and-shoulders image of a woman with a blonde bob appears on the screen beside her. 'We've released an image of a suspect, Poppy Byford, a senior procurement officer for the NHS. She was flagged in a search for orders for laboratory equipment used for the propagation of cell culture. She hasn't turned up for work today.'

'That horse has bolted,' Lee says.

'Fowle has manufactured the flu virus,' Jude says. 'Now it's about the means of dispersal.'

'Somewhere public and rammed with people,' Lee says. He looks around. 'Where's Bala?'

No one replies.

Jude spots his weapons and tac-vest stacked neatly against the wall at the back of the room and wonders whether he might soon need them.

Kirsty is caught in the press of people pouring like floodwater into the underground station, through the electronic turnstiles and down the escalators onto the platforms. She's cold and getting colder, her muscles ache, and her head is pounding as if her brain is smacking against the inside of her skull. She sways and almost falls forward on the escalator, but Grigor's hands are gripping her shoulders.

'Easy, girl,' he croaks, with sweat running off his forehead. 'We're nearly there.'

'You're infected too, you fuckin' spanner.'

'What's that?'

'You're sick.'

He laughs. The fool believes in Fowle's bullshit vaccination story.

At the foot of the escalator, they are carried towards the southbound platform, where the trains are heading for Waterloo, just three stops away, the city's busiest station. The first train that comes is already packed to bursting and they are nowhere near the front. Her eyes keep opening and closing. It's like staring through a mosquito net. She feels the wind surging out of the tunnel as another train approaches just a couple of minutes later. The doors open. Grigor uses his bulk to shoulder his way to the front and squeeze her into the crowded carriage. The doors close behind her. They start with a jolt, and she sways with the rattling motion of the carriage. She opens her mouth to issue a dire warning, but no words come out. Instead, she starts coughing. Once she starts, she can't stop. Hands are waving in her face.

Several people are swearing. Everything is spinning. Grigor is no longer holding her up. Maybe he didn't get in the carriage with her. Does he really think he's immune? She slides to the floor amongst a thicket of legs. People are trying to move away but are pushed back. A woman stumbles and falls across her. Her legs get bent backwards and she starts screaming that she's got no air. At least Kirsty has stopped coughing. Her throat feels like a junkie's carpet. She really should have done a better job of escaping when she had the chance. She's going to miss her dad's patter and her mum's morning rolls with bacon and egg, and a tattie scone as garnish. There's something not right about her green curry and no time to fix it now. She wishes that she could cup Jude's sweet face in her hands, or his balls for that matter. She's spent too much of her life without a reliable shag.

The train shudders to a halt at the next station. The doors whoosh open. Kirsty and the woman on top of her are in the way. No one can get in or out with them there. Eventually, she is picked up and dragged out onto the platform.

It's all just random thoughts now.

She wishes that she could say purple burglar alarm without bungling it. What do you mean ma accent's exotic? I'm from North Lanarkshire, no' the fucking Bahamas.

With a jolt the train starts again and leaves the station.

She can feel her limbs being moved like a puppet. She's absolutely freezing. Her head feels like it's going to explode.

The last thing she hears is someone calling for a doctor.

'Prime Minister,' Jemima Connick cuts in on the briefing room screen, 'facial recognition identified Kirsty McIntyre and Grigor Muir entering Piccadilly Circus underground station less than three minutes ago. I'm asking your permission to enact Operation Carcer with immediate effect.'

Lee glances at the Cabinet Secretary. 'Op Carcer?'

'Operation Carcer was designed in response to a biological attack involving the release of a communicable disease on the underground system,' the Cabinet Secretary replies, 'and involves stopping the trains and locking the entrance gates to the stations.'

Lee frowns. 'Trapping the people underground?'

'Until they can be screened and receive treatment in quarantine conditions, Prime Minister,' Jemima adds.

Jude is rooted to the spot, grappling with the implications of the decision that Lee's about to make. Trapping Kirsty under the ground with the flu.

'It's barbaric,' Lee says.

Jemima's face is hard. 'It's necessary to prevent the spread of infection.'

'The Civil Contingencies Act gives you the authority to restrict movement of people in times of a severe emergency,' the Cabinet

Secretary tells Lee. 'You need to make your decision now, Prime Minister. The consequences of delay are likely to be catastrophic.'

All at once everything comes unbound: Jude grips the edge of a table while a floodtide rises from his core, through his torso and shoulders, and into his head. His breath becomes ragged. He feels tears running down his face.

Lee looks at Jude with regret on his face.

'Do it,' he says.

Jemima nods in acknowledgement of the order. She speaks to someone off screen. She glances back at the screen. 'Prime Minister, we need to redeploy armed police from the north end of the Whitehall barricade to secure the Charing Cross station exits.'

'Absolutely not,' the Cabinet Secretary says.

'The army can hold the line,' Munro says.

'Do it,' Lee says.

On the screens they have a panoramic view of Whitehall from the blimp and the Apache helicopter gunship circling above, and they watch armed police moving north up Whitehall towards Trafalgar Square and the blue flashing lights of multiple vehicles converging.

Kirsty is lying at the entrance to a tunnel at Charing Cross, blocking one of the main access routes to and from the platform, and an anxious crowd is massing either side of her. She can feel the sensation of leaving her body and rising above it. Looking down, she can see a medical student kneeling in front of her performing compressions, his hands on her chest acting as a bellows, dispersing the droplets of virus in the confined space.

*Not good.*

There is a cacophony of voices: people further into the station are shouting. The escalators have stopped moving. Word is passed down that Underground staff have locked the steel gates at the station entrances and retreated to the control room. There is more shouting when the southbound train that just left backs out of the tunnel. The people inside stare out at the crowd on the platform, but the doors remain closed.

There is an announcement on the speakers: 'Due to a health incident the station has been closed. Please remain calm and do not attempt to leave the station. The emergency services are on their way.'

In the seconds before the repeaters are switched off and the mobile phone network goes down, many of the people on the platform see a news flash alerting them to a bio-weapon attack on the Bakerloo Line. A few can download a video in which Kirsty claims responsibility for death and destruction on an unimaginable scale.

'I am chaos,' she says on their screens.

Someone recognises her.

Panicked, the crowd tries to flee. On the surface people are crushed against the gates at the street entrances.

The city is full of sirens.

Grigor doesn't make it to the gates before they are locked. Fearful of being trapped in the concourse, he fights his way back down the stairs between the escalators. He feels terrible and he has come to the bitter realisation that Kirsty was right. He is infected.

Guy deceived him.

He head-butts someone who won't move out the way quickly enough and the hapless victim falls back into someone behind them and soon there is a cascade of people tumbling down the stairs. Grigor presses on. He scrambles across a pile of people at the bottom and pushes through a surging crowd onto the northbound platform where a train is stalled. He puts his head down and rams his way to the end of the platform, where he jumps onto the track.

He heads into the darkness.

The air in the tunnel is stale and heavy and his clothes are soaked with sweat. Despite the soreness of his throat, he can taste the steel in the dust in the air and he can hear water dripping from the ceiling.

He begins to shiver as he stumbles on.

After what seems a very long time, he spots torches in the tunnel ahead. He rejoices when he sees that they are approaching. He opens his mouth to greet them, but his throat is burning, and it comes out as a croak.

Soon they are shouting at him.

He has his arms out. 'Save me!'

They open fire. The first bullet strikes him in his left shoulder and spins him around. The second strikes him between the shoulder blades. He falls face down on the tracks.

# 69

# The battle for Whitehall

Lee's close protection team bracket him and yet still he is the tallest man in the room.

'We need to move you to the Pindar Complex immediately,' Darren tells him.

Lee is outraged. 'You're going to lock me in a basement?'

'Standard procedure in the event of a bio-weapon attack,' Denzell adds.

'Continuity of authority, responsibility and accountability is paramount, Prime Minister,' the Cabinet Secretary explains, patiently. 'The Chief of the Defence Staff is already there along with the Defence Secretary.'

'We need to move you now,' Darren says.

One of the redcaps makes the mistake of putting a hand on Lee's shoulder and is rewarded with a look that promises violence.

'Find Bala,' Lee implores Jude. 'Do that for me.'

Jude nods. He'd do anything not to have to think about Kirsty down in the underground station. 'I'll do it.'

There's a flash on the screen from a missile strike, and a ripple of explosions as reactive armour detonates on the outer skin of the Challenger tank on the northern barricade.

'Bravo One One; contact!' the tank commander reports.

A flash as another missile strikes the tank. It reverses, trailing a cloud of diesel smoke and gobbets of burning explosives, and comes to a sudden halt outside the Cabinet Office, less than forty metres from where they are standing.

'Zero; Viper. I see two enemy on the roof of a building on the north side of the square,' the Apache commander reports. 'It looks like they're about to fire again. Request permission to engage?'

'Zero Alpha; engage,' Munro snaps.

The gunship opens fire, raking the windows of the National Portrait Gallery restaurant, the cannon rounds like hammer blows over the speakers. Seconds later, an incendiary warhead detonates against the barricade and molten sparks billow skywards. A burning soldier runs south down Whitehall.

'You need to go now, Prime Minister,' Munro says.

From the briefing room they go down a corridor and through a locked door that is the entrance to the tunnels below. Darren guides Lee into the elevator with Denzell and the Cabinet Secretary while the others go through the emergency exit and down the stairs.

'As soon as we get to Pindar, you'll be able to resume command and control,' the Cabinet Secretary tells him in a reassuring tone as they descend. 'Op Carcer gives us the best chance to stop the assault, contain the outbreak and reassert civil authority.'

The doors open and Lee is again surrounded and hustled down an iron-ribbed corridor.

'Zero, this is Viper,' the Apache gunship's commander says. 'I can't distinguish between friendly and enemy combatants.'

'Zero Alpha; roger, hold fire,' Munro says from COBRA.

The live feeds from the blimp and the gunship's cameras are chaotic and hard for Jude to decipher. There is a scrum of emergency vehicles outside the entrance to Charing Cross station and across Trafalgar Square. Several of them are burning and smoke is drifting outwards. Gunfire on Whitehall suggests that the barricade has been breached.

A man dressed as a police firearms officer dashes out of the smoke and posts a grenade down the barrel of the Challenger. Moments later there's a white flash and burning thermite and barium nitrate spray out of the barrel.

'Bravo One One; breech foul!'

'I'll head to No. 10,' Jude says, putting on his tac-vest. He ejects and reinserts the magazines in his rifle and pistol.

Munro speaks to one of the COBRA staff: 'Tell the guard on

the door to let Mr Lyon through.' He nods at Jude. 'Be careful. Any one of them could be an illegal.'

Lee and his entourage turn a corner into the Q tunnel and Guy Fowle is striding towards them, flanked by armed police in CBRN suits. Denzell steps in front of Lee. Without breaking stride, Guy raises his pistol and opens fire.

Denzell is hit.

'Fall back!'

Hands grab Lee and pull him backwards. Someone drops smoke. Gunfire is deafening in the echoing concrete space.

A flash-bang goes off.

Lee stumbles across a body and falls while rounds ricochet off the walls above him. Someone drags him by his collar until he shakes them off, rolls over and springs up. They run a short way and then he is steered right into a tunnel.

Behind them there are three explosions in quick succession and a rolling wave of smoke travels down the Q tunnel and pursues them towards Downing Street.

'The National Grid is reporting that its super-transformers are out of phase and rapidly connecting and disconnecting to the grid,' a COBRA staff member says. 'They are expecting the grid to collapse within minutes. It's not just the grid, the damage to synchronous induction motors will wreck machinery every-where . . . factories, pipeline facilities, communication networks.'

'Close down the grid,' Munro says. 'Switch to generator power.'

He feels the detonation of satchel charges beneath Whitehall as a shudder in his ankles and knees.

'We've lost touch with the Pindar Complex.'

'And the Prime Minister?'

'Is retreating to Downing Street under fire.'

'We need reinforcement. Open the doors to the Cabinet Office and bring the quick reaction force inside.'

'We've lost control of the gates at the front and back of Downing Street and the mantrap gates at the entrance to the Cabinet Office.

We've lost control of all above-ground entry and exit points. They have electronically sealed and cannot be manually opened. We're locked in with no way out.'

Munro growls. 'Get that other tank up here and tell it to blow the bloody doors open.'

Jude feels the underground explosion as he is walking down the corridor, having passed through the green baize door at the entrance to No. 10. The door to the Principal Private Secretary's office is open and the room is empty. Jude slips past and advances across the hallway towards the atrium of the main staircase, which is bathed in light from the skylight in the roof. He lifts his rifle, craning his neck to see the levels above.

Ready to fire.

He starts climbing, keeping close to the wall, the etchings of Prime Ministers at his back. On the first-floor landing, he passes the open doors to the White Room where he sparred with Lee just days before. The door to the Pillard Room is closed. He flings it open and rolls across the room, coming up in a crouch beside one of the pillars with his gun out in front of him.

The TV crew are in a frightened huddle in one corner.

'Stay there,' he tells them.

He goes back out onto the landing and continues up the stairs to the second floor, past photographs of more recent Prime Ministers, to where the PM's flat is located. The door is open. He drops his carbine on its sling and draws his pistol. He goes in and moves from room to room with the pistol up to aim, scanning left and right, keeping an eye on the corners.

He finds Bala in the open-plan kitchen-cum-living-room.

'Lee didn't mean for this to happen,' she tells him, staring down the muzzle of his pistol before looking him in the eyes. 'Fowle left him with no choice.'

# 70

# Death in the library

Munro watches on the screen as the Challenger tank from the southern barricade drives north on Whitehall with troops advancing alongside the tracks, using it for cover. It judders to a halt outside the Cabinet Office and the turret swivels until the gun is pointing at the entrance.

The gun fires a HESH round through the front door at the mantrap gate. The explosive flattens against the gate and detonates, creating a shock wave that ejects scabs of polycarbonate glass at supersonic speeds that punch through the walls in COBRA. A scab shatters one of the wall screens and plaster dust rains down from the ceiling.

A second round shatters the gate entirely.

'Bala!' Lee shouts as he is propelled towards the main staircase at the centre of a scrum of redcaps. He last saw her after the broadcast, heading upstairs to the flat to change.

Behind him, there is an explosion as a demolition charge blows open the door to the tunnels. The redcaps drop more smoke grenades, and they climb the stairs with the rising cloud of red smoke.

'Bala!'

They reach the first landing just as Fowle and his team reach the bottom of the main staircase.

'This way,' Roger says. 'We'll go out through No. 11.'

Lee is dragged against his will by the sheer press of people around him away from the staircase and towards the front of the building.

'Bala!'

★    ★    ★

Jude can hear Lee shouting for her from the floor below.

'How long have you known?' he asks her.

Bala looks devastated. 'He told me last night. He's so sorry about Kirsty.'

He struggles to understand what she means by that.

'More than anything, he wants you to kill Fowle,' she pleads with him. 'Please.'

He hears gunfire from the ground floor.

He turns his back on her and heads out of the flat onto the landing as the ceiling is sprayed with bullets and a flash-bang goes off somewhere below him.

He waits a moment and then steps over to the railing and fires three round bursts into the rising smoke, aiming for the turning points in the landings below, moving to a new firing position between each burst. He steps back and reloads.

Bullets strike the iron railings a few feet from him and ricochet into the ceiling.

He moves back along the landing watching for rents in the smoke, firing controlled bursts.

As Lee passes a passage on his left, someone opens fire from the top of the back stairs by the Breakfast Room and a redcap directly beside him is hit. He now has several people's blood on him but as far as he can tell he is unharmed.

More smoke.

They pass a lift on the left and a bathroom on the right, and Lee is lifted off his feet as they go down a short flight of stairs. They hurry along a corridor towards the front of the house, which has a door that connects it to No. 11. When they reach it, they find that the steel door is locked.

'I'll blow it open,' a redcap says. 'Get clear!'

Lee is propelled into the library as a demolition charge is attached to the door. He shakes himself loose and demands to go back into the house to find Bala and kill Fowle.

'You can come back when it's time to redecorate,' Darren tells him.

They all crouch. The explosives detonate, blowing the door out onto the No. 11 staircase.

'Let's go.'

The redcap who placed the charge is first through the door. He is knocked on his back. Bullets chew up the floorboards and spall the polycarbonate glass of the library windows.

Guy is crouching on the main staircase with Alysha beside him.

Vera has reached the control room in the office beside the entrance hall and confirmed over the radio that she has control of the internal surveillance cameras. Maksim is on the back stairs, in a flanking move intended to cut off any lines of retreat, and Yaroslav and Anatoly are further up the stairs exchanging fire with a gunman in a commanding position on the top floor by the Prime Minister's flat.

Guy waits until the next time the gunman reloads, and darts up onto the first-floor landing with Alysha behind him. They run along the first corridor in pursuit of Lee. When they reach Maksim, he is kneeling in cover at the entrance to the lift. He has pinned down Lee and what remains of his close protection team in the library.

Guy looks at Alysha. Her aura is like a bonfire.

'It's time.'

She searches his face. 'I love you.'

They both know that he is incapable of love, but he says it, nonetheless. 'I love you.'

She closes her gold-flecked eyes and opens them again.

He nods. She sprints down the corridor and into the library and detonates the suicide vest.

Lee rises from the midst of the bodies that sheltered him with one hand hanging off like a child's glove on a string.

'I wondered if this would feel like something,' Guy tells him. There is blood spatter everywhere and ball-bearings in the walls and the ceiling, and the buckled polycarbonate windows. 'But it doesn't feel any different.'

Lee is lost in the moment, hearing almost nothing at all, just the white noise in his ears and the beckoning oblivion.

Guy draws his K-Bar. He prefers the intimacy of a knife. He kneels beside a redcap who is gasping with ball-bearings embedded in his flesh. He gently cups the man's head and swiftly cuts his throat.

'That's better,' he says when it's quiet again. He cleans the knife on the man's sleeve and stands up. 'I'm glad that you were my Prime Minister.'

Guy steps up to him and drives the knife into his throat.

When it's done and the knife is back in its sheath, he asks Vera if Jude Lyon is in the building and is pleased when he learns that Jude is the mystery gunman on the top floor. Guy had no real plan beyond this point. He could try to make it through the back gate on Downing Street using his pass and into St James's Park, but he doubts that he'd get much further. He's thought about finding Winston Churchill's brown leather armchair, which he's been told is marked with furious scratches made by the great man's fingernails, and sitting in it until the time comes to detonate his vest. What else is there to achieve? He has released a virus that will kill several billion people worldwide.

He is the greatest mass murderer in history: the raging darkness inside him is almost quenched. He's all out of demons.

'Boss?'

Anatoly is in the doorway, waiting for further orders. Guy takes the RFID pass from around his neck and flings it away. He unzips the suicide vest and shrugs himself out of it.

'What are you going to do?' Anatoly asks.

'I'm going to kill Jude Lyon.' Guy taps his phone a few times, releasing the money in escrow, and makes them all, however briefly, very rich. 'You can go.'

Anatoly nods and leaves.

He raises his carbine and walks back to the main staircase, heading for the Prime Minister's flat.

# 71

## *Give what's left of me away*

Guy finds Yaroslav slumped against the wood panelling with a crimson smear following him down the wall. A litter of bullet casings, broken glass, torn etchings, and shattered wooden frames surrounds him on the stairs.

Guy steps over him with his gun raised like a medieval archer. Above him, he sees the flash of movement as Jude changes positions. He opens fire, a three-round burst to see what follows: two rounds by way of return from a pistol.

He smiles. Jude is being careful with his ammunition.

There is more gunfire from the ground floor, which Guy assumes is the remnants of his team battling their way out. Someone pops smoke at the base of the staircase and it rises to envelop him.

He sprints upwards, taking the stairs two at a time, turns on a landing between floors, and two bullets spall the polycarbonate glass behind him, narrowly missing his head.

He hears the distinctive click of a dry fire. The trigger pulled but no bullet in the chamber. No more ammo.

Jude disappears into the PM's flat.

Guy goes fast though the door and ahead of him, at the end of the narrow hallway, a door slams shut. He runs forward with his gun raised, ready to fire.

Near the end, Jude steps out of an alcove and kicks Guy's leg from under him while pushing the barrel of the carbine upwards. Guy's finger tight on the trigger, the bullets tattooing the ceiling. Deafening noise. They fall together in a rain of plaster dust onto the carpet, all hands on the rifle, until the magazine is empty.

Letting go of the barrel, Jude elbows Guy in the face. Guy grabs him around the neck in a guillotine hold and tries to wrap his legs around him. Jude rolls back and forth, and kicks against the wall, flipping a partial somersault that breaks Guy's grip.

For a moment, no part of them is touching. Guy springs to his feet and draws his pistol in a single fluid motion. Jude slaps it out of his hand. It bounces off a skirting board.

Guy lashes out with his left fist and when Jude blocks with his forearm, Guy steps inside his guard, his elbow striking Jude in the face. He keeps going, his right hip and shoulder slamming into Jude, propelling him through the door into the roving searchlight of a helicopter hovering outside the window. Jude windmills and falls over the back of a sofa, colliding with an ironing board.

Guy draws his knife. He looks exultant.

'I'll slice you quick.'

Rising, Jude grabs the nearest thing, an iron.

After two quick steps, Guy thrusts with the knife in a flat stab. Jude blocks it with crossed forearms and smashes the base of the iron into the side of Guy's face with a satisfying thwack. Guy staggers back out of reach with blood running down his face. Jude throws the iron at him and backs up into the kitchen, grabbing a knife from a block on the counter.

Guy is still smiling, even though his right eye is lopsided, his skull fractured above and below the socket. The helicopter is out of sight above the roof, and they are back in the shadows.

Guy charges.

Jude defends himself, flicking out with the knife in an X-pattern several times, careful not to overreach, keeping his free hand close to his chest and pulling the knife in after each flick. He cuts Guy's forearms, on the right and the left, and when Guy throws a kick, he slashes him across the calf. Undeterred, Guy grabs Jude's knife hand and uses the knife in his own hand to stab high and low like a sewing machine, bouncing Jude against the kitchen cabinets, the tip of the blade repeatedly catching in the Kevlar of Jude's vest.

Guy growls in frustration as Jude throws the capture and slides sideways out of his grasp. Crockery cascades out of the cabinets and shatters on the floor.

Guy strides forward and thrusts at Jude's neck. Jude grabs Guy's knife hand and stabs upwards with his own knife like a pitchfork, aiming for Guy's groin. Guy blocks it and for a moment they are gripping each other's fists. Then Guy twists Jude's knife arm outwards and knees him in the torso, knocking him back a step. He slips Jude's grip, reaches over with his knife, running it down the outside of Jude's right palm and stripping Jude's knife away.

Guy presses his advantage with an inside kick, a left cross and a kick to the chest. Jude is slammed into a cupboard, the melamine shattering against his shoulders. He staggers sideways with his knife out of reach on the floor, while the contents of the cupboard, a mop and a broom, spill out.

Jude takes advantage of Guy wiping the blood out of his eyes to grab the broom, moving swiftly into the open space of the living area where he can use it most effectively. He stamps on the end to snap the broom head off and he has a fighting staff in his hands.

Guy is grinning at him through a mask of blood.

'You're too late to save anyone.'

Jude lashes out, striking him on the temple.

Guy reels.

Jude swings the staff right to left, aiming at his head again. This time, Guy ducks under the blow and lunges with the knife. Exposed, Jude takes his hand off the staff to raise his forearm and block the thrust. Their forearms slide and Jude feels the sharp pain of the knife slicing through to the bone as Guy pulls back.

Rolling with the pain, Jude tugs the staff across his back and down in a scything motion aimed at Guy's head, feeling it slide through his blood-slick fingers. Guy leans back and bats the stick away. On the return swing, Guy grabs the staff and pushes it over his head with his left hand while striking the centre of the staff with the base of his right palm, snapping it in two. He flings the end behind him.

They reset.

Jude switches hands for a better grip. Guy may still have a knife, but Jude now has a two-foot-long stave with a broken end and a sharp point. He's pretty sure he can hear boots hitting the roof as soldiers abseil down.

Soon it will be over.

Guy lunges, and Jude blocks him, delivering two blows with the stave: the first to Guy's fingers as Jude steps back and the second, coming in from the opposite direction, to his knuckles. Jude follows the block with a left-handed trap, grabbing the forearm of Guy's knife hand and pushing downwards. They spin like a top, Jude hammering Guy several times on the back of his head and the front of his legs, and finally the tendons of his forearm, knocking the knife out of his hand.

Jude leans back on his heel to give himself enough room to stab him in the neck with the stave and as he swings in, Guy uses both hands to block him. He head-butts Jude, grabs him around the neck, pivots and throws him to the ground with his hip. He smashes his knee into Jude's ribs and pulls the stave out of his hand.

As quick as that, Jude is defeated. He is on his back on the carpet, struggling to breathe with Guy's knee pressing into his fractured ribs. Guy is holding the stave like an ice pick above his exposed throat, about to strike.

'You failed.'

Because he's a product of this damp and often beautiful island, Jude falls back on manners and that most over-used of words . . . sorry. He's sorry to Kirsty for failing to rescue her, to Yulia and his employers for not killing Fowle at Sizewell, to Gretchen and Rosanna, to his sisters for too many historic failings to mention and to his nieces for not being there at those future moments in their lives that they will cherish. And close on the back of his apology, the thought that of all words that a man could scatter about so randomly in his final moments, sorry is probably not the worst.

He feels a sensation unexpectedly like peace.

*I am ready.*

# 72

# The aftermath

A gunshot.

It unfolds in slow motion, a change of expression: from blood-lust to incomprehension, Guy gulps like a shark and topples sideways with blood bubbling out of his throat. Jude looks back over his shoulder at Bala, who is standing, aiming Guy's pistol.

Slowly, painfully, Jude climbs to his feet. He feels debris slide off his shoulders and the blood running cold down his right arm. He limps over to Bala and puts his bloody hand on top of the pistol and lowers it, so that the barrel faces the ground.

'Thank you,' he says as she starts to shake. He puts his good arm around her as she buries her head in his shoulder.

He wonders if Lee has survived. It seems unlikely.

Within moments, the flat is full of armed men in black. Jude and Bala are surrounded and escorted out of the flat and down two flights of one of the back staircases and along the corridor to the Cabinet Office, where they are separated. She heads outside and he is taken to the COBRA complex.

'Well done, Jude,' Munro tells him as he is steered into a chair. 'You kept them pinned down on the stairs long enough for us to get reinforcements into the building. We don't think any of them have escaped.'

'And the Prime Minister?'

'Dead. The Deputy Prime Minister is on her way here now.'

A paramedic kneels in front of Jude and opens a trauma kit. He is pleased to see that there are so many bandages. He thinks he's going to need them.

'We think Op Carcer is containing the outbreak,' Munro tells him. 'The Nightingale hospital at the ExCeL Centre is on standby to receive the infected and quarantine them. We'll start emptying the underground stations as soon as we've got the transport in place. We're pretty sure that your friend Kirsty is on a southbound platform at Charing Cross. We'll find her.'

Jude nods. *But will she be alive?*

'GCHQ are working with the National Grid, National Rail and air traffic control to identify boot persistence mechanisms and strip out the malware from their operating systems,' Munro adds. 'We're hoping to return some power to the city within a couple of hours.'

Tamar arrives while Jude's having his forehead stitched. An injury that he didn't know he had.

'That'll leave a scar.' She nods to Munro, who is talking to Jemima Connick on the big screen, and walks over to look at Jude. 'Is he concussed?'

'He doesn't seem to be,' the paramedic replies.

'Lyons have thick heads,' she tells him.

'He has fractured ribs and severed tendons in his arm,' the paramedic says, tying off the last stitch. 'He needs to go to a hospital.'

Ignoring him, Jude asks her, 'How was your day?'

'Not an eventful as yours, obviously,' she replies. 'I have to say your flatmate Sanjay is really growing on me.'

'Get me out of this seat.'

The paramedic protests but Jude waves him away. Tamar helps him up, careful not to jar his injuries. A chest compression harness is holding a flail of ribcage in place and containing some of the pain. His bandaged forearm is throbbing.

'I'll put him in an ambulance,' Tamar says.

They leave through the shattered mantrap gates and walk out onto Whitehall with Jude leaning on Tamar's shoulder. There is a row of ambulances on the far side of the road, and a tented first-aid station has been set up in the street. He can see Bala standing outside one of the tents with a foil blanket around her shoulders.

'You're bloody lucky to be alive,' Tamar says.

He doesn't believe in luck. It's confirmation bias and magical thinking. He believes that the world is hazardous, and survival is a matter of chance, in this case because of a young trans woman whose concerned father taught her to shoot.

'Come on,' he tells her, steering away from the ambulances and towards the northern barricade.

'They won't let you through.'

'I want to see,' he tells her.

They walk past the two tanks, their crews brewing tea in the narrow gap between them, and through a breach in the charred and mangled barricade. At the edge of Trafalgar Square, armed police in CBRN suits and gas masks are guarding freshly erected crowd control barriers

'Don't come any closer,' one of the sentries warns them.

From where they are standing, they watch as medics and firemen in bright yellow bio-hazard suits escort lines of commuters in face masks up out of the exit on the south-east side of the square and towards waiting buses. Further across the square towards Charing Cross, ambulances are being loaded with casualties on stretchers.

'They'll find her and treat her,' Tamar tells him. 'She can survive this.'

He does not dare to hope.

# 73

## A clear day

For Jude, the story ends as it started more than a decade before, with a rendition.

Two weeks have passed since the attack on Downing Street and Jude is standing, dappled by blue flashing lights, beside the runway at RAF Lakenheath. There is a convoy of armoured vehicles full of armed men and women waiting behind him on the tarmac.

All this for one passenger.

The first time, he was waiting on the runway at Karachi and there were three passengers – an innocent man, his pregnant wife, and their unborn child – about to be sent to Syria. Nasruddin al-Raqqah was accused of causing the death of twenty-five British soldiers in an ambush in Iraq. It was misdirection: the ambush was entirely Guy Fowle's doing. Nasruddin's only involvement was being coerced into delivering a video message claiming responsibility for the attack. But that was enough to make him top of the UK's most wanted list. He was one more arbitrary statistic in the War on Terror, which has proven much more effective at incubating pitiless enemies and punishing innocent victims than it has at creating global consensus on freedoms or the rule of law.

This time, Jude's in rough shape and the Americans have sent a bigger plane, a C130 Hercules, and, like the Brits, they're not taking any chances: there is a fighter jet as escort, an F22 Raptor with external fuel tanks for added range.

Everyone knows that Guy Fowle has enough crypto to subvert entire nations.

The Hercules corkscrews in, ejecting chaff, while the Raptor circles. It slam-dunks and spins to a halt in front of Jude with its spoilers raised and its engines roaring. Huge Americans march down the ramp in matt-black Hazmat suits, as bold as the Emperor's Sardaukar, coming to a halt several metres short.

Jude raises his left hand and on his signal the paramedics open the doors of the ambulance behind him. Guy Fowle is eased out of the back and wheeled across the tarmac on a stretcher trolley. He is prone in a bright orange emergency bio-bag that makes him look like a huge pupa: a venomous insect waiting to be born.

Jude has been assured that Guy's been given enough tranquilliser to prevent that happening, but Jude only has to raise his bandaged right arm and a sniper on the control tower will take the shot.

As the stretcher passes, Jude looks down through the transparent window and Guy's eyes roll up and for a moment focus. The hatred burns through the bloody scribble of his eyeballs.

It's all Jude can do to refrain from raising his arm. Instead, he looks away at the huddle of plane spotters on the far side of the perimeter fence.

He was not informed that Guy had survived until five days after the attack. At the time of the call, he was standing in an Intensive Care Unit on one side of a wall of plastic sheeting. On the other side, Kirsty was lying connected to a ventilator, in a chemically induced coma, with acute hypoxemic respiratory failure. It's still touch and go whether she will survive.

'We can't send Guy back to Belmarsh,' Chuka told him, after breaking the news, 'and there's nowhere else here or in any of the overseas territories that's secure enough for him to go.'

'Where are they taking him?'

'They're not saying.'

'And we're not asking?'

'The fewer people that know his location the better.'

What has it come to, his immediate thought, that we can't trust ourselves to keep him locked up?

Jude's phone vibrates. He opens a custodial document from the New York attorney general's office and taps on the link to sign. He's still learning to open and close his fist and hold simple items like pens, so his fingertip signature on the screen looks even less intelligible than usual. He presses *submit*.

The exchange is complete. He'd have preferred a menu option that said 'dump in the Atlantic Ocean'.

He watches the careful choreography as the paramedics step back from the trolley and the Americans advance.

If there is a crumb of comfort to be taken from Guy's survival, it is that he must live the rest of his life with the knowledge that his attempt to cause a global pandemic failed. Thousands have died and thousands more are likely to die but the outbreak has been contained. As for his attempt to cause a war: Russia has not taken any more bites out of its neighbours. Military exercises churn on and the Doomsday Clock is closer to midnight than at any time since the Cuban Missile Crisis but neither side has yet opened fire.

The day after Jude learned that Guy Fowle was still alive, a young Russian woman calling herself Natasha appeared at the entrance to Sanjay's apartment with a USB stick. Jude made her coffee using Sanjay's beloved 'bells-and-whistles' machine and listened while she explained what the stick contained. Once GCHQ had got over their understandable fear of Russians with USB sticks, they were overjoyed at the trove of data recovered from the damaged servers in Franz Josef Land.

As for Yulia, there is no news. She is presumed dead in an explosion that no one in Russia or the West is in a hurry to acknowledge.

'I trusted Yulia,' Natasha told Jude with the coffee mug cupped in both her hands, as if she was still thawing out after the Arctic, 'and she trusted you.'

Jude watches the Americans wheel the stretcher onto the waiting plane and the ramp slowly close behind it. The plane does a one-hundred-and-eighty-degree turn and heads back out onto the runway. It accelerates and takes off, climbing steeply.

He watches as it grows smaller and smaller until it is a mere speck and then nothing at all.